Sometimes a Light

"Rich in details . . . Christy Award–winning Turner's latest is a perfect book for those who enjoy faith-focused, emotion-packed reading." —*Booklist*

"A bittersweet, introspective tale of a widower's internal journey through grief." —*Publishers Weekly*

Winter Birds

"Beautiful writing full of wisdom, literary allusions, and stylistic elegance . . . Its quiet but compelling plot, realistic characters, and sly humor made me wish it were twice as long. It reminds me of Marilynne Robinson's *Gilead*." —*Blog Critics*

"Turner brilliantly weaves together the threads of Shakespeare's plays, [television] sitcoms, birds and their habits, and the deaths of celebrities gleaned from *Time* magazine's obituary section as she unfolds the story . . . Genuine humor and well-crafted characters make this a memorable and inspiring novel." —*Publishers Weekly*

"[Turner] writes with elegant precision, and the leisurely pacing of the book perfectly captures the lengthened days of the aging. Understated and unsentimental, *Winter Birds* is a quietly memorable novel." —*Touchstone*

Some Wildflower in My Heart

"Achieves a literary excellence seldom seen in any novel. Like a rich dessert, this is not a book to devour, but to take one chapter at a time, with ample time to reflect and digest." —*Moody Magazine*

continued . . .

"Turner's skillful touch comes alive in the domestic details, recalling the work of Anne Tyler and Elizabeth Berg."

—*The Greenville (SC) News*

No Dark Valley

"The always-thoughtful Turner turns in another solid performance with *No Dark Valley* . . . [Turner is] a fine stylist, and the device of Celia's casting herself as the heroine of the novel she's living through is charming throughout."

—*Booklist*

"Lovely writing . . . Fans will recognize characters from [Turner's] previous novels, such as the Christy Award–winner *A Garden to Keep*."

—*Publishers Weekly*

"Turner writes splendid dialogue . . . Her narrative is engrossing."

—*RT Book Reviews*

A Garden to Keep

"The characters are well-developed, and their struggles are real, not saccharine."

—*Publishers Weekly*

"I couldn't put it down."

—*RT Book Reviews*

Suncatchers

"Turner's development of Eldeen Rafferty is perfect . . . Turner's strength as a writer is characterization."

—*Hope Is the Word*

to see the MOON AGAIN

Jamie Langston Turner

BERKLEY BOOKS, NEW YORK

THE BERKLEY PUBLISHING GROUP
Published by the Penguin Group
Penguin Group (USA) LLC
375 Hudson Street, New York, New York 10014

USA • Canada • UK • Ireland • Australia • New Zealand • India • South Africa • China

penguin.com

A Penguin Random House Company

This book is an original publication of The Berkley Publishing Group.

Library of Congress Cataloging-in-Publication Data

Turner, Jamie L.
To see the moon again / Jamie Langston Turner. — First edition.
pages cm
ISBN 978-0-425-25302-1
1. Single women—Fiction.   2. Women college teachers—Fiction.   3. Nieces—Fiction.
4. Guilt—Fiction.   5. Domestic fiction.   I. Title.
PS3570.U717T83   2014
813'.6—dc23
2014002711

PUBLISHING HISTORY
Berkley trade paperback edition / September 2014

PRINTED IN THE UNITED STATES OF AMERICA

10 9 8 7 6 5 4 3 2 1

Cover photograph of "chain of lights"© Plainpicture / Elektrons08.
Cover design by Sarah Oberrender.
Text design by Kristin del Rosario.

Before your daddy was born, I observed babies from a safe distance, judging them to be cute miniature people with enviable privileges, such as the freedom to stare at others openly. Up close, however, I was intimidated by them—they seemed so helpless yet were little tyrants when it came to taking over a grown person's entire life. I respected them for their importance to the future of society, of course, since babies always end up as adults if given enough time, and I was even quite fond of several of them, my nephews and nieces in particular, whose parents took them home after brief, enjoyable visits.

But when your daddy was born, I lost my heart to a baby, totally, permanently. Wonderful years followed as I reveled in every phase of motherhood. Now and then someone would say, "Just *wait* till you have grandchildren." I wasn't in any hurry for that, however, for I had observed grandparents, too, and had come to the conclusion that most of them had no sense of social awareness. What else would explain their endless monologues about their grandchildren's extraordinary charms, always accompanied by far too many photos?

And then your daddy grew up, married your beautiful mother, and the two of you were born, first Svana and, four years later, Kjell. I still remember the two moments in time, one in April and the other in December, when we learned you would be joining our family. I loved you both instantly, long before I knew your names. I knew your names before I saw you. I saw you before I held you. And when I held you, I didn't know what had hit me. I thought my life was rich and overflowing before you came, but I found that there was a whole enormous reservoir just waiting for you to fill it.

Thank you, my dear grandchildren, for the abundant joy you give without even trying. It will be a long time before you're old enough to read a book like this, but when you are, I want you to imagine your Ooma writing this page of dedication, stopping often to gaze at your photos and smile over the two of you and your extraordinary charms.

· chapter 1 ·

THE IMPORTANCE OF PLACE

On the last class day of the spring term, Julia Rich was heading home in her big blue boat of a Buick along the familiar route she could have driven blindfolded. As she neared Ivy Dale Lane, where she lived, she once again reminded herself of two things. First, that many other professors worldwide not only had endured what she was facing but had actually enjoyed it and, second, that most of her current colleagues would gladly trade places with her right now. Neither of these reminders, however, helped to settle her mind.

She slowed her Buick as she turned onto Ivy Dale, a narrow, tree-lined street less than a mile from the campus of Millard-Temple University, where she taught. At one time numbers of faculty members had lived here, but now only Julia and one other remained—a French teacher named Dr. Boyer. He was an odd, nervous sort of man, a Charlie Chaplin look-alike, who never said "hello" to her, only a prim, tight-lipped "*bonjour*," though more recently he had not spoken to her at all. She suspected that he resented her being granted a sabbatical ahead of him. Or maybe he avoided her because he felt sorry for her, as others now did.

As soon as her house came into view, she slowed even more. It was an old habit—the initial sighting, then the intentional deferral of her arrival as she took it all in. It was a small stone house with the charm of a storybook cottage. She and Matthew had driven past it one day before they were married. "Stop," she had said. "There, look at that one. I want to live there someday."

When it came up for sale a few years later, Matthew had arranged to buy it as a surprise for her. Those were the days when he was doing anything he could to make her happy, an enterprise he persisted in long after every effort had proved futile. Once they moved in and discovered the extent of the work it needed, it had lost some of its storybook charm, at least for Matthew, who did most of the labor himself. But Julia had loved it straight through the years of repairs and renovations. Even now there were times when she would be away from home and would suddenly think of the stone house on Ivy Dale and be flooded with something close to gladness. In many ways her house had taken the place of children in her life, the way some people's pets did.

She parked in the circular drive in front and took a few moments to let her eyes sweep the yard from one end to the other. Spring had come to South Carolina early this year, wet and mild. Daffodils, hyacinth, dogwoods, azaleas—all had bloomed in a spectacle of color. And now the irises were opening, soon to be followed by peonies, lilies, roses.

She walked around to the back door to let herself in, then locked it behind her. The answering machine in the kitchen was blinking, so she stepped out of her shoes at the door, laid her briefcase on the table, and walked to the phone. She knew who it was, of course. Since last August, her sister, Pamela, had worried incessantly about Julia's living alone and had called daily to check up on her. Because she didn't work, Pamela had time on her hands, and because her children were both grown, she needed someone else to mother. It didn't matter that she was younger than Julia by five years. She had always had the manner of an overseer, even as a child.

If Julia wasn't home when she called, Pamela left a message, usually constructed around a warning of some kind: *Always check the backseat of your car before getting in, don't order with a credit card over the phone, wear flat shoes in case you need to run.* She often included reports of tragic outcomes for people she had heard about who failed to follow these rules.

Julia almost pressed the button to listen, but she stopped. She was bone-tired and mentally spent. She wasn't in the mood to hear her sister's voice reminding her that evil prowled the earth. She turned and went to her bedroom instead. She took off her skirt, removed her jewelry, pulled her sweater over her head, and took her time putting everything away in its place. From the hook on the back of the bathroom door, she took her housecoat, slipped it on, and snapped it up.

Even as she did these things, she was thinking of the hours ahead. Since it was the last Friday night of the school year, she had no papers to grade. The evening gaped before her, with no plans to fill it, which was part of the reason for her present unrest. By putting on her housecoat, she realized she had already decided not to take a walk, which was one way to spend an hour or so now that Daylight Saving Time was in effect.

But for now she had supper to think about. On her teaching days she often ate a substantial lunch in the faculty cafeteria on campus and only snacked in the evening. Today, however, she hadn't felt like walking over to the cafeteria, choosing her food, sitting at the same corner table with Marcy Kingsley, her only real friend among her colleagues. Today had been a day of reflection. She had stayed in her office between her morning and afternoon classes. When Marcy had stopped by to get her, she had begged off, claiming a headache.

She had bought a bag of pretzels from the vending machine and busied herself going through the bottom drawer of her desk, discarding entire folders of old papers and ditto masters. Ditto masters—dozens and dozens of them, some handwritten. It was hard to believe she had hung on to such antiquities so long. Afterward she had run new copies of an exam, cleaned out the top desk drawer, dusted her bookshelves.

And then, because she still had a half hour left before her three o'clock class, she had sat at her desk with her door cracked, listening to the graduate teaching assistants socializing in the hallway. They were as eager for summer as the undergrads. Not one of them had yet wished her well during the coming year. By now they had probably forgotten all about the announcement in the February faculty meeting, after which there had been a pattering of polite applause for the two professors chosen for sabbaticals—Julia and Harry Tobias, who taught psychology.

Julia didn't fully understand the selection process, but she knew it was a committee decision and that the words "having distinguished yourself by the length and quality of your service" had been used by Dean Moorehead when he first informed her of the award privately. Though he didn't add the words "and because of your recent personal difficulties," he might as well have, for Julia was certain a measure of pity had also figured into the committee's choice.

Though she had pretended to be pleased and honored, it was mostly shock she had felt. That, and the beginnings of worry as she tried to take in what it would mean to the comforting structure of her life to have a year off. Long ago she had resigned herself to the mischief of time, for though a year could pass swiftly, the days within that year could seem endless. And each day included a night.

Stepping into her bedroom slippers, she thought of all the nights like this she would have to fill in the coming year. She was struck with the urgent need to write up a list of projects she wanted to complete and places she wanted to visit. That would be one thing to do tonight.

B ACK in the kitchen, she opened the freezer. Earlier in the week she had put up a dish of leftovers, which she pulled out now and put in the microwave to defrost.

She looked again at the blinking light of the telephone, but walked past it into the living room—a comfortable room, well decorated with an eclectic mix of fine old furniture and modern accessories. Above the stone hearth hung a large, colorful framed collage made of scraps of old road maps, travel brochures, and envelopes with canceled postage stamps. It was one of the few things Matthew had bought for the house that she liked. She made herself stop and look at it now, as she often did, to prove that she held no grudge against him, that her world was still intact.

She turned on the television and listened to the news for a minute, then lowered the volume and turned on the CD player. The sounds of Dvořák filled the room.

She walked back to the bathroom to wash off her makeup. Glancing into the mirror above the sink, she saw a long purple smear on her chin. She rubbed at it with her index finger and got some of it off.

She suddenly remembered the folder of old ditto masters she had leafed through in her office that afternoon. The mark on her chin must have come from those. Purple ditto ink—amazing that it could still be picked up and transferred after all those years of sitting in a folder.

As she stared at her face, it came to her that she must have had the purple streak on her chin when she met her afternoon class. Her ten students in Writing Fiction must have seen it. When she stepped off the dais to deliver her farewell remarks, they must have been reminded of all the old people they knew who went around with spots on their clothing and tufts of hair sticking out at funny angles.

At one point in her little speech, Julia had paused and looked toward the transom window above the door. Such an occasion called for a little drama, as it was no ordinary final day of class, at least not for her. "Remember this," she had said when she resumed. "Writers must be close observers of people." They must have wanted to laugh at that. "And of places," she had added after another dramatic pause. "Particularly your own native soil, into which you must keep digging deeper." She knew they would recognize the last part as a quotation from Flannery O'Connor, the woman Julia considered the best Southern writer of all time.

Looking at her watch, she saw that the bell would ring in two minutes. Time now for the real news. Stepping a little closer to the students, she said, "Some of you may have heard a rumor that I won't be teaching at Millard-Temple next year."

No dropped jaws, but she could see a sudden return of interest. All eyes were on Julia.

"It's true," she said. "I have been granted a sabbatical, which simply means I will get paid to read, to write, to travel, to do whatever I choose for a year." She glanced up at the transom window again and nodded slowly. "It's an opportunity not everyone gets."

"You going on a cruise?" Aaron Clements asked. This drew laughter.

"Maybe," Julia said. "Or maybe I'll travel in the States. Visit some of the big cities I've never seen." It was impossible to think she had lived fifty-four years and never been to Chicago or New York City, had never really wanted to. "Or maybe I'll just stay home and be lazy," she said. "Watch old movies and read and clean out a cupboard every now and then."

They smiled, though she could tell their thoughts were already drifting elsewhere. She hurried on. "Others will cover my courses next year, and I'll return a year from this fall."

"Who'll teach Southern Writers?" someone said.

"An adjunct from Clemson," Julia said. "You'll like him. He's a Faulkner man."

The bell rang. The students looked uncertain, as if wondering whether it would be rude to gather their things and bolt for the door.

"All right, off with you," Julia said. "I'll see you here again on Monday for your exam." She had already announced the essay topic. What she hadn't told them, of course, was that she wouldn't read the essays, wouldn't even skim the first pages, but would take them all home and gently place them in the trash can.

And the whole time they must have been sitting there thinking, *What* is *that on her face?* Maybe they thought it was a bruise. That would be better than if they thought it was a smudge she had failed to notice.

And the student who had come to see her in her office less than an hour ago—she must have seen the purple mark, too.

Julia had been sitting at her desk after class, thinking about how much she would miss coming here for the next year. She loved her office—her massive oak desk, the wooden file cabinet, the high ceiling, the window that faced the fountains. It pleased her to know it wouldn't be assigned to anyone else during her sabbatical. Everything could be kept in place. She imagined herself sneaking over at nighttime to sit here in the dark.

Turning to the window, she watched the students crossing the footbridge between Simmons Hall and the Snack Shop. Everyone walked differently on the last day of class. Every step said, *Let me out of here, I'm dying for summer.* On the sidewalk outside her window, two girls stopped to talk, and one of them gave a whoop of laughter as they bent their heads over a cell phone.

And then there had been a light tap at her door. She turned and saw a form silhouetted through the large pane of frosted glass. "Come in," she called.

The door opened partway, and she saw a face. "Dr. Rich?"

Julia recognized her at once. "Come in, Kelly," she said, standing.

The girl opened the door farther and stepped inside. Kelly Kovatch was one of the few bright lights in Julia's morning class of Creative Writing sophomores this semester. A tall, pretty girl, quiet and demure the way girls used to be.

"Will you have a seat?" Julia said, nodding toward the old library chair she used for student conferences. Julia sat back down at her desk and swung her chair around to face the girl.

"I can't stay long," Kelly said. "I need to be at work soon." She pushed her dark hair behind one ear. Unlike the disarray so many girls favored these days on the tops of their heads, hers was a neat, tidy hairstyle from an earlier era—longer than a bob but not quite a pageboy. She took a deep breath and continued. "I came to tell you something about the short story I wrote for your class. You probably don't remember which one was mine, but it . . ."

"Of course I remember. It was about the father and his teenage son, whose driving lesson was a fiasco."

The girl's eyes widened. "Yes. That was it." She looked directly at Julia and swallowed. "Well, I need to confess something. It . . . wasn't really my work."

She could have no way of knowing what effect her words would have. For a long moment Julia stopped breathing but never took her eyes off the girl. "What do you mean?" she asked at last.

Kelly sighed and shook her head. "Well, I turned in that story for a class called *Creative* Writing, but I didn't really create it. The whole conversation in the garage really happened, almost verbatim. It was my own father and one of my brothers. And the part about the paint buckets and the garden hose—that really happened, too. And the spare tire and the bag of flour and the scorched hot dogs—those, too. I'm ashamed to say . . ." She trailed off and looked down at her hands, then added softly, ". . . well, I never even told them I was using them for my story. I just did it."

Julia was afraid the girl might be crying, but when she lifted her face, her eyes were dry, her voice steady. "I keep remembering what you said before we ever started writing our stories about how important it was to *transform* a real-life experience before trying to use it in fiction, and . . . well, I didn't—and so I'm not sure I deserve the grade you gave me. I feel awful—I don't know what to call what I did. Exploitation or plagiarism or . . ." She broke off again.

Such innocence and probity astounded Julia. And shamed her. She swiveled her chair around to face the bookcases, and after a brief silence she spoke. "Kelly, that's not called plagiarism or exploitation. It's called being smart enough to recognize good material when you see and hear it." She swung her chair around again to face the girl. "You don't need to confess. You simply need to be grateful that your father and brother did and said those things while you were nearby and that you had the good sense to remember them and to realize what a fine story you could make out of them."

A smile of disbelief slowly spread across the girl's face. "You have no idea how much I've dreaded this. I was prepared to . . . well, I was prepared for the worst." She glanced at her watch, then stood up. "Thank you, Dr. Rich. This is a very happy ending to what I was afraid might be a very sad story."

Julia stood also. "Writers get their ideas from many places, Kelly—sometimes right under their noses. So stay alert—and keep writing. Please keep writing."

Kelly nodded. "I will, I promise." At the door she turned around. "I hope you enjoy your sabbatical, Dr. Rich. And I hope I can take another class from you after you get back."

After she left, Julia thought of other things she could have said to her. But it was too late now. Like so often in the past, words she should have said were left unspoken. But this time maybe it wasn't such a bad thing. If she had talked longer, it would have only given Kelly more time to stare at the smear across her chin.

J ULIA looked away from the mirror now. She turned on the water at the sink and ran it till it was hot. Then she lathered her hands with soap and rubbed her face for a long time, then scrubbed her chin hard with a washcloth and dried it with a towel. No mild cleansing foam today. It didn't matter anyway. All the little lines and wrinkles would keep coming regardless of how she washed her face. More and more of them. You could buy every age-defying cream on the market, but not one of them was a match for time. She picked up her brush and examined it, something she did more often these days, for her hair was not only graying at an alarming rate but also thinning. Once a month she colored it herself, but nothing could be done about replacing what fell out.

She and Marcy Kingsley had observed old Dr. Kohler in the cafeteria recently. Dr. Kohler, her hair a frail white web, had taught Shakespeare at Millard-Temple since time immemorial. She liked to joke that her students thought she had known Shakespeare personally. Very deliberately she had made her way down the cafeteria line that day, then had taken her tray to a table by the window, where two rookie English teachers were already seated. Within minutes they had excused themselves, and Dr. Kohler had eaten her lunch alone, staring out the window.

"She must've spent a lot of time in the sun when she was younger,"

Marcy had said. "When I start looking like that, I don't think I'll have the nerve to go out in public. Especially not to stand up in front of a class of *college* students." Julia hadn't said anything, but her sympathies were with Dr. Kohler. Marcy was only forty-three, but it would dawn on her sooner or later that a woman couldn't stay inside and hide her wrinkles from the world. There wasn't a thing you could do about growing old. You just had to keep going.

T HE microwave was finished when Julia got back to the kitchen, so she reset it to cook on low and started it again. She poured a glass of sweet tea, took a long drink, and then refilled it. She knew she shouldn't drink more than a single glass, since caffeine kept her awake if she drank it this late in the day. But tomorrow was Saturday, so she could sleep later. If she could sleep at all—that was often a problem, caffeine or not.

She walked back to the living room to get a magazine and brought it back to the kitchen. It was an issue of *The Atlantic* from months ago that she had never even opened. Only one of many things that had gone unattended since last August.

She stopped at the counter beside the blinking telephone. As much as she wanted to ignore it, she knew she couldn't much longer. She briefly considered deleting the message without listening to it, but she knew there would always be the niggling thought that Pamela might actually have said something important this time. The only way to get rid of it was to go ahead and play it.

She sighed and pressed the button.

But it wasn't Pamela. "Hey, Aunt Julia," a voice said, just short of a shout. "This is Carmen." There were crackling, popping sounds in the background like distant gunfire. "I know you're probably surprised to hear from *me*. It's been a long time. Like almost forever." She laughed. "Well, okay, more like never."

Julia couldn't have been more stunned if the telephone had sud-denly caught fire. Carmen? Her brother's Carmen? The little girl he had fathered with some waitress he'd met at a truck stop out west? She didn't know of any other Carmen. She tried to calculate how old the girl would be now, but she was having trouble think-ing. The last she had heard, Carmen had dropped out of high school, left her mother's trailer in Wyoming, and fled to Canada with her boyfriend. That must have been five years ago now. Maybe not that long, maybe longer.

"Anyway, I hope this is the right number!" the voice said. Now it sounded like someone was shaking a large piece of sheet metal right beside the telephone. "I called information. Hang on, I can't hear." There was the sound of clomping footsteps, then a whoosh-ing sound like a high wind through a tunnel, then the slam of a door, and the voice was back. "There, now, that's better. Anyway, I've been riding around on a sailboat for a little bit with this friend I met, and we docked down here in Charleston. So now the ride's over, and I said to myself, hey, I've got an aunt somewhere down here, so why don't I call her up and tell her I might come see her. So that's what I'm doing." She laughed, a single hoarse "Ha!"

Julia felt a sudden panic. If this indeed was her niece Carmen, she didn't want to see her, not now or ever. She had no desire to be reminded of her brother, Jeremiah, who had made more than his share of mistakes during his life, impregnating a waitress in Wyo-ming being only one of many. And neither did she want to be reminded of her own poor choices in regard to Jeremiah.

"I don't know *when* exactly I can come," the voice said. "But maybe next week. I need to work out some things first. I got your address from Lulu a while back, so if I . . ." There was a burst of static, and Julia missed the next words. Then came a muffled shout in the background. "In a minute!" the girl said. "I'm on the phone!"

By now Julia was convinced that the voice belonged to her

niece, for Lulu had been the name of the waitress in Wyoming—
exactly the kind of name a truck stop waitress would have, the same
kind of woman who would let her daughter call her by her first
name. What a horrible thing if this girl really did show up on Julia's
doorstep next week. She couldn't let that happen.

The voice continued. "Sorry, I need to hang up and help somebody, but maybe I'll see you soon. I need to get some ducks in a row
before I . . ." There was a loud bump and another shout, not a
happy one. Carmen sighed into the phone. "I've got to go now."
And that was the end. She hung up without saying good-bye.

Julia quickly reviewed the call log, but the only entry read *Unknown Name*, with no phone number. Dismayed, she stood staring
at the phone. This couldn't be happening. She hated the thought of
having company, period—someone invading her space. But she especially hated the thought of this particular company.

When the microwave beeped, she was still rooted in the same
place, still looking at the telephone, her hand over her mouth. The
call had come at a little past two that afternoon. Almost four hours
ago. What if Carmen was already busy getting her ducks in a row?

Julia replayed the entire message, her sense of foreboding increasing every second. She had seen a picture of Carmen only once—a
snaggletoothed child with a pale, sweet face, a dimpled smile, and
wildly curly blond hair. But that had been many years ago now.

Slowly she walked to the microwave and took out the dish. It
was only lukewarm, so she put it back in. She couldn't think of what
to do next. Maybe Pamela had a phone number for Carmen, though
Julia knew that was highly improbable. Pamela had never wanted
anything to do with anyone in Wyoming, their own brother
included. She had told Julia not to respond to Lulu's first letter
twelve years ago, the letter she had received not long after Lulu's
phone call claiming that Jeremiah had died of a gunshot wound
from a stray bullet while hunting.

"She just wants money," Pamela had said. "How do we know she's telling the truth? People like that are always looking for a handout. We don't know how Jeremiah died or even *if* he died—she might be making the whole thing up. Why would we take her word for it? Somebody like that, she probably doesn't even know who that child's father really is."

But one look at the picture Lulu had enclosed with the letter, and nobody could deny Jeremiah was her father. No judge with eyes in his head would have bothered ordering a DNA test. After Pamela saw the photo for herself, she never again expressed doubt, though she continued to urge Julia not to write Lulu back.

But something in the letter had compelled her to answer. For one thing, Julia had truly loved her brother, more than she loved her sister if the truth were known. For another, Lulu's mention of Jeremiah's "papers" had intrigued her. Julia had written back and sent her money for shipping. A thousand times since then she wished she hadn't, but she had. And just like growing old, there wasn't a thing she could do about it now. The box had eventually arrived, and what was done was done. Other letters had followed over the years, but Julia had never again written back.

Quickly she walked back to the phone now and punched in Pamela's number. It rang six times before the answering machine turned on. Of course—wasn't that the way life went? Pamela was always interrupting Julia's life to talk about absolutely nothing, but the one time Julia actually wanted to talk to her, she wasn't home. "Call me right away," she said testily and then hung up.

She walked back into the living room and saw on the television screen a building engulfed in black smoke. Part of her took it as an omen that something catastrophic was about to happen in her life right now, yet the other, more rational part of her argued that a phone call from a niece she had never met was no cause to over-react.

She went back to the kitchen and tried to collect her thoughts. First she would sit at the table and eat her supper. That was a starting point. And as she ate, she would listen to the rest of the *Slavonic Dances* and try to read a story in *The Atlantic* as she waited for Pamela to call back. Then she would watch something on television, make a tentative list of things to do during her sabbatical, and eventually go to bed.

She walked to the window above the sink. The stone house was laid out in a modified L shape, the two ends extending slightly perpendicular to the middle of the house so that from where she stood now, she could see all the way across the front yard to the iris bed beneath her bedroom window at the opposite end—the same flower bed where Matthew had collapsed one day late last summer.

There was a time when she had thought of her house on Ivy Dale as a lookout on the world—at least all she wanted to see of the world—but lately she had begun to feel that her view of life was diminishing into something the size of a postcard, and not one bearing a cheerful message either.

She turned and looked toward the microwave, watching the seconds count down.

chapter 2

IN THE EVENT OF RAIN

Julia was in the middle of a dream when she woke with a start the next morning. Unlike many of her dreams, she could remember this one. She had been at the edge of a lake, calling to a little girl on the other side: "No, don't send them over!" But one by one the child put them into the water—yellow rubber ducks, all lined up in a row. She scooted along the ground, giving each one a little push into the water. And as the wind drove them rapidly to the shore where Julia stood, she saw that these were no comical Aflac ducks. These had menacing orange bills and black eyes filled with hatred.

She tried to laugh away her fear, reminding herself that dreams were like the stories she taught in her literature classes—not to be taken literally, of course, but not too symbolically either. She was of the mind that too many teachers ruined literature for their students, leading them to view a story as a captured prisoner tied to a post and flogged until it yielded its identity, its *meaning*.

Pamela had never called back the night before, but Julia had left two more messages. She went into the kitchen now and checked the answering machine. Nothing. No message on her cell phone either. This was very uncharacteristic of Pamela, who considered her phone as necessary as food and water. Maybe she and Butch had gone to another one of the tacky bluegrass festivals they loved so much. Or maybe she was visiting one of her children, though she hadn't mentioned doing that until midsummer, when the new grandbaby was due. Even then, she always had her cell phone with her.

Julia dialed her home phone again, but hung up as soon as the answering machine came on. She briefly considered calling Butch since she had his cell number, but she had no desire to have any kind of conversation with her brother-in-law. She would call him only if she got truly desperate.

Well, she couldn't sit by the telephone all day waiting. She started the coffee, then returned to her bedroom to get dressed. A nice long walk after breakfast—that was what she needed. She had taken to walking after Matthew's death, finding it useful for both filling time and easing her mind.

It was almost ten o'clock when she finally set out. She took her cell phone along, though Pamela probably wouldn't think to try her cell number since Julia so rarely had it turned on—a subject of Pamela's frequent complaints.

Ivy Dale was a picturesque setting for the stone house. The trees had leafed out early this year, already forming a canopy overhead. Even on the hottest days of summer, the street seemed cool and peaceful, though today there seemed to be something unnatural and ominous about so much shade on a sunny morning.

A car was coming toward Julia, moving slowly as if looking for an address. She felt a weight in the pit of her stomach. She had thought about Carmen all through the night. Every time she woke up, she remembered her words: *I don't know when exactly I can come. But maybe next week.* Since today was Saturday, did that mean the week starting tomorrow?

The car passed. The driver was a man, no one Julia knew. She came to the end of Ivy Dale and decided suddenly to take a different route today. She turned right and walked a block to a street named Placid Place, which ran parallel to Ivy Dale. This was the way she went whenever she walked to the campus of Millard-Temple, which wasn't often.

There were some interesting old houses along Placid Place, though several of them had been divided into student apartments in recent years, which was exactly the reason Julia usually avoided this area. She didn't like the way the neighborhood had changed from earlier days, and she certainly didn't want to run into students on the weekend, especially her own students. It was Saturday, though, so most of them were probably still asleep after the usual Friday night partying. Final exams might be starting on Monday, but the average student wasn't going to let that interfere with his weekend.

Sure enough, there was no sign of activity along Placid Place, at least not current activity. One porch was littered with articles of clothing and beer cans. A lone sneaker hung by its laces from the mailbox, and a Chinese take-out carton sat on the bottom step, its lid open, chopsticks sticking out the top. Julia tried to imagine how the original owner of this once-stately old home would feel if he saw it now.

S HE picked up her pace. Well rehearsed in not thinking about things she didn't want to think about, she fell back on an old strategy. She imagined a storage room with dozens of boxes, the kinds of boxes with nice, tight-fitting lids. For now she would put Carmen in a box and close it snugly.

Since she still hadn't made a list of projects to undertake during her sabbatical, she could start that now as she walked, then write it down later when she got home.

Clean the screened back porch—that was a good place to begin. After months of winter winds and rain, it was always dirty by late spring. After the porch, she would tackle all the closets. Not that any of them were terribly messy, especially not Matthew's. Though she had cleared out the drawers of his bureau and desk, all of them uncommonly tidy for a man, for anyone really, she had not opened the door of his closet since the day after he died, when she had to choose a suit to bury him in.

She also needed to sort through all the bookshelves and kitchen cupboards and . . . suddenly she felt her cell phone vibrate. She took it out of her pocket and saw that it was from Pamela. Finally.

She flipped it open. "Where have you been?"

"Amazing—you actually have your cell phone on." Pamela's voice sounded weak and scratchy.

"Are you sick?" Julia said.

"Why did you call? What's the matter? You don't ever call."

"Do you have a cold?"

"I wish that's all it was," Pamela said. "I've been sick as a dog." She broke off to cough, a prolonged crackly cough that sounded like somebody grappling with a large cellophane bag.

"Are you taking something?"

"Yes, I'm taking something. A bunch of things. I've been drugged out of my mind for three days. All I've been doing is sleeping. But what's *wrong*? Why did you call and leave all those messages? Butch said you sounded mad on the answering machine."

"I wasn't mad," Julia said. "I just needed to talk to you. I need to know if you have a phone number for Carmen."

There was a pause. "Carmen? You mean . . ." Pamela choked on whatever she tried to say next and started coughing again, deep and hacky. Finally she caught her breath. "You mean, as in our brother Jeremiah and that truck stop woman? *That* Carmen?"

"How many other Carmens do you know?" Julia said.

"What do you want to call *her* for?"

"I don't want to, but I need to." Pamela started to say something, but Julia stopped her. "Don't talk, just listen." And she told her about the phone message, every detail she could remember. "So I've got to get in touch with her. She can't come here. That can't happen. Not now, not ever." She realized suddenly that she had stopped walking and was waving one hand around. She was standing in front of a three-story house with peeling green paint, where a girl was lounging on a porch swing in what looked like her underwear. She was holding a cup of something in one hand, and she was staring at Julia.

Julia hoped she hadn't overheard anything. She would hate to have it spread around campus that Dr. Rich was standing on a sidewalk yelling at someone on the telephone. She lowered her voice and resumed walking. "So you're sure you don't have a number for her?"

"Why would I have her number?" Pamela asked. "I've never talked to her in my whole life, not once. How about her mother? Did you try her?"

If Julia needed any proof that she hadn't been thinking straight, this was it. Even though it was probably a dead-end idea, the thought of trying to get in touch with Lulu hadn't crossed her mind. She wasn't going to admit it to Pamela, however. Pamela loved to point out how she might not have a doctoral degree like Julia, but she did have an abundance of common sense—as if a person couldn't have both.

And it was true that she was very smart, very capable. She did things Julia had to pay people to do—things like painting shutters, planting flowers and shrubs, doing their own taxes. Most of these skills, though, were the result of marrying a sloppy, overweight man like Butch. To be fair, Julia didn't really know him, had seen him only three times in person and in a few photos. "I can do anything a man can do," Pamela often said, which Julia interpreted as *If I don't do it, it won't get done.*

"I don't have Lulu's number," Julia said. "I never did. And I don't know her address either. I didn't keep any of her letters."

"Butch can probably track her down on the Internet," Pamela said. The computer was the one area, the only one, in which Butch was competent.

Julia laughed. "So what's he going to do—Google 'Lulu in Wyoming'? She might be living anywhere by now. And we don't even know her last name. Whenever she wrote me, she just signed her name Lulu. I'm sure she and Jeremiah never married."

"Well, okay, then, I guess you can just wait and ask Carmen how to get in touch with her when she shows up," Pamela said.

Julia sighed. "Of course, it's easy for you to joke about this since you're not the one whose doorbell she might be ringing any day now."

"Sorry, Jules. My head feels like a mush melon. I just can't think right now. I wish I had a . . ." She stopped for another coughing fit, then blew her nose. "Hey, I can't talk anymore right now, but I'll call back later. You going to be home tonight? We can figure out something." Her voice sounded weaker now, only a croaky whisper, though Julia suspected her of putting on.

"No, don't bother," Julia said. "Just go back to sleep and get well. Good-bye." She closed her phone and put it back in her pocket.

Well, so much for that. She suddenly realized how much she had been counting on her sister's help. Though Pamela's specialty

was disaster prevention, she was also good in an unexpected crisis—
for example, sweeping onto the scene after Matthew's death
without waiting to be asked, then supervising and reorganizing
Julia's life for weeks thereafter. And before that, when their parents
both died within months of each other, it was Pamela who showed
up to help, who made all the final arrangements and cleared out
their house. So how could it be that now, faced with a matter of
relatively minor importance compared to a death, she had nothing
to offer?

A FEW minutes later Julia came to a street corner. She could
turn right and head back home, or turn left toward the college. Or she could continue going straight on Placid Place, which
would eventually lead to a new subdivision with a small lake and
golf course, where several of the younger Millard-Temple professors lived. She stood there for a moment before deciding to keep
going straight.

She hadn't gone far, however, before regretting her decision. A
boy came bounding down the front steps of an old brick house
wearing a black T-shirt and jeans with holes in both knees. Julia
recognized him at once—he had sat on the back row in her Creative Writing class all semester—and she saw that he recognized
her, too. He ran both hands over his hair, which, as usual, was in
need of a good combing. Julia wished she had spent more time on
her own hair and makeup this morning. She didn't like her students
to see her when she wasn't put together, not even a student like
this one.

Too close to ignore her, the boy bobbed his head and said, "Dr.
Rich." Frowning, he darted a glance at his car by the curb, as if
worried that she might waylay him with a lecture about the differ-

ent types of irony in drama or the rhyme scheme of a ballad, but she had no intention of doing so. He hadn't appeared the least interested in anything she had said in class all semester, so she had nothing to say to him now.

"Hello, Mr. Vincent," she said with a curt nod as she continued walking. Seconds later, his car started and she heard the heavy bass thumps of his music as he sped past her.

She kept walking, eventually passing the city limits sign, where the sidewalk ended and Placid Place changed its name to Chapel Road. Beyond a little bridge she stepped onto the bike path and kept going. The road was wider now, the houses scattered farther apart.

Returning to her list of projects to undertake during her sabbatical, she thought of all her teaching materials she was still using from fifteen or twenty years ago. Marcy Kingsley had recently converted all of her class presentations for British Literature to PowerPoint slides and had told Julia she would show her how. "It makes taking notes so much easier for the students," she had said.

Julia was convinced that too many things were made easier for students these days. If they couldn't figure out how to take notes from a professor's lecture, they didn't belong in college. Besides that, she knew what happened with technology. Something new would come along and PowerPoint would become passé. It probably already had. But she might give it a try anyway. First she would need to retype all her notes and handouts—that would be a good way to take up time.

And she probably ought to travel some, even though she had no urge to do so except on a very limited basis. For example, she did want to drive to Milledgeville, Georgia, again to visit Andalusia, the home of Flannery O'Connor—a trip she had taken several times in the past. There was something inspiring about the house and farm, something that reminded her that a plain, confined life could count for something, or rather, that what appeared to be a plain, confined life could in fact be spacious and well furnished if one kept her mind active and open.

She felt the splash of a raindrop on her arm and looked up, startled that she could have been oblivious to the clouds gathering overhead. She wondered if there had been thunder she hadn't heard. Further, how could she have missed the forecast, something she usually consulted morning and night? More proof that her thoughts were in disarray.

More raindrops were falling, leaving dark splotches on her shirt. She began walking faster. An old chapel stood back from the road just ahead. She could wait out the storm there. The wind suddenly picked up with a fury. If she hadn't been witnessing it with her own eyes, she never would have believed the sky could burst open so suddenly. By the time she reached the covered entrance of the chapel, actually running the last hundred yards, she was soaked.

Standing against the door, panting, she watched the rain fall in sheets and felt the spray against her face. She had never liked being out in the rain the way some people did, had never really liked rain at all, not even from indoors.

A tired old memory came back to her now, across the span of nearly fifty years. It wasn't her worst memory, but one of her earliest and most vivid. She was standing with her back against the door of an old brick building, just as she was now. It was the last day of school, so it must have been early June, and her mother had just dropped her off at the front door of the elementary school in Nadine, Alabama. There had been more angry words and tears at the breakfast table, then only the two of them riding silently in the car, neither offering comfort to the other, and now she was late to school again.

It was raining heavily that day, and Julia had stood at the door of the school, first watching her mother drive away and then turning to look at the soggy playground, where flags and markers were set up for races and games. It was a day she had looked forward to for many weeks, barely able to concentrate on anything else, not even on her achievement tests, which, though only in first grade, she understood to be very important to her father. But she had tried to rise above her excitement and do her best, for she knew the test results would be included in her final report card, which the teacher would hand out at the end of school on the last day.

Before that, however, there were prizes to be won during the Field Day activities, an event that had already been rescheduled once for inclement weather. A fast runner, Julia had pinned all her hopes on winning a race and bringing home a blue ribbon. She had imagined a look of pride and approval spreading across her father's face, a hand laid on her head, maybe a word of praise.

But it was raining and showed no signs of letting up. The sky was gray, the playground full of puddles. And it was the last day of school. Even at the age of six, she knew a lost cause when she saw one. She didn't know certain words, but she knew the concepts. She knew this meant wholesale cancellation, not postponement. Time had run out. There was no contingency plan, and there would be no prize to take home.

Out on Chapel Road now, cars had slowed. The rain had slacked off some but was still falling steadily. She had no umbrella, of course. She had her cell phone but could think of no one she wanted to call for help. Marcy would come, she knew that, but she didn't want to hear her cheerful, idle chatter all the way home—"You're all wet, girlfriend!" and "What in the world were you doing all the way out here?" and all the rest of it.

So she would stay here and watch the rain until it stopped. Then she would slosh her way back home, change out of her wet clothes, and . . . well, she didn't want to think past that. There was nothing to anticipate at home, nothing good.

But what of it? She had known dreary days before and would certainly know them again. There was no sure way to plan for the unforeseeable, no way to avert misfortune or guarantee shelter in the event of rain. At least this time she had found a small, dry place for refuge.

· *chapter 3* ·

Nothing Solid and Sure

Days later, as Julia turned onto Ivy Dale after giving an exam, she realized that the phone message from Carmen had completely changed the way she arrived home.

Gone was the sense of breathing more easily as she proceeded down her quiet, shaded street, of slowly shedding the carefully calculated way she conducted herself away from home, of letting her eyes settle on the stone house, dropping whatever worries she had at the time to admire yet again the steep pitch of the roof, the dark red shutters and front door, the way the two ends of the house angled politely toward each other, the stone walkway Matthew had laid, the lamppost by the circular driveway, the ivy-covered mailbox.

She still saw all of these things, but only in an absentminded way. They gave her no sense of well-being. Not even the gnarly trunk of the Japanese maple afforded her much joy, or the irises unfolding daily under her bedroom window.

Now, from the moment she turned onto Ivy Dale, she strained forward, looking for a car parked in her driveway or someone at the front door. All looked safe right now, however, so she pulled into the driveway, not the circular one in front but the original one that shot straight to the garage at the rear of the house.

In the kitchen the red light on the answering machine was blinking again. Carmen's phone message was having its effect here, too. No more waiting till later. A phone call might require immediate action. She walked directly to the phone. Unlike only days ago, she was now relieved to hear her sister's voice. Though still hoarse, it sounded better than it had last week.

"Hey there, Jules. Call me. Butch did find Lulu, and you won't believe it—she's listed as Lulu *Frederickson*. So either she really did marry Jeremiah or else she just took his name without bothering, which wouldn't surprise me."

Julia called her back at once. Pamela answered after the first ring and began talking as if in the middle of a conversation.

"And the town is Painted Horse, Wyoming. I found it on a map. I've got her address and phone number. You have a pencil? You think she really married him?"

"Who knows?" Julia said. "I wonder if she moved. Seems like Painted Horse is a name I would remember."

"Well, anyway, it's still a trailer," Pamela said. "Butch found that out in the personal property listings."

Julia took down the information and told Pamela she would let her know if she got in touch with Lulu. But Pamela wasn't ready to hang up. Starved for conversation after her long fast, she rushed into a news report about a woman being held up at an ATM. But Julia didn't let her get far. She had to hang up, she told her. She had a phone call to make. There was no time to waste.

• • •

I T was almost three o'clock, but it would be two hours earlier in
Wyoming. She had no idea whether Lulu had a job. Maybe she
was still a waitress. More likely she had quit working by now and
was on welfare.

She punched in the numbers quickly, and, remarkably, someone
answered. At first Julia wondered if she might have called Pamela back
by mistake, for it was a woman's voice, low and husky like Pamela's sick
voice. But it sounded like an older voice, and not a very cordial one.

As there was no one to impress in Painted Horse, Wyoming,
Julia didn't bother with preliminaries. "Hello," she said in a busi-
nesslike tone. "I'm trying to get in touch with someone named
Lulu, and I was given this number. Is this Lulu?"

There was no reply at first, then a short laugh, and then,
"Nuh-uh, this is Ida. You wanting Lulu? Lulu Frederickson?"

Julia wondered if Lulu was a common name in Painted Horse.
"Yes, that Lulu," she said. She couldn't make herself put the two
names together.

"Who is this? What you wanting Lulu for?"

"I need to contact her daughter. It's urgent. I was hoping Lulu
would give me a phone number for her."

Another coarse laugh. "Which daughter you talking about?"

This shouldn't have surprised Julia, but it did. She should have
known a woman like Lulu would have several children, probably by
several different fathers.

"Carmen," she said.

"Who is this?" the voice asked again. "Is something the matter
with Carmen? You know where she's at?"

Julia spoke briskly as if to convey the need for answers, not
more questions. "My name is Julia Rich. My brother, Jeremiah, was
Carmen's father. I need to talk with Carmen right away."

"Jerry was your brother?"

"Yes, I'm Jeremiah Frederickson's sister. One of them. And I need to get in touch with Carmen." And then, as if someone from Wyoming needed clarification, she added, "I'm Carmen's aunt."

"Well, you're not the only one that wants to talk to her. I do, too. I got a thing or two to tell her."

Julia's heart sank. "You don't know how to reach her?"

"Nobody does."

"Not even her mother?"

"Lulu's dead."

Julia wasn't sure she had heard right. "But . . . we found a listing for her with this phone number."

"Folks can die sudden."

"When . . . did this happen? Does Carmen know?"

"That's what I just got through saying. Nobody knows where she's at. Funeral was a week ago." It struck Julia that the woman didn't seem particularly sad about any of this, only inconvenienced.

This was bad news, of course. Not because Lulu meant anything to Julia personally but because any hope of contacting Carmen was now dashed. But she couldn't help being curious. "What happened? Was it an accident of some kind?"

"Well, for sure she didn't *mean* to die." The woman coughed, a smoker's deep, rolling cough. "She give out sudden. Real bad off. Couldn't get her breath."

It struck Julia that this woman sounded more like a native of the Deep South than the West. She could be one of the people routinely interviewed on the local ten o'clock news here in South Carolina: "Yep, we was a'layin' in the bed sleepin' when they was a loud boom and 'fore we knowed it we didn't have no roof." These people were usually missing at least one front tooth and often had a bad eye.

She said, "Was it . . . heart trouble?"

"Just up and died," the woman said.

Julia wondered if everyone in Wyoming spoke so cryptically. She heard a sudden high whistling sound in the background. "Water's boiling," the woman said. "I got to go tend it."

"Wait, please. I'm very sorry to hear about all this, but are you absolutely sure you don't have any idea how to reach Carmen? No cell phone? No address? Nothing at all?"

"She used to call Lulu some, but Lulu never did call her. Carmen, she was footloose. Trekked around a lot. She come back here once, just a day, then lit out again. Told Effie she was going to Oregon. Or maybe it was Ohio." Julia doubted that this woman even knew the two states were in opposite directions from Wyoming.

Julia sighed. "Oh." Then, though it didn't matter at all, she asked, "Who's Effie?"

"Lulu's sister. Half sister. Lulu was the oldest." There was a thump in the background, and the whistling sound stopped.

"And you're . . . their mother?" Julia asked.

"Practically same as."

Julia decided not to follow up on this. She had a sudden vision of the three women—Lulu, Effie, and . . . had she said *Ida*?—soft-fleshed, disheveled, and slack-jawed, sitting on a dilapidated sofa in a trailer, engrossed in a soap opera, eating nachos and beef jerky. She knew she was being unfair, assuming the worst about people she had never met, but she also knew she was probably right.

She couldn't resist one last try. "So you can't think of anyone at all who might know how to reach Carmen? Or how about a place she might have worked recently? Or maybe Effie would know something?"

There was a sudden frantic yipping in the background, along with loud thuds, as of someone trying to kick down a door. "He's not allowed in!" the woman shouted. "You let him in, you'll be the one cleaning up his nasty turds." She coughed another deep, racking cough. To Julia she said, "*Nobody* knows where she's at. Nobody means *nobody*. Effie can't help. She's bad sick, half out of her mind." There was more barking in the background, then the sound of breaking glass. "Now look what you've gone and—" And suddenly the line was dead.

Julia slowly closed her cell phone and stood in her kitchen a long moment, trying to absorb the setback, trying not to think ahead to the eventual, inevitable slam of a car door, the sound of a knock on the door or the chime of the doorbell, the sight of a stranger on her front step.

WHEN at last she came back to herself, she was still standing in the same spot, staring at the backsplash above the sink. It was something she often found herself doing—studying the rows of small multicolored tiles, looking for but never finding a repeating pattern. The whole length of it was just a random mix, though something Matthew had "designed," as he had liked to say. In Julia's opinion, such a design could have been drawn up by a child—a blind one.

She knew there was a parallel here to the course her whole life had taken, except there was no one to claim the role of designer for that sad piece of work. Hers was a life of echoes and shadows. No pattern, nothing solid and sure.

Slowly she walked back toward her bedroom, trying hard to think of something, just one thing, she could latch on to as the dimmest flicker of hope in this whole situation with Carmen. Only one thought presented itself: At least if Carmen did call her back or, worse, did show up in person, Julia could get rid of her by saying her family needed her immediately back in Wyoming. She could hustle her to the airport, buy her a plane ticket, and get her on the next flight out.

In the meantime, she would fill up the next days and weeks with comings and goings, as many as she could think of, until enough time had elapsed that she felt safe again. In case Carmen did come sometime soon, Julia was going to try her best not to be at home. And if she did happen to be here, she could always pretend she wasn't. There was no law that said you had to open your door if someone knocked.

Julia changed out of her teaching clothes into a crisp pink shirt and a pair of tan slacks. As afternoon seemed a particularly likely time for an out-of-town visitor to arrive, she had already devised a plan for the next several hours. She would run by the library and get a couple of books she had put on reserve as well as a movie Marcy had recommended, then go to the mall for a wedding gift for Dean Moorehead's daughter. She would take her time selecting it and having it gift-wrapped. Then she would stop somewhere to eat, and if she read one of the library books as she ate, the way she saw other people doing in restaurants, she could stretch it out even longer.

She ran a brush through her hair, dabbed on some lipstick, and left the house a few minutes later. As she backed cautiously out of the driveway in her Buick, an ancient pickup truck lurched to a stop at the curb. No clutching at the heart, though, since she recognized it at once as belonging to Gil, her yardman. Gil did a lot more than mow the lawn. A "lawn sculptor"—that's what he called himself on his business card. A droll little man with a luxuriant mustache, he had a disconcerting habit of blinking constantly whenever he spoke, which thankfully wasn't often. But he was very fastidious, very dependable, not to mention reasonable in price, so she was willing to allow him any eccentricity.

Though Matthew had made a hobby of puttering in the flower beds himself, he had hired Gil years ago, one of several forward-looking arrangements he had made for upkeep at home when his job started requiring him to travel more. Julia sometimes thought of such arrangements as credits on her husband's ledger page, though they in no way canceled the long list he had left in the other column after his death. It was a conflicted sort of gratitude she felt even now, colored as it was by the discovery of his many debts, which had become her debts.

She still remembered the day after Matthew's funeral, when certain financial horrors were beginning to come to light. Pamela had gone through Matthew's desk and dug out bills, statements, receipts, and one insurance policy, ironically small considering the fact that Matthew was in the insurance business. Pam had sorted through them all and put them in order, then entered everything on a spreadsheet. As Julia stood at the desk and stared at the figures displayed on the computer screen, she heard two things simultaneously: first, Pamela's voice saying, "I'll help you get through this, Jules, but I have to tell you it looks like he left you in a mess," and, second, a lawn mower starting up right outside the window.

Looking out the window that day, Julia had seen Gil in his baggy work pants and red suspenders, his broad-brimmed hat pulled down low over his eyes, maneuvering the mower around the base of an oak tree. And she remembered Pamela following her eyes to the window, then saying, "At least you don't have to worry about your yard along with everything else right now—well, except *paying* him to do it."

And that wasn't the end of it. After Pamela finally packed up and left, Julia had found several dozen handwritten IOUs in an old cigar box, all neatly printed, dated, and signed by Matthew—debts to his card-playing friends, totaling over six thousand dollars, all of which she had insisted on settling out of pride.

JULIA waved to Gil now, but he made no sign of having seen her, though she knew he had. She stopped her car and pulled forward onto the circular drive, then eased out onto Ivy Dale and turned in the direction of the library. She and Gil didn't converse often, as there was little to talk about. They had a routine, and he stuck to his part. She stuck to hers, too, which was to mail him a check at the beginning of every month.

As she pulled away from the stone house, Julia glanced at Gil in her rearview mirror and thought again about what a colorful character he would make for a story. Tweak him a little, of course, add a limp perhaps, make him more talkative with some quirky speech patterns, maybe give him a more distinctive name, something more obviously foreign, and perhaps a characteristic odor—garlic or cabbage or curry.

She thought, too, of other people in her life who could also be cast as story characters: Marcy Kingsley, Dr. Boyer the French teacher, old Dr. Kohler, even her sister Pamela, and Pamela's big sloth of a husband, Butch. And Ida from Wyoming. But it would take a better writer than herself, not just someone with a good eye for detecting idiosyncrasies. A real writer had to be able to create, not just imitate and exaggerate.

More than once when mentioning her upcoming sabbatical, Dean Moorehead had said to her in his soft, earnest voice, "We know you'll enjoy some extra time for writing," which she had taken to mean, *We expect to see you published again.*

But publication was another one of those things Julia didn't want to think about. She tried to push the thought away, but it pushed back this time, then began to settle in. She knew her few scholarly essays and two stories didn't count for much in academia, especially considering the origin of the stories. No one knew about all that, however, and there was certainly nothing to be gained by allowing herself to dwell on it again.

To her credit, she was a good teacher, a proven teacher, an *excellent* teacher in fact, perfectly capable and fair in her critique of student writing. No one could deny that she had much to offer in

the classroom, whether she ever published again or not. Unfortunately, however, publication carried a great deal of weight with
deans and department chairs. She knew they were waiting for her
to deliver again. She had told her dean a couple of years ago that
she was "working on" a novel. What she didn't tell him was that the
only work she had done on it had taken place in her head. She
hadn't actually written down the first word.

Sitting at a stoplight or eating breakfast or walking across
campus, she might think of a perfect opening, but as soon as she
picked up a pen or sat down at her computer, doubt set in. She
might make several tries but by the end rejected them all as too
stilted, too bland, too pretentious, too something. And then an old
worry: Maybe she had read those exact words somewhere else and
was only recalling them. She had the kind of memory that could do
that. And even if she could write her own decent opening, where
would she go from there? The thought of advancing beyond the
first page was terrifying, like walking to the edge of a chasm and
leaping.

Shame and fear—they made a debilitating pair. The closing
words of one of her two published stories came to her now: *He saw
her on the loading dock, waiting for him in the rain, the steam rising
about her like an unholy incense.* She knew she could recite most of
the sentences before that, too, all the way back to the first one.
That was how well she knew the story. Backward and forward, as
they said.

It was a good story, perfectly balanced between suggestion and
revelation, with complex characters and a strong ending. But it
wasn't her own, except for the title.

· chapter 4 ·

PRAGMATIC JUSTIFICATIONS

Sitting in her Buick at the public library, Julia studied the towering oak tree near the entrance, the roots of which had heaved the sidewalk upward until it cracked. It had been that way for years. Evidently no one was concerned enough to do anything about it. Library patrons simply skirted that section of the sidewalk. All it would take would be an accident and a lawsuit, and then something would be done.

When Julia had first received the box of Jeremiah's papers eleven years ago, theft was the furthest thing from her mind. She had never stolen from anyone, but the fact that it was from her own brother made it worse. And it didn't matter that he was dead and would never know. Somehow that made it worse, too.

She remembered well the shock of Lulu's long-ago phone call with the news that Jeremiah had been shot and had died instantly. And before Julia could even get her breath to ask about the funeral, Lulu had gone on to tell her that it had happened four days earlier, that he had already been cremated and his ashes scattered somewhere in the Grand Teton National Forest.

Pamela had been furious. "First of all, she waits *four* days to tell us? And then she just *throws* him to the wind?"

By this time, their father had been merely existing for almost two decades, his body refusing to follow where his mind had gone, and their mother was worn out from caring for him night and day. When Julia told her about Jeremiah, she received the news mutely, as if she had lost so much already there were no words left to say, as if this were just the epilogue of the long tragedy called life.

Julia thought she might have dropped the phone from shock. "Are you there, Mother?" she asked after moments of silence.

"Yes." Barely a whisper.

"Did you hear me?"

"Yes."

"Will you tell . . . him?"

"No."

This was consistent with the mother Julia had known all her life, always serving, forbearing, shielding. Even now, though her husband's mind and heart were hollowed out, she wanted to spare him the grief she knew he would feel if he could. For above all else in life, Jeremiah had been his one shining prize, not that he ever put it into words, or showed it in any way.

Julia always wondered if somehow in the black cave of her father's mind he had sensed a tremor in the earth the day her mother learned of Jeremiah's death, something that told him all was lost, for within days he took a sudden downward turn and two weeks later Julia received a phone call from her mother. Her father had died in his sleep. Pamela was there to help.

And Pamela was there again two months after that when their mother died. It was one of the saddest things Julia could imagine— that her mother, finally and blessedly relieved after decades as her father's full-time caregiver, not to mention full-time receiver of his every foul mood and unkind word, was allowed no respite at the end of her life. No time to travel, to redecorate her house, to go shopping, to get up in the morning and plan a whole day of doing exactly what she wanted to do. Julia's only hope was that if her mother had by chance been assigned a parcel of real estate in the heaven she claimed to believe in, maybe the landlord there would give her nice accommodations with a scenic view and free rent.

She and Matthew had driven to both funerals in Alabama, but only for the day each time. Pamela did all the real work before and after—the arranging and paying and cleaning and selling and all the rest of it. Julia fell back on her teaching as an excuse, though she knew she could have asked for, and been granted, time off. But Pamela didn't play the martyr, just took it on willingly and, of course, efficiently. Julia knew it was something a lot of sisters would still be bringing up. But Pamela didn't. She understood the real reason Julia couldn't come, the thing they never talked about.

OVER the years Julia had tried to blame her misjudgment in the matter of Jeremiah's papers on the fact that it had been such a confusing time, losing her brother and both parents so close together. But she knew emotions didn't suddenly erase a person's understanding of right and wrong, that good people in stressful times rose above temptation every day.

It all started with the letter she received months after Jeremiah's death, mailed from somewhere in Wyoming, signed, simply, "Lulu." She was surprised at the quality of the writing itself, though the stationery had been a sheet of notebook paper. The letter stated that Lulu had "stacks of Jerry's papers," which she wanted to send to Julia since "Jerry always said you were the one who could appreciate them and would know what to do with them."

Suggesting that the packaging and postage would be a hardship since "Jerry didn't have insurance and things are tight," Lulu asked if Julia wanted her to "go to the trouble of mailing them, or just dispose of them." She would wait a few weeks, she said, and if she didn't hear anything, she would "assume the latter."

Julia wrote her back, of course—addressing the envelope the same way the letter was signed, to "Lulu," and though Pamela advised her not to, she enclosed a check. Sometime later a box appeared at the front door of the stone house. It was a box that at one time had held a television, a fact from which Julia deduced that though money was supposedly tight, it appeared that Lulu was able to scrape together enough for one of life's real essentials.

So those were the facts. One, two, three deaths, all within a few months. Then a box of handwritten manuscripts—short stories, essays, a novella, and a lengthy memoir titled *Lost Boy*. It was the memoir that filled in the gap between the hot summer night Julia had last heard her seventeen-year-old brother slam the door of his bedroom in Alabama and the day over twenty years later when he finally called his mother on the telephone to tell her he was living in Wyoming with a woman named Lulu and their little girl, who was six.

The memoir made fascinating reading, like a novel, with a hero she would have loved even if he hadn't been her own brother. When she took it out of the box that first day, Julia read it straight through without stopping. Though she realized the potential for distorting the truth when penning one's own life story, she also recognized in Jeremiah's writing something remarkable. Even if certain details were overstated—though she had no way of knowing whether they were—her brother was a poet with words.

She had seen glimpses of it when he was growing up, of course, in his book reports and English papers, whenever he took the trouble to do them, but this was different. It was mature writing by someone who had somehow mastered the narrative art without apparently having been taught.

The knowledge affected her in two ways. First, she was proud, as anyone is proud of a family member who performs well, though she knew it was a selfish kind of pride, the kind whereby one sees a relative's achievement as a reminder that he shares the same superior gene pool. Second, she was angry that Jeremiah, who had slouched his way only through eleventh grade, could put words together as well as she could. Further evidence of the fundamental unfairness of life. She had always tried so desperately to meet their father's high standards, while Jeremiah, the apple of his eye, never appeared to care whether he measured up, in fact seemed to make a game of falling short.

The memoir ended abruptly after fast-forwarding over a great deal of time, as if tired of itself. No more lush, detail-rich passages, only a small breath of white space followed by a flat summary: *And one September day I arrived in Wyoming, where a woman's heart opened to me and I found home at last. We had a child, a beautiful little girl, and it came to pass in the fullness of time that I returned to the faith of my mother.*

That was all. Stymied, Julia read the closing sentence many times. She never would have guessed that "the faith of my mother" was a place to which Jeremiah would return, for she couldn't remember that he had ever been there in the first place. In his youth, he, like Julia, had had no use for their mother's faith. He saw it as a defect that enabled their father's tyranny, for submission was a key ingredient of her particular faith. But so was love. And prayer—their mother took to heart the admonition to "pray without ceasing."

The faith of their mother was not embraced by their father, though the two of them had met at a tent revival in the early fifties, where her father was song leader and soloist for a traveling evangelist. Her mother, sitting on the front row between her parents, had caught his eye, as he had caught hers. Julia wondered if there were signs, had her mother's eye not been so dazzled by his handsome exterior, that his heart was not in his work, that the words he sang meant nothing to him, that he had simply secured a job where he might meet pretty, easy-to-manipulate young women.

After they married, he told her he wanted sons. That she bore him only one was a disappointment he never let her forget. As children, Julia and Pamela never had to wonder where they stood in their father's affection, for he never tried to pretend that he esteemed his daughters as much as his son.

Though, to be sure, he had a strange way of showing his esteem for Jeremiah. The two of them, father and son, were so much alike they could have been twins if time could erase an age difference of thirty years. Yet as far back as Julia could remember, there had been conflict.

Her mother had often wrung her hands over it, called it a Frederickson family trait. "Your father and his father never did see eye to eye either," she told Julia once, "and the same with his father and grandfather—it's something in the Frederickson men that can't just let each other *be*. The fathers always have to be striving and picking at the sons." Julia wondered if her mother really did believe the striving and picking were aimed only at Jeremiah. Didn't she hear the way their father talked to them *all*? Or maybe she just meant that Jeremiah was the only one who ever fought back.

Though their battles were many and fierce, there was a softness in Jeremiah that her father didn't have. Not softness in the sense of weakness, but gentleness, toward women, babies, animals, and anything beautiful, even everyday beauty—a wildflower, a leaf, a robin. Running deep beneath all the things they shared, which were many—good looks, intelligence, verbal wit, musical giftedness, physical strength—there was this one enormous difference. And it seemed to be the thing her father couldn't abide, the thing he kept trying to root out.

If judging only by her last memory of the two of them together, Julia might be tempted to say that her father had succeeded, for there was nothing gentle about her brother that sultry July night. Not when their argument first erupted, not when Jeremiah hurled a chair against the wall, not when he answered his father's tirade curse for curse, not when he slammed the door of his room so hard the wood splintered, not when he turned his music up as loud as it would go and threw things around inside his room.

By early morning he was gone and never came back. On the kitchen table he left his mother a pink rosebud from the bush by the back door and a note that said simply, *I love you, Mom, I always will, but I have to leave before I turn into him. I'll see you again one day. Promise.* Pamela had found both flower and note in a small jewelry case in her mother's dresser after her death, the brown papery bud detached from the stem, the note worn from handling.

Within her brother's papers, Julia saw sure evidence of the gentleness her father had so hated but had failed to eradicate. All these lovely words—she wondered if they had cost him effort, or had just wafted into his mind as a breeze through an open window.

And though Julia hated to admit it, the anger evoked by her brother's writing gave rise to another emotion: envy. She found herself wishing she had written these words. So what if her dissertation had been praised as a "masterpiece of writing, both scholarly and artistic"? Academic writing had only been a hoop in the dog and pony show of higher learning, and she had jumped through it, with one goal in mind: to qualify for a college teaching position. It certainly wasn't the kind of writing she really wanted to do.

In her first years as a new teacher, she submitted papers and essays to various literary periodicals to fulfill the standards expected of faculty members in the arts and sciences at Millard-Temple. Several were accepted for publication. But it was her love of fiction that continued to grow, especially the short stories of Flannery O'Connor. She fed her obsession by reading these stories over and over. This was the kind of fiction she wanted to write someday—startling and mysterious and comical all at once.

The day she received the box from Lulu and first read Jeremiah's stories, something else hit her hard: What was she waiting for? She had already been teaching for fifteen years. If her younger brother had written things like these, why hadn't she? She had gone through hard times, but what of it? So had he. Anyway, hard times were no excuse for not writing. If anything, they should be fodder.

She nearly lost heart that day. She imagined a drag race, with her car stalled at the starting line while Jeremiah's and everyone else's sped around and around the track.

Time passed, not much, and then one day she was sitting in the living room of the stone house, reading through one of Jeremiah's stories again, this time penciling in a few changes, as if she were a magazine editor and someone she didn't know had submitted this piece.

A VAN swung into the library parking lot now and pulled into the spot next to Julia's Buick. The back door slid open and four children clambered out, all of them holding armfuls of books. A woman got out from the driver's side and ambled toward the library, the children trailing after her, all talking at once. One of them, a skinny boy with shaggy white-blond hair, was hopping on one foot.

What's wrong with you? Settle down! Can't you just walk like all the normal children in the world do?—it was amazing how words you hadn't heard for almost half a century could come back so clearly.

Starting with his first step, Jeremiah's constant motion had been only one of their father's many complaints against him.

Julia took a piece of paper out of her purse and looked at it. On it were written the titles of the movie and the books she was going to pick up here at the library. It was getting stuffy in the car, so she opened the door. But still she didn't get out.

The woman and three of the children were almost to the door of the library now, but the towheaded boy was down on all fours beside the broken sidewalk, peering into a crack, his books strewn about him on the ground.

Keep up! Watch what you're doing! Why can't you stick to one thing?

Julia suddenly wondered if over the years the roots of the oak tree had gradually applied more and more pressure until one day the sidewalk had all at once broken apart with a sound like a discharging cannon, or whether it had happened silently. She wondered if even now the cracks were still growing, if someone could monitor them around the clock and, with measuring tools, could actually chart them widening, lengthening.

A FTER she had been through Jeremiah's story several times that day, revising a word here, adding a transitional phrase there, changing the title, she had looked up from the sofa where she sat in the living room. On the coffee table in front of her was a trial issue of a new regional literary magazine titled *Green River* that had come in the mail the day before. She decided on the spot to submit the story there.

She typed it from the handwritten pages, very carefully, and proofread it multiple times. Up to the end, she planned to submit the story with the same byline he had neatly printed at the top of every page—*J. Frederickson*. Or at least that was what she told herself now. She had prepared the mailing envelope, thinking about other magazines she could try if this one didn't want it. As it turned out, *Green River* did want it, and they published it without making a single change.

What she couldn't remember was what had gone through her mind in the seconds right before printing off the final copy, the exact moment when she lifted her hands above the computer keyboard and added another name to the end of *J. Frederickson* to make it *J. Frederickson Rich*.

Maybe she had been plotting to do this all along, or maybe the thought came to her at the very end in a rush of pragmatic justifications piling up one on top of the other: *Contemporary magazines prefer to publish stories by living writers.* And *After all, this would be in a trash heap in Wyoming by now if I hadn't ransomed it from Lulu.* And *My editing made it what it is.* And *Jeremiah wouldn't care who got the credit.* And *Tenure requires publishing.* And, of course, *No one will ever know the difference.* All of which missed the point completely.

A N old woman was slowly exiting the library using a cane. In her other hand she carried a quilted tote, bulging with books. She crept to a car in a nearby handicapped space and proceeded to get her books, her cane, and herself inside. It struck Julia that here was a woman of courage whose limitations didn't stop her from venturing forth to get what she wanted. Yet she defrauded no one in the process.

Julia sighed and glanced down again at the paper in her hand. One of the titles she had written down was another how-to book that a colleague in the English department had recommended—*On Writing: A Memoir of the Craft*, by Stephen King, of all people. So now she would go inside, check it out, take it home, and read it. She put one foot out of the car. She couldn't begin to count the number of how-to books she had read, always delaying the action of writing for a little more preparation.

She got out and headed for the entrance, thoroughly peeved that she had allowed herself to be trapped once again in all these depressing memories. Perhaps they had served one purpose, however, by increasing her resolve to avoid Carmen. For how could you bear to look at a child, knowing you had stolen from her father?

· chapter 5 ·

LIKE PRECIOUS CARGO

Three more days passed without incident. No dreaded phone calls or knocks on the door of the stone house, at least not while Julia was home. She began to hope that Carmen had already come and gone or had given up her plan to visit, had decided instead to get back on the boat with her friend and perhaps sail to South America.

Julia gave her last exam, finished reporting her grades, and then on Friday afternoon put on her black academic cap and gown to march in the graduation procession. The faculty members flanked the students as they filed into the auditorium, then parted from them and sat on the platform in rows facing the graduates and their families.

Julia found herself listening and watching more attentively this time, knowing she would be absent from the ceremony next year. It came to her that her sabbatical was a rare opportunity in more ways than one, a warm-up exercise for retirement. She found her senses on high alert—the trumpet fanfare sounded louder than usual, the colors of the flags borne in at the head of the procession seemed brighter, the excitement more palpable.

Usually during the conferring of degrees that followed the commencement address, Julia listened carefully to each graduate's name as it was announced. Sometimes, just to have something to do, she even checked them off one at a time in the printed program, adding asterisks beside the names of students she had taught. Today, however, she had no interest in that. Already she felt a detachment from campus proceedings, as if observing from a great height.

She knew it was due to more than her imminent sabbatical. Part of it was a recurring sense of dismay that time could have swept her up and so quickly deposited her at the end of another school year, seated here with other gray, stodgy professors. But even more than that, she felt somehow shaken by the sight of so many happy faces in the audience. The graduates, yes, but more than these, the parents and grandparents. It was a line of thought she didn't want to allow, a box she wanted to keep the lid on.

I N Julia's youth, parenthood was always the cornerstone of whatever future she imagined for herself, in spite of the fact that her own parents did little to cast it in a positive light. Though she might become other things, too, she knew she would surely be the mother of children. Maybe it was only an extension of her lifelong impulse to revise the unsatisfactory, but regardless of its source, it was a persistent dream—to be half of a happy team of parents such as those she saw on television or occasionally in the homes of neighbors and friends, sometimes even in public places among strangers.

And it was at the beginning of graduate school that she at last began to feel that the dream might be within reach. She met a boy—college students were still referred to as boys and girls in those days—in a class called Research and Writing. They started dating, then going steady—another obsolete term. Victor Hart was his name, and he was working toward a doctoral degree in history. At some point they began to talk of marriage.

Victor was smart, not only in the global sense of understanding how the universe was put together but also in subtle, intuitive ways often thought to be a woman's purview. He knew in an instant when she was troubled, for example, had an instinct for whether silence or coaxing was called for, was a dispenser of the understated but perfect compliment: *I see the world reflected in your eyes, Your voice is like a fresh clear morning, You create solace when you enter a room, I admire your truthfulness.* But it was her truthfulness that fell short in the end. She let him go, or rather sent him away, without ever telling him why.

A few days after defending her dissertation, on her way from Texas to her new teaching position in South Carolina, she had stopped at her parents' home in Alabama, and all was destroyed in a flash. The Christmas wedding she and Victor had talked about never came to pass. He called, he wrote, he tried to see her, but she shut him out. She couldn't marry, she told him. Not now, not ever. No, there was nothing to explain; she had simply changed her mind. She never breathed a word about what had happened to her in Alabama.

When she did marry, years later and against her better judgment, it was not Victor. Matthew Rich was the man she married, though not the man she loved. And not the man to whom she bore children. That part of marriage never happened.

At unexpected times Victor still came to mind. She remembered meals they had cooked together, books they had read, concerts they had attended. She knew he had moved back to his home state of California, for she had read an item in an alumni newsletter years ago: *Victor Hart lives in Zion Park, CA, where he chairs the history department at South Chester University. His wife, Laura, is a systems analyst.*

Julia wasn't sure what a systems analyst was, but she wondered what kind of woman Laura Hart was, whether she had given Victor children. Sometimes she wondered if Victor ever thought about the girl named Julia Frederickson he had once claimed to love, the creator of solace with the reflecting eyes and the fresh, clear voice, whose truthfulness he admired.

A s she was exiting the auditorium, Marcy called her name. Julia turned around and waited for her. Marcy already had her cap off. "Am I glad that's over. Good speech, though, and so *short*! Remember the year that old fogy went on forever and then started over at the beginning of his speech? It was like he was in a loop he couldn't get out of." She was trying to fluff her hair. "I hate these caps. Ring around the hairdo."

The lawns were already flooding with graduates and their families, everyone laughing, posing for snapshots, giving high fives. Some of the teachers posted themselves at certain locations every year after graduation so that students could find them, introduce them to their parents, have pictures taken with them. Julia had never taken such a chance, however, for she had no confidence that anyone would come by. She and Marcy agreed on this point and usually made plans to go somewhere to eat as soon as they could take off their regalia and get away from campus.

As they walked toward Simmons Hall together, Marcy described what the other teachers seated on her row were doing during the ceremony. Seated farther back than Julia, those on Marcy's row could get away with more. Julia caught only snatches of what she was saying—someone was working a Sudoku puzzle, someone else was reading a paperback book. No doubt another was texting, someone else dozing—all the same predictable back-row behaviors the younger teachers either had picked up from their students or had never outgrown themselves. In previous years, Julia had felt indignant over such reports, but today she could muster nothing beyond indifference.

In her office she removed her hairpins and took off her cap, then her robe. She laid her cap back in the bottom drawer of her file cabinet and hung her robe on the coat hook behind her door, where it would wait until she needed it again.

She was touching up her hair when Marcy appeared again with an armful of books and folders, her computer bag slung over one shoulder. "All set? You're riding with me this time. I'll dump this stuff in the backseat."

Julia started to argue but changed her mind. Riding with Marcy, though always an exercise in patience, would necessitate a trip back to campus to get her car, which would give her a good reason to return to her office. She thought she might spend some time here this evening after they ate—a sort of private observance to close the school year and usher in her sabbatical.

It was almost four thirty by the time they made their way through the campus traffic and were finally seated in a place called Sticky Fingers in downtown Greenville, a drive of some thirty minutes, during which Marcy sprang it on Julia that this was to be her treat—an end-of-year, beginning-of-sabbatical, I'll-miss-you celebration.

Though not a sentimental person, Julia suddenly realized that she would look back fondly on this outing with her friend. For years she had taken Marcy for granted, had even been annoyed with her on a regular basis, but now it struck her that she would miss seeing her, eating with her, hearing her stories and gossip.

As a friend, Marcy deserved more credit than Julia gave her. She made few demands and not only excused small slights but seemed to have no memory of them afterward. Further, she was clearly bright, though she seemed to think she had been hired at Millard-

Temple only by some stroke of luck. She often expressed wonder that someone with Julia's mind would stoop to be her friend. "Don't say things like that," Julia had told her more than once. "You're the one who knows Brit Lit inside out."

But Marcy would always laugh and counter with something like "What I know about Brit Lit could maybe fill a demitasse, but don't ask me anything about any other kind of lit. I'm the one who thought Hiawatha was a girl, remember."

They continued to look at the menu after the waitress took their drink orders, Marcy reading aloud and exclaiming over the various items. By now Julia was already being reminded that Marcy's cheerfulness was hard to take for long stretches. Somehow she willed herself to relax, however. She was in no hurry. The more time here, the less time at home. She faded in and out of Marcy's outflow of talk, occasionally providing an answer to a question or filling a pause with a brief remark.

At one point Marcy stopped, slapped the table on both sides of her plate of ribs, and said, "Shoot, girl, I'm going to miss you next year! Who's going to listen to me? Larry's going to miss you, too, I'll tell you—he'll be the one who has to sit through all my saved-up words at the end of the day. Poor guy, he'll be begging for the condensed edition!" Larry was Marcy's husband, about whom Julia knew more than she cared to. Most of it was good, however, for according to Marcy, Larry was "a husband to die for."

Afterward they walked all the way down Main Street to the Liberty Bridge, a cantilevered affair over the Reedy River. They stopped in a few of the shops along the way and got ice cream at one of them. When Marcy dropped her off by her car back at the college almost three hours later, Julia allowed an awkward hug before she opened the door to get out. Marcy put a hand on her arm. "Hey, kiddo, you seem a little down. You going to be okay?"

Julia nodded. "Oh, sure, I'll be fine."

"It's been a hard year for you," Marcy said. "You deserve some time off." She cocked her head. "So, what are you going to do with yourself?"

They had been over this ground before, but only in general terms. "Oh, a little of this and that," Julia said.

Marcy waited a moment to see if there was more, then said, "Well, I'll tell you what I'd do if I had a year off. I'd go back to Kansas and spend a whole month in the town where I grew up. I'd drive by my old house at least once a day and visit my old schools and the grocery store and the library and the church and the park and my granddaddy's barber shop and all the rest of it. I'd relive my whole childhood, right up to the day I got married and had to start being a boring old adult." She laughed. "How about you—you going back home for a little bit?"

The question only proved how little Marcy knew about her, though, in all fairness, it more accurately proved how little Julia had shared with her. She shook her head. "No, I won't be doing that. Nobody's there anymore."

Marcy smiled at her. "Well, if you need anything, you'll holler, won't you? Don't be a stranger. Keep in touch, okay? I'll sure be lonesome eating by myself in the cafeteria every day. Can we have lunch together sometimes?"

Julia felt suddenly very tired. Talkative people wore her out, especially when so much of the talk was in the form of questions. She nodded. "Sure, I'll be around. Give me a call."

"I'll do it!" Marcy said. "Bye now, girlfriend! Don't forget me! Have fun!" She waved, blew a kiss, and as she pulled away gave several toots of her horn. Julia watched her turn the corner and head toward the front gate. Such an innocent soul, Marcy. It was amazing that she had such a friend.

After Marcy's car disappeared from sight, Julia went inside Simmons Hall and sat in her office with the blinds open until she could see night falling over the campus. She left the light off so as not to attract attention, in case anyone else happened to be in the building on the evening of graduation day. Presently she heard the slam of a door down the hall, then laughter, followed by "I'm so out of here!" And then all was quiet for a long time.

At last she rose from her desk, walked to the door, and took a long look around her office. In the months to come, she knew she would think of it often, as a familiar land where she had once lived and one to which she longed to return. Out in the hall she tested the doorknob to make sure it was locked before heading down the dark hallway.

O VER the next week Pamela continued to call every evening with the same question: "Did she come yet?" She also said things like, "Well, you need to get on with your life. You're too tense. I think you ought to pack a suitcase and come see me for a couple of weeks. Sisters *do* usually visit each other, you know."

As if it would ease anybody's tension to spend a week in the same house with an inveterate nail biter like Pamela. Julia always thanked her but declined, claiming she was too tired to pack a suitcase. She hadn't told Pamela about her sabbatical yet because she dreaded hearing all the questions, all the advice about how she should use the time, especially more hints about visits.

As the days wore on, she began to allow herself to believe that the threat of Carmen was past. She wasn't ready yet to open Matthew's closet, but she busied herself cleaning the back porch and kitchen cupboards, getting her teaching wardrobe washed and pressed and properly stored, watching movies, taking long walks, going back and forth to the library.

She began reading late into the night. She finished two books about writing, even took some notes to integrate into her lectures.

Her colleague had been right about the Stephen King book—it was very good, even though King said bluntly that nobody really needed how-to books in order to learn to write well. You could learn everything you needed to know, he said, by reading and paying attention and rubbing shoulders with people in the normal course of living and working. And by writing, of course. You had to write a lot to learn to write well.

And this frothy-sounding principle from the other book by a writer she had never heard of: "To achieve the highest mark in fiction, the writer himself must live life fully." She wrote that down, too. Though insipid, it could launch a class discussion: *What does it mean to live life fully?*

Somewhere in the back of Julia's mind during the reading of these two books, an intention had formed. She had to write a story of her own and get it published. If she didn't, she could never hope to put to rest her fear and guilt over Jeremiah's stories. Not that writing a good story would absolve her, but maybe it would clear her mind, gain her a few more nights of sleep, or at least a few nights of more sleep.

Many years ago she had read a description of guilt that had stuck with her, the gist of it being that guilt is an irresistible thing humans latch on to and carry around like precious cargo. She thought it might have been in a Steinbeck novel, though she couldn't remember which one. She had read the passage many times, then had closed the book never to finish it.

ON the second Saturday morning in June, Julia rose early, having decided sometime during the night to drive to Andalusia in Milledgeville, Georgia, today. It would take seven hours of driving time altogether, and then the walking tour. Not only would it get her out of the house in case Carmen came, but she would also be able to list the trip under "Professional Growth and Development" in the next update of her faculty portfolio.

Besides visiting Andalusia, she had made another decision during the night: If she could get through another week safely, she would put Carmen completely out of her mind and get on with the summer.

She dressed quickly, ate a little breakfast, printed out directions, and by eight o'clock was locking the back door of the stone house. She got into the Buick, set the trip odometer, and pulled away from Ivy Dale, none of it with much enthusiasm. For some reason, this trip felt more like something she needed to do rather than wanted to.

Heading toward the interstate, she made another decision: Today she would try to live life fully. She had heard the phrase many times before running across it in the book, of course, and even though it was a cliché, it might be something to take up her mind today. She knew it probably started with a positive attitude—another nebulous concept, with a whiff of false virtue about it, one of those traits she associated with shallow naïve people. But it couldn't hurt. It might be fun to become a different person for a day.

The day promised to be a fine, sunny one—there, that was a start on a positive attitude. And the summer was spread out before her, and an entire year after that. She reminded herself again that many of her colleagues would love to be in her place, getting paid for all that time to do whatever they wanted to do.

As she settled into the flow of traffic, another idea returned to her, something else she had thought of during the previous night—that after this refresher drive to Andalusia she could perhaps plan a trip along the eastern seaboard. New England was full of authors' homes. Such a trip would certainly give her something to show for her year out of the classroom. Besides courage to leave her comfort zone, it would require research and preparation, not to mention careful budgeting, and then the trip itself would occupy a great deal of time and in the end provide her with even more professional activities to list in her portfolio. And maybe ideas for stories, too.

The miles passed agreeably enough. Before long she tuned the radio to *Weekend Edition* on NPR and listened for a while to a woman from Australia talking about the year she spent as a doctor in the African bush. "I've never liked change," the woman said in her starchy, clipped accent. "I was absolutely petrified, but now I'm gratified that I did it." Here was inspiration—a woman who was afraid to leave her comfort zone but did it anyway and was glad afterward.

Shortly there followed a story about a restaurant in Tennessee called the Critter Hutch, specializing in dishes featuring squirrel, possum, and rabbit. "Fried is the cooking method of choice here at the Critter Hutch," the radio narrator said. In the background were kitchen sounds—clanging metal, whirring mixers, sizzling grills, running water, shouting, clattering, thunking. Though Julia had no interest in actually eating at the Critter Hutch, she suddenly wished she could see it. What a wonder—the world was full of such diverse people, even in neighboring states. Maybe she should make a list of some of these places for day trips. Tennessee wasn't that far away.

T HE radio soon became only background noise as Julia fell to remembering. Matthew's people had lived in Tennessee. He had taken her there the first Christmas after they were married. As she recalled, the relatives she had met on that trip were just the type to eat possum and squirrel. By then the grandmother who had raised Matthew was in failing health in a nursing home called Quiet Acres. They had gone to see her.

A bizarre but curiously tender scene came to Julia's mind. The grandmother, whom Matthew had always spoken of as Gran, was a wisp of a woman, part Cherokee, with sharp features, skin like old leather, and a long tangle of yellow-gray hair.

When they entered her room, Gran was staring hard at the door as if willing someone to appear. "Oh, bless us, you're here, Matty," she said, her voice a high-pitched warble yet oddly commanding. "Come over here quick." She raised a twisted hand toward her bedside table. "Look inside there and get that jar."

There was only one jar in the drawer, and Matthew took it out. It was a jar of hair removal cream. "You got to do this, Matty." She touched a clawlike finger to her jawline. "I got these old whiskers down here, but my hands are too crippled up to do anything."

Matthew had held back. "I brought Julia to meet you, Gran," he said. He cast a look at Julia that said, *Help me out here.* But Julia stayed where she was, at the foot of the bed. She must have spoken the usual niceties—*Glad to meet you, I've heard so much about you*— but Gran had eyes only for Matthew.

"Nurses here can't do squat," Gran said. "Only one I like—a colored girl. All the rest I got no use for. Don't reckon half of them ever even went to nursing school." She pushed herself up higher on her pillows. "Go on, Matty, get a washrag from the sink and wet it. It tells you how to do it on the jar."

Julia remembered little else about that trip to Tennessee, but she could still see Matthew sitting on the edge of his grandmother's bed, smoothing cream onto her face and then gently wiping it off. Afterward he brushed the tangles out of her hair. Julia hadn't thought much about the incident at the time, but it struck her now as a marvel. She wondered why she couldn't have learned to love a man like that, couldn't have at least tried. It was at unguarded moments like this that she felt the impact of her carelessness, her failure to notice important things.

Well, Matthew had been careless, too, leaving her saddled with so many debts that she'd been forced to deplete almost every resource, even most of her modest inheritance. She had always trusted him to pay the bills and keep their accounts in order. After all, as an insurance adjuster, he worked with numbers every day. It was incredible to think she had known so little about their finances, that she had no idea, for example, about the bad investments or the other two credit cards Matthew used besides the one they shared, and that he routinely robbed one to pay the other. Electronic equipment, expensive clothes, things for the house, a new car every couple of years—nothing that worried her at the time, but all of which added up to a lot of money.

When all the debts were finally settled, she considered it a mercy that she was able to keep the stone house and her Buick. That she had enough each month to pay Gil the yardman was a luxury.

But she had already strayed from her purpose—these weren't positive thoughts. She couldn't let herself start going over all of that. It was in the past. With Pamela's help, she had paid every debt. Except for her monthly mortgage, she owed no one. There, that was a happy thought. Her accounts were clear, with some left over.

There was no way to know how word of her financial difficulty had leaked out, but such news always did. Even though she had been spared the public ignominy of foreclosure or bankruptcy, Julia could still see in people's eyes that they knew she had fallen to reduced circumstances. She wanted to wear a sign around her neck: *Don't feel sorry for me. I am completely solvent.*

She turned the radio up a little. ". . . and though they've recently received sharp criticism from animal rights activists, for now the Critter Hutch is still open for lunch and supper six days a week," the reporter was saying. Well, of course, the whole world could be overrun with squirrels and rabbits, with ten possums lying dead along every country mile, but there would always be some PETA fanatic ready to stage a protest over killing them for food.

Julia turned the radio off and popped an audiocassette into the tape player. Respighi's *Pines of Rome*—that would do. She didn't mind being one of the few people who still had a collection of audiocassettes and still drove a car with a cassette player. It was a perfectly legitimate way to listen to music. It occurred to her that perhaps she could go to Rome someday and see the Coliseum and the Vatican and the catacombs and the Pantheon. And whatever else was there. Aside from the stereotypical things—the Eiffel Tower in Paris, Big Ben in London, the canals in Venice—she knew so little of the world. Surely part of living life fully had to be visiting other countries.

Or she could read about them—that would be free, although inferior to the real thing and certainly not the most aggressive way to combat provinciality. Still, armchair travel could be another way to fill the long hours of the coming year.

S HE pulled into the entrance at Andalusia before noon and made her way to the broad steps leading up to the house. A short video about Flannery O'Connor ran continuously in one of the back rooms, and this was where she decided to start. Though none of it was new information to her, she never grew tired of it. After that she took her time walking through the house. She stood at the doorway of O'Connor's bedroom a long time, imagining the author bent over her typewriter every morning.

On the wide screened front porch, she sat in a rocking chair a good while, looking out over the same landscape O'Connor had observed decades earlier. She left the house and strolled among the various outbuildings, then walked down to the pond and along the road for a piece, imagining what it must have been like when O'Connor lived here, when the sweetness of purple wisteria hung in the air and peacocks roosted in the trees at night.

A strange hobby for a single woman to have had—raising noisy, showy peacocks—but O'Connor had owned as many as fifty at a time. Recently the foundation had reinstated a moderate number of the birds at Andalusia, no doubt hoping to attract more tourists. As Julia walked around the property, she observed them closely, musing over the astounding inequity between the plain-looking females and the males dragging their ridiculously magnificent tails behind them. She remembered reading somewhere that a peacock's nighttime screech sounded like someone crying, "Help!"

She finally left Andalusia and drove through the town of Milledgeville, past the college O'Connor attended, her childhood home, the old Sanford Tea House where she used to dine, the church where she attended daily mass, the cemetery where she was buried.

It was well after three o'clock by the time she started home. The trip had been a good idea. As she had hoped, the old fascination had returned and Andalusia had worked its spell on her.

FOR the next week it rained off and on every day, with sudden gusts of wind whipping up and clouds letting loose torrential downpours that flooded creeks and basements. Most days it rained two or three times, loud sustained drummings on the roof. Once a storm broke in the middle of the night, after Julia had finally fallen asleep, the lightning so intense and prolonged that she could have read in bed without the lamp. Twice the power went off for several hours. "Someone better build an ark," a weatherman on television said.

Julia stayed close to home, and when at the end of the week the rain subsided, her spirits lifted, not simply because the sun had at last appeared through the clouds but also because her final week of waiting was up and Carmen had not come. And wasn't that the way it went? The worries you allowed to consume you usually never came to pass, at least not while you were looking for them. It was the ordinary days you had to watch out for, the insignificant moments you never before considered as threats. Those could turn your world upside down.

It happened two weeks later, on an otherwise unremarkable Saturday, the last day of June. Julia had run to the grocery store for a few things and on her way home turned the radio to NPR just long enough to hear that it was Click and Clack, the Tappet Brothers—the call-in program about car trouble. As she wasn't interested in hearing the brothers crack jokes about slipping clutches, worn axles, and the like, she turned it off almost immediately, but not before she heard a woman caller ask, "What could be causing the horn of my 1999 Ford Explorer to honk at random intervals all by itself?" It was a question the two brothers would get around to answering eventually, but only after a great deal of foolishness.

When she arrived at the stone house, she pulled her Buick around to the back, got out with her two bags of groceries, stepped into the screened porch, and bent her head to fit her key into the back door. A momentary presumption upon a common, everyday act. And just as the key slipped into the lock, a voice spoke from behind her.

"Hey, Aunt Julia. I hope you don't mind me waiting here on your glider."

· chapter 6 ·

NO USEFUL PLAN

How did one prepare herself to see her brother's face in a girl's body? In a story, the moment might be accompanied by a gasp and the dropping of the grocery bags. The same in a movie, with a camera zoom and a slow-motion sequence of the various items scattering across the floor. In real life, it appeared that one simply turned into a statue and stared.

In all her prior imaginings of Carmen's arrival, Julia had never considered this one: that the girl would be waiting on the back porch for her. Though too late now for scolding herself, she did it anyway. She should have been prepared. She should have known that an uninvited guest wouldn't hesitate to come around to the back, wouldn't let an unlocked screen door stand in her way.

Nor had she stopped to think that Carmen would now be close to the same age as Jeremiah was when he left home. The girl could have no way of knowing how much she looked like him. Same build, tall and thin. Even the clothes she was wearing—T-shirt, jeans, black All-Star Cons—could have been his, though he wouldn't have worn a shirt ripped at the shoulder. Torn clothing wasn't part of the fashion scene back then.

Carmen stood in front of the glider, shifting her weight from one foot to the other, rubbing her hands up and down the sides of her jeans. The curly blond hair was Jeremiah's, too, in fact almost the same length he had worn his in the seventies, when their father had railed against the hippie look, which was exactly the look Jeremiah had adopted. Except for the ripped shirt, however, the girl had an innocent, wholesome look, like someone who had grown up on a farm in the Midwest. Nothing of the counterculture in her appearance, nothing to mark her as a teenager with a troubled history—no pink hair, bizarre piercings, skull-and-crossbones tattoos, at least none that could be seen.

Julia wondered if the girl's mother had felt slighted whenever she looked at her and saw nothing of herself, only Jeremiah. The wide-set eyes were his also, and the spatter of freckles across the nose and the smile that dimpled at one corner. It appeared to be a forced smile, though, not one related to gladness, and it began to falter as the silence grew longer.

"I guess you got my phone message a while back?" Carmen said, putting a hand to her ear like a phone and wiggling it. "I was going to call again, but . . . well, I couldn't." And then, as if there might be some question, "I'm Carmen." She laughed nervously. "I guess we never officially met. Or unofficially either."

As it would serve no purpose to pretend she hadn't gotten the message, Julia said, "Yes, I got it, but it was so long ago now that I thought you must have changed your plans." The door into the kitchen was unlocked and standing ajar now. She couldn't remember opening it, but she must have, for her keys were dangling from the doorknob. She removed them and dropped them back into her purse, then stepped away from the door and placed a hand on the back of the wicker rocking chair.

"Well, I was going to come sooner," the girl said, "but some things happened. Some . . . lamentable things." She sat down on the glider again, as if understanding that an invitation to come inside wasn't imminent.

Lamentable—strange that she would say that. It was exactly the kind of formal word Jeremiah would have dropped into an otherwise simple, colorless sentence. Julia set the bags of groceries on the floor. It didn't matter that it was hot out here on the porch, that there were things in the bags that needed to go in the refrigerator. Something clear and forthright needed to be said, and there wasn't a minute to waste.

"I talked to your grandmother a month or so ago," Julia said. "She needed to get in touch with you. She had some things to tell you." Julia hoped she didn't sound too eager.

"My grandmother?" The girl's confusion looked genuine.

"She said her name was Ida."

Carmen made a scoffing noise. "Oh—Ida. She's not my grandmother."

Julia let this pass. "Have you talked with anybody at home recently?" she said.

Carmen frowned. "Home? If you're talking about Wyoming, no."

"Well, I'm afraid Ida has some bad news," Julia said. "I still have her number. I'll go get it so you can call her."

Carmen shook her head. "Wait, no, I'm going to have to decline that offer. Just so you know, Ida has a way of taking liberties with the truth. She loves to pass along bad news. Somebody stubs their toe, she'll say they're paralyzed from the waist down." She looked down and studied a thumbnail. "Did she tell you what this bad news was?"

"Yes, she did, and in this case I don't think she could make it sound worse than it is. It's about Lulu."

Carmen looked up. "What about her?"

• • •

J ULIA held back a moment. She knew the bearer of such news should speak softly, show compassion. A touch of the hand, a hug—those would be appropriate. But she made no move. She took a breath and said it plainly, gently. "Lulu died. Probably six or seven weeks ago now."

Carmen stared at her. She swallowed hard but didn't flinch. She appeared to be processing the information, but reserving belief.

Julia set her purse on the floor beside the bags of groceries and walked over to the glider. She sat down but kept her distance. "How old are you?" she said.

Carmen looked puzzled, as if stumped by the relevance of the question. *Your mother died. How old are you?*

"I mean, you're so young to have lost both of your parents," Julia said.

"I'm twenty," Carmen said.

Maybe it was true, though she looked considerably younger than that. "Well, I'm very sorry about your mother," Julia said. "That's a hard thing." She reached her hand out and laid it on the glider cushion, close to Carmen but not touching her.

The girl turned her face away. "We weren't close," and after a moment, "not for a long time. One thing Lulu knew how to do was hold a grudge." She sighed. "But she had cause."

Julia didn't know what she was expecting, but it wasn't this dull acceptance. Obviously, a little guidance was needed, a little pressure. "Well, I know you'll want to go back to Wyoming for a while," she said. "I think there may be some things of your mother's they want you to have. I can help you buy a plane ticket and get you on your way. I can let them know you're coming. They're waiting for you."

Carmen turned swiftly. Her words came out in a rush. "Waiting for me? You don't understand. They don't have any use for me back there, none of them. It all changed after Daddy died. And I can't think of one single thing of Lulu's that . . ." Her eyes suddenly filled with tears, and she looked away again. With the torn sleeve of her shirt, she roughly blotted each eye.

Julia's mind was racing. She had to remain firm. She spoke again. "Well, this is what's known as a family emergency, Carmen. When something big like this happens, you sometimes have to do things you don't want to do. You don't have to stay out there indefinitely, but you need to go pay your respects to your mother and the rest of the family. It's the only decent thing to do." She couldn't see Carmen's face to judge the effect of her words. She waited a moment, then added, "If you're really twenty, you're an adult. You have to make yourself do the right thing." She suddenly remembered something else. "Ida said your aunt Effie is very low, too. Maybe she's already gone."

Carmen turned back to face her. "If Ida said it, it probably just means Effie has a cold." She breathed in sharply and said, "Effie almost killed Lulu once. That time was an accident, but another time she went after Daddy with her bare hands. She had a horrible temper. Explosive. Nuclear." She enunciated the last word carefully.

Julia could hardly take all of this in, but Carmen didn't stop. "And why did you say *if* I'm really twenty? Don't you believe me?" She looked away. "You're . . . different than I thought you'd be. Daddy used to talk about you like you were some kind of . . ." Either the word eluded her or she decided not to say it. "But I'm probably not exactly what you were expecting either."

Julia stood to her feet to signify that her mind was made up, that she wasn't going to be diverted by minor points. "Well, I'll go inside now and check for airline tickets. You can wait out here." She picked up her purse and the bags of groceries and was stepping inside the kitchen door when something occurred to her. She turned around and looked back at Carmen, then at the floor around the glider. "Where are your bags?"

Carmen looked up at the ceiling fan. "I don't have any."

"What do you mean, you don't have any?"

Carmen's eyes were following the slow rotation of the fan blades. "Your fan's not set right," she said. "It's going the wrong direction for summer."

"Did you fly here?" Julia said. "Did they lose your luggage?"

Carmen shook her head.

"Then where is it?"

There was no response.

Julia set her things down again and came back to sit on the glider. Suddenly the situation seemed more dire. She couldn't explain why, but it seemed to her that a runaway showing up on your doorstep with a suitcase was one thing, whereas a runaway showing up with only the clothes on her back was another. Though *runaway* was hardly the right word when the girl had left home years ago. But surely she had belongings of some kind somewhere. You didn't just wander around for years without anything at all. A backpack, a tote, a paper bag, something.

She tried to calm herself. "All right now, what has happened, Carmen? We can't go any further until you tell me where your things are." It was a weak, illogical ultimatum, and they both knew it. If "go any further" meant "make arrangements for you to leave," Carmen would hardly be interested in cooperating.

The girl closed her eyes and shook her head slowly. Not stubbornly, but wearily.

Julia raised her voice. "How did you get here? Weren't you in Charleston when you called? Did somebody give you a ride here?"

Carmen nodded, one quick jerk of her head. She quickly swiped a finger under each eye. Then she looked straight at Julia, lifted her chin, and said, "I hitchhiked."

Julia spoke the first words that came to her mind, spoke them emphatically. "Girls don't hitchhike," though what she really meant was *Nice girls don't hitchhike, girls with any sense at all don't hitchhike, girls who want to live to see tomorrow don't hitchhike.*

"Well, they do sometimes," Carmen said. It wasn't a challenging tone. "Sometimes they start out walking and they walk for a long, long time until they're just about ready to fall down, and then they finally give in and decide to take their chances." She paused. "Truck drivers are the most trustworthy—that's what I've found."

J ULIA'S desperation was mounting with every second. This qualified as a genuine crisis. She took in a deep breath and released it slowly. "So did you leave your things in the car you were riding in?"

"It was a pickup truck," Carmen said. "The inside of it smelled like rotten eggs."

"Okay, so you left your things in the truck you were riding in?"

"Not on purpose," Carmen said. She was flexing her fingers as if trying to work out a stiffness.

Julia tried to sound patient, though it was a mixture of anger and panic she felt. "So you have nothing? Nothing at all? Not even a toothbrush?" She heard the pitch of her voice rising.

Carmen stood up and fished in the pocket of her jeans. She brought out a few wadded dollar bills and dropped them on the glider seat beside Julia. She fished again and brought out two more. She reached into the other pocket and pulled out a small, scuffed New Testament and dropped it on top of the bills. "I had another dollar," she said, "but I bought a Frosty last night." She sat back down. "The lady didn't charge me tax."

Julia stared at the bills. "I don't want your money," she finally said. But Carmen left it where it was.

All powers of reasoning seemed to have flown. Julia had taken in all the facts of the situation, yet no useful plan had emerged. A food chopper brain, that was what she had right now. It was a favorite self-deprecating joke of Flannery O'Connor's—the kind of mind where everything went in but only minced pieces came out.

There were only a few options, none of them good. Julia obviously couldn't leave the girl out here on the porch all day and into the night. But taking her inside was inviting trouble, all sorts of messy, complicated trouble that would go on and on. She couldn't do that. But how could she send her away with nothing? Or send her away with *something*, for that matter? Now that she had sat out here and talked with her, it seemed that she had passed the point when that was possible.

All at once Pamela came to mind. What would her smart, sensible, go-getter of a sister do in her place? And right in the wake of that thought came a plan. Yes, maybe she could send the girl away after all. She could go inside right now and get together a travel bag for Carmen, and then send her off to Pamela in Twin Lakes, Virginia. After all, Pamela was Carmen's aunt, too.

Julia felt the smallest stirring of hope. This might work. Twin Lakes didn't have its own airport, but it did have a bus station, not far from Pamela's house, in fact. And Pamela had a daughter not much older than Carmen, so surely she was better equipped than Julia to figure out what to do with her, would probably enjoy the challenge—another success to add to the long list of other things she had set right in the lives of her friends and family. As for Julia, she would gladly listen to Pamela boast for the rest of her days on earth about how she had fixed the problem of Carmen, if only she would.

She quickly reviewed the steps of the plan, revising as she went. She would go inside and call the bus station first, then collect some toiletries, then come back out and give Carmen a good excuse for why she couldn't keep her here. Or maybe she should give her the excuse first, as soon as she thought of one, so that Carmen wouldn't get her hopes up about staying here tonight. Then if there were hours to while away before the bus left, they could go shopping for a few more necessities—a new shirt maybe. She would wait until Carmen was actually on her way before calling Pamela to let her know where and what time to meet her.

Julia looked at her watch. It was just before eleven in the morning. If everything fell into place, Carmen could be on her way well before suppertime, perhaps even shortly after lunch.

Lunch. Julia suddenly wondered if Carmen had eaten anything since the Frosty. The girl was leaning forward now, staring at the floor, clutching the edge of the glider seat, as if it took effort to hold herself upright.

Something twisted inside Julia, like hunger, though she knew it wasn't that. How many times, she wondered, had this child been at the mercy of others? How had she kept body and soul together? Where had she slept the night before, and the night before that? And though Julia didn't want to know the answers to any of these questions, she couldn't shake them from her mind.

A thought forced itself upon her, so powerful the words might have been spoken aloud: *Jeremiah, what am I doing to you?* The words from his memoir flashed into her mind: *We had a child, a beautiful little girl.* And Carmen's words from minutes earlier: *Daddy used to talk about you like you were some kind of . . .* Julia couldn't imagine what word went in the blank.

"What have you eaten today?" Julia asked her, and she knew the answer before it came.

"Nothing."

Julia suppressed a sigh. "Well, let's go get something. Give me a minute to put these things in the refrigerator." This wasn't a commitment, she reminded herself as she stepped inside. She wasn't bringing the girl into her house. She was only going to take her somewhere and buy her some lunch. They could eat a quick bite, and then she could proceed with the plan to send her to Pamela.

But already, the plan felt shaky. The bus station here in Beckett had closed a few years ago, but she knew there had to be one over in Greenville. She would have to get directions, which was easy enough, but what if there wasn't a bus headed to Virginia anytime today? Maybe she should check instead on airports in other towns close to Twin Lakes, Virginia.

But all at once, just as she opened the refrigerator door, she remembered something else, something that put an end to the plan, at least for now: Pamela wasn't home. Her daughter-in-law's baby had arrived two weeks early, and she had just left for Louisiana to help out. She wouldn't be back for a week.

Slowly Julia set the milk inside the refrigerator next to the orange juice, then used up more time by rearranging some things. No new plan came to mind, but maybe she would think of one while they ate. If she were a religious woman, now would be the time to pray to that end, but unlike Jeremiah, she had never returned to the faith of their mother. That kind of faith had never interested her in the least, tied up as it was with her mother's abject servitude and her father's bouts of rage.

She closed the refrigerator. She studied the three doorways out of the kitchen: one leading into the dining room; another into the living room; and the last one, through which she had just come. She heard the echo of her own words: *When something big like this happens, you sometimes have to do things you don't want to do. It's the only decent thing to do.* And something her mother used to say—*You just have to keep going forward*—though in her mother's case going forward was never linked to real progress, only to yet another act of groveling at her husband's feet.

In Julia's case, for now, it meant walking to the door leading to the back porch, where Carmen waited.

THEY drove to Del's Deli near campus. It wasn't far from Ivy Dale Lane, and the service was fast. Although it was a popular hangout for students during the school year, Julia was counting on a slim crowd since it was summer and an hour before noon. She was relieved as they stepped inside to see that she was right. Only one other table was occupied at the present, by a middle-aged couple apparently waiting for their food.

After giving Carmen time to read the menu board, Julia ordered first, more than she usually ordered and more than she wanted, to encourage Carmen to eat heartily. If she had to feed the girl before she left, she meant to do it right.

She sent Carmen to get drinks and choose a table while she paid. Then there were napkins and straws to get. Through the mirror behind the condiment station, she saw Carmen looking at her, her face expressionless as her eyes studied her from head to toe.

She joined the girl at the table, wishing she hadn't picked the one right beside the middle-aged couple. But on second thought, that might work to her advantage. With others so close, maybe Carmen wouldn't talk. Maybe she would only want to eat, and that would be fine. Talking was dangerous. It could lead to knowing too much.

Carmen picked up a straw, jabbed it upright against the tabletop, and slid the paper off. She stuck the straw into her water and drank nearly half of it.

Julia felt a pang of shame for not having offered the girl a drink of water at home, or the use of the bathroom. "You could have something else besides water," she said. "They have good sweet tea here."

Carmen shook her head. "That's okay. I like water." She took another long drink.

"It wouldn't be a bad drive at all from Greenville," the woman at the next table said. She had the kind of voice that could be called sultry, and she talked rapidly, with crisp diction. Definitely not a native of the South.

"But it would get old," the man said. "And if your first class started at nine, you'd get caught in all the morning traffic."

The woman laughed. "Yes, all the morning traffic."

"Hey, don't make fun of our morning traffic," the man said.

"Oh, I think your morning traffic is lovely," the woman said. Just then a teenage boy in a red Del's Deli T-shirt set a salad and sandwich on their table.

Carmen was looking around at the walls, which were crowded with a miscellany of old advertisements for things like Brylcreem Hair Tonic and Barq's Strawberry Soda as well as old road signs and several pieces of real art. Del, the owner of the shop, allowed local artists to display things they wanted to sell, usually leftovers from student art shows.

Several large paintings had dark Gothic themes. One of them depicted a phantomlike woman drifting through a dense forest with bats flying overhead. Another was a moonlit scene of an enormous purple spider in a black pool. It was easy to understand why no one had bought these pieces.

Carmen was staring at a painting of a castle silhouetted on a cliff. Without looking at Julia, she said, "You have a husband, don't you?"

"I did, but he died," Julia said.

Carmen looked at her, surprised. "He did? When?"

"Last August."

"How?"

Julia laid her hand over her heart and patted it. "Heart attack. It was fast."

"In his sleep?" Carmen asked.

"No," Julia said. "In the front yard. He was planting flowers." She looked away to indicate she didn't want to talk further about it.

"I'm sorry," Carmen said. Silence followed, and she seemed to be done with the subject. Then she sighed and said, "I was planting flowers when Lulu came out and called me in to tell me Daddy was dead."

Julia was instantly doubtful. "Planting flowers in October?" She didn't know much about Wyoming, but October couldn't be the right season for planting anything.

Something flared briefly in Carmen's eyes as she recognized another challenge to her truthfulness, but she let it go and nodded slowly. "Daddy had helped me rig up this little portable greenhouse for a science project in school. I couldn't really fit inside, but I could sort of crawl halfway in and do what I needed to, then close it back up tight. I had some beans growing in one big pot and some potatoes in another one, and I was planting some wildflowers when Lulu came out the back door and called me in. She was crying."

These were exactly the kinds of details Julia didn't want to hear, the whole reason she didn't want to talk. She didn't want to imagine Carmen as a child, crawling around inside a makeshift greenhouse Jeremiah had built for her. She didn't want to think about her planting things in October, hoping they would grow during the long winter. Or about her mother calling her to come in, for that only made Julia wonder what words Lulu had used and what it must have been like for a little girl to receive that kind of news about a father such as Jeremiah must have been.

I LIKE the looks of the campus," the woman at the next table said. She was petite, with large, dark eyes and a short, ragged haircut of the sort that Julia had always wished she had the nerve to try.

The woman's face showed signs of wear, but there was a comfortable kind of beauty about it.

"It's okay, I guess," the man said. "It's small."

"Tobias said I could use all his notes," she said.

The man laughed. "He was joking, right? As if you need somebody else's notes to teach a course like that. Good grief, does he know you've written books? How many has he written?"

"I don't know," she said. "It's not something you ask a person."

"Well, it's an insult. Like asking Babe Ruth to coach a Little League ball team. Or Einstein to teach junior high math. You could teach that course in your sleep." He gave a scornful laugh. "So is Tobias the guy's first name or last?"

"Does it matter?" the woman said. "Listen, I think this is one of those things that's meant to be. The way I just happened to run into him that day and he just happened to mention they hadn't found anybody to fill in for his class yet. And besides that, I need to be busy. I can't just sit around. I want to do this, Ben." She spoke the last words slowly, emphatically.

Besides Julia's natural curiosity about other people's conversations, this one was especially interesting, for it sounded as if the woman might be referring to Harry Tobias—the psychology professor at Millard-Temple who, along with Julia, had been granted a sabbatical for the coming year.

The man at the next table reached over and touched the tip of the woman's nose with his finger. "Vibrant Vera. I value you too much to vex you. If you want to stay home, fine. If not, that's fine, too."

"Good, I'll get the ball rolling," the woman said.

Julia was always amused at the silly things grown people said. But the man's last words weren't silly at all: *If you want to stay home, fine. If not, that's fine, too.* It was the kind of thing she could imagine

Matthew having said, though never in a public place where someone might have overheard. Julia suddenly wished she could tell Vibrant Vera to appreciate this man.

The boy in the red T-shirt appeared again, holding two more plates. "I got a club sandwich with fries, and a soup and wrap combo," he said. Carmen took the sandwich and set it down, then removed the long toothpick and examined each layer. Julia busied herself stirring her soup, testing it, sprinkling it with pepper. Then she took a bite of her wrap to encourage Carmen to do the same, but when she looked across the table, Carmen's eyes were closed, her lips moving, her hands touching the sides of her plate as if to make sure it didn't go anywhere.

Julia felt like groaning. Evidently her brother had not only returned to the faith of his mother but had also dragged his daughter along with him. Or maybe Carmen was only pretending to pray, making a show of piety in order to gain sympathy.

Her prayer, if that was what it was, was brief. She fell to eating in a way that made it obvious she was hungry.

There was more laughter at the next table. "Oh, sure," the woman said. "I've never heard of *that* Tobias in my whole life. I think you just make half of this stuff up."

"No, it's true," the man said. "Well, maybe not true, but it's a real story. With a happy ending, too."

It suddenly occurred to Julia that although they both wore wedding bands, this couple couldn't be married to each other and still interact this way at their age. Or maybe they were newly married. The whole thing was more than a little weird—that she would be sitting right next to someone in Del's Deli who might cover Harry Tobias's classes while he took his sabbatical concurrent with her own.

Carmen was still concentrating on her food. And here was another defiance of probability, Julia thought—that her brother's daughter, virtually a stranger, would somehow in her long miles of wayfaring from Wyoming end up on Julia's back porch in Beckett, South Carolina, one Saturday morning in June. And without a stitch of extra clothing, not even a bar of soap or a comb.

She looked away, her eyes landing on an old road sign on the wall: *Danger Ahead—Bridge Out.* Too bad there hadn't been a sign on Ivy Dale this morning when she had come home with her groceries: *Danger Ahead—Girl on Back Porch.*

chapter 7

THE DEEPEST PART OF NIGHT

Carmen had already eaten almost half of her sandwich, but she paused now and set it down on her plate as if suddenly aware that she was violating the rules of etiquette by eating so fast. She wiped her mouth carefully and took another drink of water, then picked up a few French fries. "Do you have any children?" she asked Julia. "Daddy didn't think you did." She bit the tip off a French fry and chewed it, then ate the rest of it quickly in small bites, her eyes fixed on Julia the whole time.

"He was right," Julia said, and before Carmen could respond, she asked, "Do you have any brothers or sisters?"

Carmen bit into another French fry. "Not any that really count. Lulu was married before she knew Daddy, so she already had two kids, but they lived in Casper with their grandmother, so I didn't know them. Their daddy was mean to Lulu. To everybody, really. He was Effie's stepbrother."

She picked up her sandwich again. "So I was the only one at home. With Daddy and Lulu, I mean. Until Daddy died, and then relatives I'd never heard of started showing up, most of them from Arkansas. That's where Lulu was from." She took a bite of her sandwich and chewed it slowly. "Some of them overstayed their welcome. It was pretty . . . horrendous at times." She took another swig of water. "Lulu was older than Daddy. I guess you already knew that."

More information Julia didn't want, but that was what came of asking questions. The facts were hard to sort out. Effie was Lulu's half sister. And Lulu had once been married to her half sister's stepbrother? So where did Ida fit in? She wondered how much older Lulu was than Jeremiah, but she wasn't going to ask any more questions. She would just be quiet and try to think of the next thing to do.

"Does Aunt Pamela have curly hair, or is it straight like yours?" Carmen asked.

"Straight, like our mother's. Jeremiah was the only one who got the curls." She wished the girl would quit talking and just eat.

"What was she like—your mother?"

This was not a subject Julia wanted to talk about in Del's Deli or anywhere else. "Your daddy must have told you about her," she said.

Carmen nodded. She set her sandwich down again and took a crunchy bite of her pickle spear. "But not much. He cried one time when he talked about her. I remember that. Said he couldn't forgive himself for abandoning her. That was the word he used—*abandon*. I'd never heard the word before, but it was so lonely-sounding I never forgot it." She finished the rest of her water. "I never knew either one of my grandmothers. Lulu's real mother died a long time ago. She was . . ." She broke off suddenly and leaned closer. "How did Lulu die? Did they tell you?"

"I didn't get all the details," Julia said. "It happened suddenly, Ida said." And then, in case the girl had forgotten, "Effie may have died by now, too."

Carmen went back to her sandwich. Presently she continued. "Lulu was always making excuses for her. Poor Effie—nothing but hard knocks all her life. She was sick as a kid, she had a lisp, she was picked on in school, men treated her dirty, on and on. It was always something. Effie couldn't be held responsible for anything she did."

Julia didn't know what to say to any of this. This whole family dynamic sounded like a low-class reality show. How her intelligent, talented brother could have gotten involved with people like that both mystified and saddened her.

There was a sudden commotion as a young woman and small child entered Del's Deli. The child was crying loudly and trying to wrest himself away from his mother, but she managed to pull him inside so that the door could shut, at which point his wails were amplified. The woman's face was impassive as she held him firmly and looked toward the menu board. It was a tolerant yet embarrassed look, the same kind of look Julia had seen on the faces of pet owners holding their dogs on leashes beside mailboxes.

The boy in the red T-shirt came out from behind the counter bearing a lollipop. He stooped down and waved it in front of the child, who stopped crying immediately and snatched it.

Carmen took the lid off her cup and got up. She had eaten the last of her sandwich by now, and only a few French fries and half the pickle remained on her plate. "You want more to drink?" she asked Julia. She took both cups for refills, and when she came back, she said, "So let me get this straight. Ida said Lulu died, but she didn't say how?"

An idea came to Julia. "No," she said, "but it could have been the result of a doctor's error or something that went wrong at a hospital. If so, there might be a malpractice suit under way." Though good taste forbade going further, she did it anyway. "Families often get large settlements from such things. You would want to be there if that happened." And she couldn't resist adding, "Anyway, Lulu must have had a will of some kind. There's probably some money that's rightfully yours."

Carmen shook her head and spoke as if it were a closed subject. "No, no money. Even if there were, they'd make sure I didn't get any of it. And why would I want it?" Though Julia could think of several good answers, she said nothing.

When the girl's plate was clean, Julia said, "I can't eat the other half of my sandwich. Do you want it?"

Carmen nodded. "Sure." She ate it quickly, then said, "Thanks for lunch." She picked up the long toothpick on her plate and twirled it between her fingers, then touched the little red cellophane ruffle around the top of it and laughed. "Very funny. A fancy toothpick." On their way out, she spotted the cowbell mounted on the wall beside the door, a piece of rope tied to it. There was a printed sign above it: *Ring me if you like Del's Deli*. Carmen pulled the cord, and a loud clank resonated.

As they walked to the car, Julia noticed the girl's ripped shirt again. Okay, that could be the next thing. She could take her somewhere and buy her a new shirt. And after that maybe the next thing would come to her.

I T was during the darkest hours of morning several days later when Julia first heard the sound. It wasn't the sound itself that awakened her, for it was faint and far away, the kind of sound that would go unnoticed if one were asleep. But she wasn't asleep. She had been, but only for a brief time and not deeply. It had become a nighttime pattern long before Carmen arrived on the scene— short, restless naps followed by long wide-awake stretches of lying in bed, trying various methods of getting back to sleep.

She had tried both physical and mental strategies. On this particular night, in the few minutes before she heard the sound, she was trying a technique advocated by a New Age fitness trainer she had run across on daytime television several weeks ago, in which one contemplated his five senses one at a time, listing his own favorite sensory impressions in each category.

She wasn't actually going through the exercise herself, only remembering how ridiculous the trainer had looked and sounded as he lay on a mat with his eyes closed, wearing his red and black spandex, droning on and on with all seriousness about memorable sights he had seen: ghostly clouds snagged like old witches' hair across a haunted mountainside, smooth pearly stones in the burbling brook that ran through his grandfather's pasture, and so forth. Julia felt sure somebody else had written the lines for him. She remembered how funny it seemed for a grown man to use the word *burbling*.

Another idea came to her. Sometimes if she tried to compile lists, she could weary herself into sleep. The Debussy preludes, for instance. She always started with the longer titles, some of which sounded like poetry. *Sounds and Perfumes Mingle in the Evening Air.*

That was as far as she got, however, for it was at that exact moment that she became aware of the sound. At first she thought it was coming from outdoors, perhaps from a neighbor's tomcat that often prowled around. The noise stopped for a while but then resumed, softer now. She thought of other things it could be. A dog howling at the moon. Something with a squeaky wheel being rolled down the street. A high-pitched radio frequency. A beginning violin player.

It stopped again, for a longer time, long enough for Julia to start trying to simulate the rapid eye movements that usually preceded sleep. She had read somewhere that if you closed your eyes and then moved them around in circles very fast, you could eventually trick yourself into falling asleep.

But she heard the sound again, and though it was even softer now, she suddenly sat up in bed. Maybe it was inside the house. She waited a few seconds and then slowly pushed the covers back and walked to the door, where she stood listening. She heard nothing. The guest room where Carmen was sleeping was at the end of the short hallway, across from the other bathroom and diagonal to Julia's bedroom.

She opened her bedroom door cautiously and looked out. All was dark and quiet. She stepped into the hall and moved toward the guest room but stopped a few feet away. The hardwood floor was bad to creak at this end of the hall. She stood very still for a long time but heard nothing. Just as she turned to go back, however, she heard it again, from behind Carmen's door—a long, soft wail, as of pleasure or pain past telling. And then a soft bump. Julia hurried back to her room and closed the door. Moments later she heard the sound of water running in the hall bathroom, then the flush of the toilet, and all was quiet again.

THE problem of Carmen had not been fixed. After buying her two new shirts and some underwear at Sears on Saturday, they had stopped by a drugstore for some toiletries. After that, with a sense of defeat, Julia realized that the only thing left to do was to take her home. She made it clear, however, that there was a limit. A week—she could stay that long while she decided "what to do next." She stated it firmly. Carmen had nodded distractedly but said nothing.

Whole days had somehow passed, three of them, and June had turned into July. But there appeared to be no solution in sight, no evidence whatsoever that the girl was making other plans, even though Julia had left her cell phone out and told her she could use it. She also offered the use of her laptop, but Carmen hadn't touched either one. Each day she stayed in the guest room for long hours with the door closed, even during the daytime. Maybe she was reading the magazines and books she had asked to take from the living room. Or maybe she was sleeping, for there was never a sound from behind the door. Until tonight.

Yesterday she hadn't emerged until well after lunchtime, wearing an old pair of Julia's pajamas. Julia had told her to help herself to any of the things in the guest room closet, her holding place for clothes she was tired of and ready to donate to Goodwill. Carmen came into the kitchen, where Julia was cleaning out the refrigerator, and said, "What day of the week is it?"

A few minutes later she came back out dressed, said she was going for a walk, and disappeared for over two hours. Upon returning, she pointed across the backyard and said, "There's a college over in that direction. I guess that must be where you teach. Especially since I found an office with your name on the door."

She sometimes looked at whatever was on television but not with much interest. One day she stood in front of the shelves of CDs for a long time, reading the labels, and several times she went into the backyard and sat on the bank of the creek. Another day Julia looked out the kitchen window and saw her several houses away talking to Dr. Boyer, the French teacher, in his front yard, and another time stood by the mailbox conversing at length with a woman pushing a stroller. She came in later with a cosmetics catalog, which she left on the kitchen counter.

Since Saturday Julia had moved about the house nervously, as if she were the guest. She tried to keep herself busy with small projects but constantly lost her train of thought and failed to finish any of them—she straightened one dresser drawer, sorted through part of the linen closet, polished some of her good shoes, reorganized the top compartment of her jewelry box. Carmen asked once if she could help with anything but didn't offer again after Julia told her no, she had her own way of doing things. The thought of working side by side with the girl made her fearful. It would seem too much like an acceptance of her presence, could perhaps be interpreted as an invitation to extend her stay. Carmen might think of it as payment for her room and board. And, of course, if they worked together, they would have to talk.

Not that they didn't talk now. There were always the inevitable conversations at mealtimes, though Julia tried to get through those as quickly as possible. A few times she had eaten early, by herself, rushing to finish before Carmen appeared in the kitchen, then waving toward the stove and telling her to take whatever she wanted.

It was too early to tell whether Carmen was naturally talkative or if she was only forcing herself to be friendly. Either way she was full of questions, some uncomfortable, some merely strange: "What was your husband like?" "Do you wear contacts or are your eyes really that green?" "Have you ever seen an armadillo?" "Have you ever been to an opera?" "Do you ever look at doors and wonder who first thought of *hinges*?" And this one: "Isn't *eating* a funny thing? I mean, putting stuff into your mouth and . . . masticating it, then *swallowing* it?"

Brief answers, or none, instead of discouraging her, only left time for more questions, more random comments, often as if talking to herself. One morning, between bites of oatmeal, for example, she said, "Exchanging the truth for a lie and worshiping the creature more than the creator." Whatever that was supposed to mean. Another time, "A rider named Faithful upon a white horse." Though Julia felt no obligation to respond to such things, it was unsettling not to know what might come next. She could have tolerated the girl's presence better had the two of them silently occupied their own spaces within the house, as this was a way of living already familiar to her from the years of her marriage.

They went to Target to get Carmen more socks and a second

pair of jeans. Julia had no intention of outfitting her completely, but, on the other hand, you couldn't expect someone to keep wearing the same things day after day. When they carried the bags into the house afterward, Carmen said, without looking at Julia, "Thank you for these, but I don't like to live off other people's generosity. I'll pay you back." Julia had merely shaken her head dismissively. She couldn't really say what she was thinking: *The best payment will be when you leave.*

She had no idea what was going through Carmen's mind concerning the weeks ahead. She wanted to ask her point-blank if she was making any progress with long-term plans, but she was too afraid of the answer she would get. Things certainly couldn't continue like this, Julia knew that, but she had promised a week, so she would hold on till Saturday before taking further action, though she couldn't imagine what kind of further action was even possible if the girl refused to leave.

As for Pamela, she had little to offer. A reversal had taken place. Because she had suddenly stopped calling every day, Julia had taken to calling her instead. Every time they talked, however, Pamela spoke in a hasty, absentminded way, claiming that she needed to get back to the new baby, who was usually crying in the background. According to Pamela, he wasn't taking to breast-feeding and had lost too much weight since they brought him home, so the doctor had instructed them to feed him formula with a dropper every two hours. They were all having trouble sleeping, she said, and her daughter-in-law, convinced that everything was her fault, was crying almost as much as the baby.

Before the end of each conversation, Pamela rushed through the same advice concerning Carmen: "Just tell her you have somewhere you have to go, so she *has* to leave." She reminded Julia that the invitation to come to her house for a visit was still open. "I'll be home on Sunday. Just say you can't change your plans, somebody's counting on you." It was the kind of advice easier to give than to follow, to tell someone to leave your house, especially someone related to you, someone with no car, no money, no home, no job, not even a suitcase.

No more sounds came from down the hall, so apparently Carmen was done crying—for there could be no question that that was what she had been doing. Julia turned on her bedside lamp and got back into bed. Another tip for sleeplessness was to turn on the light and do something until you started to feel sleepy, reading being at the top of the list of recommendations. She had a novel on the table, one with a dense meandering opening. So far she had found nothing in it to interest her, though the book had been a fixture on the *New York Times* bestseller list for weeks. She kept having to reread the same pages each time she picked it up. Lean, clean story lines didn't seem to be in vogue these days. Even now she couldn't remember anything about this one except that the main character was a U.S. senator who was in a hospital in Russia for some reason.

She opened the novel, read the sentence *Medieval Icelandic sagas had been Saul's passion since before the Cold War ended*, and immediately closed it again.

She took another book from the table, titled *From Life to Fiction*, its premise being that a writer didn't need anything but his own familiar experiences to write fresh, unforgettable stories. She let it fall open and read a sentence: *Tap into your parents' stories—the ones you've heard since you were a child.*

Her childhood wasn't anything she wanted to think about, especially not in the deepest part of night. Her parents hadn't been the kind to tell stories anyway. Her father's only references to the past were for the purpose of pointing out how soft and lazy children today were compared to when he was their age, when he rose at dawn, walked five miles to school, worked in the fields, and all the rest. Julia had never gotten a new pair of shoes without having to hear all over again about the cardboard cutouts he had put inside his shoes as a child when his soles wore out.

Behind his back, and a few times to his face, Jeremiah had made fun. "And did you put gravy on the rest of the cardboard and eat it for supper?" he had asked one time. There had been no end of shouting and things being flung about that night. Julia remembered it clearly, for that was the time her father had gotten Jeremiah in a choke hold. And who knew what might have happened had her mother not fallen on the floor, weeping and praying aloud?

There were no bedtime stories growing up, though sometimes at night Jeremiah and Pamela would crawl into bed with Julia and she would read to them, very quietly, with a flashlight.

There was the one story her mother told her, however, that summer day in the kitchen while they were snapping, blanching, and freezing green beans. In the living room Julia's father was sounding notes on the piano, working as always on his endless compilation of folk songs, his only pastime since his accident.

Her mother had lifted her gaze from the pot of boiling water and stared at the doorway through which the tune of "Listen to the Mocking Bird" was stopping and starting. "He was traveling with that evangelist," she had half whispered, "leading the music and singing solos and playing his accordion, and I sat in the front row between my parents every night that whole week. I remember how my heart fluttered every time I thought he might be looking at me. I was only seventeen."

She had spoken with a tone of utter bewilderment, as if trying to figure out how she could have gone from a beginning like that to her current state of slipping out to attend church by herself on Sunday mornings, though not every week. She must have planned those Sundays with great forethought, spacing them out and steeling herself for what would follow, for experience had taught her, had taught them all, what was to be suffered afterward—first, specific grievances about the quality of Sunday dinner that day, followed by more general ones about women who failed to put their families first, about the weakness of character evidenced by anyone who leaned on a "religious crutch," about the place in hell reserved for hypocritical, slick-haired, fire-and-brimstone preachers. All of this bellowed by their father, between large mouthfuls of the dinner he had just pronounced unfit for human consumption, and endured mutely by their mother, who had risen early to prepare it. Going to church was, in Julia's memory, the only step her mother ever took outside the rigid boundaries set by her father.

She looked back at the book she was holding now. How odd, and inexpressibly sad, she thought, that her mother had told but one story. And what a story—that her father could have ever been young and dashing, her mother seventeen and in love with him.

Julia closed the book and stared at the black-and-white photograph on the cover—a man walking down a dirt road holding the hand of a barefoot child. Julia recalled only a single time she had felt her father's approval. She wasn't yet old enough to go to school, and Jeremiah was only a toddler. Pamela hadn't been born yet. They were in a yard somewhere, not their own. She was playing tag and hide-and-seek with other children while the grown-ups talked. One of the adults called to her father, "Your girl is a fast runner. Look at her go." And her father had swung her up to his shoulders and sung a few bars of "Yes, Sir, That's My Baby" in his perfectly pitched bass voice while everybody laughed and clapped.

One morning sometime later he went to work like always but didn't come home for weeks. Her mother told her there had been an accident on the assembly line, and her father was in the hospital. After that he never held a job again, never lifted her up on his shoulders again, or sang or laughed. It was as if another father had come home from the hospital.

J ULIA looked at the clock. Though there was no good time to be thinking about her father, this had to be one of the worst times. She ran her finger over the title of the book before setting it back on the nightstand. *From Life to Fiction*. She marveled again that Jeremiah had been able to write such beautiful fiction. He had borne the worst of their father's wrath, had wandered for years without a place to call home, yet somehow had risen above it all to write not just passably but brilliantly.

And now his daughter was here in Julia's house, making sounds in the night. No doubt it was for her father that she wept. Or maybe for her mother, more recently dead. Most likely for both.

Julia turned off the lamp beside her bed. A grave truth came to her as she laid her head on her pillow. She had given in too easily last week by allowing the girl to stay. She should have hardened her heart and pointed her to the door. Now she was stuck, for how could she ever send her away after hearing her weep in the night?

chapter 8

DISTANCE, NOT SPEED

Carmen didn't give the impression of a high school dropout. She was smart, not only in an encyclopedic way—offhandedly making reference to things like tectonic plate shifts, Odysseus, and the sixty-two moons of Saturn—but also in the art of ingratiating herself. Though it was subtle ingratiation, Julia suspected she knew exactly what she was doing.

The girl had already opened Matthew's toolbox on the back porch, something Julia had never done, and found a screwdriver, with which she tightened the handles on two saucepans that had been an aggravation to Julia for months. One day she went through the house and reversed the direction of all the ceiling fans, and another day she oiled the glider on the back porch to make it quit squeaking. She washed the Buick and vacuumed out the interior, swept both driveways, scrubbed down the outdoor grill, and rolled the garbage can out to the curb and back.

And then Friday came. That morning Carmen announced that she was going to walk to the library over at the college. When she came back, she ate a sandwich on the back porch and then went to her room and closed the door. She came out three hours later and left again. She didn't say where she was going this time, and Julia didn't ask.

It was early evening now. Though Fridays usually dragged, the hours had flown today. Julia ordered a pizza to be delivered. It seemed like a good thing for a Friday night, hopefully the last Friday night Carmen would be here. After this, she told herself, Friday nights would be normal again. Deep down, however, part of her wasn't so sure she liked what she remembered of normal Friday nights, the same part of her that was getting used to the girl's presence in the stone house.

In many ways it seemed that Carmen had been here much longer than a week, but not because she was a difficult houseguest. She made no clutter, helped without being asked, provided pleasant company when she wasn't asking too many questions.

Julia turned the oven on low so she could keep the pizza warm when it came and then began putting together a salad. Whereas she had once fretted over how to get rid of Carmen—amazingly, only days ago—she now fell to worrying about what was to become of the girl. And more immediately, where was she right now? Over and over she glanced out the kitchen window toward the street. It came to her that if Carmen had some kind of accident, no one would know what phone number to call since, as far as she knew, the girl had no identification on her.

What if she had taken Julia's limit of a week to mean that a Saturday arrival required a Friday departure? What if she was gone for good, leaving the same way she had arrived—with only the clothes on her back? She might be out on the highway right now, hitchhiking again. Julia suddenly felt awash with guilt—this would be a new regret to bear for the rest of her life, to add to all the old ones.

And so when she looked up a few minutes later and saw Carmen turning from the street into the driveway, her relief was great. The girl's head was down, her thumbs hooked inside her jeans pockets. She was walking slowly, as if bearing a weight. Julia reached over and turned off the light above the sink.

By now she knew the girl's face well. Even though she permitted herself only glances, the frequency of them had added up to familiarity. In the past she had noticed that when brothers and sisters looked alike, sometimes even in the case of twins, what was handsome in the boy didn't always translate into beauty in the girl. Or what was pretty in a girl looked weak and unfinished in a boy. Jeremiah and Carmen weren't siblings, of course, but it was hard for Julia to think of them as father and daughter since her last memory of Jeremiah was as a teenager. At any rate, the same smile, the same eyes, the same profusion of blond curls wore equally well on both of them.

It was difficult to see the face of a family member the way others saw it, but Julia remembered how often during his teen years people had spoken of Jeremiah as handsome. When she was younger, she had sometimes resented the fact that her brother had gotten it all. Not that she and Pamela were slouches, but Jeremiah was undeniably the gold medalist among them. He was even a personality at school. Everybody knew who he was and liked him, even though he didn't seem to care whether they did. Julia couldn't remember that he had ever had a best friend. For certain he had never brought anyone home. Pamela was the only one who had ever done that.

Genes were funny things. Julia didn't know how anyone could use them to argue for an intelligent designer, at least not a fair one—not when the best genes aligned themselves in the same child, the one who didn't seem to appreciate them at all.

There was one exception, however, one wayward superior gene that had somehow shown up in Julia: She could run fast, faster even than Jeremiah, whose track triumphs had been only in distance races. *Only*—a curious modifier for someone who had set a high school record in the state of Alabama for the mile run when he was fifteen. A short time later, however, he had shrugged it all off and dropped out of track, probably because he saw how much his achievement meant to his father, who had been a distance runner himself.

By then Julia had already quit the girls' track team, but for the opposite reason—because her father didn't care enough. Her wins never earned his praise. "Short-wick running," he called the sprints. In his way of thinking, distance, not speed, was the real test of mettle. She had tried other ways of pleasing him, but anything Jeremiah did eclipsed her best efforts, and after he left home, her father lost interest in life altogether, though he was trapped in it for many more years.

Julia turned the water on and held a colander of mixed greens under it. As she did so, Carmen stopped in the driveway and turned around to look back at the street. She stood there a moment, then lifted one hand as if gesturing, as if conversing with someone, though there was no one else there. But the girl was given to talking to herself—Julia had heard her in her bedroom and caught her at it on the back porch several times. Carmen lifted both hands now and tipped her head to look up, as if to check for rain. But above the trees the sky was a strong, unclouded blue.

From the back, with both hands raised, the girl looked lean and tapered, like a statuette on a trophy. Julia wondered if she had excelled in sports the way her father had. Maybe she was a good distance runner. Or maybe her only distance running had been when she left home at the age of sixteen, which wouldn't have given her much time to set high school records.

Julia knew that if she stood in the driveway as Carmen was doing right now, no one looking out the window would think of a figure on a trophy, not the way her weight was slowly redistributing itself around her waistline these days. She needed to do something physical—more than just a daily walk. Earlier in the summer, before Carmen's arrival had interrupted her list-making of projects for the coming year, she had briefly entertained the thought of joining a fitness club. The idea of spending money to jog on a treadmill or pedal a stationary bicycle didn't interest her, but swimming and water aerobics did, except for the embarrassment of wearing a swimsuit in the company of others.

A few times she had thought about taking up running again. Not long ago she had received a flyer in the mail about an upcoming fall event called Carolina Senior Showdown over in Greenville, in which people fifty and older could sign up to compete in various sports, foot races included. She wondered if there would be paramedics on hand in case one of the runners keeled over. She had thrown the brochure away, but she still thought about it from time to time and wished she had the courage to enter.

CARMEN turned back around and continued walking toward the house, still slowly. It came to Julia that whereas she had doubted the girl's age only a week earlier, she now had no trouble believing her. Her deft and graceful hands, her close observing and listening, the way she quickly changed the subject when she sensed resistance or unease, the turning away of her eyes as if afraid of what might be read in them—all of these spoke of a woman, not a girl. And her words, the colorful ones she slipped in as she talked—words like *decimate, cogent, moribund, vilify*—always used sparingly yet precisely, and always preceded by a slight pause as if reviewing the definition, weighing it against the possibility of error.

She stopped again, then walked back to the circular drive. When she came to the short walkway that led to the front door—the walkway made of stones Matthew had cut with a masonry saw—she faced the house and stood looking at it from one end to the other as if taking in every feature. Neither smiling nor frowning, she studied it the way an architect would, or an appraiser, or a photographer intent on light and angle.

We had a beautiful little girl. Jeremiah had been right about that. Not a description Julia had ever heard applied to herself. Hers were average looks, from head to toe—she knew that. Average everything. Even her weight was right in the middle of the recommended range, something Pamela often complained about. "You don't even try!" she would say. "It's not fair. I can walk by a plate of cookies and feel another roll around my middle." Pamela would scoff if Julia were to share her concerns about her waistline.

She pulled back from the window and returned to her cutting board to slice into a green pepper. She wondered what Carmen was thinking as she studied the stone house, whether she was saddened by the thought of leaving it. Most likely she was sad about other things that had nothing to do with Julia and the stone house. Maybe her chief sadness was that she was all alone in the world.

There had been no more sounds of weeping in the nighttime, not after Julia remembered that her clock radio had sound effects. For the past three nights, she had chosen the sound of ocean waves when she went to bed. Maybe that was the reason she had dreamed about being on a whaling ship the first night, a dream she remembered the next morning and mentioned to Carmen over breakfast. Carmen had smiled and asked if they had run across the Great White One.

A pizza delivery car slowly approached the stone house and turned into the circular drive. Julia wiped her hands and picked up the money she had set out. When she opened the front door, Carmen was talking to the driver. The back door of the car stood open, and several pizzas were stacked inside zipped bags beside a child's car seat. There was a child in the seat, but all Julia could see was two little feet kicking up and down.

The delivery woman grinned as she handed Carmen the pizza. "Better check it," she said. She jerked her head back toward the car. "He's bad to sneak bites."

LATER, at the table, Carmen was quiet. She ate a few bites of pizza and nibbled halfheartedly at her salad. Finally she put her fork down. "I'll be out of your hair tomorrow," she said, her tone neutral, light. She didn't look at Julia but addressed the door leading into the living room.

How strange it was, Julia thought, that these were words she would have welcomed only a few days ago. Now she could think of nothing to say.

Carmen took a drink of her Coke. "I can be gone by noon if that's okay." Her words were deliberate, almost rehearsed, but courteous, with no trace of hard feelings. "I appreciate your hospitality. It's been a very nice . . . respite."

"Where will you go?" Julia said. She heard the combative tone of her voice and tried to moderate it. "Do you have a plan? Something specific, I mean? A friend or another relative somewhere? I can help you with plane fare."

"Oh, I've got some things in mind," Carmen said. "Some waters to test, some tracks to follow. A man to see about a bull. I'll be okay."

"A bull?" Julia said.

Carmen gave a half smile. "It's something Daddy used to say. He'd say he was off to see a man about a bull, and then be gone for a few weeks. He could do almost any kind of work. Lulu would always cry when he left, but she knew when he came back he'd have money, and usually a nice present for her."

Julia knew the girl was trying to divert her, that she had no plan. "Where will you go?" she said again.

Carmen shook her head. "You think I'm going to tell? No, thank you, I don't want to be followed."

They stared at each other for a long moment. *This is a face you'll miss seeing*, Julia thought.

Carmen was the first to look away. She picked up the piece of pizza on her plate and started talking. "I think this is the best pizza I've ever had except for one time in . . . I think it was Minnesota." She took a small bite and chewed as she continued talking. "It was in the middle of winter, and this old Indian woman made it from scratch at this place called Mister Luke's. Just a hole in the wall in this little town I don't even remember the name of." She peeled off a piece of pepperoni and ate it by itself. "Ojibwa—that was the tribe she was from." She said the word again: "*O-jib-wa*. Isn't that an interesting word? Sure not something you'd expect to see—an old *Ojibwa* woman twirling a pizza crust around her head." A yap of laughter and she hurried on. "The place was close to a lake—all frozen over, little kids sliding on it. Or maybe it was in Wisconsin, I don't know. I've been around, seen a lot of places." She took another quick bite. "And maybe it wasn't Mister Luke's after all—that might have been a different town. It could've been the Snack Den in Iron River—that one was by a lake, too, I'm pretty sure of that, but. . .

"Carmen, stop it. Stop talking."

The girl stopped and looked at Julia. She was still chewing.

"I can't let you leave," Julia said. "Not yet."

Carmen frowned. "Why?"

But Julia had no answer, hadn't even known she was going to say those words. The question hung in the air for a moment. "Well, what I mean," she said, "is you're not ready to go anywhere yet. I still need to get some things together for you—like a suitcase for starters." She was making this up as she went. "You can't travel anywhere carrying your things in a plastic bag."

"I don't need things," Carmen said. "Naked came I, and naked shall I return. In a manner of speaking." She flashed a smile at Julia. "I've seen Walden Pond, did you know that? In fact, I lived near there for a few weeks last spring. A few very chilly weeks. In spartan simplicity. Henry Thoreau would've approved, I think. Wasn't he the one who said we're a ruined nation because of too much stuff? Simplify, simplify, simplify, keep your accounts on your thumbnail, strip away everything superficial and . . . superfluous. Reduce life to the essentials. Instead of three meals a day, why not . . ."

"Carmen, stop it. What happened?" It came out much louder than Julia intended.

Carmen stared at her, evidently as surprised by the question as by the intensity.

"What happened . . . *when*?" she finally said.

But Julia couldn't begin to explain what she meant. Her mind was in a tumult. She wasn't referring to a specific incident, of course. It was instead a sudden hunger to know the answers to all the questions she hadn't asked, and all the ones she hadn't yet thought of asking, about all the years of Carmen's life. She was appalled to feel her eyes brimming with tears. She couldn't re-member the last time she had cried. She clamped her hand over her mouth and squeezed her eyes shut.

After a long silence Carmen pushed her chair back and stood. She moved to Julia and stooped down beside her, laying a hand on her arm. "I'm sorry. It's been too much having me here. I can go tonight. You don't need to get me anything else. You've done so much for me already."

How can this be? Julia wondered. How can I be sitting here while this *child* comforts me? She opened her eyes and saw her empty plate on the table, her bowl of half-eaten salad, her half-empty glass of soda. She looked across the kitchen and saw the microwave on the counter, the colored tiles of the backsplash, the sink, all the same things she saw every day and knew so well. But she couldn't bring herself to look at the girl kneeling at her side.

"Here, here's your napkin." Carmen held it out.

Julia took it and wiped her eyes. "I'm okay now," she said. "I don't know what came over me. I think I'm just tired. I didn't sleep much last night."

Carmen stood up. "Well, it's my fault. I need to go."

Julia pointed to the chair. "No, you need to sit down. Please, Carmen. I have some questions . . . they might take a little while. If you don't mind."

· chapter 9 ·

SHARPER FOCUS

Carmen's answers were thorough and, to the best of Julia's judgment, honest. The things that had happened to her were indeed lamentable, and many. She refused to answer no question. If there was a certain sense afterward of secrets undisclosed, Julia took responsibility, for not asking the questions that would have revealed them.

It would be difficult to rank the sadnesses in Carmen's life if drawing up a "Top Ten" list, though Jeremiah's death when she was nine would surely be first. That event had sliced her life in two, like a piece of fruit, separating the good half from the bruised. Her mother's emotional unraveling had begun almost immediately, as well as a sudden influx of loosely connected relatives claiming concern for Lulu. The trailer was soon bursting with people Carmen barely knew, among them Ida and Effie.

As Jeremiah had always been considered an interloper among Lulu's kin, his child was by association viewed in the same light, a nuisance at best, but more often made to feel as if she were somehow directly responsible for this upheaval in her mother's life. Apparently no one recognized it as an upheaval in her life also.

With the loss of her father and, for all purposes, her mother, she was in many ways an orphan. Some of Carmen's elementary teachers took an interest in her—she was bright and diligent—but it was a limited kind of interest, for at the end of every school day and every school year, she always had to go home, such as it was. At first some of the people from the church she had attended with Jeremiah called and came by, but were soon made to understand from Ida and Effie that their help was neither welcome nor needed. With no one to take her to church, Carmen quit going.

"Were you ever . . . abused by a man?" Julia asked her at one point. From Carmen's answer to this question, her besetting flaw was clear: She had wanted love so desperately that she had trusted too easily. Either that, or she had carried a sign around that read *Take Advantage of Me.*

But they were only *attempted* abuses, Carmen pointed out, not fully realized—a fact she cited as a "blessing." The first time was when she was only eleven, at the hands of one of the assorted relatives passing through the trailer—a lowlife cousin of Lulu's they called Jayhawk, who tried to force himself on Carmen when no one else was at home. Though Lulu's mind was disengaged by this point, her motherly instincts were jarred loose by what she saw that day when she walked in, and as she scrambled to get Jeremiah's shotgun down from the wall, Jayhawk had time to run. He disappeared, no charges were pressed, and this incident, like others, melted into the background of Carmen's childhood.

Then there was the science teacher later, in eighth grade, who also tried to take liberties with her, the kind that eventually got him fired. Ida and Effie had little sympathy, were of the opinion that Carmen had probably brought it on herself, and Carmen was so confounded she was afraid they might be right. After all, hadn't she eagerly gone to his office almost every day after school? Hadn't she smiled whenever she felt his eyes on her in class? Lulu's distress after the incident was such that she stayed in bed for a week, during which time Carmen wasn't allowed to see or speak to her.

Afterward, some of her classmates, especially the boys, called her names that implied she was fast and easy. The science teacher had been a popular one, so Carmen was held accountable for the replacement teacher, a grim moon-faced woman with the unfortunate name of Mrs. Plugg, whom no one liked.

And in tenth grade some of these same boys gathered around her after school one day. They had her shirt off when the janitor came down to the stairwell to see what was going on. They were all suspended for several days and thereafter invented quieter methods of tormenting her.

Julia asked about friends. Carmen shook her head. "Kids don't seem to like other kids who try too hard," she said. "I guess I was too different. I didn't fit in." It angered Julia to think of it—a beautiful, smart, friendly child, rejected. Children could be as cruel as fate, collectively turning on the appointed outcast, feeding off each other's meanness. Julia had seen it happen sometimes even among college students.

As time went on, Carmen took refuge in the warm, bright, populated land of books. That, and stories she made up. Sometimes she wrote them down, but more often she simply played them out in her mind. That way Effie didn't make fun of them and Ida didn't scold her for wasting paper.

O NE thing she said landed heavily on Julia's conscience. "I used to spend hours imagining what you were like," Carmen told her. "I made up things about you. Told people I had an aunt in South Carolina who wanted me to come live with her. Said you

were rich. I sort of justified the lie because of your last name. I told
them your husband was a bank president, and he was always buying
you things like new cars and diamonds. One time for no reason at
all he got you a chocolate Monopoly set." She shrugged. "I was just
trying to impress people. I didn't really care if you were rich or not."

It shamed Julia to realize that while her niece was constructing
dreams about her, never once had she herself paused to consider
what the girl's life would be like after losing her father or whether
she might step forward and help in any way.

"Did he do that?" Carmen asked. "Buy you presents for no
reason?"

Julia nodded. It was true, especially during the first several
years of their marriage. There were many gifts, though not as ex-
travagant as Carmen's stories claimed. But Julia didn't like to think
about any of that, especially her ingratitude. "But no more questions from you now," she said. "I'm not done with mine yet."

Carmen's recall of details was extraordinary. She had a keen
mind for names, numbers, chronology. She knew about the first
letter Lulu sent Julia. She also remembered well the day Julia's
check came in the return mail. She remembered the wrangling at
home that day, too, with both Effie and Ida arguing for cashing the
check and throwing the box of papers in the garbage can where
they belonged.

But she also remembered riding to the post office with Lulu the
next day to mail the box to Julia. "Ida and Effie were furious," she
said. "Lulu didn't buck them very often. Mostly she did whatever
they said. Ida and Effie, they made a formidable duo, let me tell
you. Relentless and . . . indefatigable. I just tried to stay out of
their way."

With both Effie and Ida taking up permanent residence in the
trailer, Carmen was evicted from her bedroom and relegated to the
living room sofa, where she slept for six years, until she lost even

that with another downward turn in her bleak life: a short, ill-fated relationship with a boy named Tig Henderson, who showed up in Painted Horse the summer after she finished tenth grade. She was sixteen, and he was twenty. She believed everything he said, starting with his promise to love her forever. "I wanted so much to be the most important person in somebody's life," she said. Tig was very convincing, told her he had a good job offer from an uncle in Alberta if they could only find a car to drive up there. In Canada, he said, teenagers could get married without a parent's consent, so that was the first thing they would do when they got there.

"I told him kissing and anything else was off-limits till we got married. Daddy had told me never to let another man kiss me unless he was my husband—that's what a good girl I was. Dumb, too. Tig played me like a toy drum. Acted like he agreed with everything I was saying. I don't think he was even interested in girls, really. He just needed an . . . accomplice."

He laid out a plan to Carmen, and before sunrise one morning, while everyone in the trailer was asleep, she scraped together all the money she could find, including the cash Lulu kept in a mason jar for groceries and emergencies, some five hundred dollars in all. She also took Jeremiah's old guitar and Effie's car keys, along with her car, and met Tig down behind the old coal mine. They headed north toward the Canadian border.

She made a face. "So, you see, I wouldn't kiss, but I would steal—how stupid is that? He didn't have any uncle in Canada or any job offer. He only wanted to hide out up there. He'd done something he could go to jail for—I found all that out later. That's why he always freaked out over cops." She laughed. "He sure had me pegged. Gullible with a capital G. He must've had a hard time keeping a straight face."

Several days later, after ditching the car, crossing the border on foot, and walking for endless miles in the middle of nowhere,

Carmen woke up one morning to find Tig gone, along with all her money and Jeremiah's guitar. "No note or anything," she said. "But at least he left my backpack."

Julia had already identified these "at least" statements as an annoying habit, this latching on to a minor point as a ray of cheer in an otherwise miserable situation. As if leaving her backpack could in any way make up for the boy's treachery.

THOUGH part of Julia wanted to cover her ears, another part wanted to hear it all in one sitting. And so after each answer, another question followed. Carmen spoke candidly of the years since Tig, but in a rush of words now, as if she needed to relieve herself of the truth as soon as possible. She began telling the facts more simply, stripped of detail. A CliffsNotes version of a lonely, wretched adolescence.

The exact sequence of events became a jumble in Julia's mind, mostly because her questions ranged far and wide in no particular order. There was no limit to the ways the girl had been lied to, lied about, rejected, cheated, disappointed—all of them strewn along the road of her short life like miles of wreckage after a collision— yet also interspersed along the way, according to Carmen, were countless mercies: at least *this*, at least *that*. A messy plot, with two driving forces—the girl's literal fight to survive and her quest to find a good man to take her father's place. But this was Julia's assessment, not Carmen's.

She had traveled light, moving about a good deal, by bus, train, hitchhiking, taking whatever work she could get from anybody who didn't ask a lot of questions. From Canada, she had returned to Montana, then headed to the Dakotas and down to Nebraska and west into Colorado. She slept on cots, couches, concrete floors, bare ground, occasionally in a real bed, but rarely in one place for very long.

One day outside Denver she thought about the trailer in Painted Horse, Wyoming, which seemed like a haven of tranquillity in comparison to her life as a vagrant, so she made her way back there. "But it didn't turn out exactly like the Prodigal Son story in the Bible," she said. They wouldn't let her in. Effie said she was calling the sheriff to lock her up. Lulu came to the window crying and told her she'd made her bed, now go lie in it.

From there she headed east, passed through Kansas City, then St. Louis, traveled north through Minnesota and Wisconsin, lived in the Chicago area for a while, worked at a meatpacking plant in Ohio, and eventually ended up in New England, where she had lived for the last three and a half years. She had done every kind of work imaginable—each job "an answer to prayer," as she called it. Everything from cleaning bathrooms to babysitting for a family with nine foster children.

She studied her hands as if remembering how much work nine children required. "That was a hard job," she said, "but I loved it. It lasted only a couple of weeks, though. The parents thought the kids were getting too attached to me."

"So answers to prayer can fizzle fast," Julia said.

"But something else opened up after that," Carmen said quickly. "It always did." She looked at Julia for a long moment, her blue eyes unblinking. "I guess prayer must sound pretty silly to you."

Julia said nothing. What need was there to reply? Surely after such a rehearsal of her life, the girl could see for herself how futile her prayers had been.

More questions, more answers. At some point Carmen had started going to church again, wherever she happened to be. She liked small churches best, had met "saints like you wouldn't believe." She had even joined a church in Connecticut. "They let me clean on Saturdays and help in the nursery on Sundays," she said.

Julia almost laughed. How kind of them to let her do their dirty work. She didn't say it, though.

The questions continued, and Carmen grew visibly weary. Sometimes she answered with a single word. Had she ever finished high school? *No.* So just to clarify, she had never been a victim of sexual abuse that resulted in pregnancy? A slight pause, then a firm *No.* Did she have any personal identification? A social security card? No card, but she knew her number. And, of course, no birth certificate? *No.*

How had her shirt gotten torn? This question seemed to confuse Carmen at first until she understood that Julia had leapt forward in time to her arrival here at the stone house only a week ago. Perhaps sensing that the questions were almost over, she sat up straighter and summarized this most recent misfortune, the one that had left her without even her backpack. "But it was really ratty by now anyway," she said. Once again it had involved a man, a seemingly nice man who wore gray ostrich cowboy boots with silver toe plates. She had been fooled by the boots since all the cowboys she had ever known in Wyoming were gentlemen, and since Jeremiah had worn boots with silver toe plates. Evidently gullibility was still an issue.

From her brief account, it sounded to Julia as if she had been lucky to get off with only a torn shirt, and she told her so. But Carmen objected to the word *lucky.* Her explanation: Of the many jobs she had held, one was at a karate school, where she often observed evening classes before starting her custodial work. Evidently she had observed well, for when the man pulled onto a gravel road and made his first move, she took him by surprise. "I think I might have broken his nose," she said. He doubled over, both hands to his face, at which point she opened the door and ran.

"So God prepared me for that," she said "by giving me some free karate lessons."

Julia shook her head at this. If God was so gracious, she asked, why didn't he spare her the attack altogether? Why didn't he provide a ride for her with a kind woman who gave her money and a good, warm meal instead of a bad man who turned on her and left her stranded on a deserted country road?

Carmen answered promptly. "He sometimes lets us suffer the consequences of our foolish choices to teach us lessons." She leaned forward. "And anyway, he did provide a kind woman who gave me food and clothes, and a place to sleep besides. He led me here to you."

Julia could only stare at her. There was no way to reconcile such simple-minded Sunday school ignorance with the girl's obvious intelligence and with what she had been through. If one of her students had written a story with a character like this girl, Julia's criticism would have been ruthless: *Are you writing fantasy or realism? Either way, the character is unbelievable. Try for convincing complexity.*

So here was another reason she needed to stay—so that Julia could try to adjust her faulty thinking, open her eyes to the real world. She would start out with something very basic. For example, the fact that good things could usually be traced to identifiable causes, such as hard work or natural aptitude, but bad things often happened for no reason. Watch the news any night of the week for proof. In the lives of people as a whole, the ratio of abrupt calamity to sudden good fortune was maybe fifty to one, probably more like a hundred to one, maybe higher.

She would try to help the girl understand the need for bold, positive action in order to make more good things happen instead of depending on will-o'-the-wispy things like prayer.

B Y the time the talk at the kitchen table was done, the sky had gone from blue to mauve. With the overhead light off, the kitchen was growing dim, yet Julia had the strange sense of seeing

Carmen in sharper focus. Perhaps it was because for the first time she was allowing herself a long, close, head-on look at the girl.

Carmen was the first to rise from the table. Picking up her glass, she went to the sink and filled it with water, then drank it down all at once. Julia turned on the overhead light and started clearing the table.

Carmen said, "A light that shines in a dark place makes everything visible."

Julia had no reply for this. She carefully placed the plates and bowls and glasses between the spokes and ribs of the dishwasher as Carmen gathered up the silverware and wiped the table. They moved back and forth slowly, deliberately, without talking. Julia put away the leftover pizza, and Carmen took the empty box out to the recycle bin.

"You probably want me to leave more than ever now," Carmen said at last. "Now that you know all those things about me." She was standing in the doorway leading into the living room, the expression on her face guarded. One thing she must have learned, finally, was not to hope too quickly.

In an instant Julia's thoughts settled themselves into one perfectly clear resolution: *She must not suffer again.* But just as quickly the truth came to her: *I have no power over suffering, hers or mine or anyone else's. No one does. What will happen will happen.*

Julia turned and began wiping the countertops. She spoke slowly. "No, I don't want you to leave. I want you to stay."

There was a long silence before Carmen replied. "I've been praying you'd say that, but now I can't think of anything to say back."

Another silence as Julia absorbed the fact that God was getting credit for her change of heart. Well, no matter.

"I believe in angels," Carmen said. "Guardian angels."

"No doubt," Julia said. She continued wiping the counter.

"If they got paid, mine would be rich, even at minimum wage."

Julia said nothing. She was wiping the same spot over and over now.

"And if they got overtime, he'd be a billionaire. Or she. Well, *it*—angels really aren't male or female, you know. They neither marry nor are given in marriage."

Obviously, there was no predicting what would come out of this girl's mouth next. After all the hard, plain words of the past couple of hours, now these frivolous ones.

Julia knew it was her turn to say something. Something wise and meaningful. She imagined an empty dialogue bubble above her head, waiting to be filled in. She knew the girl was still at the doorway, and she turned to face her.

Somehow Carmen had gone from standing up to sitting down, folded up inside the door frame, her back against one side, her feet against the other. Her face was buried in her hands, but she made no sound.

Displays of emotion always embarrassed Julia. She could only be grateful that Carmen hadn't rushed at her, embraced her, and burst into sobs. She turned back to the sink and took her time rinsing the dishcloth, wringing it out, hanging it over the dish drainer to dry. She looked out the window and cleared her throat. "I noticed that house down by Dr. Boyer's has a *Sold* sign on it now," she said. So much for wise and meaningful.

"It's a couple in their forties," Carmen said. "He works at the post office, and she's a kindergarten teacher." Her voice sounded steady, so maybe her tears were already over.

Or maybe she needed a little more time. "Well, I wish the one across the street would sell," Julia said, still facing the window. "It's been empty for almost three months. At least someone could come mow the lawn. It's not the most scenic view."

"A woman went through it yesterday with a real estate guy," Carmen said. "She was in an SUV with a Florida license."

Julia laughed. "Where does she work?"

"I don't know, but I'm guessing something medical. She had on blue scrubs and white rubber-soled shoes."

Julia said, "Well, I'm going to sit on the back porch and read a little while."

Carmen got to her feet. "Uh, Aunt Julia, there's more . . . if you want to ask more questions. I mean, I didn't tell you every detail, so . . ."

Julia held up a hand. "No, we've talked a long time. You've told me enough."

Carmen hesitated, then said, "Well, maybe I'll take a warm bath if it's okay."

Julia nodded, and Carmen turned and left. Seconds later Julia heard the tub water running in the hall bath. She couldn't name all the feelings inside her right now, but she knew one of them was fear at the thought of how close she had come to turning the girl out. And another was relief that she hadn't. And mixed in was a good bit of anxiety about how all of this was going to work.

· chapter 10 ·

SINGING TO PLANTS

July and August passed in a swelter of record-breaking temperatures, but the first week of September brought with it a welcome mildness. They needed rain, but at least there was a break in the heat, a reminder that cooler days were coming. Of all the seasons, Julia had always liked fall best, with its colorful drifts of leaves and earlier evenings. She also liked fall because it was when school started again and she could return to her comfortable routine. Not this year, of course, but every passing season would bring her closer.

She was feeling especially restless right now since it was the first week of classes at Millard-Temple and she wondered how her courses were going. She wished she could make herself invisible and sit in on some of them. On second thought, she didn't wish that at all, for what if the interim teacher was too good, what if his lectures were too engaging, the students too attentive? No, it was safer to pretend that things were going poorly, that the best students were waiting for her return to sign up for her classes.

It was the Friday after Labor Day, going on toward lunchtime, and Julia and Carmen were sitting on the back porch together, Carmen on the glider looking through job listings in the newspaper and Julia in the wicker rocking chair with a book of essays in her lap. The radio was on, tuned in to NPR, and Stravinsky's *Firebird Suite* was playing, though too softly for its full effect.

"Hey, here's a job I could do," Carmen said from the glider. "It's a companion for an elderly gentleman. That's what the ad says—'companion needed for elderly gentleman.' Isn't that quaint? That might be interesting." She took a slurpy sip of her coffee, which was mostly warm milk with a dribble of coffee and lots of sugar.

Julia looked up from her book. "Interesting? More like dangerous. Remember the elderly gentleman who was on the news the other night for killing his neighbor and dumping his body in a well?" The man had looked like a harmless old grandfather.

Carmen cocked her head toward the radio. "Wait, did you hear that? Didn't that part sound like something from *Peer Gynt*? I wonder if Stravinsky did that on purpose? Who came first—Stravinsky or Grieg?" She looked over at Julia expectantly.

Julia had heard nothing that sounded like *Peer Gynt*, but she hadn't been listening closely. "Grieg, I think," she said, "but I'm not sure. I'm not the expert on music you seem to think I am."

Carmen looked back at the newspaper. "The ad says 'Good pay,' so he must be rich."

"*And* the elderly gentleman in Columbia," Julia said, "who ran the meth lab and had a whole stockpile of explosives he was planning to use to blow up the governor's mansion . . . remember him?" They had seen him on television a few nights ago, being led from his house in handcuffs, the stereotypical Southern redneck. Scruffy beard, missing teeth, beer belly, wife-beater shirt.

Carmen took another sip of her coffee. "But nobody like that would advertise for a companion, would they? He didn't look like he knew any words that big." She set her mug down. "And don't forget that poor old man in Greenville who drove his car into the Burger King and killed those two people. Of course, you have to feel sorry for somebody like that. He wasn't a *criminal*. It must be a horrible thing to live with—running over somebody by accident that way."

How quickly a conversation could go awry. Julia pretended to be reading again. Maybe Carmen would take the hint and stop talking. Or at least change the subject.

But she didn't. "If he'd had somebody to drive him around," she continued, "it wouldn't have happened. If he'd had a companion like me, for example, he could have said, 'Hey, Carmen, I need you to take me to Burger King.' And I would've said, 'Okay, sure, Mr. Elderly Gentleman with slow reflexes, I have my driver's license now, so hop on in, let's go.'" She picked up the paper and rattled it. "So, see, I might save somebody's life by answering this ad. Or maybe a bunch of people. Maybe this elderly gentleman is going to smash into a playground full of children if he doesn't get a companion to drive him around, or . . ."

Julia broke in. "That reminds me. I'm going to need you to drive to the post office after lunch to mail that package for me." The driver's license was a new acquisition for Carmen, as were a new social security card and a copy of her birth certificate from the county seat in Wyoming where she had been born. She was especially proud of the driver's license. Almost daily now she ran some kind of errand for Julia.

"Sure," Carmen said. "And don't worry, I'm not going to answer any ad to be a man's companion, elderly or otherwise." She turned over several pages to the crossword puzzle, then neatly folded the newspaper back and picked up a pencil.

"There's really no need for you to rush into a job," Julia said.

"It's not as if you've been lazing around all summer. You've kept busy around here." And it was true. The girl had made herself useful not only at the stone house but also at other houses up and down Ivy Dale.

W ITH Carmen, you knew why it was called *striking* up a conversation. She didn't hold back. She knew most of the neighbors by name now. She had washed their cars, mowed their yards, weeded their gardens, even helped a single mother and her two little girls move into the house across the street.

She often played with the girls in their yard for hours on Saturdays to keep them out from under their mother's feet. Julia sometimes watched her from the kitchen window as she gave them piggyback rides, taught them jump rope jingles, drew chalk pictures with them in the driveway, read books to them on the front steps.

After learning about Dr. Boyer's knee replacement surgery, Carmen had offered to walk his dog, bring his mail and newspaper to the door, and get his groceries. Over the past two months she had exchanged more words with Dr. Boyer than Julia herself had in over twenty years. Almost daily she came home with a new French phrase, something she had asked him to write down for her.

A few weeks ago she had even rung the doorbell of "the White Ark"—Julia's name for a two-story monstrosity erected ten years ago in an empty lot on the east end of Ivy Dale, which looked totally out of place among the smaller, older, more tastefully appointed homes. The residents of the White Ark were a reclusive older couple who rarely showed themselves outdoors. Year-round their eaves were strung with Christmas lights, the kind that were supposed to look like icicles, and until very recently a collapsed inflatable Santa had been puddled in their front yard, a mass of dirty red-and-white plastic, which was the purpose of Carmen's visit.

The woman who answered the door that day opened it only a few inches and, without saying a word, shook her head at Carmen's offer to clean and fold the Santa, then shut the door firmly. The next day, however, the Santa was gone from the yard and part of the red plastic could be seen spilling out the top of the garbage can in the driveway.

"That woman has the palest, bluest eyes," Carmen had told Julia, "like one of those Siberian husky dogs. She looked a little . . . furtive. But, you know, she might be deaf now that I think about the way she stared at my mouth while I was talking. And she has a kind of a hooked nose—*aquiline*, is that the word? She's tiny, with this long, wavy silvery hair. But kind of pretty, in an odd, dreamy sort of way, like a confused fairy who's forgotten how to fly, and . . ." These descriptions could go on and on.

All this from a fifteen-second conversation through a three-inch crack. Carmen could make a story out of a stick lying on the ground. Sometime recently she had taken to writing things in an empty journal she had found on one of the bookshelves. Julia had no idea what she wrote. Maybe it was simply a diary of things she did and saw every day, like descriptions of neighbors with aquiline noses.

She studied the girl now, carefully penciling in letters on the crossword puzzle. She always went slowly so as not to have to erase anything. She was sitting with one leg tucked under her, the other swinging back and forth. Her shoelaces were untied but bunched up between the eyelets so the ends didn't dangle and trip her. She claimed that tied laces made her feel trapped in her shoes. These were new sneakers, but not expensive ones. She had refused the ones Julia had wanted to buy her, insisting that she didn't want any at all if she couldn't have the cheap ones.

Julia wasn't ready to drop the subject of a job. "In fact," she said, "you've stayed so busy I'm going to run out of projects around here before long."

Carmen said nothing. She was frowning now, tapping her pencil against her foot. "'Dr. Johnson's pal'?" she said. "Seven letters, the fourth one is a *w*."

"Boswell," Julia said. "He wrote a biography of Samuel Johnson."

Carmen gave a sniffy laugh as she filled the letters in. "Okay, thanks. I wouldn't know either one of them if I met them on the street."

"You won't be meeting them on the street. They've both been dead for over two hundred years."

"Yeah?" The girl looked up. "Have you ever thought about how everybody's skeleton looks basically the same? I mean, there are little differences in size and all that, but if you just had everybody's skeleton lined up side by side, it would be impossible to tell a famous person like Barack Obama from a mailman named Joe Schmoe. You know?"

"I can't say I've ever thought about it," Julia said. Carmen could be very silly—Julia had told her so more than once. At other times she was witty in a way you knew wasn't accidental. Other days, she was neither silly nor witty, but grave and tense as if listening for something. But even on her quiet days she was polite, always polite.

JULIA went back to her book. She turned a few pages and saw an essay by Edith Wharton. She liked Edith Wharton. It came to her now that she would like to read *Ethan Frome* again. She couldn't remember much about the plot except that it involved a young girl and an older man and it was set in New England. Maybe she and Carmen could read the book together.

She suddenly thought of something else that had been on her mind for many weeks now. This seemed like the right time to mention it, as it would support her point about a job.

"You don't want to get a full-time job right now anyway," she said. She didn't expect an answer, for Carmen was slow to speak when she thought there might be more coming.

Head down, Carmen kept her eyes on the paper, but she was clearly waiting, her pencil poised above the puzzle.

"I want to take a trip sometime in October," Julia continued, "and I'd like you to go with me. You wouldn't want to have to ask an employer for time off so soon."

Carmen looked up. "What kind of trip?" She looked worried, as if she thought Julia might be broaching the subject of a trip to Wyoming again.

"To New England," Julia said. "I'd like to visit the homes of some American authors during my sabbatical. That part of the country is full of them. Frost, Hawthorne, Melville, Dickinson, Mark Twain . . . well, you already know—you lived up there."

Carmen wrinkled her nose and shook her head. "You can go. I'll stay here and work. I'll help pay for all the things you'll have to charge on your credit card."

"I thought you liked New England. You're always talking about all the history up there."

"*It was the best of times, it was the worst of times,*" Carmen said. "I know, I know, that's Dickens. His house isn't up there."

"Well, I don't want to go by myself," Julia said. "There are other homes I want to see, too. Edith Wharton and Henry Wadsworth Longfellow and Harriet Beecher Stowe and Louisa May Alcott and . . ."

"I once met somebody who slept in Louisa May Alcott's bed," Carmen said.

At times Julia ignored these leaps in a conversation, but at other times the new turn was irresistible, as now.

Julia closed her book. "What are you talking about?"

It was a girl Carmen had met on a train somewhere in New England. This girl—Fawna was her name—was "bumming around for the summer doing random stuff just for fun." One day she went on a guided tour through Orchard House in Concord, Massachusetts, the house where Louisa May Alcott lived when she wrote *Little Women*. Somehow Fawna managed to slip into one of the groups without paying, and then she kept the guide off balance the whole time by asking funny questions like what they used for toilet tissue back then.

When the guide was finished with her speeches in the upstairs bedrooms and everybody else moved back downstairs, Fawna stayed behind and hid under Louisa's bed, waiting for the house to be locked up for the night. Or so she said.

"Why?" Julia said.

"She hated that tour guide. She said the woman talked so fast nobody could understand her. And she didn't have an ounce of fun in her bones, got all mad about the questions, told Fawna she was out of order and couldn't ask any more."

"So she hid under the bed to get even with a tour guide?"

"Yeah, I know, it was dumb. But it was hilarious the way she told it. She tried on an old dress that was on top of the bed, and she sat at Louisa May Alcott's desk, and she went through all the books in the bookcase and drew pictures of Charlie Brown and Snoopy in them. She could draw all the *Peanuts* characters perfectly. She showed me. And she took a ceramic owl off a shelf as a keepsake. I think Louisa May Alcott collected owls."

"Sounds like she was stringing you along," Julia said.

"She showed me the owl." Carmen laughed. "Yeah, I know, she could've been totally making it all up. Maybe the owl came from Walmart. But I think she really did it. That girl was crazy. She took a picture on her phone of herself sitting at the desk wearing the dress. She showed me that, too, but it was kind of dark and blurry."

Julia said, "A place like that would have some kind of security system."

Carmen shrugged. "But she didn't break in, see, so why would an alarm go off? In the morning she just hid under the bed again and waited for the tours to start so she could crawl out and blend in with them. She said it was a different guide that day. He was nicer and talked slower."

Julia rocked back and forth ever so slightly in her wicker chair, studying Carmen for any small sign that she might be teasing.

Carmen shot her a wide-eyed, innocent smile and took another sip of her coffee before bending over the crossword puzzle again.

"Then there's always the possibility," Julia said, "that you never met anybody named Fawna on a train. Maybe this is just another one of your stories."

"I still think about her," Carmen said without looking up. "Lots of times I stop and say, 'I wonder where Fawna is now and what she's doing?'" She chewed on her bottom lip for a moment. "Oh, I know this one. It's easy. Five letters, starting with A. 'Tree kin to birch.' A-s-p-e-n, aspen." She looked up and smiled. "That's the name of a ski resort in Colorado, too, did you know that?"

JULIA got up and went inside. She returned the book of essays to the shelf in the living room and came back to the porch door. "How about going somewhere for a quick lunch?" she said. "You drive, and then we can run by the post office and library."

Carmen put the newspaper and pencil aside. "Okay, but my treat this time. Dr. Boyer paid me yesterday." She stood up and stretched. "I've been to Mark Twain's house. Did I ever tell you that? I didn't sneak in, though. I paid. Did you know Mark Twain's bed was switched around backward? He slept with his head up against the footboard and his feet down by the headboard. Said he wasn't going to spend all that money on a fancy carved headboard unless he could look at it while he was in bed." She laughed. "Funny

guy, Mark Twain." Then, abruptly serious, she added, "Too bad he
was such . . . an infidel."

Julia went to get her purse. When she returned, Carmen was
stooped in front of the plant stand by the screen door, singing to
one of the African violets, the one that was supposed to have frilly
fuchsia flowers, though it hadn't yet bloomed. They had recently
heard a story on NPR about a former opera singer who experi-
mented with her prizewinning houseplants by singing to them in
different languages. She claimed that singing in French produced
the largest blooms. Carmen had been fascinated by the story.

"*Ouvrez votre coeur, petite fleur, et chantez-nous une belle chanson,*"
she was singing now, over and over. It was the refrain of a song she
had learned from her father, in English of course, but she had asked
Dr. Boyer to write it down for her in French. *Open your heart, little
flower, and sing us a beautiful song.*

· *chapter 11* ·

FROM EAST TO WEST

A few weeks later, Julia was in Matthew's bedroom in the middle of the night. She didn't hear the door open, but suddenly Carmen was standing there, squinting against the light in an oversized gray T-shirt and black pajama pants.

"Aunt Julia, are you okay? You need some help with those?"

Julia dumped the armful of sport coats onto the bed, which was already covered with other clothing: suits, shirts, pants, neckties.

"No, but thanks anyway," Julia said. "I couldn't sleep again, so I thought I'd get up and put myself to work." She put a hand on top of the rollers in her hair. "I know I'm a sight. I wasn't expecting company. Sorry I woke you up."

Carmen shook her head. "I woke myself up. Then I saw the light under the door."

Julia picked up a necktie she had dropped on the floor and added it to the others on the bed. "Goodness knows I've put this project off long enough. I thought maybe it would force me to get moti-vated if I emptied the whole closet first."

"Do you put those things in your hair every night?" Carmen asked. "Maybe that's why you can't sleep."

Julia said, "Some of us have to get our curls the hard way."

Carmen walked over to the bed. "All these clothes belonged to one man?" She touched the sport coat on top, a brown wool herringbone. "Daddy had one suit. Just one. It was dark blue."

Julia was surprised he'd had even one suit. From what Carmen said, Jeremiah had hired himself out as a ranch hand most of the time, doing things Julia had seen only on old television westerns—herding cattle, mending fences, branding. And taming wild horses—he had been especially good at that, she said. Also rodeo contests, which was highly unusual for someone who hadn't grown up going to rodeos.

"Lulu was obsessed with that suit after he died," Carmen continued. "Like it wasn't just Daddy's suit, it was *Daddy* in some eerie way."

She moved over to the pile of neckties. "A pool of iridescent fish," she said. "Psychedelic eels." She ran a hand through them. "Daddy had only one tie I can remember. Blue with yellow crescents. When you think about it, ties are sort of funny—these long, skinny things men hang around their necks. Who do you suppose ever thought that up? Hey, look, here's one that matches my pajamas." She pulled out a light gray one imprinted with small black and red triangles and draped it around her neck, then moved to the mirror to study the effect.

"Anyway," she continued, "Lulu was already starting to have problems before Daddy died. She would get all nervous over the littlest things. Daddy always explained it away—said she was just tired." She paused. "After he died, she started wearing his suit."

In all the questions Julia had asked, Lulu was a subject she had always avoided. She knew she blamed Lulu for things that weren't her fault—such as the fact that Jeremiah had settled in the West and never once come back home. And even, somehow, the fact that he went hunting and got himself killed. And certainly the fact that he hadn't had a proper funeral, only a scattering of his ashes to the wind. He hadn't even needed his one suit to be buried in.

But now this fact—that Lulu wore his suit after he died. Though Julia didn't want to soften toward her, she couldn't help it. Such a sad thought—a woman so emotionally unsteady that she began wearing her husband's suit.

"Ida and Effie had fits about it," Carmen said, "but she kept right on wearing it."

"Wasn't it too big?" Julia asked.

Carmen nodded. "She was shorter than you, and mostly skin and bones. She pretty much quit eating after Daddy died. But she didn't care if the coat was big. She just rolled up the sleeves and said she liked it that way. The pants had to be just right, though—she tore them completely apart and remade them. Spent days on them. She was always real particular about how things fit her around the waist." She laughed. "And hips. Ida used to call her Snake Hips."

This came as a surprise to Julia, for every time she had imagined her brother and Lulu over the years, she had always pictured Lulu as a large woman—broad-beamed, thick-waisted, big-breasted, heavy makeup over coarse features, big braying laugh. She had always wondered how her brother could have been attracted to such a woman.

She carried the last armload of sport coats to the bed and deposited them on top of the others. Now for the shoes, all lined up in color groups on the closet floor, each pair neatly polished and fitted with stretchers. This didn't include the running shoes, sneakers, and other casual shoes on the revolving shoe tree.

She began moving them out of the closet, two pairs at a time, and setting them in rows, side by side, next to the desk. She hadn't realized there were so many. Matthew had been partial to lace-ups, though he had six pairs of loafers, too. Expensive brands, all of them, and none of them showed much wear.

Carmen pulled a red necktie out of the pile and studied its checkerboard design. "How could one person wear all these?" she said.

"One at a time," Julia said.

"What are you going to do with them all?"

"Good question," Julia said. The easiest thing, of course, would be to fill up the trunk and backseat of the Buick and take the whole lot to the Salvation Army or Goodwill, as she had done months ago with most of the things in his bureau drawers. But she also knew she could sell the clothes on the bed if she wanted to go to the trouble. There was a consignment shop over in Greenville that specialized in high-end men's clothing.

Carmen held up another necktie, a royal blue paisley. "Hey, could I have some of these?"

"What for?"

"For a skirt," Carmen said. She went on to describe a skirt she had seen a Millard-Temple girl wearing on campus, the whole thing made out of neckties sewn together side by side, with the wider pointed ends forming a saw-tooth hem. She was sure she could find instructions on the Internet. As with all young people, computer skills came easily for Carmen. Somehow these things seemed to be programmed into their brains at birth.

"It sounds like something from the hippie era," Julia said. "Something you'd wear with love beads and go-go boots. But . . . do you sew?"

Well, yes, as a matter of fact, she did, a little. Another one of her jobs in New England had been at a dry cleaners, where she picked up some free sewing lessons from the alterations woman. She asked Julia about an old sewing machine she had seen in the bottom of the linen closet.

"I haven't used that in years," Julia said. "I don't even know if it still works. Wait, don't tell me . . . you probably had a job repairing sewing machines, too, right?"

Carmen laughed. "No, but I did rebuild alternators one time for a couple of months." She pulled out another tie with interlocking silver and lime green hexagons. "I think I'd want this one somewhere in front," she said, "maybe next to this one." And she held up another one, rust-orange with wavy yellow and brown stripes.

Julia looked away quickly. A single visual image, only a glance, and suddenly you could be yanked out of the present and back to a different time and place, somewhere you had no desire to be. The rust-orange necktie was one Julia had stared at across a restaurant table as Matthew talked. Over twenty years ago—that was how long it would have been.

THEY had been married almost five years at the time. It wasn't a special occasion—not a birthday or Valentine's Day or their anniversary. Just a regular weekday in early spring, as she recalled. On the days she taught an afternoon class, Matthew was in charge of supper. She was rarely hungry at night and could have gone without anything, but those were the early years of their marriage, when Matthew still thought there must be some kind of connection between his effort and her happiness. And so he put himself on kitchen duty two days a week, which also meant their sitting down to eat together, something else she could have done without at the end of a long day.

That evening, however, when she got home, he wasn't wearing his jeans as usual, nor was he working on some home repair project while supper warmed in the oven. He was still dressed in his suit and necktie, sitting on the couch in the living room, watching the news and waiting for her. He had reservations for seven o'clock, he said, at a restaurant in Greenville called the Open Hearth. It was one of his favorite places.

She wasn't in the least interested in going out for dinner in the middle of the week, but something kept her from refusing, maybe the fact that he had reserved a table. He followed her back to the bedroom, where she set her briefcase down and took out the set of freshman themes she had been planning to grade that night. She placed them on her dresser with a sigh.

"Hard day?" Matthew asked.

She didn't look at him. "About like usual."

"Maybe you should cut back to half time," he said. It was an old subject, but one he hadn't mentioned in a while. The way he said it now, though gently, suggested the possibility of a renewed campaign.

She said nothing but turned and went into the bathroom.

"If we leave in about ten minutes, that'll get us there on time," he said through the closed door.

Her argument against working half time was always the same. They needed her income to pay for the house and all the work he was doing on it. And though she never told him this part, the thought of staying home scared her. She was a teacher. That was the only life she knew. She wouldn't know what to do with herself if she had entire days at home. The two afternoons she had now were enough for her. Many Saturdays she went to campus to work in her office, and sometimes Sundays, too.

When she came out of the bathroom, Matthew was looking into the mirror above her dresser, straightening his tie, the rust-orange one with yellow and brown stripes. He rubbed his hands together, gave her a hopeful smile through the mirror, and said he was in the mood for a steak.

The idea came to her suddenly that maybe he had good news of some kind. Maybe Mr. Carrier, his boss, had finally asked him to be a partner. That was something he had been hoping for. He had been with the insurance company for twelve years now. Or maybe they had landed a corporate contract and Mr. Carrier was giving everyone a big bonus.

He walked to the bedroom door, then paused and looked back at her. She made him wait while she pumped a dollop of hand cream into her palm and applied it slowly, working it between her fingers, over the backs of her hands, around her wrists. He turned and left, as if he knew she would never come as long as he stood there. And he was right. She waited another few moments and then followed him.

AT the restaurant, he pressed her to order a full meal, though all she really wanted was an appetizer. "We can take home whatever you don't eat," he said, which was what he always said. She knew he was planning ahead. Restaurant leftovers were a staple for the nights he was on supper duty.

She didn't remember now what she had eaten that night, but Matthew had a steak, charbroiled exactly as he liked it, which was barely. She could still see it bleeding onto the white plate. He made a few attempts at small talk while they ate their salads, but when the entrées came, he fell silent and gave his full attention to eating. Not in an uncouth way, though. Matthew might have grown up in eastern Tennessee, but he had somehow emerged from the hills with impeccable table manners.

She was beginning to think it was just a craving for steak that had motivated the drive to Greenville, but at last the moment came when she learned the real reason.

The restaurant was still moderately full of other diners, for the Open Hearth was the kind of place with a loyal clientele, people with money who ate their dinners late. The interior had been remodeled since the last time they were here—classy touches such as black-framed sepia photographs hanging by long silver chains along the walls, a bank of ferns in a stone planter against the plate glass window, small light fixtures with mica shades suspended above each table, emitting an amber glow. Easy-listening music played softly, piano and strings.

The waitress took their plates. Matthew asked for a cup of decaf coffee, but Julia declined. He also ordered a slice of key lime pie, a dessert he knew Julia liked, and requested two forks. When it came, he slid it to the middle, then reached forward and took a bite onto his fork.

He ate it slowly, then set his fork down and spoke. "I have something to ask you."

Julia felt a quickening of her pulse. She lifted her eyes to his necktie but no higher. Matthew picked up his coffee and took a sip, then put it down and patted his mouth with his napkin. Julia still hadn't taken a bite of the pie.

But he didn't ask his question right away. First, he told a humorous anecdote about one of his coworkers at the insurance office, the newest employee and one he mentioned frequently. Chet Ambrose, a dyed-in-the-wool Southern boy who had been married less than a year, had come to work that morning with the news that he and his wife were expecting a baby. He had announced it to the entire office, then inverted the empty pockets of his suit pants and said, "See, I'm flat broke. We still have college loans to pay off. A baby was *not* in the plan!" All of which elicited laughter, but not as much as the next part: "We can't figure out how it happened."

As Matthew talked, Julia kept her eyes on his tie. The stripes wouldn't be still, and the orange had turned into an indiscriminate color that had no name. She knew now what the question was going to be, and there was nothing she could do to stop it. It was coming, as surely as the sun would rise tomorrow and make its way from east to west. And she had no answer ready, none except *No*, which she knew was not the answer he wanted to hear.

He finally stopped talking and leaned forward. "Julia," he said. He waited till she lifted her eyes, and then it came. "Please, can we talk about children?"

I WOULD probably need about thirty, I'm guessing," Carmen said. She had already laid a dozen or so neckties across the back of a chair.

Julia picked up the last two pairs of shoes from the closet floor and added them to the others beside the desk. She ran a finger over the top of a black loafer and left a trail through the fine film of dust. How curious, she thought, that dust could get inside a closet with the door closed.

I T was almost three o'clock in the morning when Julia finally crawled back into bed. Carmen had returned to her bedroom over an hour ago, and the house was quiet, except for the sounds of gentle rain coming from Julia's clock radio. Over the past weeks, she had switched from "Ocean Waves" to "Spring Showers." There was no evidence at all that the sounds helped her sleep better, but at least they kept her from straining to hear noises down the hall.

She arranged the covers, then rearranged them, then did the same with the pillows, then finally lay still and closed her eyes. A few minutes later she adjusted the volume of the spring showers to make them more like a summer downpour. She waited for twenty minutes before getting up to take a sleeping tablet, but she was still awake an hour later, still thinking about the look on Matthew's face some twenty years earlier, as the light of hope dimmed. No anger, only puzzlement, then disbelief, then resignation, all within the space of a few seconds.

By the time they got home that night, his face was wiped clean of any expression. Not that she studied it at any length, but a side-long glance at a stoplight a few blocks from Ivy Dale Lane told her all. He had taken in the answer she had whispered fiercely, tearfully over the dessert they left unfinished—*No, I can't, please don't ask that, I can't!*—and now, having seen all the years ahead in light of her words, he had apparently erased a dream. He seemed to know that her answer was permanent, that there were no compromises such as adoption to be considered, for he hadn't pressured her at the restaurant or in the car, nor was he ever to bring it up again.

And he never again mentioned Chet Ambrose and his wife's pregnancy. Over a year later at Mr. Carrier's retirement dinner, Chet was there holding a blue-eyed baby girl in a bright pink romper and matching headband, which she kept yanking off and stuffing into her mouth. All evening Julia avoided looking at them or at Chet's high-spirited wife, who, when she wasn't laughing, was digging around in the diaper bag and pulling out one thing or another. And Julia also avoided looking at Matthew that evening, for she didn't want to see his eyes following Chet and Estella—that was the baby's name—all around the room.

Time and again the thought had come to her since Matthew's death that he had treated her better than she deserved, accommodating her every preference. He saw to it that she never had to state a wish more than once, whether for something requiring a great deal of expense and labor, such as the circular drive, or something more easily granted, such as putting his dirty work clothes on top of the washing machine instead of inside the hamper.

Julia sat up in bed again and turned on the light. She picked up the folded program on her nightstand to look at it once more. It was one of the few things she had found while going through Matthew's clothing. As in most other things in his world, other than his debts, Matthew's pockets were in order.

She had pulled the program, along with a ticket stub, out of the breast pocket of a suit coat. It was only a folded leaflet on plain white paper, obviously a low-budget piece of work. The title on the front—*The Adventures of Tom Sawyer*—was off center, and the hand-drawn illustration of a freckle-faced boy in a straw hat and overalls appeared to be the work of a child. Inside, the name Geoffrey Long was circled in the cast of characters, and beside it in labored cursive was a penciled signature—*Geoffrey "Huckleberry" Long*, with a note scrawled beneath it: *Thanks for coming, Mr. Matt.*

Julia didn't know anybody named Geoffrey Long, and she had never heard any child call him "Mr. Matt" either. She turned back to the front and studied the program again. The location was an elementary school in Greenville, and the date was on a Friday night in November almost two years ago, the time seven o'clock P.M. Once again she was reminded of how little she really knew of Matthew's life.

She tried to imagine what that particular Friday night would have been like. Had the two of them eaten dinner together at home before he went to the play? Friday suppers were usually paltry. A good one might include both soup and sandwiches, but most often it was one or the other. Or had he called her, as he often did on Fridays, and said he was working to finish up some things in the office and would grab something to eat on his way home, if she didn't mind? Which she never did.

And what had she done that evening? Graded another stack of papers? Or watched a movie? Maybe she had turned on the gas logs in the living room against the November chill and listened to the radio.

By that point in their marriage, Matthew had learned not to ask if she wanted to go anywhere on Friday night. The answer would always be the same. She was tired. She wanted to stay in. Many Friday nights she lay on the sofa, television muted, a CD playing softly, and read until she fell asleep, usually long after Matthew went to bed. When she woke, sometime in the early hours of morning, she would get up and move to her bedroom.

But what about when Matthew had come home that night? He always greeted her kindly if she was awake, asked her the standard polite questions. Was she feeling all right? Was she tired? Had it been a good day? Could he get her anything from the kitchen? And if she pretended to be asleep, which she often did, he always stood by the sofa for a moment, then touched something belonging to her—the blanket, her book, her sleeve, occasionally her hair—before walking back to his bedroom. He never disturbed her by speaking, never presumed to turn the television off. But even if she had been asleep that night, or pretended to be, why hadn't he told her the next day about going to Geoffrey Long's school play? Or had he mentioned it and she simply hadn't paid attention?

Well, enough of all that. She slapped the printed program back onto the nightstand. The Tom Sawyer play was over and done. The curtain had come down, the audience had applauded, and Matthew had dropped dead in the flower bed less than a year later. Why should she be lying awake full of pity for him that he had gone by himself alone one Friday night to see a children's play?

But that brought up another question: *Had* he gone by himself? She had turned his pockets inside out to check for another ticket stub, but there was only the one. What would she have done if she had found two? What *could* she have done, besides wonder for the rest of her life who had gone with him? And even if she had found incriminating evidence—a lipstick smear on a handkerchief, an earring, a note written in a feminine hand—what then?

She picked up the play program again and smelled it—no scent of perfume there. She put it down, turned out the light, and lay back down. And who would have blamed Matthew for wanting the companionship of a woman who desired his company, who listened and responded to whatever he said, who welcomed his touch? At the time Julia might have flown into a fit and played the victim, but she'd had a year now to reflect on what it must have been like for the man who was her husband. She had no idea how he had coped in a marriage like theirs, and, to be truthful, it was easier not to know.

But she couldn't get the picture out of her mind. Matthew, sitting among parents and grandparents in a school auditorium on a Friday night, watching an amateur production of *Tom Sawyer*, smiling and laughing at all the right times, staying afterward to talk to the boy named Geoffrey, asking him to sign his program, then driving home to the stone house, silent and empty except for Julia.

She flopped over and repositioned herself among the covers and pillows. She hated it when she did this—wallowed in regrets she couldn't do a thing about. And right now it was more than the play, of course, though that discovery had added weight to the memory of Matthew's question at the restaurant, put to her with such deference and hope: *Please, can we talk about children?* Matthew, always the gentleman.

It was a perfectly fair question for him to ask—a man married five years and well into his forties by then. They had never talked about having a family before they married, though she had known from the way he observed and interacted with other people's children that he wanted his own someday. For that reason, if for no other, she should never have married him. At the very least, she should have disclosed her intentions regarding children and allowed him to give her up. But selfishness had won. The thoughts of a husband and the security of marriage had been suddenly appealing in a way that caught her by surprise.

She had made no outright promises, but she knew she had led

him to believe they could be as happy as other couples, as she indeed had hoped they could. She was almost thirty when they married, he eight years older. "Mystery Woman" was what he called her
during the months of their courtship.

THEY first met at a concert of the Brahms *Requiem* sung by the
Greenville Chorale. Matthew arrived at the last minute,
shortly before the lights went down, and hastily took the seat next
to her because it was on the aisle and empty. But not twenty seconds later, the rightful seat holder arrived—a tall black-haired
woman in a mink stole, the kind where the little mink encircled her
neck, its jaws clamped onto its tail—and as the lights were dim-
ming said, quite loudly, "You, sir, are in my seat."

They had laughed about it afterward, when he caught up with
Julia in the lobby and introduced himself as "Matthew Rich, ejectee
of the seat next to yours." They went to a McDonald's between
Traveler's Rest and Greenville and sat across from each other while
they had soft-serve ice cream sundaes.

Almost a year later, at a much nicer restaurant, after another
concert for which he held a legitimate ticket for the seat next to
hers, he made a winsome speech starting with "We make a perfect
pair, you know. Mystery Woman and Rich Man." He had a ring in
his pocket, and somehow before they parted for the night, the ring
was on her finger.

She should have told him then, or a dozen times before or a
dozen times after. But she kept silent and allowed plans to go forward for a small, private summer wedding. And one thing followed
another, as they always do in a marriage, until one day five years
later her thoughtful husband arranged a dinner date. Once again
they sat at a table in a restaurant, and this time he asked, "Please,
can we talk about children?"

And she gave her answer, which must have shocked him for only an instant before it settled into his mind as a confirmation that theirs had never been and would never be a marriage made in heaven, that the Mystery Woman who was his wife had turned into a cold case with no clues.

chapter 12

THE SEVENTH PICTURE

Sometime later, still in the dark of early morning, Julia awoke with tears on her face. It was an old dream she knew by heart. No sound at first, only images. Not a movie kind of dream, but an old slide show.

The pictures always flashed into her mind in quick succession. The first was the house where she grew up, a two-story gray-shingled house in Nadine, Alabama. It was an August afternoon, and she was on her way from Texas, where she had just defended her doctoral dissertation, to her new teaching position in South Carolina. She would soon be twenty-eight years old.

She was sitting in her car in the driveway, staring at the house she hadn't seen for almost nine years. It had a neglected, vacant look, though she knew her parents had occupied it every day since she had last been here. And now she was returning to lay her academic trophies at her father's feet. At last she had achieved something that outshone anything Jeremiah had ever done, as far as she knew. By then Jeremiah had been gone almost as long as she had, without a word of communication.

The second picture in the slide show dream was her mother's face, wrecked by time and toil, her eyes filled with fear to see who might be knocking at the kitchen door, beside which still grew the old rosebush, one spent rose dropping wilted petals. She peered out from behind the dingy, gauzy curtain, and for a moment Julia thought it was someone else looking out at her, a hired housekeeper perhaps. And then the door slowly swung open and she saw it was her mother—unkempt hair, empty eyes, a woolen scarf wrapped around her neck in the hottest part of summer. Barely fifty, yet the face of an old woman. It was like looking at a familiar building that had been vandalized.

The third picture was even worse, for it precipitated all the horror that followed. Her father's face showed the same signs of ruin as her mother's, though in his case it was a building not only vandalized but also boarded up, long deserted. Deep depression was what ailed him, according to her mother. That and his bad back and his crippling arthritis, which had worsened to the point that he had given up everything, even his compilation of folk songs. Most days now he didn't get out of bed.

Suddenly the slide show had audio. Her father's voice was un-impaired, a fact Julia perceived as soon as she stepped across the threshold into the kitchen that day, for she could hear him roaring from another room about what he was going to do to her mother if she didn't bring him a glass of orange juice right then.

He was still shouting when Julia approached his bed a few moments later. When she saw his face, contorted by rage and pain, she knew immediately that this trip home was a doomed effort. He stopped midsentence, his eyes pitiless as death, and when he spoke again, it was clear that there was still no favor to be found in his sight. Turning his face to the wall, he said, "Oh, it's you," as if he couldn't stand the sight of her, though she knew it was more likely only disappointment that Jeremiah wasn't the one standing by his bed.

AFTERWARD, she and her mother had quarreled at some length in the kitchen, a quarrel such as they had never had before, all the more intense because it was conducted in near-whispers. With endlessly sad years and troubled memories piled high on both sides, it would have been hard for anyone listening to tell what they were arguing about. Back and forth they went, not waiting for the other to finish. Even now Julia recalled feeling only a vague, un-focused fury over everything—her own physical exhaustion, her father's rejection, both old and new, the fact that he was now bed-ridden coupled with her mother's failure to forewarn her, the whole dreary atmosphere in this house where intimidation was like an-other occupant, so powerful that they dared not speak aloud.

"Why didn't you tell me he was getting worse?" This was Julia's first question after stalking into the kitchen from her father's bed-room. Her mother's reply was full of rancor: "Getting worse? He's been getting worse ever since you were old enough to remember. Did you think he might be getting better? And anyway, you never asked. Pam was the only one who ever called or came to visit." This wasn't the mother Julia had grown up with.

But in other ways she was the same. At this point in the slide show, an image of her mother's Bible appeared, lying on the kitchen table beside a place mat littered with crumbs and stained with old food, her mother's hand resting on the cover as they argued. It was the same Bible she had always had, its cover as limp as an old dishrag.

When Julia's eyes fell on the Bible, she dragged it into the argument, too, her words spiteful, mindless, barely coherent, still whispered feverishly: *"That!"* She pointed to it. "So how much peace has it given you after you sacrificed your own children for a man like *him*? You did this to yourself! You could have gotten out years ago—and now see what he's done to you, to all of us!"

There was more, of course, both given and received, much of it repeated as the argument climaxed and then gradually lost steam.

Julia finally stopped and collapsed into a chair at the table. Her mother came toward her. At first Julia thought she meant to touch her, comfort her, but she only held out a paper napkin, then sat down and laid her hand on her Bible again. "This has been my strength through the years. This was the holy voice that told me to stay true to my marriage vows. I would give my life for this book." She wasn't whispering anymore, but speaking as if to herself. "It's the same book that warns about an unruly tongue. I'm sorry for all the things I just said."

Julia stopped whispering, too, but her words were low and hard, spoken from between clenched teeth. "Any book that tells you to subject innocent children to a man like him isn't worth the paper it's printed on."

"You were all three strong, smart children," her mother said. "I'm not saying I couldn't have done better by you, but I knew you would all make it somehow." Her hand was still resting on the Bible. "I knew he wouldn't if I left him."

Julia didn't know whether to laugh or cry. She pointed to the bedroom. "You call that *making it*?" She stood from her chair. "And *you*—have you *made it*? Is this how your God rewards you for being trampled on all those years?"

She had originally meant to stay overnight, had wished a million times that she had gotten herself under control, had set aside her pride and self-pity and called a truce, had taken her mother in her arms to beg forgiveness for her thoughtless words, had tried to ease her burdened soul for at least a few hours before leaving. But she hadn't. She didn't even tell her why she had come. Her doctoral degree suddenly seemed worthless.

The fifth picture was her mother's face at the kitchen door once more, looking out at Julia, who was sitting in her car again, one fist clutching her keys, the other pressed to her mouth, her breath coming fast. It was a beseeching look on her mother's face, as if she wanted to open the door and call Julia back in but knew there was no use trying.

And then a movement at the bedroom window—the one facing the driveway. It was her father's room. What effort it had cost him to make his way from the bed to the window she would never know, but that was the next picture—no face but a large, knotted hand on the heavy damask drape.

A sudden leaving of her senses followed. Julia fumbled for the right key, inserted it into the ignition, turned it hard. The engine caught; she jammed the gearshift into reverse and shot backward.

At this point in the slide show, she felt a sudden soft resistance against the tires of her car, nothing alarming at first, more like the sensation of running over a thick branch or a garbage can lid. Maybe if she had immediately applied the brakes, had gotten out to see what it was, maybe the rest of her life would have been different. Or maybe not. Maybe the damage was already done by the rear wheels before the front ones struck. At any rate, she didn't stop, not until she reached the end of the driveway and saw what lay crumpled in front of her.

THIS was the seventh picture, the one so horrible that ever afterward she feared falling asleep and seeing it during the night. And feeling and hearing it. Suddenly the volume on the audio was turned up high. All at once the neighborhood, usually so quiet with such a little bit of traffic, was filled with sound. Sirens keening, people from all directions running, shouting, and then above it all, heart-rending wails.

The child himself made no sound at all. It was too late for that. His plastic three-wheeler lay on its side several feet away, the front wheel only slightly out of alignment, one of the back ones still turning slowly. A fact cruel beyond belief—that cheap yellow plastic was more durable than human flesh.

Now, as always after the bad dreams, her father's old songs came to torment her, always the saddest of them, and always the saddest words of the saddest songs: *Poor boy, you're bound to die. They sobbed and they sighed, and they bitterly cried. Oh, father, father, dig my grave, go dig it deep and narrow.*

J ULIA got up, took another sleeping pill, and went back to bed. At last she slept. When she woke hours later, she could tell it was late, but she continued to lie there, marveling that sleep had fallen upon her at last and delivered her once more to a new day.

With the sunshine leaking into her bedroom around the draperies, it came to her again that it was a charitable universe that operated this way, whereby daylight always returned, even after the worst nights. And the fact that after such nights she could rise again and push away enough of her old guilt to function almost normally—this was a gift for which she had no explanation. She always accepted it with gratitude, though she always felt guilty for doing so. There were certain sins one had no right to forget.

She folded back the covers and tentatively set her feet on the floor. Still solid beneath her. Slowly she stood up and walked to the window, then opened the drapes and blinds. And here was her own front yard looking as it did every other morning, except for the garden hose, which was unwrapped from its caddy behind the azalea bushes and stretched to the corner of the house. She walked across the hall to Matthew's bedroom and looked out the window. Everything in the backyard looked the same, too, except for Carmen lying flat on her back in the grass near the creek bank, one arm thrown over her eyes, one knee propped up with her new fishing hat perched on top of it.

The hat was something the girl had run across while clearing Matthew's fishing gear out of the garage. After putting it through the washer, she had decorated it with numbers of colorful lures, jellylike worms, and bobbers, all of which dangled from the brim. She had left a space in front just wide enough for an unobstructed view.

Carmen stirred now and swatted something on her arm. She sat up and squinted at the sun, then lay down again. Apparently she was tending the garden hose, which ran all the way across the backyard to the creek bank, where a few hydrangea bushes still bore blue blooms, stragglers she was coddling. She had to know their days were numbered. Even now, during the last week of September, the mornings and evenings were noticeably cooler, though daytime temperatures still climbed into the eighties. But the first frost would come, as it always did, and then winter.

She moved closer to the window. In the birdbath, a blue jay was fluttering in and out of the water, flapping its wings. A breeze was lifting the leaves of the trees, and overhead the clouds were floating across a sea of sky, robustly blue. Julia looked back at Carmen. Blue jeans and a blue T-shirt. A conspiracy of blue this morning.

CARMEN had been quieter than usual the last couple of days. Perhaps she was dreading the New England trip, which she had finally agreed to, reluctantly. Maybe she was thinking of all those hours together in such close company—in the car, in motel rooms, on a plane. It was certainly something Julia had thought about.

Whatever it was, the girl clearly had something on her mind, again. Yesterday she had cut a dozen red roses from the trellis alongside the garage and had spent a long time arranging them in a white pitcher on the kitchen table. Julia had almost pointed out the bad timing. They were leaving in a few days and would only have to throw them out. But she had said nothing.

Carmen rolled over on her stomach now and crawled over to move the hose to the base of another bush, then lay down on her back again, spread-eagle, her head thrown back, her hat on the ground beside her. She lifted one arm and waved it about. Such a movement could have been entirely void of feeling, or motivated by joy, but Julia interpreted it as despair. She wished she could read the girl's mind.

At Pamela's insistence, the route for the trip had been slightly modified. Julia had planned all along that she and Carmen would rent a car and drive since her Buick got poor gas mileage. Before beginning their tour of authors' homes, they would stop for a day of sightseeing in four cities: D.C., Philadelphia, New York, and Boston. They would end the authors' tour in Hartford, Connecticut, and from there would fly home. By then, Julia figured, even Carmen would be tired of driving.

The change was only on the front end of the trip. Now they were leaving South Carolina a day earlier than originally planned so they could stop by Pamela's house in Twin Lakes, Virginia. "It's no fair that you get her all to yourself," Pamela had told Julia more than once in recent weeks. "She's my niece, too, you know."

This from the same person who only months earlier had said things like "Just tell her she *has* to leave," who predicted disaster when Julia told her the girl was staying, who threatened to drive down from Twin Lakes to give Julia a lesson in "how to say no," and who told Julia to lock up her jewelry, her good silver, and anything else portable that could be pawned for cash. Also the same person who said, "All right, have it your way, I wash my hands of all responsibility"—her last words before all communication ceased.

But only for two weeks. One afternoon in early August, Pamela's dark green van had pulled into the circular drive of the stone house. Julia's only surprise when she looked out the kitchen window and saw who was ringing the doorbell was that her sister had held off so long. "Where is she?" Pamela had demanded as soon as Julia opened the front door. "Have you gotten rid of her yet?" Her eyes scanned the living room, as if checking for missing art objects and other valuables.

This from the same person who a few days later left great wet blots of tears on Carmen's T-shirt as she said good-bye and climbed into her van to return home, who over the following weeks asked to speak with Carmen at the end of every phone call, or sometimes at the beginning, who repeatedly begged her to come visit "Aunt Pam and Uncle Butch in Virginia."

JULIA turned away from the window and went back to her bedroom to get dressed. The next time she looked out, Carmen was standing up, her hat on her head, dragging the hose back toward the front of the house. When Julia went to the kitchen for coffee, she watched Carmen rewind the hose. When she finished, she shook her head vigorously so that the fishing lures danced. Julia wished she wouldn't do that. Though she had snipped all the barbs off, the hooks were still sharp.

Suddenly the girl looked up at the sky, then turned and headed down the driveway toward the street, moving quickly as if late for an appointment, still wearing the hat. Now that Julia thought about it, the hat could be a sign that the girl's spirits were lifting, for she usually didn't wear anything playful on her sad days.

All at once something fell into place in Julia's mind. This wasn't the first time she had seen Carmen leave the house this way, walking with the same sense of purpose instead of her usual moderate pace. No sooner had this thought come to her than the probability of a pattern presented itself: She was quite sure the time of day was always the same—late morning. And the direction—on these days, wasn't it true that the girl always turned left at the end of the driveway instead of right as she most often did?

Not a second later Carmen came to the street and turned left. She soon disappeared from sight, still walking swiftly, as if on a mission. This meant she probably wasn't headed to the college since this way would take her twice as long. Julia thought through the possibilities. The streets to the west were mostly residential, some of the homes rundown. Tucked among them stood the old Presbyterian church on a big corner lot and a smaller Baptist one two blocks away. Neither of these was the one Carmen had chosen as her church, though. That one was on the east side of town and much smaller. Beyond the Baptist church were the elementary school, a set of apartments, and a feeble attempt at a shopping strip—a Laundromat, a convenience store, and a doughnut shop. After that the town gave up and turned into open fields and scrubby stands of pine and poplar, with a few farmhouses and barns scattered here and there along the old highway.

So where was Carmen going? Julia tried to remember how long these westward excursions had lasted in the past and how the girl had behaved upon returning home. And how many there had been. It was hard to believe she hadn't noticed the pattern before, for she was always curious about the girl's comings and goings, though she tried to give the impression she wasn't. She liked to think that this was one reason they were so compatible—they allowed each other space, respected each other's privacy.

And often enough there was no cause to wonder, for Carmen sometimes spoke openly of where she was going or where she had been—to the college campus, to the public library, to a park, a church, a store, a neighbor's house. So why was she sneaking away now? Well, maybe not sneaking. Maybe there was some simple explanation. Maybe she was doing yard work or odd jobs for someone in that direction. If so, that might be cause for secrecy since Julia had told her more than once that it would be safer to work only at houses at this end of Ivy Dale.

Throughout her life, Julia's brand of worry had never been the teapot variety—starting slow, heating gradually, steadily, before a brief boil, then a quick cooldown. It had always been more like a natural disaster—an earthquake, a volcanic eruption, a tornado. Her worry exploded now. What if Carmen had once again trusted unwisely and gotten herself into another dangerous situation?

She was in the Buick within minutes. Her heart pounded as she drove down Ivy Dale, all sorts of disturbing scenarios running through her mind. If she saw the girl on the sidewalk—and she couldn't bear the thought of *not* seeing her—she would pull over and watch from a distance, then creep along to see where she went. And if she saw her go into a . . . but suddenly her plotting ceased, for she saw her. Not from behind, however. Carmen was coming directly toward her, apparently already returning from wherever she had gone, or having changed her mind about going.

Well, this was awkward. There would be little chance of avoiding her notice, though Julia held out hope at first. Carmen was walking more slowly now, looking up into the trees, her lips moving as if talking to herself, one hand sweeping back and forth. Oh, so that was it—only another of her prayer walks.

But then, just when Julia was almost past, Carmen glanced

toward the street and saw the Buick. She stopped and made binoculars out of her hands, peered through them, and then cheerfully waved. There was nothing for Julia to do but stop and roll down her window. "I had a sudden craving," she said. "I'm going to the doughnut shop. Do you want one, too?"

"Well, okay, I guess so," Carmen said, more polite than eager, for she rarely ate sweets. She got into the car, humming something. As they passed the Presbyterian preschool, a line of children was leaving the play area, heading toward a side door. One little boy lagged behind, leaping about and slashing the air with a stick he was carrying. A woman came from the front of the line and took the stick away, then held his hand and walked with him.

Julia pulled over to the side of the street and applied the brakes. "I don't want a doughnut," she said, looking straight ahead. "I just made that up. I was out looking for you." She sighed. "I got worried and let my imagination get carried away."

Carmen let out a low whistle. "Seriously? It's been forever since anybody worried about me. Lulu used to when I was little. And Daddy did, too, but he didn't wring his hands and fuss out loud like Lulu did." She tapped a finger on the dashboard. "Daddy used to call me Bob—did I ever tell you that? My middle name is Roberta."

Julia made herself look at Carmen. "Well, Bob, I should have told you the truth to start with. I shouldn't . . . equivocate." *Lie* was a hard word to say. "It's a bad habit I have, and I don't want to do it anymore. I don't even like doughnuts, really."

"Me neither." Carmen held her gaze for a moment, then jiggled her head to make the fishing lures shake. "I could make you a hat like this. Want me to?"

Julia smiled. "Thanks, but I'll pass." She took her foot off the brake, and the Buick rolled forward a few inches.

Carmen put a hand on her arm. "Wait, Aunt Julia. Can I ask you a question?"

Julia felt a prickle of dread, but she stopped the car and put it in park. "Well, sure." She rolled down both of the front windows and turned off the engine, for she knew Carmen's questions were usually plural, not singular.

CARMEN looked over at the church. All the children were inside now. She took off her fishing hat and set it on the seat between them. "Sitting in front of the Westside Presbyterian Church," she said to Julia, "Carmen asked her aunt a probing question." She turned back to Julia and gave a nervous laugh. "Do you ever have this funny feeling like you're not really *here*?" She pointed both index fingers down. "I'm not just talking about here in this car, but just wherever you happen to be. Like this person"—she lifted both hands and stared at them—"isn't really *you*? And all this stuff around you"—she touched the door handle, motioned outside toward the sidewalk, the treetops and church steeple—"is just in a *picture* or something?"

"Is this your probing question?" Julia asked. She was suddenly struck with the oddest sensation that what Carmen had just put into words was indeed something she had felt before, many times.

Carmen made a face. "Sitting in front of Westside Presbyterian Church," she said again, "Carmen started stalling with other questions because she was halfway afraid to ask her aunt Julia the *real* question."

Julia raised her eyebrows. "And Aunt Julia said to Carmen, 'Afraid of what? Not of me, I hope. Please tell me you're not afraid of *me*.' After which Aunt Julia waited for Carmen to answer."

Carmen smiled but didn't reply immediately. She looked at the church again. The side door opened, and another line of children appeared. These looked even younger than the other group. They were holding on to a rope as they slowly made their way down the long sidewalk to the playground. One of them tripped and fell, and the child on either side went down, too—a modified domino effect.

"There they are," Carmen said. "They're late coming out today. I thought I'd missed them." She watched for a moment, then turned back to Julia and took a deep breath. "No, not afraid of you—I just don't want to upset you. You might think I'm being nosy." She laughed. "Well, I guess I am."

"Go ahead and ask your question," Julia said. "I need to get home before sundown."

The line of rope-holders had come to a halt now, and a woman rushed forward to help the three children to their feet, one of whom was crying. Another woman, a large one wearing a polka-dot smock, was standing at the front of the line, holding the end of the rope, her other hand raised like a policeman stopping traffic. Near the back of the line, a little girl in denim dungarees let go of the rope and plopped down on the sidewalk.

Julia looked away and fixed her eyes on the steering wheel. Suddenly she wished she could retract her last words and replace them with *Well, then, let's don't go there. Just save that question for another time.* She should have turned on the radio, then gunned the engine and headed straight home. But, no, she had chosen this time to be warm and inviting, even teasing, parking the car as if she had all the time in the world. *Go ahead and ask your question,* she had said. And now Carmen had shifted in her seat to face her, and there was no way to stop whatever was coming.

"Did you ever . . ." The girl cleared her throat longer than could possibly be necessary. ". . . did you ever wish you had . . . a child of your own?"

Of course. It was inevitable. There had been a few close calls before, timid advances toward the subject, but Julia had always held them off by diversionary tactics and Carmen had always retreated. But now this. And Julia had no one but herself to blame. She had set the whole thing in motion. She was the one who had panicked, had flown out of the house to track Carmen down, had tried to cover up with a falsehood. She was the one who had pulled over in front of a church—a church with a daycare, of course—and proceeded to deliver a principled little confession about telling the truth and not pretending anymore, and then, for good measure, had pressed Carmen to *ask her question*.

She stared hard at her hands in her lap, thinking how wonderful it would be if she really wasn't the person attached to them, if the Buick and the church and the children were only things in a picture. But she was here, and a question had been asked. Truth seemed to be the only choice.

"Yes, there was a time when I did wish that," she said, knowing that her answer, instead of closing doors, would throw them wide open. "But many years ago I . . . did something. I forfeited my right to motherhood."

NEITHER of them spoke for a long moment, though there were other sounds: the children's voices at play like the twittering of birds, the rhythmic swish of a broom as a woman swept her front steps across the street, the barking of a dog farther away, the throb of a small-engine airplane overhead.

At length Julia turned to look at Carmen. "It was all a very long time ago." She looked down at Carmen's fishing hat on the seat and touched the brim. "Nothing to be done about it now. It was my fault, but I didn't mean for it to happen. I could have easily prevented it, but . . . well, I didn't. I'll tell you about it if you want me to." She started the car. "At home, though. Not here."

"I'm so sorry," Carmen said softly. "You don't have to. I shouldn't have . . ." She stared out her window as Julia turned the car around and headed back to the stone house.

Two blocks from home, they passed a house with a wraparound porch. Wind chimes of every variety hung along the eaves.

The windows of the Buick were still down, and they stopped and listened a moment. It struck Julia that though the visual effect was whimsical, the choir of wind chimes wasn't as harmonious and lilting a sound as one might expect.

"I like to walk this way whenever the wind is blowing," Carmen said, nodding toward the house.

Other mournful words of her father's old songs came to Julia's mind. *Hang your head over, hear the wind blow. Look down, look down that lonesome road. Nobody else can walk it for you, you've got to walk it by yourself.*

A car horn beeped behind them. Julia raised a hand out the window and then drove on toward home.

chapter 13

THE BEATEN PATH

Julia was still in bed when the phone rang early Saturday morning. "I hope you don't come dragging in after dark," Pamela said. "I sure wish you would stay two nights instead of just one. We'll barely have any time to visit. We're grilling out for supper." All the same things she had been saying for the past week. "Are the suitcases in the car yet? What time are you leaving?"

"After Carmen gets home," Julia said.

"Gets home? Where is she?"

"Here right now, but she's headed to church soon," Julia said.

Pamela groaned. "Church—*today*? It's Saturday."

"The Sunday school classes are putting on a play about Moses and the Israelites tomorrow. She volunteered to do the props."

Pamela gave a derisive laugh. "The *props*? Like what? The golden calf?"

"No, just manna and stone tablets. The manna was easy, but the stone tablets took a little work. She made them out of foam."

Pamela said, "That ought to make a real convincing sound

when Moses throws them down." She laughed again. "How are they going to manage the plagues? And the parting of the Red Sea?" Julia knew Pamela was only flaunting her knowledge of Bible stories. She never missed a chance to let it be known that she had taken her children to church and Sunday school when they were growing up.

Julia gave her time to finish laughing. "Are you done now? Because if you are, I need to hang up. I have to get ready for a trip."

"Did you get the oil checked in your car?" Pamela asked. "You could burn up your engine if you . . ."

"I told you, we're renting a car," Julia said. "We're picking it up at noon."

"Well, still, it wouldn't hurt to check the oil, and the tire pressure, too. And the heat and air—make sure that . . . wait, did you say *noon*? You're not leaving till *noon*?"

Julia finally got off the phone with her, but not before Pamela once again dropped a hint to be invited along on the authors' tour: "I've heard the colors are supposed to be especially good this year. That's something I've always wanted to do—visit New England during October." Julia knew that the wistful sigh was meant to be heard.

"Well, we won't be able to get away at all today if I don't get off the phone," Julia said. "We'll see you when we get there." And she hung up. She couldn't imagine having Pamela along for the whole trip. This overnight visit at her house was going to be bad enough.

J ULIA was driving the first leg of the trip. They had been on the road over an hour, listening to a program called *From the Top* on NPR, featuring especially talented young musicians.

"Did you ever take music lessons?" Carmen said.

Julia nodded. "Piano. Your father could play circles around me, though." She remembered how she dreaded practicing, not because of the practice itself—she had actually loved playing the piano—but because of her father's tutorials shouted from the other room, always ending sooner or later with "Stop! You're slaughtering it! No more!"

They passed a billboard: *FIREWORKS AND PEACHES NEXT EXIT*. Evidently North Carolina was no different from every other state in the South, all of which were full of such signs that stayed up year-round.

"I never heard Daddy play the piano," Carmen said, "but you knew he played the guitar, right? He taught me a little. He got me a little plastic ukulele when I was only four." She positioned her left hand on an imaginary fret and made strumming motions with her right. "Isn't *ukulele* a cool word? Has a little Hawaiian twang." She said it again. "*U-ku-le-le*."

"Your father could have played any instrument he picked up," Julia said. She turned the radio off. "Okay, want to start reading now?"

Carmen reached to the backseat and got a book titled *Masterworks of Short Fiction*. It was Julia's idea that they use some of their road time reading aloud. For this purpose, she had selected an anthology of short stories and the novella *Ethan Frome*, which she wanted to save for after they visited Edith Wharton's home in Massachusetts. They would listen to the radio, too, of course, as well as the CDs she had brought along.

The truck traffic was heavy along this stretch, but Julia's driving strategy was to set the cruise control at sixty and stay in the right lane. This meant, of course, that most other vehicles, including eighteen-wheelers, were whizzing past their rented Honda. That was fine with her. She was in no hurry to get to Pamela's. A red Corvette convertible flew by, then whipped in front of her to pass a car that wouldn't give up the middle lane.

The stories in the *Masterworks* book were arranged in alphabetical order according to the authors' last names. Julia had assumed they would start with the first story and continue in order, but Carmen opened the book and ran her finger down the table of contents, then stopped suddenly and laughed. "Well, how about that? I should've known. Here's a story you probably know from memory—let's do it first." And she turned to Flannery O'Connor's "A Good Man Is Hard to Find."

Julia had actually hoped to be the one to read this story aloud since it was one of her four favorites by Flannery O'Connor. But this might be better after all. Now that she thought about it, she couldn't remember ever hearing it read aloud by someone else, though she herself had done it numbers of times.

CARMEN cleared her throat and plunged in. Julia wished later that she had a recording, not necessarily of the story itself, though Carmen was an expressive, fluent reader, but it was the girl's commentary along the way she wished she could replay.

After the first page, it was, simply, "She's a good writer. Very funny, very compact." On the next page she remarked that it felt odd to be riding in a car reading a story about a family riding in a car. She also said she had a bad feeling about the cat hidden in the basket on the floor of the backseat. "That cat is going to cause trouble, you wait and see," she said, as if Julia didn't already know.

She stopped and laughed heartily after the sentence *In case of an accident, anyone seeing her dead on the highway would know at once that she was a lady.* "I did laundry for a woman in Rhode Island just like that," she said. "She wore this lacy pink underwear whenever she went out in case she ended up in the emergency room."

On the next page Carmen paused and said, "So I guess the grandmother's never going to get a real name besides 'the grandmother,' right?" But she didn't wait for an answer. After the part about Mr. Teagarden and the watermelon, she stopped again and laughed, and when the monkey sprang into the chinaberry tree a little later, she laughed even harder, then said admiringly, "Who would ever think of putting something like that in a story?"

She thought June Star was especially funny, said she used to know a little girl exactly like her. When the Misfit was mentioned again on the fifth page, she said, "Uh-oh . . . portentous. Is he going to show up at the end?" But she kept reading, quite fast, rarely faltering over a word.

Julia hoped the traffic wouldn't be this bad the whole way. She had thought the roads would be clearer traveling on Saturday. Right now she was hemmed in on all three sides by trucks, with two more lined up behind the one that was passing her. She wasn't going to let herself get pressured into joining the passing game, though. There was no need to rush. She knew there was a rhythm to freeway traffic. This little bottleneck would loosen eventually. Anyway, it was a fine day for traveling—overcast with an expected high of sixty—and she was listening to one of her favorite stories.

The description of the accident tickled Carmen, especially the way it started, with the cat leaping out of the basket onto Bailey's shoulder, "clinging to his neck like a caterpillar." She laughed at some length over that phrase, and the grandmother's "I believe I have injured an organ."

But that was the last time she laughed. When the three men in the black car showed up and the grandmother recognized the driver, Carmen stopped and threw her head back. "Oh, no, I knew it. It's him. I don't think I want to read any further." But she kept going, only slower now, as all the family members were marched off into the dark woods except the grandmother. Carmen didn't even smile when the Misfit said his father died in "nineteen ought nineteen," and when the last three gunshots were fired, she paused and gave a low half moan before reading the final few paragraphs.

Julia found that she was clutching the steering wheel tightly, her neck tense. Somehow the story seemed more violent this time than it ever had before. Perhaps it was due to the fact that she wasn't seeing the words on the page. Free from the physical process of reading, maybe her mind translated the words into more powerful images. Or maybe the story was colored this time by Carmen's remarks or by her slower pace at the end. Whereas it had never before quite seemed like anything that could really happen, this time it struck her with the force of some gruesome report on the evening news. She was suddenly reminded that horrible things could happen to real people on road trips.

The blue light of a police car was flashing up ahead, and as they passed it, Julia saw the red Corvette pulled onto the shoulder of the road. The driver was handing the officer something out the window.

Carmen inhaled deeply and let out a long sigh. "Wow. Are all her stories this . . . harrowing?"

"Well, no," Julia said, regretting now that this was the story they had started with. She didn't want Carmen to think she enjoyed stories about old women getting shot by escaped convicts. She wished one of O'Connor's milder stories had been included in the book rather than this one. Even the one about Hulga Hopewell and her wooden leg would have been better.

And after Carmen's next words, she wished it more than ever. "Okay, I have a question," the girl said. "Maybe I'm imagining things, but it seems to me that Flannery O'Connor is sort of interested in religion. I mean, even the title of the story, right? 'A Good Man Is Hard to Find'—well, yeah, like *impossible*, if we're talking about man's natural . . . depravity. You think that's what she was getting at?"

Julia had no desire to discuss man's natural depravity. "Maybe, maybe not," she said.

"Well, they're all sinners, not just the Misfit," Carmen said. "Even the grandmother—she goes from being this very funny character to sort of pathetic, you know? Sort of . . . fatuous. She's this selfish old hypocrite that gets them on the wrong road first, and then gets them all killed. But then at the end when she finally sees the truth about herself and him and everybody else—well, it's too late then for . . . grace. I don't know, though—is *that* what's going on?"

In Julia's years of teaching, whenever a student offered some insight beyond his years, her first thought was always to suspect it was not his own, that he had read it in a journal or online critique and was just trying to show off. But Carmen's comment had come so spontaneously that Julia was forced to accept it as genuine. She tried not to act as surprised as she felt.

Depravity, hypocrisy, grace—these were Flannery O'Connor's bread and butter in the way of themes, but how could a high school dropout extract all of this? In one reading, no less? And how could she nail the grandmother's character so precisely when so many readers saw her as purely comic or purely evil?

S HE felt Carmen's eyes on her, as if waiting for an answer, though Julia couldn't think of what the question was. "Her fiction is very complex," she finally said.

"But do all her stories have this kind of *religious* slant?" Carmen said. "I wouldn't expect you to like stories like that."

Julia couldn't remember now why she had ever thought reading stories aloud in the car was a good idea. "I guess you could say," she replied slowly, "I like her stories in spite of her religion, not because of it. A good story can always be enjoyed on different levels, both literal and figurative."

Carmen laughed. "Oh, Aunt Julia, I just love the way you talk. I know there's no way I could ever learn everything you know." She paused. "You know, that part when the grandmother told the Misfit he was one of her *babies*? Well, I wonder if . . ."

Thankfully, Julia didn't have to hear what Carmen wondered, for at that very moment a distraction appeared in the form of a flashing message on a portable signboard along the side of the road: *TRAF-FIC SLOWING AHEAD.* Carmen stopped talking and pointed to it. Seconds later, they came to the top of a small rise and saw a long line of vehicles bumper to bumper in all three lanes ahead of them as far as they could see. They soon came to a complete stop.

All at once this didn't seem like a welcome distraction at all. Sitting in traffic would mean more time for Carmen to ask questions. Julia sighed. "Must be an accident up there somewhere."

Carmen seemed to have forgotten about the story already as she unbuckled her seat belt and reached into the backseat. "A GPS would sure come in handy right now," she said, "but at least we've got this." She pulled out the road atlas, opened it, and found the map for North Carolina.

Julia had declined the GPS offer from the rental place. The most advanced travel aid she ever used was MapQuest, of which she had, in fact, availed herself for this trip. Inside a folder, which was now tucked between the driver's seat and console, were many pages of MapQuest directions for all the planned stops along their route. They crept ahead a few feet and stopped again. Loud rap music was coming from a car nearby.

Carmen pointed ahead. "There's an exit coming up. Let's get off and see what happens, okay?" She sounded excited. Sudden glitches always seemed to rev up her can-do spirit.

Julia wasn't at all excited. Deviating from a prescribed route had always been equated with risk in her way of thinking. And risk could so easily mean failure.

They crept a little farther. Up ahead several cars were taking the exit.

Carmen looked back at the atlas. "Yeah, this should work," she said. "We can take this exit and then—well, I guess Highway 21 runs up the right general direction. Maybe we can pick up the interstate again somewhere around Statesville."

Julia wasn't comforted by the girl's word choices—*should work, I guess, general direction, maybe.*

Carmen glanced up. "You could go ahead and get off on the shoulder now, Aunt Julia. That would get us to the exit quicker. Other cars are doing it, see?"

"Those people probably live out that direction somewhere," Julia said. "They probably know every inch of those back roads."

"Well, then, if we get turned around, we can stop and ask one of them where we are," Carmen said cheerfully.

Julia looked over at the opposite side of the interstate, where drivers were freely traveling toward their destinations, then looked again at all the lanes of traffic in front of her. No sign of a break. Behind her more and more cars were joining the backup. She looked at the car next to her, where a man was pounding on the steering wheel and shouting animatedly.

She didn't look at Carmen but was very aware of her presence. *You've kept yourself in a box for half of your life, all because of an accident.* It was something the girl had said just days ago, all the while weeping copious tears, after Julia told her about the child whose life she had taken. *You don't understand the definition of* accident, Julia had replied, dry-eyed, for she had cried all the tears she could cry many years ago.

And at some point Carmen had said this: *You're too hard on yourself, Aunt Julia. You're punishing yourself for no good reason. It won't bring the boy back.* As if anyone her age could understand the weight of such a crime and what kind of punishment was appropriate.

Nothing could bring the boy back—that much was true. But some offenders deserved no amnesty, she told the girl. Certain sins were beyond atonement.

S OMEWHERE up ahead a car honked, then another, and a whole spate of honks ensued, different pitches and timbres—blares, beeps, toots, blasts—a cacophony of vented frustration. It sounded like a beginning band warming up.

Julia could feel the girl looking at her. More horns were joining in from all sides. It was amusing, really, to think that these were all adults.

Carmen raised her voice. "You don't want to sit in the middle of this, do you?"

No, Julia didn't want to sit here. She took a quick look behind, then checked the right side-view mirror, cautiously pulled out of her lane onto the shoulder, and slowly proceeded to the exit.

Carmen tapped her index fingers together. "And the crowd applauded wildly as Dr. Julia Rich bravely took a step off the beaten path," she said. She directed Julia to turn right at the stop sign, and as they traveled down the road, the sound of the car horns behind them gradually faded.

Julia couldn't help thinking of the fact that this was exactly the mistake the family in O'Connor's story had made: getting off the beaten path. They had taken a hilly red dirt road and ended up getting murdered by a psychopath. Well, this wasn't a hilly dirt road. Not yet at least.

They drove for almost a mile before they saw a sign verifying that they were on Highway 21 North. It was just a plain, two-lane paved road leading . . . well, somewhere. Every road led somewhere.

· *chapter 14* ·

ANOTHER CLOUDBURST

"See? That worked out," Carmen said as they pulled into Pamela's driveway a few minutes past five o'clock. "We didn't lose much time at all."

Julia had to admit that the detour had turned out much better than she expected. She had almost forgotten how much was lost when traveling by interstate—all the local color of small towns and the surrounding countryside, such as the ramshackle diner named The Big Bad Wolf's Barbecue Pit and the backyard clothesline on which were hanging a half dozen of the largest men's jockey shorts she had ever seen, plus one pair of jumbo boxers, black with red lips printed all over them. Carmen had laughed at that and said, "Aw, look, somebody loves him," then had taken several pictures of the clothesline with Julia's camera.

The front door of Pamela's house flew open, and Pamela stepped out onto the porch, waving with both hands. She was wearing an old-fashioned bibbed apron over a dark blue sweat suit and sporting a new hairstyle: a little round shrub of tight brown curls—inspired by Carmen's hair, she had told them over the phone. "Come on in!" she called. "We've been waiting! It's all ready to eat!"

Inside, dinner was indeed ready and waiting, and within minutes they were hustled in and the four of them were seated around the dining room table, elegantly set with china, silver, candles, and cloth napkins. Since the last time Julia had seen Butch, he had grown a beard and mustache so that he now resembled a caveman more than ever—a middle-aged caveman going gray. He was wearing a faded turquoise T-shirt with *Cooper County Senior Athletes Cycling Club* printed on it. It was clear from its snug fit over his ample stomach that he was no longer an active member of the club.

Pamela began bringing in platters of food, talking the whole time. "I just *love* a formal dinner," she said, "where you pass things around in serving dishes." She jerked her head toward Butch. "We hardly ever eat this way anymore because *somebody* is always too impatient."

Either Butch didn't hear her or he was too busy illustrating her point as he stabbed two thick pieces of grilled pork and deposited them onto his plate.

Finally all the dishes were passed, and the meal commenced. Right away Pamela introduced a subject dear to her heart: her grandchildren. She bragged in general for a while, then zeroed in on their oldest grandson, Cody, who wasn't even five yet but already knew how to log on to a computer using his father's password, had even found his way to the Lego website one day. From Cody, she worked her way down the ranks, detailing the skill set of each child, even the baby, who, to hear her tell it, was far ahead of other three-month-olds.

Carmen was all ears and eyes and smiles. Anyone watching her would think she really was interested in all of this. And, knowing her, she probably was.

Pamela's talk moved to her two grown children. Even when she stopped long enough to ask Carmen or Julia a question, she managed to make it a quick transition: "So did you finish the props for the Sunday school play?" she asked Carmen, but then allowed only a sentence or two before, "I remember a Christmas play Bobby and Kendra were in at church when they were kids. The two of them were a *donkey* in the nativity scene, and I had to make them a costume. Neither one of them wanted to be the tail, of course, so we had to make them flip a coin."

Carmen laughed. "I get it—heads or tails. Who won?"

"Bobby got tails," Pamela said. "To this day he still talks about it. Says it was bad enough being a jackass, but it warped him for life being a jackass's . . . well, rear end."

Butch gave a snort of laughter. To this point he hadn't contributed a word to the conversation, of course. Ensconced at the head of the table, he was hunkered over, his hairy forearms flanking his plate. He was attending to his corn now. Ignoring the special little holders beside his plate, he simply picked the corn up with his hands and rolled it around on top of the butter in Pamela's fancy butter dish.

For being so untidy, however, he proved remarkably neat and systematic as he swiftly mowed his way down each row with a great deal of noisy crunching, always returning to the same end to start again. Julia kept imagining the ding of a typewriter bell. He stopped midway to take a long swig of his tea before getting back to work. By now his mustache and beard were flecked with bits of corn.

"Did I ever tell you how *thrifty* Kendra is?" Pamela said to Julia, and off she went, telling how Kendra made her own soap and baby wipes and granola.

When Pamela went to the kitchen for more rolls, Carmen took the opportunity to ask Butch a few questions: what kind of work he did, if he liked to read, where he grew up. Julia was surprised at his answers—he sounded far more intelligent than she had ever given him credit for.

When the meal was finally finished, Pamela looked at her watch and sighed. "It's already after six. This is *so* frustrating to have you for only a few hours! We're going to play a game after supper, then have dessert later. I sure wish you'd gotten here earlier."

"Some people wish their lives away," Butch said.

Pamela ignored this. She picked up some dishes and started for the kitchen, calling back, "I tried a new recipe for dessert. Something called Chocolate Satin Decadence. Don't even *ask* how much butter it called for!"

Butch looked at Julia and Carmen. "That means she's getting ready to tell you."

"Snuff out the candles, Butch!" Pamela shouted from the kitchen. "And put on some music! We can listen to it while we clean things up."

As Butch rose from the table, Julia knew exactly what kind of music it would be. And she was right. Soon a twangy song could be heard from another room, quite loud, with the repeating phrase "a hundred years from now." Julia didn't like to think of herself as a musical snob, but she knew she probably was. In her opinion, a little bit of bluegrass and country went a long way. Some of the titles were ridiculous. "All My Exes Live in Texas," for example, and "Satan's Jewel Crown."

As they worked, Carmen made the mistake of asking some questions about bluegrass music, and soon the dishes were forgotten. Pamela dragged out two shoeboxes full of photos taken at festivals and concerts they had attended over the years and spread the pictures out over the kitchen table. Before long they were all seated again as she and Butch told story after story, interrupting each other frequently to argue over details.

Carmen said, "What about this one?" and held up a photo in which a much thinner Butch and an obviously pregnant Pamela stood with their arms around each other in front of an elevated platform with a banner across the back that read *Sugar Pop and the Honey-Hill Express*. "Oh, I was a running joke that whole night," Pamela said. "We were sitting right down front, and after every song Sugar Pop would point at me and say, 'Hey, you still hanging in there, little lady?' He even asked if there was a doctor in the house just in case, and there was—but only a dentist."

"A chiropractor, not a dentist," Butch said.

"No, it was a dentist." They debated this at some length.

Pamela picked up another photo. "This one was on our very first date—Pete Chisholm and the Mighty Fines. I'd never had such fun in my life. It was like a brand-new world after all those years of listening to nothing but *folk songs* plunked out on a piano." She rolled her eyes at Julia. "And, of course, Mother had those favorite hymns of hers, too." She paused. "Which she sang only when she could get away with it."

"I wonder if those were the same hymns Daddy used to sing to me," Carmen said. "He knew all the verses. And a lot of folk songs, too."

Pamela put both hands over her heart. "Oh, sweetheart, your daddy had a voice like pure liquid gold. I always knew he could've made it big as a singer if he hadn't . . ." She suddenly looked as if she might break down and cry.

Butch laid a finger on one of the photos on the table. "This gal right here," he said, "she could *whistle*. She did these bird trills during 'Wings of Bright Feathers' that made you think you were inside a dang bird sanctuary. Remember her?" He pushed the photo toward Pamela.

Pamela picked the picture up and held it close. "Oh, it just tore my heart out," she said. "Absolutely tore my heart right out." Julia assumed she was talking about the woman who did bird trills until she added, "I was only fourteen when he left home. It was like he died. And that's what I wanted to do, too—just shrivel up and die. I cried myself to sleep every night." She dropped the photo among the others on the table and buried her face in her arms.

During the silence that followed, a question hit Julia hard: What had she done to comfort her little sister in the wake of their brother's disappearance? Well, she knew the answer to that. Nothing. The real question was why. And she knew the answer to that, too. She had been too busy thinking of herself. She had gone back to college a few weeks later and had stayed away for the next nine years. She tried to imagine now what it must have been like to be the only child left at home, in such a home as theirs.

Butch patted Pamela's arm and picked up another photo. "And this here is Horace Pitts," he said loudly. "He sang tenor with the Mountain Laurel Boys, and their encore was always 'Fly Away Yonder Where the Wind Blows Sweet.' On one whole stanza Horace would hum and whistle at the same time in two-part harmony."

Pamela's head snapped up, and she glared at him, her eyes filled with tears. "What in the world are you talking about? You must be losing your mind. Benny Bellis was the one who always sang 'Fly Away Yonder,' *not* Horace Pitts. You're thinking of 'Tread Soft on My Bruised Heart'—that's the one the Mountain Laurel Boys always ended with."

The dispute didn't last long, for Butch soon conceded—so quickly, in fact, that Julia felt sure his error must have been intentional. Butch handed the photo to Pamela, who studied it briefly. "That Horace Pitts was sure a handsome man," she said. "He was engaged to be married, but he got hit on his motorcycle a week before the wedding. He wasn't wearing a helmet." She proceeded to quote some statistics about helmets and motorcycle fatalities, then pushed the two shoeboxes over to Butch and said, "Here, put the pictures back in." She stood up and clapped her hands. "Okay, chop-chop, let's finish getting things cleaned up so we can play some Rook!"

B UTCH and Carmen disappeared to the dining room to clear the rest of the table. Thankfully, the music had stopped by now. Julia heard Butch talking. Carmen laughed and said something, and then they both laughed.

"It's funny," Pamela said. "Butch doesn't usually warm up that fast to strangers." Julia was tempted to point out that he didn't warm up to people who weren't strangers either, like his own wife's sister. But she knew the logical response to that, since his own wife's sister had never shown the least interest in him. Over the years she had exchanged maybe a dozen words with him, the few times she had called Pamela and he had answered the phone. Until Carmen asked him about his job tonight, Julia hadn't even known what kind of work he did except it had something to do with computers and he had an office at home.

The only things she knew about him came from comments Pamela had made, mostly about unfavorable aspects of his character. At least those were the comments Julia had stored away. She thought of something now Matthew told her once, during a rare argument over something she couldn't remember: *You always hear what you want to hear.*

"I sure hope you've given some thought to Carmen's education," Pamela was saying. "She can't do much of anything unless she at least has a high school diploma. She could get a GED without much trouble. You can probably get those online now."

As usual, Pamela seemed to think she was the possessor of

knowledge no one else had thought of. "We've already talked about that," Julia told her.

"So is she going to do it?" Pamela said. "If I were you, I'd get her started on it as soon as you get back home from this trip. The longer she puts it off, the harder it'll be."

"She knows it's important," Julia said. "She plans to do it." She knew she should go ahead and tell Pamela they had already paid the money and gotten Carmen enrolled in an online course of study, that it had been Carmen's idea to begin with, that she intended to take the test by spring, but she didn't say any of that either.

They worked in silence for a while. More music started in the other room.

"Turn that up a little!" Pamela called. "Hey, you two, is everything off the table?" The music got louder, and she started singing along as she put up leftovers: *If blue is the color of lonesome*, all the way through to the end. *And left me to cry all alone.*

It still seemed like such a contradiction to Julia that her sister, so cautionary and well-armed with practical tips, so quick to spot error, could give in to such trite mush in her music and reexperience the same sappy, banal scenarios time and again. But then, maybe it made a certain kind of sense. Maybe it was simply Pamela's way of acknowledging that the circumstances of life couldn't always be corralled and managed and that when the severest blows were dealt, as they so often would be, the time for advice was past and all one could do was mourn with the mournful.

Eventually the supper things were cleared away. Butch dug the Rook cards out of a drawer in the kitchen, and they all sat down at the table. Maybe things would have proceeded calmly if Pamela hadn't said, "Did I tell you that everything we had for supper was one of Mother's recipes?"

And if Carmen hadn't said *this*: "She must've been a good cook."

A simple statement that could have been answered with a simple

yes or no, but naturally Pamela couldn't stop at that. She started listing all her favorite dishes among the ones her mother cooked, many
of which Julia couldn't even recall. "Oh, and she made this chicken
spaghetti I just *loved*," she said. Her smile suddenly vanished. "But
Daddy didn't—at least that's what he told her one day after she'd been
making it for years and years. She served it for supper that night, and
he knocked his plate off the table and told her it tasted like . . ."

And suddenly, another hairpin turn of emotion. Before they
knew what had happened, Pamela was in tears again. "Oh, she had
such a *hard, sad* life!" she said.

We all did, Julia wanted to say. She said nothing, though, nor did
she cry.

Pamela continued. "She told me once that she always felt responsible for Daddy's accident. He woke up sick that day, but she
talked him into going to work since he didn't have any more sick
days left and they needed the money. If he had just stayed home,
everything could've been different. But he didn't and she . . ." Fresh
tears followed.

Julia took this in. Here was something she had never known,
something their mother had for some reason chosen to tell only
Pamela, and Pamela for some reason had never told her.

Butch stared at the table, chewing on the inside of his mouth,
occasionally reaching over to pat Pamela's hand, as if this were a
play they had rehearsed many times and he was listening to her
lines again. Carmen, her eyes full of commiseration, apologized for
bringing up a touchy subject.

"But you didn't, honey, you didn't!" Pamela said. "I set myself
up for it, going through all her old recipes like I did. And wearing
this again." She fingered the piping around the bib of her apron. "It
used to be hers." At last she wound down and took several deep,
shuddering breaths. With her red eyes and short mop of tight curls,
she looked like an overgrown child, vulnerable and a little foolish.

There was a long silence, and then Carmen said, "I didn't know any of that. Daddy never told me much except that his relationship with his father was . . . acrimonious. He called his mother a few times—I remember once when he put me on the phone and told me to say something. I must've been seven or eight. So I told her all about some dinosaur bones somebody had just dug up near Painted Horse. But she never said a word back. Daddy said not to feel bad, she was probably crying, but I didn't see how dinosaur bones were anything to cry about."

At that Pamela broke into laughter—the giddy kind that went on too long to be real. "Well, goodness, I sure know how to be a wet blanket, don't I?" She wiped her eyes and waved her arms about. "Here, let's clear the air of all the doom and gloom. Okay, now, does anybody want to play Rook? I warn you, Butch and I are *really* good." Her voice was thin and bright, like something breakable. "Maybe we should split up so we're not partners, but whoever gets Butch, whoa, watch out. He's a *maniac* when it comes to bidding. You remember how to play, don't you, Jules?" She was talking breathlessly now, and Butch was watching her, no expression on his face.

Julia nodded. Rook sounded much safer than sitting around talking, running the risk of another cloudburst of emotion. It was decided that Julia and Pamela would team up against Butch and Carmen. Butch reviewed the rules aloud while Pamela went to get a pencil and scorepad.

I T was almost ten o'clock when Pamela stood up and, with a dramatic flourish, laid down her last card, then emitted a whoop of victory. She had saved the right color, yielding a windfall of all the remaining points plus the kitty, not only setting Butch, who had taken the bid, but also pushing the score for herself and Julia to 505. "We did it, we did it!" she cried, raising her palm to Julia for a high five. "We took them *down!*" She pushed her chair back and did a little jig, which rattled the dishes in the china hutch against the wall.

"Careful, you might rupture something," Butch said. "My fault," he said to Carmen. "I flubbed up when I trumped in on that measly fourteen in the third hand." He went on to review each hand after that, ending with "And she knew my off-suit was black, so she saved her high one." He turned to Pamela, who was still bobbing around in a circle, waving both hands. "You must've had a ton of black."

"I did, I did!" She started a modified cancan, though lifting her foot only a few inches with each kick. Her sweat pants were a size too small so that more was jiggling than just the dishes in the china hutch. "Time for a celebration!" she said as she danced over to the refrigerator to get the Chocolate Satin Decadence.

Later when Julia and Carmen were getting ready for bed in the guest room, they clearly heard Pamela say to Butch across the hall, "You can't shower till morning. I don't want them running out of hot water tonight." And Butch's answer was just as clear: "I told you that dinky hot water tank wasn't big enough when we bought it." Then he said, "Hey, what's wrong, sugar? Your feet hurting again? Here, come to Daddy. Lie down and let me rub them for you." And there was a soft click as their bedroom door closed.

Carmen nodded, smiling. "I suspected all along they liked each other a lot more than they were letting on. But you probably already knew that."

Julia said nothing. She was too busy wondering how a twenty-year-old could read between the lines so much better than someone in her fifties with a PhD.

THEY got away after breakfast the next morning. On the front porch Carmen hugged both Pamela and Butch. "I never had aunts and uncles," she said. "Not real ones. Or cousins either—I really want to meet Bobby and Kendra sometime. And Cody and Starla and Eleanor and little Jesse." As they pulled out of the driveway, she called to Butch, "That was just a fluke last night. We'll win the next Rook game!"

"Oh, no, you won't!" Pamela said. "You just wait and see—right, Jules?" She gave a little yelp, then swung her hip sideways and bumped against Butch, who grimaced and pretended to be hurt. He was wearing a bright orange T-shirt with a big black question mark printed on the front and a pair of pants held up by suspenders—pants so roomy that it suddenly made Julia wonder if he used to be even larger.

Julia slowly backed out into the street, then allowed herself one last look. Pamela's round face had fallen, and she was holding her apron up against the corner of one eye. Something pulled at Julia's heart, seeing her sister standing there, wearing the same tight sweat pants as last night, her springy curls hugging her head like a nubby knitted cap. Butch moved closer and put an arm around her.

Carmen twisted herself around and waved to them until they were lost to sight. After a moment of silence, she sighed and said, "I sure like them." She laughed. "Aunt Pamela is sort of . . . mercurial, isn't she?"

Already the image of her sister standing on the porch of the small brick house had begun to fade in Julia's mind, yet off and on throughout the rest of the day, for some reason, she kept seeing the big black question mark on Butch's shirt.

chapter 15

RUGGED OPTIMISM

It was a cool day. High in the pale blue sky, small lumpy white clouds were laid out in long rows, as if someone had run a wide rake through them. The hillsides in Virginia were showing more fall color than in South Carolina, though it still wouldn't peak here for another couple of weeks.

Somewhere on the freeway in Virginia, Carmen chose a CD of Ferde Grofé's *Grand Canyon Suite* to play, but first she took the insert out of the CD case to read about the piece. "Okay, listen to this. Here was his inspiration." And she read aloud: "*The richness of the land and the rugged optimism of its people fired my imagination.* I like that," she said. "Rugged optimism." She said the words slowly, distinctly. "And this is nice, too. Listen. *But this music is your music, and mine only in the highly technical sense that a copyright has been filed away with my name on it.*" She turned to Julia. "Don't you just love that? Doesn't it show what a big heart he must have had?"

That was Carmen, always looking for the best in people. To Julia it sounded like the kind of statement someone would carefully craft to market himself as noble and generous. She would like to ask Ferde Grofé what he did with the money he earned from the *Grand Canyon Suite*. Had he given all of that to the American people, too?

They rode in silence for several minutes as Carmen continued to study the insert. It was a pleasant pattern they had already fallen into: periods of quiet between the CDs and radio. And the talking, of course. Perhaps more talking than Julia would have chosen, yet she had to give Carmen credit—she could take a hint when Julia was ready to be done.

"I went to the Grand Canyon one time," Carmen said now. "It was one of the few trips we took when I was a kid. We rode there in Daddy's pickup truck and stayed two nights in a motel. But we never did it again. It made Lulu too nervous to be away from home." She closed the insert, then studied the picture on the front, an artist's rendering of the Grand Canyon at sunset. "Did you ever go on any trips when you were growing up? I don't remember Daddy ever talking about it if you did."

The casual tone was a ploy, something the girl had obviously discovered to be more successful for getting answers to her questions, especially questions concerning Julia's childhood, about which she seemed genuinely interested, though Julia knew that her greater interest was in Jeremiah's childhood. Head bent, Carmen pretended to be very busy trying to fit the insert back into the case, as if she didn't much care whether Julia answered or not.

Julia wasn't fooled, but she answered the question anyway. "Only one I can remember," she said.

"Yeah? Where did you go?" Carmen asked.

So Julia told her.

As navigator, her mother had had only one tool—road maps, the uncooperative ones that would never fold back up the right way. Unfortunately, some of them were also out of date, which, along with the hubbub of having three children in the car, resulted in more than one wrong turn. Her father's way of dealing with such errors was to pummel the dashboard and steering wheel while shouting insults at her mother, the children, other drivers, and the people who made the road maps.

It was the only family trip they ever took after her father's accident. All the way from Alabama to Missouri to visit her mother's parents, and all the way back again. Julia realized now that her father must have been under tremendous physical duress the whole time he was driving—an activity expressly forbidden by his doctor, whom he always referred to as "Peabrain Peters." As a child, however, she was aware of only one thing: her deep fear that the trip would never end or that none of them would still be alive when it did.

She remembered cowering in the backseat, never relaxing for a minute, trying to shush Jeremiah, who kept saying he was thirsty or hungry or needed to go to the bathroom. He couldn't have been more than five, but already he and their father were at odds. When their father threatened at one point to make them all get out and walk, Jeremiah spoke up at once. There was no way Julia could stop him fast enough. "But Grandma and Grandpa wouldn't like it if *you* got there and we weren't with you," he said in his clear, flutelike voice. It wasn't exactly sarcasm, or sass, but simply a bright child's way of noting the humor in an adult's silly statement. But because almost anything Jeremiah ever said was assigned to the broad category of "impertinence," their father took immediate offense.

Julia remembered how wildly the car had swerved on the two-lane road, accompanied by a horn blast from an oncoming car, as her father swung an arm into the backseat, trying to make contact with some part of Jeremiah's body. He hit Julia's Chatty Cathy doll instead, knocking her onto the floor and activating her voice. "Let's have a party!" the doll said. Jeremiah made the mistake of giggling at this, and their father slammed on the brakes and careened off the road. The car stopped at a crazy angle, the nose aimed down into a wide shallow ditch.

Their father must have realized the difficulty of administering a spanking in such close quarters, especially since he seemed to have pulled a muscle and raised a welt on his hand, for he proceeded to deliver only a tongue-lashing about "back talk," in which he included everyone in the car, even Julia's doll that didn't know when to keep her blankety-blank mouth shut.

For Jeremiah, scoldings were so routine by now that he generally failed to be attentive, much less impressed, often putting him in double jeopardy: a spanking for the original crime and another for contempt of court. But not this time. Her father never even turned around to see Jeremiah laying both sticky hands against the window and tracing around them with his tongue.

Julia remembered very little of the actual visit with her grandparents. She had seen them only a few times in her life, had never before been to their house, though they always sent nice presents for birthdays and Christmas. They were the ones, in fact, who had given her the Chatty Cathy doll for her last birthday. She had only vague memories of them: her grandmother's large, soft lap and sad, droopy eyes, her grandfather's stooped posture and his fondness for peppermints. She remembered sleeping in a white room with two white beds and yellow striped curtains. And she remembered saying good-bye, being pressed close to her grandmother, smelling her talcum powder and feeling her shake as she wept.

On the way back, her mother drove the car, with all three children jammed elbow to elbow in the front seat while their father lay on the backseat updating them every two minutes as to the degree of his discomfort and the further damage to his back.

"Pamela was the lucky one on that trip," Julia said to Carmen. "She was too young to remember it."

Carmen was quiet for a moment before venturing, "The part

about the doll is pretty funny—but I can say that because it didn't happen to me." She turned to look out the window. "Daddy was such a different kind of father from that. It's hard to see how the two of them could've been related, isn't it?"

"It was the accident," Julia said. "My father never got over it. Not physically, not mentally, not emotionally. He took it out on the world, and since it was our misfortune to be stuck in the same house with him, we bore the brunt of it." Even as she said it, she realized that this was something she had never before put into words. To Carmen it must have sounded like a prelude to forgiveness, or the act itself, though Julia knew she was in no way capable of ever doing that.

Carmen seemed to be thinking this over, but then she said, "I actually remember Daddy telling me about that doll of yours—I'm sure you already know why." She didn't wait for a reply. "What other things could your Chatty Cathy say?" This, too, was typical of the girl, buying time, suspending the discussion of something important by circling back to a trivial detail.

But trivial details were fine with Julia. She didn't want to talk about her father anymore. "Oh, let's see—she could say, 'Tell me a story' and 'Please brush my hair' and 'Let's play house' and 'May I have a cookie?' Those were some I remember. And 'I love you.'"

She could have told Carmen that her Chatty Cathy doll mysteriously lost her voice shortly after the trip, that one day when she went to pull the ring behind the doll's neck, there was nothing to pull. The ring was gone, with only an empty pinhole where the string used to be. But there was no reason to get into all that—her mother's dissolving into tears when she saw it, Julia's own inconsolable grief, the fact that she never said a word to her father for fear that next time she might find one of the doll's limbs missing, or the pretty blue eyes that opened and closed, or the blond hair on her head, or her whole head. To think that she had a father who would

do such a thing filled her with horror and shame. And a great deal
of anger, which she took care to conceal.

She had loved the doll before that, but thereafter she loved her
obsessively, with a sentimentality born of pity, as one would love a
blind puppy. From that day on, Julia stayed in her bedroom more
than ever, and she took to hiding Chatty Cathy whenever she
wasn't home. She never carried the doll out in public after that, for
she didn't want to run the risk of exposing her handicap to others.

Well, goodness, enough of all that, she told herself now. You
couldn't go through life whimpering over a little thing like a doll.
Such was life. She had gone through much worse things than a
broken doll. And so had other people. She glanced over at Carmen,
who was staring into space, her lips pursed as if whistling, though
no sound came out.

J ULIA wanted to be behind the wheel of a car as little as possible
in the four major cities they would be visiting before beginning
their authors' tour. To this end she had instructed Carmen during
the planning stages to find hotels within walking distance of the
main tourist attractions. They would locate their hotel, park there,
and then do their sightseeing on foot. Or if they couldn't walk
somewhere, they could take a taxi, maybe a subway or bus if they
could figure out the right one.

Washington, D.C., was the first stop. They could only sample
it, of course, so it was a matter of selecting. The National Zoo was
Julia's choice, an easy one after learning that Carmen had never
been to a zoo. After some deliberation, Carmen chose the National
Mall. Even then, they would have to keep moving to see them both.

After arriving in the city, finding their hotel, and eating lunch,
they walked to the Mall and spent the afternoon visiting the mon-
uments and war memorials. "It's a shame, isn't it?" Carmen said as

they stood on the steps of the Lincoln Memorial, looking across the Reflecting Pool to the Washington Monument. "To be able to see such a little bit, when you could spend days and days here. It feels sort of like a . . . desecration, doesn't it?"

At the World War II Memorial, they separated briefly while Julia moved around the oval walkway taking pictures of the arches, pillars, fountains. When she returned to the Pacific Tower, she found Carmen bent down in front of an old man in a wheelchair, listening, nodding earnestly. "This is Clarence Baker," she said when she looked up and saw Julia, "and this is Clarence Baker, Jr." She gestured toward the younger man at his side. "They're both veterans—World War II and Vietnam." The old man lifted a finger and said something with great vigor, though indistinguishable. It was then that Julia saw the tears coursing down his face.

Carmen took one of the old man's hands in hers. "Thank you for what you did for our country." She looked up at his son. "Thank you both. You're true heroes." She patted the old man's hand gently and smiled. "And thank you for sharing all those things with me," she said. "We owe you so much."

"What was he telling you?" Julia said as they walked away.

"I don't know," Carmen said. "I couldn't understand any of it, but his son said he fought in the Pacific and was in the Bataan Death March."

THE next morning they took the Metro to the National Zoo. They started at the Cheetah Conservation Station and wound their way down Olmsted Walk to the emus, then the elephants, the small mammals, the apes, reptiles, lions, and tigers. After the Kids' Farm, they started back toward the front entrance, stopping by Lemur Island, Gibbon Ridge, and Beaver Valley. In Julia's opinion, the whole experience verged on sensory overload—sights, sounds, smells. Even touch, for Carmen insisted on joining the children who were petting the goats at the Kids' Farm.

They took their time, stopping all along the way for Carmen to sketch pictures of animals in her journal while Julia took notes in hers. They ended near the entrance again, saving the Bird House and Asia Trail for last, and it was here, along the Asia Trail, where something unforgettable happened. Julia knew the lemurs and clouded leopards and otters and flamingos and all the rest would fall out of her mind eventually, but this was the memory she would keep.

It was midafternoon. Along the stone walk near the giant panda house, they heard a commotion ahead of them, but not the sounds of animals this time. As they approached, they saw what was happening. A young woman some thirty feet away was trying to get a little girl into a double stroller, where a docile baby was already installed. The girl, perhaps three, was throwing a fit. Not just the garden variety, but a royal hissy fit, as Pamela would say.

The mother snapped the child's lap belt and pushed the stroller forward, but the child unsnapped it and lunged out, shrieking, "Papa! Papa!" then took off down the walkway in a gangly but purposeful gallop. The mother, a slight woman but stronger than she looked, and very quick, plucked her up and reinstated her in the stroller, amid much screaming and churning of arms and legs, and the whole cycle started again. The mother never raised her voice, but remained focused and seemingly unperturbed, whispering in the child's ear when she picked her up. As if the child could hear anything but her own screams.

Everyone along this part of the Asia Trail was curious, of course, Julia included, though she knew it was an unflattering commentary on human nature that such spectacles always made onlookers feel superior. Some people were only sneaking glances, but others were gawking openly, some of them stopping in their tracks to do so, drifting together in little clumps and remarking audibly: *Can you believe that? I know what that child needs. Kids today— parents let them run the show.*

And then, all of a sudden, from right beside Julia, came Carmen's commanding voice: "Come on, people, let's don't just stand here! Let's pitch in and help her!" She burst into action, sprinting ahead. Julia followed, more than a little embarrassed. As they drew near, the child flung herself onto the walkway, rolling onto her back this time, kicking, pumping her arms and legs, screeching, gasping over and over, "Papa! Papa!"

With one hand on the stroller, the young mother knelt near her, but far enough away to avoid getting hit or bitten. She was pleading with the child. Carmen touched the woman's arm, and she looked up, startled. "I can push the stroller so you can carry her," Carmen said. "Maybe she'll calm down that way." She nodded toward a bench. "Or maybe we can move over there and sit down. Will she let you hold her?"

The mother shook her head. "At these times she does not want me. I cannot reason with her." She spoke with an accent. She looked back to her daughter and said something in what sounded like French. Carmen knelt down beside her close to the child, whose eyes were tightly shut. She was still crying and writhing but appeared to be winding down. "Hey, there, kiddo," Carmen said, "what's up? *Bonjour, ma petite. Tu es tres jolie. Je m'appelle Carmen.*"

As if Carmen had flipped a switch, the child went still and opened her eyes. She stuck her thumb in her mouth and began sucking furiously, glaring up at her. "I don't really speak French," Carmen said to the mother. "I have a neighbor who's a French teacher. He taught me a few words." The mother gave a wan smile and reached over to push the child's hair away from her face. The girl swatted at her hand angrily.

A short, bald man came forward, holding out his hand. "Here's a piece of candy. Would that help?" Julia took the candy and handed it to the mother, who gave another weak smile. A teenager appeared: "I could do some magic tricks for her. I do shows for kids' parties all the time. I'm a ventriloquist, too." A woman with a little girl of her own offered a stuffed bear. "Would she like to see Gumpo? Mary Beth will let her hold him. He's very soft and huggable." Another woman knelt down in front of the baby, who had by now begun to fuss. She rocked the stroller a little and made soft clicking sounds out the side of her mouth. "Does he have a pacifier?" she asked.

The mother dug a bottle out of a stroller pouch. "This is what he wants." At the sight of it, the baby let out little mewls of longing.

And this was how it came to be that Carmen sat on a bench along the Asia Trail at the National Zoo one day in early October, with a little girl named Josette in her lap, beside the child's mother and baby brother, while a small crowd stood around watching a teenage boy pull coins out of people's ears and carry on a funny conversation with Gumpo the stuffed bear. It was like a scene in an old movie—the kind where good things materialize on cue. A warm and fuzzy moment. If Julia hadn't seen it with her own eyes, she never would have believed it could happen in a public place in this day and age.

Before they parted, Josette's mother told Carmen and Julia what had triggered Josette's temper tantrum. It was a short story, and very sad. At the zoo not half an hour earlier, Josette had seen a man in the crowd—a stranger, but tall and bearded like her father, wearing a dark wool cap like his—and she thought it was her father. All in the world she wanted was for him to pick her up and hold her and carry her home. The saddest part of the story was this: "My husband went away three months ago," the mother told them. "He has not come back or called. He does not want us any longer. How do you tell this to a child?"

• • •

THEY took the Metro from the zoo back to the National Mall and found a nice restaurant for dinner. Carmen tore open another packet of sugar to add to her tea, for they had apparently reached the Land of Unsweetened Tea. She stirred it for a long time. At length she sighed and said, "I'll never forget Josette."

Julia nodded. She knew nothing could have aroused Carmen's pity more than a little girl who wanted her father. The waiter brought a covered basket to the table, lifted out two small, crusty loaves with a pair of silver tongs, and set them on the bread plates.

"I hope she'll see her papa again," Carmen said, "but I'm so afraid she won't."

Julia nodded again.

"I don't see how a man can do that—leave his wife and children," Carmen said. She stirred her tea a little more. "There's just so much you can't do anything about, isn't there? Except pray."

Julia said nothing. She knew Carmen would do that with or without her encouragement, had probably already done so, in fact.

Carmen took a bite of her salad and chewed thoughtfully. "The zoo was an interesting place," she said after a few moments, "but I liked the mall a lot better. In fact, I don't think I ever want to go to a zoo again."

Julia took another piece of bread onto her plate. "Why is that?"

"All those animals," Carmen said, "living there just so people can come stare at them. It doesn't matter how nice it is and how well they take care of the animals, it's just not . . . *home*, you know? It's not a very happy place."

So now she was feeling sorry for elephants and tigers and orangutans. Julia should have foreseen this. Anyone with Carmen's history would have strong feelings about the importance of a real home.

Julia thought of trying to inject a little humor: *Hey, how about a little rugged optimism here? Or prayer—you're good at that. You can pray for an earthquake so all the animals will get loose.* But the moment didn't call for humor. She saw Carmen's journal, tucked inside her shoulder bag hanging on the back of her chair. "But you liked the animals, didn't you?" she said to the girl. "May I see your pictures?"

"They're not done yet," Carmen said. "I've got to fill them in some more." But she got her journal out, opened it, and passed it across the table. On the page was a picture of a meerkat standing upright on its hind legs, holding its front paws together primly. Its upturned mouth simulated a smile. An amazingly good drawing, which was no surprise to Julia, for she had seen the girl's pictures before, and Jeremiah's long before that. Besides the caption *Meerkat*, the only words on the page were coming out of the animal's mouth, in a cartoon bubble: *Best burrows are in Africa, not D.C.*

"There's one on the next page, too, but it's not as good," Carmen said. Julia turned to it and saw a red panda eating bamboo leaves. Above its head, another cartoon bubble, and inside this one: *Take me home to China.*

Julia flipped through other pages and saw rough sketches of an oryx, a siamang, a Przewalski's horse. Naturally, Carmen would choose out-of-the-ordinary animals to draw. She smiled and handed the journal back, then took out her own and opened it. "Your journal is going to be a lot more fun to look through than mine. Here's my page about the red panda." She read her summary aloud: "Red panda. Resembles raccoon. Long, bushy tail—covers itself when sleeping. Native to China. Eats bamboo leaves. Adult leads solitary life. Endangered species."

She stopped there, deciding not to read the last part: *Cub born last year died at 3 wks. Survival rate for cubs born in captivity 50%.*

· chapter 16 ·

PEOPLE LIVING THEIR LIVES

As the trip north unfolded in front of her eyes, Julia began to recognize the moments she would carry with her through life. *This is one*, she would say to herself. *You will remember this.*

She continued to record facts about the places they visited, but in one sense the trip, the real one, was unrelated to the expansion of her mind concerning historical and cultural matters. There was that part of the trip, of course, but the sights and sounds and heritage of the Northeast, though constantly before her, were thrown into a secondary role. They were like eye-catching sets and costumes in the play, worthy in their own right yet no substitute for the text—or for what could be called the greater beauty of a play: the subtext.

Being together twenty-four hours a day cast a spotlight on Carmen's idiosyncrasies. For example, her attitude toward food continued to be purely practical with little anticipation or in-the-moment enjoyment, as if she knew eating was necessary for life, like sleeping or breathing, but certainly nothing to spend time thinking about. She ate slowly, only small portions and one food at a time, moving clockwise around her plate, turning the plate so that what she was eating was always closest to her.

From an analytical point of view, it didn't fit with Carmen's history. If food had often been hard to come by, as Julia knew it had, it seemed that one would fall into the habit of eating quickly, without regard to order, and in larger quantities, not knowing when or if the next meal would come. But Julia had quit analyzing, had simply come to accept it. Carmen was what she was.

Though she ate as if out of duty, she always expressed gratitude. She did occasionally remark on the color or texture of a food, but rarely the taste. She often ordered whatever Julia did, perhaps to spare herself the trouble of choosing. What seemed to interest her most at mealtimes was observing other people.

Whenever they ate at a place with self-seating, Carmen always chose a table in close proximity to a couple, sometimes without children, sometimes with, for she was interested in both couples and children, separately and as families. She was fascinated by the idea of marriage, as only the unmarried were. If the couple appeared to notice her, she would turn surreptitious. If they didn't, she would stare, but only in moderation and all the while managing never to lose her way in a conversation with Julia.

In hotel rooms, she had set ways of behaving. The first thing she always did in a new room was to look for the Gideon Bible and place it on the nightstand. Then she would scout out the facilities in the hall—ice machine, laundry room, stairways. And there were other rituals, too—the two glasses of water she always drank upon rising every morning, the five-minute showers, the one hundred sit-ups. She always hummed as she brushed her teeth.

At night she liked to put on her pajamas early. Before bed, she washed her face with soap, laid out her clothes for the next day, and hung her head over the trash can as she brushed her hair. When she finished with her hair, she looked as if she'd undergone shock treatment, but by morning it was always back in place, in a manner of speaking.

Sometimes she read her New Testament or the Gideon Bible in bed, sometimes on the floor, sometimes in the morning, or night, or both. And some days Julia didn't see her read at all. She slept on her side, with a pillow over her head. At times during the night Julia heard what she thought was whispering, whether praying or dreaming or merely talking to herself she didn't know.

There was no predicting her television preferences. She might watch the news with Julia, only halfway listening as she did something else, but commenting from time to time: "Be sure your sin will find you out." "Politicians sure don't seem like the smartest people on earth, do they?" "She'll never get a fair trial." At other times she would flip through the channels and find a movie like *Old Yeller* or a documentary about glassblowing or the Dead Sea Scrolls, and sit riveted through the whole thing.

The night before they left Philadelphia, she ran across *Nanook of the North* on television, a cinematic relic that captivated her, even though there wasn't a scrap of dialogue, only primitive-sounding music and printed captions to accompany the grainy black-and-white images. She moved to the foot of the bed for a closer view. After it ended, she said, "What contented, resourceful people the Eskimos are. Their lives are so . . . unfettered." She talked at length about the building of the igloo, especially the little window of clear ice. At times like this, Julia found it hard to think of her as an adult.

And then, with hardly a breath, she somehow segued from igloos to the tour guide they had met in Philadelphia that day—a fortyish woman with only the shortest stubble of black hair, like iron filings, and dark exotic eyes. The way she moved and used her hands made you think she must have taken ballet lessons. And the best part: her name tag said *Carmen*. She told the group that today was her first day back at work after cancer treatments. "I feel honored to share my name with somebody like that," Carmen said now. "Such courage! Can you imagine how much of that she must have? I never knew how beautiful a bald woman could be."

Julia was getting used this sort of thing. It was humorous, really, to think they had spent a day and a half touring the historic district of Philadelphia—had seen an original copy of the Constitution, had watched reenactors sign the Declaration of Independence, had walked through the Liberty Bell Center, had visited the Betsy Ross House and the U.S. Mint—and yet what was Carmen exclaiming over? A cancer survivor and an ancient film about Eskimos.

Not that she didn't appreciate the other, sometimes to an embarrassing degree. At one point that afternoon, after gazing for a long time at the inscription on the Liberty Bell—*Proclaim Liberty throughout all the Land and unto all the Inhabitants thereof*—Carmen had spread her arms wide and said, "A Bible verse on the Liberty Bell! We live in the best country in the whole wide world." Under the high ceiling, surrounded by all the stone and glass, her voice had reverberated quite loudly. People had looked at her curiously, but some of them smiled. One older woman even said, "Amen, honey!" Julia was surprised that Carmen hadn't asked everyone to join her in singing "God Bless America."

THEY arrived in New York City on a clear, sparkling afternoon and found the Warwick Hotel. Their room was on the eleventh floor, on the front of the building, overlooking the Avenue of the Americas. Julia pulled back the curtain at the window and looked down at the street crawling with traffic, relieved that they had made their way through it in one piece.

Across the street, facing the hotel, was an office building. Julia could see a woman watering a hanging plant in one office, a group of people around a table in another, and, higher up, a man standing at the window holding a cell phone. She wondered what kind of life those people led, working in a place like that, in a city like this. She wondered if any of them had been working there on 9/11, if they still had bad dreams about what might fall out of the sky. She wondered if any of them could imagine living in a small stone house in a small Southern town and teaching at a small university.

Once Carmen had scouted out the hallways, they walked to a restaurant the concierge recommended and then down toward Times Square. *I'm really in New York City*, Julia kept telling herself. The crush of people, the babble of languages, the chaos of yellow taxis, the skyscrapers, the smells of streetside food and gutters and bodies—she had read about it all, seen it on the news and in movies, had always supposed it would feel claustrophobic and dangerous, but it didn't. It felt . . . *exhilarating* was the only word that came to mind, although that sounded a little too dramatic.

Judging from the look on Carmen's face, she was as swept away by the city as Julia was. Strangely, during all the time she had lived in the Northeast, she'd never been here before. They didn't talk as they walked. They would have had to shout anyway.

THE next day they covered miles on foot. Central Park, Carnegie Hall, all the way down Fifth Avenue to St. Patrick's Cathedral, and back to the Museum of Modern Art, where they spent most of the afternoon. It wasn't a famous work by Picasso or Matisse or Seurat that most intrigued Carmen, but an enormous tapestry titled *The Thousand Longest Rivers in the World*, with the names of all 1,000 rivers in order, from the Nile to the Agusan, neatly embroidered with cotton and linen thread onto canvas.

It was near the end of the afternoon when they saw it, taking up most of a single wall in one of the gallery rooms. Frankly, it didn't interest Julia—it didn't look like art to her. If she wanted a color-less, orderly listing, she could read a telephone book. Besides, she had been on her feet long enough and was ready to get back to the hotel room. But Carmen planted herself in front of it and studied it, turning her head from side to side as she scanned each line. A teenage boy dressed in all black wandered up and stood beside her.

"Okay, number one," Carmen said, "this Alighiero Boetti guy, however you say his name, has shown a very high level of commit-ment here. I'll give him that. To start with, it must have taken a long time just to research all the rivers and make sure he had them in the right order. I mean, who measures rivers anyway?"

Carmen pointed to the printed description mounted on the wall. "It says he started it in 1976. Before everybody had computers, right? So hats off to you, Mr. Boetti."

Two middle-aged women stopped to listen. "Number two," she continued, "I sort of have a hard time believing a man really did this. I mean, *really*? Sitting down with a needle and thread?"

A young couple with a baby joined the group. The man had the baby strapped to his back like a papoose. "Is this a tour?" he asked the teenage boy.

"Number three," Carmen said, "if this Mr. Boetti really did do this, and if he was a *real* artist, I sure hope he did some other things to show off his talent because, to be honest, this just seems a little . . . well, *pedestrian* to be in an art museum."

She stepped closer and checked the printed information again. "It says he finished it in 1982, so, number four, what took him so long? Did he have to keep ripping out stitches and doing them over?"

By now two other people had come along. Julia glanced back and saw a uniformed guard moving in their direction, looking ner-vous as he talked into his lapel.

"And, number five," Carmen said, "I wonder if somewhere

along about *here*"—she paused and pointed to the Potomac, which was number 460—"he was tempted to just revise his plan and make it *The Five Hundred Longest Rivers in the World*? And his poor wife, if he had one—can't you just hear her? 'Hey, Al, can you please quit sewing and go mow the yard?' But single-minded Mr. Boetti says, 'Not now, honey, I've got to finish the Monongahela.'"

Someone laughed. "But, number seven," Carmen said, "you've still got to give the man credit for setting a monster goal and sticking with it."

"That's only number six," the teenager in black said, "and you already said that anyway."

Carmen didn't miss a beat. "Just seeing if you were listening. Okay, then, number six, think of all the . . ."

The guard stepped forward and placed a hand between Carmen and the tapestry. "You're standing too close to the art," he said sternly. He had a round, flushed face, and his uniform jacket was so tight it looked like the buttons were about to pop off. "And we need to keep things moving, too. No congregating allowed. We have fire codes."

Somebody behind Julia said, "Well, good grief, you mean there's a law against *standing* in an art museum?" and for just a moment they all stared at the guard, who must have wondered if he should call for reinforcements. But then they began dispersing.

Carmen looked at his name tag. "Maybe you can help me out, Sherman. Do you know whether this artist, Mr. Alighiero Boetti, embroidered this whole thing by himself?"

Sherman looked at the tapestry as if he'd never seen it before, but then gathered himself, rocked forward on his tiptoes, and spoke with authority: "If it says he did it, then he did."

As they walked away, Carmen said, "Well, I think he *hired* somebody to do it. Probably a woman."

• • •

THAT night after dinner they walked to the Majestic Theatre to see *The Phantom of the Opera*, and then they rounded out the day by sharing a piece of white chocolate blueberry cheesecake at Roxy's in Times Square.

Carmen had two bites, said that was enough, and pushed the plate toward Julia. She liked the overall experience of the show, she said, and thanked Julia for the whole day, then added, almost apologetically, "But *Phantom of the Opera* is really sort of a vapid story, isn't it? I mean, fantasy is fine and all, but this plot is full of holes. Like, what does the Phantom do all day and how does he stay alive? And, seriously, how could the girl fall in love with somebody like him? And how did his face get all messed up anyway? Did I miss that part?" She laughed. "I know, I'm probably the only one in the world who doesn't like it. The woman sitting next to me said it was her *tenth* time to see it."

The funny thing was that Julia didn't like it either. She liked the grandeur and glamor of it—the costumes and the sets and the masquerade scene and the experience of sitting in the balcony at a Broadway show—but the whole time she had been wishing the music weren't so boringly melodramatic, the story so complicated and sketchy at the same time. Even the name of the female lead annoyed her—Christine. She couldn't say what was wrong with it, but by the end she thoroughly hated it. She thought Christine and the creepy Phantom deserved each other. If they ever came to New York again, she would get tickets to something like *West Side Story*.

Back in their hotel room, Carmen put the finishing touches on her sketches from the day while Julia watched the news—the usual recitation of worldwide misfortune, with one exception: a man convicted of murder, having already served eight years of a life sentence, had been found innocent and set free. Or maybe that was the worst story of all, to think of what he and his family had been through during those eight wasted years. And then there was the weather report—more bad news, with nothing but rain and cold temperatures in the immediate forecast. Julia turned the television off. She was suddenly very tired.

"Here, want to see my sketches?" Carmen said. She handed Julia her journal.

Julia studied the drawings at length. The first was an old woman they had seen in the art museum, leaning on her pronged cane in front of Andy Warhol's thirty-two soup cans. The other three were people they had seen along the streets that day—a toothless vendor selling gyros, a tall African man with a gigantic yellow snake wrapped around his shoulders, and a teenage girl with orange hair and combat boots, wearing an elf costume and carrying a sparkly wand.

Julia went through them once, slowly, then again. "They're good," she said. "Very good."

Carmen was brushing out her hair now. "You could spend all day here just watching the people."

Julia laughed. "True, and I guess we know one thing now— there are freaks in other parts of the country besides the Deep South."

Carmen stopped brushing and looked up. "Freaks?" she said. "Why would you call them that?"

Julia could have tried to explain it away, but she didn't. It was just a thoughtless comment, a humorous allusion of sorts to something Flannery O'Connor had once said when asked about the characters in her stories. But it really had nothing to do with the people in Carmen's sketches.

Julia looked at them again. No, the old woman wasn't a freak. She was just an old woman standing in an art museum looking at an iconic modern American painting. And the vendor was only making an honest living. The man with the snake had been a natural comedian, with a deep radio voice and a friendly, rolling laugh. And the girl in the elf costume was having fun. She probably felt sorry for all the people like Julia wearing normal, boring clothes. They weren't freaks, any of them. They were just people living their lives.

HALF child, half adult—that was Carmen, though you never knew which you were going to get on any given day. Most often, of course, you got them both. The turnarounds could happen in the blink of an eye. While it was hard at times to think of Carmen as a grown-up, it was just as hard at other times to believe she was only twenty. Her strict routines, her sensible outlook, her frugality, her moral rectitude—sometimes Julia felt that she was in the company of her grandmother. And the girl's frequent revisiting of favorite topics, telling the same stories—this was another of her old-person habits.

Right before they turned out the light, for example, Carmen returned to a subject she continued to find irresistible—Pamela and Butch. She reviewed many of the same specifics she had covered the previous days and then once again brought up the latest news: "I finally talked him into it!" Pamela had told them on the phone just that morning, *him* being Butch of course, and *it* being a couples water exercise class at the YMCA, which was going to be their Christmas present to each other.

"How perfect is that?" Carmen said now. Julia surely hoped somebody at the YMCA understood the principle of water displacement. She imagined the swimming pool spilling over and flooding the decks when the two of them got in at the same time.

Carmen was quiet for a while, then said, "I always thought

having a sister must be the most wonderful thing in the world. Or a brother. And to think, you had one of each."

Julia turned off the lamp between the two beds. A sister and a brother—it was true, she'd had them both. But not until this moment had it ever struck her as anything to be thankful for.

They heard voices out in the hall. "I shall quote a poem as I dance with you, my lovely!" someone yelled, followed by laughter and loud thumping, and "Stop it! You're going to wake everybody up!"

After the noise subsided, Carmen spoke in the dark. "Did I ever tell you about a poem I wrote in sixth grade called 'Death Throes of an Earthworm'? The teacher said to pick a subject nobody else would think of. It was about this worm named Sebastian that got trapped on the sidewalk after it rained. He finally dried up in the shape of an S."

So now she was back to being a little girl again. Nobody's grandmother would say something like that. For some reason Julia suddenly thought of all the children who hadn't wanted to be friends with Carmen in school. She felt sorry for them. They hadn't known what they were missing.

A few seconds later Carmen said, "Aunt Julia, are you okay? Are you *laughing*?"

"I'm fine," Julia said. "Go to sleep."

"Sometimes you have to laugh to keep from crying," Carmen said. "At least I know I do."

Julia didn't answer. There was no way she was going to follow up on a statement like that at this time of night.

· chapter 17 ·

DOWN THE RIVER

Six days down, six to go. This was the thought going through Julia's mind as they set off from New York the next day and headed toward Boston. It had been her custom on the few trips she had taken with Matthew to wish the days away, yearning to return to the stone house. It was discouraging to realize she was up to her old tricks. Maybe the weather forecast had something to do with it. Maybe her attitude would improve when the sun came back out.

It didn't help that she hadn't slept well the night before. Long past midnight, eleven stories above the Avenue of the Americas, she had lain awake thinking of the man newly released from prison after the surprise turn of events: a deathbed confession by the real murderer. She could still see the image of the innocent man being escorted from the prison to a waiting car, suddenly free but looking more stunned than happy as reporters shouted questions at him.

Lying in bed, she had thought about all the irretrievable years of injustice. She thought about the jurors and the judge who had sent the man to prison for the rest of his life, and how they must

feel now. A powerful illustration of a fundamental truth: that careful weighing of facts was good and productive only insofar as the
facts were the right ones.

She had eventually drifted off to sleep, but not a deep sleep and
not for long. She had awakened sometime later, aware that Carmen
was restless. She heard the rustling of covers and moist little clicks
of lips and tongue as if the girl were mouthing words, then whispering, and a long sigh. At one point, Carmen drew in a sudden
breath and sat up in bed. "Aunt Julia, did you say something?" she
said softly. Julia didn't answer, and the girl had finally settled back
down.

I T was late Friday morning, and traffic was bound to be heavy all
the way into Boston. This would be Julia's last stint as driver.
Once they left Boston for the rural roads, she intended to turn the
wheel over to Carmen. She was more than ready to be done with
driving on freeways and in big cities.

Carmen was quiet today. Since waking and dressing, she had
been preoccupied, had spoken very little over breakfast. Currently
she was slumped down, staring out the passenger window, her right
foot propped up on her left knee. As she wiggled her foot, the laces
of her canvas sneaker flapped back and forth.

It began to rain, the kind of big splatty raindrops that precede
a downpour, and the windshield was fogging up. It was a cold day,
more like December than October. Regrettable weather since
today, rain or shine, would be their only chance to see Boston. Julia
turned the defroster on and adjusted the speed of the windshield
wipers as the rain increased.

She hoped this didn't mark the beginning of a long wet, cold
spell. In her research for the trip, she had read about such New
England Octobers of the past, when heavy rains stripped the trees

of their leaves before the autumn show. She had a sudden thought, so dire it was almost funny. What if winter paid an especially early visit to New England this year? What if they had to walk through *snow* to get to the authors' homes?

The radio was on, and Garrison Keillor began reading his daily *Writer's Almanac* segment on NPR. On this day in 1856, he said, Gustave Flaubert's first installment of *Madame Bovary* was published, though an offending passage was omitted, and in 1885 Louis Untermeyer, U.S. poet laureate from 1961 to 1963, was born. On his ninetieth birthday Untermeyer announced that he was writing his third autobiography since "the other two were premature."

As always, Garrison Keillor ended the segment by reading a poem, this one titled "Letting Go." He read it gravely, respectfully, from the first lines—*Long past childhood I carried my balloon—/ A fat red grudge on a short, dingy string, / Heavy for a thing so light*—all the way to the end: *Until one day in early winter, I let it go as the sun sank, / Watched it float skyward and melt into pink clouds.*

The soft, measured words faded away, and a sprightly Strauss waltz soon took its place. The rain had intensified by now, falling in heavy gray curtains, thrumming hard on the roof of the Honda. Julia slowed to forty-five, then forty. And still, above the sound of the rain and the thunder, and the swish of wet tires as other cars passed, the lilting waltz continued. And still the poem lingered inside the car, as if waiting to be acknowledged.

The balloon poem was an apt little metaphor, Julia mused, though nothing especially clever, certainly not profound. Forgiveness was good, even in the winter of life, even for grudges blown out of proportion. Not that it had anything to do with her. Forgiving implied repentance on the part of someone else, generally for a specific act, not for a lifetime of general misery. You couldn't forgive globally. The failures of her parents were facts of her life, as permanent as the DNA they had equipped her with. You couldn't send such offenses up into the clouds to disappear. No forgiving things like that, no forgetting.

And forgiveness assumed some kind of ongoing relationship anyway. How could she forgive two dead people, especially two dead people who never once said they were sorry? Though she should, and did, try to shut their faults out of her mind as much as possible, she felt no moral obligation to pardon them.

She paused to consider the word itself. *Forgive*—such an angular, strident sound for such a soft meaning. It should be a much prettier word since its root, *give*, was the bedrock of so much virtuous behavior—sacrifice, courtesy, respect, and, of course, love. But there was nothing to be done about the word. You couldn't go around changing all the words that didn't sound like their definitions.

Of all the people she knew, she could think of no one she needed to forgive, no one against whom she was harboring a grudge for an excusable offense. The balloon poem was well conceived, its theme valid for a good life, but she felt no prick of guilt, as she sometimes did when a poem touched on something like selflessness or honesty or fortitude.

CARMEN finally broke the silence by turning the radio down and asking a question: "Forgiveness is one of the hardest things, isn't it?" Then a pause, followed by a string of words that could only be from one source: "Pray for deliverance from the gall of bitterness and the bond of iniquity." And then, dolefully, "That's a deliverance I sure need."

Julia said nothing. She didn't want to talk, not on a rainy day in heavy traffic, certainly not about a subject like this.

Carmen either didn't read her mood or else chose not to. Still facing the window, she said, "Going all the way back to things that happened to you many years ago."

Julia felt like saying, *Stop, not one more word*. She couldn't bear the thought of another heartrending memory recalled from the girl's fatherless childhood. Anyway, it always irked her to hear young people refer to their past with a phrase like "so many years ago" when they had lived so short a time.

But Carmen continued. "Things might seem little now that you're grown, but they sure didn't when they happened." Julia gripped the wheel tighter and leaned forward to indicate that all her concentration was needed for driving. Wasted effort, for Carmen didn't notice. "Like forgiving Daddy for cutting the string off your Chatty Cathy doll," she said. "That must have been hard to do."

A moment of surprise as Julia realized whose childhood Carmen was talking about, then perplexity as she wondered how the girl knew about the incident with her doll. But had she said *Daddy*? Maybe Julia had misunderstood. A quick clarification—"I never called him Daddy," she told Carmen. "Not even Dad. I avoided calling him anything, really."

Carmen's foot quit wiggling. There was a long pause. "I meant . . . *my* daddy, not yours. You knew that, right?" She turned from the window to look at Julia.

Julia played the words over: *Like forgiving Daddy for cutting the string off your Chatty Cathy doll.* She felt like she was listening to a riddle. She glanced at the girl. "How did you know what happened to my doll?"

"Daddy told me." Carmen uncrossed her leg and sat up straighter. "When I was a little girl"—she spoke slowly, clearly—"Daddy told me what he did to your doll. He told me more than once. He said he used his mother's nail scissors with the tiny curved blades."

There was silence as Julia tried to take it in. She could feel Carmen looking at her, waiting for a response. She heard the words again: *Daddy told me what he did to your doll. He told me more than once.* Maybe it was just a matter of ambiguous pronoun reference.

The Strauss waltz had ended and something else was playing now—something Julia couldn't put a name to. Though the volume was turned down, she could hear a repeated dissonant fanfare and a lot of percussion, as if pieces of heavy machinery were flying about. Something twenty-first-century, no doubt.

Carmen turned to face Julia squarely. She spoke in a near-whisper. "You didn't think . . . *your* father did that to your doll, did you?"

"I knew my father," Julia said. "You didn't. You weren't even born when . . ."

Carmen interrupted her. "Wait, just listen." What followed was a revelation that took no more than two minutes yet turned a life-long certainty inside out. Her daddy had often told her, she said, about cutting off the voice ring of Julia's doll. He said it was the first real memory he had from childhood with a beginning, middle, and end. He never talked about it in a joking way, but always to underscore a serious truth: that the human heart was bent on mischief. And that a thoughtless act could never be undone. "I think Daddy could've made a good preacher," Carmen said. "He really knew how to drive a point home."

He hadn't expected the prank to be irreparable. In his child's mind, his only thinking ahead was to imagine a brief time of comical consternation for his big sister and then . . . what? First, the unavoidable scolding, at the very least, though that was never a deterrent to his foolish, impulsive behavior. But after that, what? Maybe an easy fix by his father, who could repair anything. Who could say what thoughts were behind the act of a five-year-old?

"He said he hardly ever saw the doll after that," Carmen continued. "He also said you never held it against him, you just treated him like it had never happened. I remember thinking you must be some kind of angel to forgive him for something like that. He liked to use that story whenever he talked to me about sin and its consequences, which he did a lot. He said it was the first time he knew how bad it felt to do something really mean to somebody else." She shook her head. "But you never even knew *he* did it? How could that be?"

A long pause. The rain was slackening, but Julia kept driving slowly, trying to find a hole in the truth Carmen claimed to be telling. At length she said, "I . . . really don't know. But my father hated that doll. I never once doubted that he did it." What a cold, blighted house of fear theirs had been, she thought, that not one word was ever exchanged about the incident. She wondered if her mother had known the truth, and her father. For sure Jeremiah had. She wondered if Jeremiah was punished.

She wondered other things—if they all thought *she* knew it, why no apology had been required, if any of them had an inkling of what she had endured. Pointless questions, all of them. The fact was that she did know now, if Carmen's report was to be trusted, and though it didn't exonerate her father from all his other unkindnesses, it did cause a revision of this particular distress. Nothing to shake the world, but evidence, if she needed it, that assumption and error were often the same.

If it weren't such a commentary on the wretchedness of family life Frederickson style, it could be something to laugh about—one of those funny discoveries grown-up siblings make in later years: *So you were the one who did that?* But it wasn't funny, though there was one part Julia could almost smile over: the fact that, without saying a word, she had received credit in Jeremiah's eyes for forgiving him, had been held up as an example to his own child, who had thought her aunt was an angel. She couldn't help wondering how she would have behaved all those years ago had she known Jeremiah was to blame. Most likely not angelically.

But what difference did any of it make now? It had happened almost fifty years ago. And subtract one hurtful act from her father's long list, it still left a multitude.

"Water under the bridge," she said. "And down the river and around the bend and on to the sea. Just a drip compared to all the real suffering people have endured in the history of mankind." She laughed lightly. "After all, what's a broken doll in comparison to . . . say, the Holocaust? Or any number of other genuine tragedies." And she meant it. She hoped Jeremiah hadn't been punished for his childish act.

"Well, yeah, but it's still sad," Carmen said. After a while she sighed and added, "Sometimes it's easier to forgive others than yourself, isn't it?" Julia gave no answer, and the girl didn't press for one.

WITHIN a few moments the music on the radio, the same piece evidently, seemed to be reaching a climax—a sustained roar underneath more clanging noises, like a freight train plowing through a crowded car lot. "Heavenly day," Julia said, and turned it off. The rain had diminished to a slow drizzle. She turned the windshield wipers to the lowest setting. The distance to Boston wasn't far, but long enough for more talking if she didn't act. "How about starting *Ethan Frome*?" she said. "It's short. We can read a couple of chapters a day and be done by the time we get to Edith Wharton's home."

Never had Carmen refused to do anything Julia had asked of her. Nor did she now, though it was obvious her heart wasn't in it. She reached into the backseat and pulled the book out, then adjusted the back of her seat and started reading.

Only after she had read the first paragraph did Julia remember how foreboding the whole introduction was. But, oddly, Carmen's spirits seemed to lift as she continued to read, though perhaps it was just an act. She began slipping in a few comments of her own, so smoothly it was hard to tell she was departing from the text. Only a few times did she trifle with the serious tone, however, as when she read the part about Ethan Frome's disfigured face: "But since he didn't want to be confused with the Phantom of the Opera," she inserted, "he decided not to wear a mask." Not for a second did she pause for a reaction but kept right on reading.

She finished chapter one, then put the book away as they were nearing Boston. "Well, that's pretty . . . lugubrious," she said. "I mean, we already know he ends up crippled." She readjusted her seat and turned to look out the window as Julia again reminded herself to give more careful thought to what they read aloud. Something light and humorous would have been a better choice on a dismal day like this. Well, too late now. They rode the rest of the way without talking. It was still drizzling lightly, and the sky showed no signs of clearing. Wet, gray fog muted the colors of the leaves.

B Y two o'clock, they were setting out on a walking tour, starting at the Boston Common. It was cold, but at least the rain had subsided to a sloppy mist. Too, they shouldn't have to contend with crowds of other tourists on a day like today.

Carmen walked with her hands jammed into the pockets of her hooded fleece, pulling out a folded sheet of directions to refer to from time to time, occasionally reading aloud a dull paragraph of explanation about one of the places, but mostly scanning the faces of the people they passed.

For almost two hours they kept to the route, hurrying through the landmarks of Boston: the Massachusetts State House, the brick row houses and gas lights along the cobblestone streets of Beacon

Hill, the Old Granary Burying Ground, the statue of Benjamin Franklin, the site of the Boston Massacre, the Old Corner Bookstore, the Old State House. Lots of old things in Boston. Somewhere along the way Carmen pointed out the famous grasshopper weather vane, but Julia knew she would never remember which building it was on since she didn't feel like jotting notes in her journal on a day like this.

It was too bad. Here they were right in the middle of so much history, yet it felt more like a bothersome homework assignment they were rushing to finish. Maybe it was the weather or maybe the fact that Boston wasn't new to Carmen. She had lived in the general vicinity at some point, had been to the city several times. Maybe they should have opted for a guided tour so she could have heard things she didn't already know.

Or maybe they were just trying to do too much in one trip. Whatever the cause, it was a shame this beautiful old city wasn't getting the attention it deserved, that there would be no memory to carry away, only a blur.

A FTER the walking tour, they ate an early dinner and headed back to their room. As they were approaching the hotel entrance, someone exited and jogged past them, a tall young man in a tan jacket, holding a newspaper over his head against the rain, which had picked up again. Carmen spun around and stared after him.

"Do you know him?" Julia asked.

Carmen shrugged. "I guess not."

They went inside to the elevators. A family was already waiting to go up—a frazzled-looking couple and three small children, one of them a baby wearing a white cap with ear flaps, tied under the chin. The man was holding the baby, and the woman had the other two, both boys, by the hand. They looked to be around two and four, and the younger one had something brown all around his mouth. The older one twisted around and looked up at Julia and Carmen, staring back and forth between them, finally settling on Carmen.

The father punched the button again and said, "These have got to be the slowest elevators in the world." The baby, looking over his shoulder, scrunched up her face and let out a wail right in his ear. He shifted her to his other arm, closer to her mother, who smiled at her and said, "It's somebody's bedtime, isn't it?" The mother had a pale, narrow face and straight, limp hair. She looked worn out, as if it were her bedtime, too.

The baby kept crying. "I knew we should've brought her stroller with us," the man said. It was then that he became aware of Julia and Carmen standing behind them. "But, hey," he said, making an attempt at joviality, "she ain't heavy, she's my baby!" He bounced her up and down, but she continued to cry. "Where's her juice?" he said a little less jovially, and the woman let go of the boys' hands and rummaged in the bag she was carrying over her shoulder. The bottle was practically empty, but the baby saw it and made frantic little whimpering sounds as she reached for it. She put it into her mouth and sucked greedily, but all she got was dry, whistling sounds.

"Here, baby doll, you've got to tip it up," the mother said. The man repositioned the baby in his arms so that she was leaning back, and she began sucking again, with more success.

Just then one of the elevators dinged and the door slowly opened. A large woman in a red capelike raincoat, holding a miniature dog in her arms, came hurrying into the lobby from outdoors and called, "Wait! Hold the door! We're going up, too!"

They all moved into the elevator, and when it was determined that they were all headed to the sixth floor, Julia began to imagine the worst—being in a room sandwiched between a screaming baby and a barking dog. Well, she had requested room changes before and wouldn't hesitate to do so again.

It was a small elevator with a mildewy smell. When the door finally closed and they began their labored ascent, there was a low-pitched grinding noise from somewhere directly above them. The two boys, enthralled by the idea of an animal in their midst, shifted their attention from Carmen to the woman with the dog. They stood on their tiptoes trying to see the dog, a curly-haired white puffball, panting and trembling in the woman's arms as she talked baby talk to it and stroked its head, her diamond rings flashing.

A strong scent of cologne began to mix with the smell of mildew as Julia watched the digital numbers of the floors light up ever so slowly. The man had been right—this was an exceedingly poky elevator. And wobbly—Julia wished there were a tactful way to suggest getting the weight distributed more evenly.

They had made it only to the third floor when the baby emptied the bottle and began fussing again, flailing her arms about. The mother handed the man the diaper bag and took the baby. She tried to calm her, but the volume of her crying escalated. It was remarkable how loud one baby could be in an elevator. The man sighed and ran a hand through his hair. "No, leave those alone!" he said to the younger boy, who had reached up and was tugging on a set of brightly colored plastic keys clipped to the diaper bag.

During all of this Carmen had said nothing, but suddenly she leaned over right in front of the baby's face and spoke to her in a Donald Duck voice. Not just quacking sounds, but actual, understandable words—"Hey, there, little girl, where did you get that pretty white cap?" Just one more example of something Julia didn't know she could do. The baby instantly froze midcry, her face still contorted, her mouth still wide open, but making no sound, only staring at Carmen instead. The little boys stared, too. The older one said, "Do that again." So she did, this time addressing the boys: "What's up, guys? My name's Donald Duck. Have you seen Mickey Mouse anywhere around here? I'm looking for him." The boys giggled.

A ND suddenly everything was more relaxed. The baby let out a string of shrill gibberish and clapped her hands together. The father leaned down and picked up the younger boy. "Oops, I guess we forgot to wipe your mouth, didn't we, buddy?" he said, laughing. The mother kissed the baby on the forehead and smiled at Carmen. "I guess I need to learn to talk like that. It sure did the trick for her." She unclipped the set of plastic keys on the diaper bag and handed them to the baby, who stuck them in her mouth. The woman turned back to Carmen. "I love your hair. Mine is just hopeless in this kind of weather. I bet yours is naturally curly, isn't it?"

Carmen nodded and jerked a thumb toward the dog. In her duck voice she said, "Me and him, same hairdo."

The woman in the red raincoat released a little arpeggio of laughter and said to her dog, "Does wittle Buffy wike the sound of the funny ducky-wucky?" Little Buffy continued to shiver, his bulging black eyes darting about nervously.

Mercifully the number 6 lit up just then, and they stopped with a clunk and a shudder. There was a brief delay before the bell chimed and the door began to slide open—just long enough for Julia to have a sudden horrible vision of the eight of them trapped inside the elevator overnight. Well, nine counting the dog.

"Here we are, folks, step lightly so the boat doesn't tip," Carmen said in her Donald Duck voice. The little boys laughed and clamored for more. The woman with the dog got off first, fluttering a hand and calling back, "Say ta-ta to everybody, Buffy!" Her coat billowed behind her like a sail as she swept down the hallway, chirping "Ta-ta! Ta-ta!"—thankfully, in the opposite direction from Julia and Carmen's room.

Julia stepped out and waited for Carmen, who held the door open for the family. The baby was still diverted by the plastic keys, now plucking at them and shaking them. Her chin was wet with drool. The man put the younger boy down outside the elevator. "Where are you ladies from?" he asked Julia, and she told him. He chuckled and said, "Up here to see some *real* fall color, huh?"

Julia was already noticing that people up here in New England were more than a little condescending in their attitudes about other parts of the country. As if fall color were a foreign concept to anyone from a state like South Carolina. "We're from *Vermont*," the man offered, in a tone that suggested it was a bedroom community of the Garden of Eden. Another benefit of the trip suddenly occurred to Julia, one she hadn't thought about until right this minute—that they would actually get a double dose of fall color this year, the early show up here and the later one at home.

Carmen was out of the elevator now, kneeling in front of both boys, who were telling her things to say in her duck voice. As they collapsed into another round of giggles, she looked up at their parents. "Sorry, you probably don't want them getting all wound up."

The woman smiled and shook her head. "That's okay. It's been sort of a disappointing day for them. For all of us, really. Thanks for making us laugh." The man started shepherding the boys down the hall, in the same direction Buffy and his owner had gone. The woman lingered a moment. "Life can sure get crazy sometimes," she said, looking after her husband and sons. "Now we'll see how it goes with all five of us sleeping in the same room. That should be interesting." She looked back at Carmen. "Thanks again. I'm glad we could ride up together."

"Me, too," Carmen said. Her eyes were on the baby. "What's her name?"

The woman untied the baby's cap and pulled it off to expose a headful of feathery down standing up as if electrically charged. "Allison," she said. "We're calling her Allie. Say bye-bye to the nice ladies, Allie." She lifted the baby's hand and waved it, then smiled again and started down the hall after her husband.

Though Julia was relieved it hadn't lasted any longer, she was glad for the elevator ride, too, since it seemed to have cheered Carmen up, at least for now. She hoped the girl's brooding spell was over. Tomorrow they would leave Boston and drive the short distance to Cambridge to see Longfellow's birthplace, then head to Derry, New Hampshire, to visit Robert Frost's home. Maybe tomorrow the sun would be shining and everything would be back to normal.

chapter 18

WHATEVER HARD TRUTH

As it turned out, there was a memory to take away from Boston after all. And when the parts finally came together, a veil was suddenly lifted on the past few months. If Carmen had been a book Julia was reading, she would have reproved herself for missing the subtleties of foreshadowing. But Carmen wasn't a book, of course. This was real life.

What happened was this. Julia unlocked the door to their hotel room, took off her jacket, and hung it over the back of a chair. Carmen stooped down by the door to remove her shoes. Julia walked over to turn on the television. She flipped through several channels until she found the evening news. She watched a moment, then turned to another channel and watched, until she decided she liked the looks and voice of the first newscaster better and went back to that one. Just as the anchorman said, "The Dow fell thirty points today," Julia sensed sudden, swift movement behind her and turned to see Carmen lying facedown on one of the beds, not crying audibly but surely crying.

She was stupefied. She stared for a moment, then turned back to the television, her thoughts whirling. At home she had heard Carmen in the night and other times had seen her fight tears, but never had she seen her give herself over to them like this. Her first impulse was to doubt appearances. Maybe the girl was just tired from all the walking. Or it could be more than physical—a deep weariness, not only of cold rainy Boston but of the whole trip, being cooped up in a room and a car, being dragged from place to place, being expected to act interested and make conversation. Maybe she just wanted to go back to South Carolina, where she could take long walks by herself and retreat to her own bedroom at night and close the door.

But as she looked at Carmen again, now clutching a fistful of the floral comforter, something told Julia there was more to this. But what could it be?

A sound from the bed—a suppressed half squeak, half sob, and a long, convulsive heaving of shoulders. Julia considered her options. She hated to intrude on anyone's sorrow. Maybe it would be best to cover the awkwardness by pretending she hadn't noticed. After all, the television was turned up loud, so Carmen might think she hadn't heard anything. Julia could disappear into the bathroom right now and take a long shower, thus giving the girl time to get herself under control.

But that was no good. Though such an act could disguise itself as politeness, Julia knew it for what it really was—cowardice. Or, maybe more to the point, selfishness. For she knew what she was hoping deep down—that she would be spared having to offer something in return for an unburdening of the soul.

A sudden image came to her mind—a kitchen accident from many years ago. Her mother had sliced her hand open with a knife while cutting up a chicken. She had cried out and dropped the knife with a clatter, then grabbed the dishcloth and held her hand over the sink. From the living room, Julia and Pamela had heard her, had both rushed into the kitchen. Julia had seen the blood and shrunk back in horror while ten-year-old Pamela had taken over.

Julia looked again at Carmen lying on the bed. Please, no open wound, she thought. Let it be bandaged in private, let grief be swallowed silently. Yet other thoughts rose. *You can't turn away from this. You have to step into the middle of it. You have no choice.*

She turned the television off and walked quickly to the bed. She sat on the edge and touched Carmen's hand. The girl moaned softly, raggedly, but turned her palm up. Julia gathered her hand into both of hers and held it tight. "Tell me," she said, and even though it wasn't exactly true, she added, "I want to know."

At length Carmen raised her head. "I don't think I can do this, Aunt Julia."

"Yes, you can. Tell me."

"The trip, I mean," Carmen said. "I don't think I can do it. I thought I could and I've tried, I really have, but I just can't. I can't be here right now. I'm sorry, but today was just awful. New England is so dark and cold and . . ."

"The weather is supposed to be nicer tomorrow," Julia said, though she knew that wasn't what she meant.

". . . and scary and depressing."

"I'm pretty sure the Salem witch trials are over."

Carmen rolled over on her side. "It's a good thing," she said with a faint smile. "They would've hanged me for sure."

"Tell me," Julia said again.

IT was a sad, sordid story. The clues had been there all along. The sounds in the night, of course. The intense interest in children. The careful observation of couples. The long walks and interludes of silence. The preoccupation with guilt and forgiveness. The early resistance over the trip to New England. The increased edginess as they neared Boston.

Even her confession at Julia's kitchen table in June, when she told about her years since leaving Wyoming—there had been clues there, too. She remembered one of the last things Carmen had said that night, stopping in the doorway: *There's more, if you want to ask more questions. I didn't tell you every detail.* And her own response: *You've told me enough.* Surely if she had pressed the girl for whatever the *more* was, the whole truth would have come out.

It was unfair, though, that the burden should have been on Julia to get to the truth. Why hadn't Carmen just come out and told her instead of waiting to be asked the right question? It could be considered a lie, her holding back. If not technically a lie, an argument could certainly be made concerning the sin of omission.

The wonder of it all, after Julia heard the truth, was that the girl still clung to prayer, still believed there was a God in heaven, still thought good men walked the earth. This could be interpreted, Julia supposed, as a faith past shaking—something to be desired. Or as a lack of basic common sense—something weak and pitiful that needed to be fixed.

CARMEN didn't rush. She sat up on the bed, Indian style, and started at the beginning. Julia sat on the other bed and listened. For the most part she reserved her questions, not wanting to extend the telling longer than necessary. Though she might have wished for fewer details as time wore on, there was a certain comfort in the protracted nature of the narrative, for it delayed the conclusion, the moment when she would possess whatever hard truth was coming.

Some of it could have been amusing if Julia weren't in such a state of dread. The introductory sentence, for example: "I was seventeen when I caught a ride in an eighteen-wheeler in Prentiss,

Massachusetts, in the middle of a New England heat wave, with a man whose arms were completely covered with tattoos of galaxies and planets." She paused a moment as if to give Julia time to digest all of this, and then continued.

It was July, and she was walking toward a field where she had heard a carnival was setting up. Her hope was to get a job of some kind for a few days before traveling southward, down the eastern seaboard. Even then, three years ago, her ultimate goal was to make her way to Julia in South Carolina.

The left shoulder of the road was tall with weeds, so she was walking on the right side, which had been mowed. Why it should matter which side of the road was mowed and which wasn't, Julia couldn't imagine, but she kept quiet and let Carmen tell it the way she wanted to.

The story continued, detail upon detail, until she finally made her way back to the part about the tattooed truck driver, who offered her a ride to Hartford, Connecticut. The truck was a gleaming white semi, but it didn't have any writing on it except for a notation in tall black letters: *110 INCHES INTERIOR HEIGHT*.

"Did I say how crazy hot it was that day?" Carmen said. "I knew a nice new truck like that would be air-conditioned." She shook her head. "So that's how I wound up in Hartford—a place I never even wanted to go."

She wandered around Hartford for two days, looking for a halfway friendly face—someone she might approach about a few chores to do, maybe a place to sleep. She had some money from her last job in Maine and some leftover snacks in her backpack. She spent the first two nights on the back porch of a crumbling house being converted into apartments, then left in the morning when the workmen started arriving. She found a park with rose gardens, a lake, a playground, and she went there with take-out food in the evenings and watched the families.

Her rule of thumb was to give a town three days, and if no work turned up, to hit the road again. On the afternoon of the third day, she passed a little mom-and-pop Mexican restaurant called Paco's Tacos, wedged between a laundromat and what used to be a drug-store but now served as a church: Faith, Hope, and Charity Taber-nacle, according to the sign in the window. On the sidewalk in front of the restaurant was a very old Hispanic man with a broom, using it as much for support as for sweeping. She asked him if she could sweep for him, told him she didn't need money, she was a champion sweeper from way back and just wanted to help. He studied her face at length, then motioned her inside. He led her back to the kitchen, spread his arms in a hopeless gesture, and said, "You help *thees*?"

The kitchen was a mess. If DHEC had dropped by right then, the restaurant would have been closed for good. The old man spoke enough English to make her understand that somebody in his family had died, or was in the process of dying, and he was trying to keep the business open with the help of two others, who were coming in for the evening shift. "You clean thees," he said, survey-ing the kitchen with his sad, watery eyes, "I pay a leetle."

And that was how Carmen landed a job as kitchen help and waitress at Paco's Tacos. Paco himself eventually got well and came back to take over, but he kept her on and let her sleep in the catch-all room they called the office. He paid her with a little cash and free meals—the kind of food she had never eaten before. "But it was fine," she said. "I ate it all—enchiladas, quesadillas, chimichan-gas, you name it. It was all okay. You can get used to anything."

S HE stayed in Hartford through the end of the year—the lon-gest she had stayed anywhere since leaving Wyoming—and what happened in those five months changed her forever, left her with guilt for a lifetime. "It's there from the time I wake up till I go to bed, and all through the night, too," she said. But she was dry-eyed as she spoke, staring down at her hands.

She looked up at Julia. "Have you ever read *The Scarlet Letter*?" Something told Julia this wasn't just one of her goofy, irrelevant questions. Carmen laughed. "Sorry, dumb question. You have a PhD in literature. Of course you've read *The Scarlet Letter*. Even I've read it. Once in tenth grade and once in a library in Chicago." She looked away. "Twice is enough."

She could have stopped there, and Julia would have known all she needed to know. On the one hand, she wanted to say, "Please, no more. I get the general drift. You can skip all the details." But on the other, she knew Carmen needed to tell it all—and, though she couldn't say why, she knew she needed to hear it.

"My story's not exactly like Hester Prynne's, though," Carmen said. "For one thing, I didn't stay at the scene of the crime. I left. And he . . . wasn't a preacher like Arthur Dimmesdale. His father was, though." She was staring at her hands again, but now her fists were clenched. "I had a baby." She looked up and said, "I hate the word *illegitimate*. A baby shouldn't ever be called that. Life is never illegitimate."

Julia couldn't take this in. That day at her kitchen table, months ago, when she had reeled off questions and Carmen had answered them—hadn't she asked about this very thing? "You told me you had never been pregnant," she said.

Carmen sighed. "I knew I was misleading you, and I've regretted that a lot." She looked away. "You asked if I'd ever gotten pregnant after a man abused me. But, see, what happened in Hartford wasn't abuse. We both knew what we were doing, and we knew it was wrong. So I told you no. It was a . . . deception. I'm sorry." Carmen hung her head.

After a long moment, Julia spoke. Though her mind was teeming with questions, there was one that had to be asked first: "Where's the baby?"

Carmen took a deep breath. "She . . . died right after she was born."

The draperies at the window were still open. It was dusk and the sky was finally clearing over Boston. Behind shreds of gray clouds were streaks of fiery orange, purple, gold. Tomorrow held the promise of sunshine, of trees aflame with autumn glory. Julia felt a sudden resentment that misery could be set against a backdrop of such beauty.

She looked back at Carmen. To think that this child had had a child—it seemed impossible.

"So now you know," Carmen said. "I'm not the good girl you thought I was, if you ever even thought that. That's not what kept me from telling you, though. There's something about admitting a sin out loud that gives you a little . . . reprieve, you know? And that's what I couldn't let happen. I needed to feel the weight of it right here every day." She thumped a fist over her heart. "I didn't want anybody's sympathy making it easier. It's a sin I need to feel the full force of. So I'll never forget."

Julia studied the girl's face before speaking. "I thought forgiveness was something religious people believed in."

Carmen answered promptly. "I do. God forgave me. Totally."

"So if God forgave you, why can't you . . ."

"Forgive myself?" Carmen said. "I don't even know what that means. You can *acknowledge* your sin, which I've done. The heart is deceitful and desperately wicked. That's straight from the Bible. I don't want to forget what I'm capable of. So if that's what you call not forgiving yourself, then, okay, I guess I can't forgive myself."

Something was wrong with such stark, relentless reasoning, but Julia couldn't put it into words. She said the only thing that came to her mind, the same words Carmen had said to her not long ago. "You're too hard on yourself."

Carmen nodded. "I need to be. It scares me sometimes when I see a family like the one we met in the elevator. I want that so much, but it has to come the right way. No cheating or shortcuts. For now that means waiting. And praying."

"And rubbing your nose in your sin whenever you get to feeling too hopeful?" Julia said.

The girl frowned. "I guess I haven't explained it very well. Hope is something you can't ever have too much of."

CARMEN got up from the bed and walked to the window. She stood looking out, her hands in her back pockets. "You want to know who he was?"

"If you want to tell me."

She came back and sat on the edge of the bed. "He came to eat at Paco's a lot. On Sundays mainly. His father preached at the church next door. The one that used to be a drugstore. It still smelled a little . . . medicinal." She wasn't trying to be funny, didn't pause for effect but kept right on talking.

The boy's name was Stephen. He played the piano at the church. He was twenty-two. He'd been to college for three years and wanted to be a music teacher but couldn't finish because of money. So he was living at home again, working for a paving company and teaching a few piano lessons to earn enough to go back.

Before long Carmen started going to the church since it was so handy. She liked the people, liked the singing and preaching.

Julia said, "And this was the church where they let you clean every week and work in the nursery?" She tried not to emphasize the word *let*, but Carmen must have picked it up.

"I volunteered," she said quickly, defensively. "They were good people. A lot of young families. They made me feel like I belonged, and I hadn't felt that way for a long time. Stephen's father was a good preacher. The way he explained Scripture—it was so clear and powerful and beautiful."

They had a little choir, and they asked her to sing a solo one Sunday. So she asked Stephen to meet her at church to practice. "And that's how it all started," she said. "Fast-forward a couple of months, and . . . well, you know. It happened two times."

Julia shook her head. "Please, you don't need to . . ."

Carmen raised her voice and kept going. "After the first time, I made up my mind to leave Hartford, just to make sure it didn't happen again. I told Paco I had an emergency and needed to quit my job, and that night I went over to clean the church so it would be ready for Sunday." She looked away, toward the window. "Stephen showed up before I finished cleaning, and he helped me get the chairs set back up. And we talked a little while, but I didn't tell him I was leaving. We even prayed together, and then . . ."

Julia stopped her again. "I don't need to hear it," though what she really meant was *I don't want to hear it*. That it must have happened at church struck her as appalling. She had a question, though. "If you loved each other, why didn't you just get married?"

Carmen dropped her head. "That's another part of it. He was going to marry somebody else. He was *pledged* to her. That's what they called it. Their families had known each other forever. It would have destroyed her, and their parents, too. She already had a wedding dress."

Julia didn't believe it for a minute. The boy had undoubtedly played on Carmen's gullibility, inventing an excuse for why he couldn't marry her—a very far-fetched one. Surely there weren't arranged marriages in the United States these days, unless the Amish or Mennonites still did that sort of thing.

"And so it happened again," Carmen said. "I was so ashamed.

Not just because it was a sin but because I . . . wanted it to happen. I loved him. And I wanted him to love me. Even if it meant breaking somebody else's heart."

"There's nothing wrong with love," Julia said.

"No, there's not," said Carmen quietly. She closed her eyes. One knee was jerking up and down. "I still dream about him sometimes." A few moments of silence, then, "I left the next morning before the sun came up. Came to Boston. Figured I could get lost in the crowd until I got back on my feet." She was speaking more slowly now. "I never went back to Hartford. He never found out about the baby." She opened her eyes and looked at Julia. "So now you know."

"Now I know," Julia said. She also knew that the preacher's son in Hartford had gotten off much easier than Arthur Dimmesdale.

CARMEN got up and walked to the foot of the bed, then turned around. "But there's another thing I need to tell you. I had trouble sleeping last night. Did you know?"

Julia nodded. "I could tell."

"There were visions and voices," Carmen said. She appeared to be perfectly serious. "I guess it started with the baby in the elevator. Later I got to thinking about the baby I lost, and then I started dreaming. I saw a little girl running through a field. And then the wind started blowing hard and she disappeared in the tall grass. But then I heard a voice whisper right in my ear, '*I walk the earth.*'" She stopped talking but didn't take her eyes off Julia. "And then I felt a hand on my face."

Julia felt a sudden deep exhaustion. She had been sitting here for a long time, listening, struggling to take it all in, to keep from discounting the parts until she had heard the whole, but now this. A nighttime chimera reported as reality.

They stared at each other until Julia finally said, "But didn't you say she died?"

"That's what they told me," Carmen said. "And I believed them. Until now. I heard a voice in my dream last night. It said, *I walk the earth*. As plain as day. It was a child's voice."

Julia said, "But didn't you . . . see her after she was born?"

"I never did," Carmen said. She sat down on the bed again. "I wasn't really . . . *with* it. It's hard to remember."

"Tell me," Julia said.

"I'll try," Carmen said. She sat for a moment, kneading her hands together. "I was in labor a long time. The midwife never left me. Her name was Luna—as in the moth. I knew her already, of course. She was sort of shy, but very nice. I trusted her."

She told the rest briefly, simply, but among the few embellishments she included were the sounds she heard that night—strong winds, heavy rain, claps of thunder. The storm went on and on, like her labor. But at last, another sound. "I heard her cry," she said. "Finally it was over. I think I must have passed out because all of a sudden I opened my eyes and couldn't hear her anymore. I asked to hold her, but she wasn't there. And Luna wasn't there either. That's when they told me something was wrong with the baby and she had died. And there was nothing they could do. They said *she*—so I knew it was a girl."

She lifted her eyes and looked at Julia. "I asked to see her, begged to hold her just one time. They said they knew what was best in these situations, they couldn't let me do that." Her voice dropped to a whisper. "They said it was too late anyway, that a whole day had passed and I had been in and out of consciousness and they had already . . . had her taken away. They wouldn't say where. They said just to think of her in heaven. They looked so sad and spoke so kindly to me. I thought they were telling the truth. Nobody would tell a lie like that."

She leaned forward, her eyes still fixed on Julia's. "But I heard her voice last night. God wouldn't play a trick like that on me. I *know* he wouldn't."

Julia didn't know any such thing. But she did know one thing without a doubt, that their New England trip had suddenly been blown completely off course.

chapter 19 ·

Sufficiently Unworthy

It was too much information too fast, like sitting in a class and having nothing to take notes with. Somehow Julia had to get her thoughts in order, remember the important things, make connections. Now there were new facts to be inserted into the timeline of the girl's snarled history. First, Carmen had had a baby. Second, the baby died, or so she was told. Third, she had a dream that the baby was living. Fourth, she believed the dream to be true. There were other facts, of course, but these were the most pertinent to the trouble at hand.

The clock on the hotel nightstand said 7:04 P.M., but it felt much later. Julia looked at Carmen, still sitting on the bed, a picture of depletion, her eyes closed, her shoulders hunched. Julia moved over to sit beside her. She put an arm around her and drew in a deep breath. "I want to help," she said.

In the months since Carmen's first appearance at the stone house, the two of them had never embraced. Such a thing would have embarrassed Julia to no end. But when Carmen threw her arms around her now, she didn't pull away.

After a few moments, Julia said, "Okay, one question at a time. Where was your baby born?"

Carmen walked over to the desk and picked up the road atlas. She flipped through it, then handed it to Julia. "There," she said, pointing. "Danforth, Massachusetts. That's where it was. Is." She traced her finger from Danforth to Boston and back again, all the way across the state, to the western edge. In a state like Massachusetts, however, not that far in actual miles.

"How did you end up there?" Julia said. "And where were you living?"

Long story, the girl said, but she would give an abridged version. From Hartford she went to Boston, where she found work caring for an old woman, bedridden in a back room of her daughter's house. Carmen asked for Sundays off, and one Sunday she walked to a nearby church. It was February now, and there was snow on the ground. Her eighteenth birthday was only days away.

Julia spoke before she could stop herself. "Did this one meet in a storefront, too?" That the girl would have gone to any church at all after Hartford revealed something disheartening about her—some weakness of mind common among people who spend their lives making the same mistakes over and over.

No, it was a stately old brick church with a stained-glass window above the front door, depicting Jesus with open arms and the words *Come Unto Me* written out in chips of colored glass under his feet. A sign from God, naturally. Beside the steps was a large brick marquee bearing the name of the pastor and associate pastor. It was the associate pastor's name that caught Carmen's attention: Harriet Dove.

So much for the abridged version, Julia thought.

By now Carmen had realized she was pregnant, and it was Harriet Dove in whom she confided. And Harriet Dove knew someone who knew the director of a small licensed, nonprofit adoption agency in Pittsfield, Massachusetts, who took in "girls in trouble," placed them in private homes to live, and covered all their expenses. Many of their referrals were from pastors and other "Christian ministries" in New England. The births were home births, attended by qualified midwives, and it was understood that the babies would be adopted.

So that was how she ended up with Babies First Mission. Julia immediately hated the place, starting with the name. What was an adoption agency doing calling itself a mission? It sounded self-righteous, which in itself was cause for suspicion. And *Babies* First? What about the mothers of the babies? Why didn't they come first?

Carmen was assigned to the home of a couple in nearby Danforth—Milo and Joyce Shelburn. Milo was the assistant director of Babies First, and he and Joyce took their turn housing girls, one at a time. The baby had been born in their home.

"And they were the ones who told you she had died?" Julia asked.

Carmen nodded.

E ARLY the next morning Julia was lying in bed, the hotel room dark, only the palest line of light at the window. Carmen spoke into the quietness. "Those miners in Chile didn't have it so bad," she said. An odd remark to start any day with, but especially a day like this, after the confession of the previous night, the long hours of talk that followed, the short hours of sleep between then and now.

Julia knew, of course, that she was referring to the Chilean miners trapped for months underground—news that was several years old now, but nevertheless fascinating to the girl. A few weeks earlier she had read a book about the ordeal and talked about it endlessly. She knew all the miners' names and ages, the hierarchy among them. She was especially intrigued by the structured life they had managed to live over two thousand feet below the surface of the earth.

"They had each other," she continued now, "plus they knew people were working to get them out even if it might take a long time." She rolled over on her side and rose on one elbow to face Julia. "When I first started reading that book, it was like, yeah, I know that feeling. Buried in a place you can't get out of." She sighed. "But they got rescued in the end."

Julia thought of something that had eluded her the night before, a point that needed to be made. "Why should there be pardon for my taking a child's life," she said, "yet none for yours of giving birth to one?" She turned toward Carmen. In the dimness she could see only the shape of her, not her face.

"Yours was an accident," Carmen said at once. "Mine wasn't."

Julia pushed the covers back and sat up. It was too early to have to choose words so carefully, but she had to say this right. She was glad there was so little light in the room. She could think better in the dark. "It's no more an accident," she said slowly, "to lose your temper and act in anger than it is to violate your conscience and act in passion. Both qualify as sin, in your terms. And whether death or birth, the consequence of each sin was unintended."

Carmen didn't move for a long moment and then flung herself onto her back again. "Oh, Aunt Julia, how do you come up with stuff like that?"

"Well, think about it," Julia said. "It seems to me that causing the death of a child is a far more serious crime than giving life to one. In my case, there's never a way of bringing that little boy back." She paused. "If your dream was true, at least your child is alive somewhere. At least we can find her."

Julia could hardly believe what she had just said. She certainly hadn't meant to say it. For one thing, she had little confidence in Carmen's dream. But the words were spoken. Not *we might be able* to find her, but *we can* find her, as if it were a plan already laid, not a mere potentiality. In all of their talk the night before, neither of them had mentioned such a thing. They had gone through the girl's confinement at the Shelburns' house, the birth, the following days, every part Carmen could remember, some of it multiple times, but had looked only at the past, not the days to come.

THEY both knew the original purpose of the trip had evaporated, of course. The drives from one author's home to another, the reservations for lodging along the way, and then the flight home—it all seemed totally trivial now, though the irony was not lost on Julia that they were scheduled to fly out of Hartford, of all places.

In the planning stages, Hartford had been a point of some mild contention between them, yet one Julia wouldn't concede for some reason. Carmen had tried to dissuade her by saying Mark Twain's house "wasn't really all that much to see," but Julia said leaving Mark Twain out of an American authors' tour was like leaving red out of the color wheel. Besides that, she said, she wanted to see that carved headboard Mark Twain used as a footboard.

But now these words: *At least we can find her.* Julia had opened her mouth, and out they had fallen, without a single thought as to how the two of them could ever do such a thing.

The room was growing lighter, and Julia could see Carmen better now. It didn't take long to realize what she was doing. Still on her back, she was turning her head slowly, deliberately from side to side on her pillow. And when she spoke, her words, too, were deliberate, and full of feeling: "She would be two years old now. Part of a family. I couldn't barge in and interrupt their lives. I couldn't and I wouldn't."

"Let's back up," Julia said. "You're forgetting something very important. If you were lied to, the baby was *stolen* from you. That was a crime in every sense of the word."

Carmen's answer was firm. "But let's back up even further. Here's something else important. I broke God's law. Do I want to break a family apart, too?"

Forget God's law for just a minute, Julia wanted to scream, but she gritted her teeth and said nothing. It was maddeningly clear that the girl had thought this through and made up her mind. And she was right up to a point. If the child was indeed alive, she had surely been adopted. And if there had been a legal adoption—well, as legal as it could be given the heinous lie—or even if by some other technicality it wasn't legal, the transfer had been made. The child was part of a family.

Julia rose from the bed and walked to the window. She pulled back the draperies and saw the shadowy outline of Boston beneath a pale amethyst sky. She wondered if they would even notice the clear skies today. She turned and went into the bathroom. Maybe a hot shower would help her think.

T HEY were downstairs by eight o'clock, sitting at a table in the small dining area with their complimentary breakfast. While Julia stirred brown sugar into her oatmeal, Carmen bowed her head. And just what, Julia wondered, would she be saying to God this morning? *Help me to feel sufficiently unworthy again today, not to forget for a minute what I did, and not to let Aunt Julia offer me even a smidge of comfort?*

They ate without talking for a while. "If nothing else, you need to find out the truth," Julia said at last.

Carmen had finished her yogurt and was opening her pint of milk. Her eyes looked even bluer today. She was wearing a turquoise corduroy shirt that used to be Julia's, along with a brown-striped sweater. Certainly nothing Julia had ever worn together, but as always the clothes looked better on Carmen than they ever had on Julia.

She glanced at Julia. "And the truth shall set you free."

Julia pondered her words. They sounded promising. She repeated them: "Yes, and the truth shall set you free."

"Look not every man on his own desires," Carmen added. "Love your neighbor as yourself. Do not use your freedom as a cloak of evil. You were called to be free, but not free to indulge your sinful nature."

Oh, only more double-talk from the Bible. "Setting aside your sinful nature," Julia said, "let's think about this logically."

Carmen didn't look like she wanted to talk about logic right now. She was having trouble getting the carton open and had taken a plastic knife to it.

Julia leaned forward. "If you never know for sure," she said, "you will always wonder. Your mind will always be unsettled, your nights full of more visions and voices, your soul a slave to uncertainty. You will never be able to give yourself wholly to any task because part of your heart will always be off somewhere, wandering about the hills and dales of possibility. Despair will surely come to darken all the days of your life."

Part of her believed everything she was saying, though another part recognized the little speech for what it was: windy oratory. It was exactly the kind of thing that used to issue forth in the middle of one of her class lectures, totally unplanned, rendered with a slight loftiness that could easily earn a professor a reputation among students as "out of touch."

At first Carmen showed no sign of having heard a word. She had succeeded in forcing a ragged opening in the top of the carton. She poured the milk in a small trickle over her Cheerios, then picked up a spoon and slowly lifted her eyes to Julia's. Sometimes, as now, when she was most serious, she set her mouth in such a way that her dimple showed. She took a deep breath. "It's been over two years," she said again. "I don't know where she is."

"But you know where she was born," Julia said. "We can start there."

Carmen shook her head. "I . . . just couldn't, Aunt Julia. You said something that day in your car, when you came looking for me. I asked you a question, and you said, 'I forfeited my right to motherhood.' Do you remember that? Well, okay, I can say the same thing."

"I have a plan," Julia said. "Hear me out. You need to *know* for sure. If she really did die, you need to know that, but if she didn't, we can find her and you can at least *see* her. From a distance. No big scene to call attention to yourself or make anybody uneasy."

The plan was still under construction, maybe completely improbable, most likely imprudent. But if they could only observe the child, maybe happily involved in play, might that not help Carmen in time come to terms with her guilt?

At least she had the girl's attention now. She was chewing slowly, her head cocked, her brow furrowed, clearly thinking over what Julia had just said.

Even now Julia was formulating a larger point she could make, something that would resonate with a person like Carmen: *If your God is merciful, as you claim,* she would say, *then surely he would show mercy to an innocent child. And surely he would allow you to see his mercy in her life.* And she would push it further. *And if he is the master of the universe, as you also claim, can he not repair as well as create? Can he not mend your sad heart?* And somehow she would link that thought with this: *Sometimes the same thing can bring good and ill. Take rain, for example. Floods can destroy things, but sometimes after rain, good things happen, too. Crops can grow and flowers bloom and rainbows spread across the sky.* Oh, yes, she could wax eloquent with a thought like this. A little bit of metaphorical lace to pretty up the speech, to draw attention away from the fact that she was touting the power and goodness of a God whose very existence she had never avowed.

But she would wait for all that. The breakfast room was starting to fill up. A couple with a sulky-looking teenage girl set their plates down at the table next to theirs. The girl had a silver ring in one nostril and straight, stiff hair the color of a radish.

"And what if . . ." Carmen started, but a yowl of dismay rose from another table nearby. Someone had just dumped a whole plate of scrambled eggs and hash browns on the floor. A worker appeared to help clean it up.

Carmen and Julia fell silent and finished their breakfast quickly.

SOMETIME later that morning they were headed west from Boston on Highway 20—the same basic route as the turnpike, but without the tolls. It wouldn't be a long trip to Danforth, under three hours.

Julia put in a CD titled *Solely Slowly*, a collection of adagio pieces—something that should make an easy background for thought as well as something to imply that she didn't want to talk. It was evidently a sentiment Carmen shared, for she put her seat back and closed her eyes.

As she drove, Julia's mind went over and over the same thoughts. She wished she knew more about the legal aspects of adoption, how the whole process worked, where the records were kept, who had access to them. There were probably different laws for different states. She had heard about open versus closed adoptions, but in a case like Carmen's there wouldn't have been such a discussion.

Even if they somehow managed to find out where the child was, no small *if*, the plan was still fraught with danger. What if they saw the child happy and healthy, well provided for by doting parents?

Wouldn't Carmen be likely to feel even more keenly the loss of what could have been hers?

Or what if they saw the child but she didn't seem happy and well cared for? Or what if their search ended with the discovery that Carmen had been told the truth, that the baby had died at birth? Another very real and unhappy possibility, one sure to reignite Carmen's thoughts about the wages of sin.

These were all questions for which there were no answers. Not on this side of the journey. Like everything else in life, you couldn't know what was at the end of the trip unless you packed your bags and set out.

They had driven less than half an hour when Carmen sat up and said, "Hey, I thought I was supposed to drive after we left Boston. I'm going to forget how if you don't let me. Besides, I can't just sit here, I need to *do* something." Julia had gotten behind the wheel out of habit, but she didn't mind trading places. The route was easy, and traffic wasn't bad, certainly nothing the girl couldn't handle. So she pulled off and Carmen took over.

The CD of *adagios* and *largos* was still playing. Maybe it had helped to discourage conversation, but it certainly hadn't provided a very soothing background, for today Julia was hearing things she had never noticed before—a flute obbligato that wailed like a cold wind down a chimney, a ponderous bass line that labored like an aging heart, a percussive effect like the whirring of bat wings, a trumpet with a scalpel edge. Even her favorite pieces—Albinoni's *Adagio in G Minor*, Massenet's *Meditation*—failed to steady her this time. Off and on for no good reason, she kept imagining a scene out of Edgar Allan Poe, a deathly slow masquerade ball with an evil presence floating among the dancers. Strange sensations for the dazzle of a perfect October day.

The plan began to seem less feasible with each passing mile,

Julia's responsibility for error more profound. She wondered if Carmen's mind was full of the same doubts. More than once she came close to raising her voice above the music: *Stop, this is all wrong. Let's rethink this.*

But each time she held back: *No, keep quiet. Stay the course.* Besides, if they didn't continue on their way to Danforth, what would they do while they waited around for their flight home? Or should they pay to change their reservations and go straight home? Or drive to Hartford and sit in a hotel for five days?

Hartford was another problem, but one Julia couldn't think about now. She had no idea how Carmen felt about returning there, whether she would want to see her old haunts or avoid them altogether. She had claimed to love the boy; maybe she thought she still did. Regardless, she must be curious about him.

But Julia could only wonder. She wouldn't think of asking such things. For herself, she felt the urge to look the boy in the eye— well, he would be twenty-five now, hardly a boy. She wanted to tell him what he had done to Carmen, tell his parents, announce it to the whole church. She couldn't imagine being so bold, but her outrage was so great she felt she could.

For now, however, Hartford would have to wait. One town, one weighty memory at a time. First, Danforth, Massachusetts. But as the last piece on the CD played—Samuel Barber's famous *Adagio for Strings*—she imagined over and over all the different ways their quest could fail.

AFTER the CD ended, they drove on in silence. Julia's mind drifted to an article she and Carmen had read weeks ago in which a backpacker across Europe had written about his travels and urged readers to "leave home and watch yourself grow." She remembered one of the last things he had said—something about the need to take a picture of yourself before leaving home so you would have a record of who you used to be, for you would certainly be someone different when you returned.

Carmen had made a joke of it at the time, had even taken pictures of the two of them. They were on Julia's cell phone right now—Carmen, lounging on the glider, clownish, her eyes crossed, tongue sticking out the side of her mouth; herself, sedate and cautious, sitting in her wicker rocking chair with a book in her lap. That day on the porch seemed like eons ago.

And now Julia had already lost her way to whatever big idea she was trying to reach. More useless woolgathering. It was so exasperating when she needed to be thinking clearly.

She must have made a sound, for Carmen glanced over. "What? Is something wrong? Are you as scared as I am?"

"There's nothing to be scared about," Julia said. "We're just going to see what we can find out." Calm and confident—that was the tone she was trying for, though she felt neither. She turned the radio on, then leaned her head back and closed her eyes. There was a sudden burst of audience laughter and applause.

It was a weekly quiz show on NPR called *Wait Wait . . . Don't Tell Me!* She listened, but not with interest. All the quiz questions seemed silly: *Which product did Vincent Price's grandfather invent? Tootsie rolls, contact lenses, or baking powder?* A year from now who would remember what the answer was? Or care?

But the radio stayed on anyway. The program ended, and another followed, called *Whad'ya Know?* More trivialities, including an interview with a professional chef who had worked at the White House for twenty years. The chef told about finding Richard Nixon in the kitchen one time making himself a sandwich at two A.M. "Another one of those late-night break-ins he liked so much," the host quipped. All the repartee was too pat, the audience laughter too quick, probably prompted by a lighted sign that read *Laugh now*. The whole thing was like a rehearsed skit.

Yet she left the program on all the way to the end.

T HEY stopped for gas in Springfield, Massachusetts, and ordered a sandwich for lunch at a place called Friendly's, where the waiter, ironically, wasn't. As she had done at every restaurant on their trip, Carmen asked for sweet tea, knowing what the answer would be but interested in the waiters' various responses. This one pointed to the packets of sugar and sweetener on the table and said tersely, "We have *those*."

They ate quickly and were done within half an hour. As they were getting back into their car outside the restaurant, a black van pulled in beside them, and a swarm of children spilled out the side doors. A big, jolly man got out of the driver's seat and started corralling them while a woman leaned into the backseat and unbuckled a toddler and a baby. Carmen waited until the way was clear and backed out slowly. Across the rear window of the black van, twelve stick-figure decals were lined up side by side—two parents, eight children, and two dogs. Julia knew Carmen saw the decals, was probably even counting them. Maybe she had a contest going and this was some kind of record.

Back on Highway 20, the opera was on now. Today it was *La Bohème*, but it was nothing Julia wanted to hear. She fell to thinking about the place where they were headed, and what had happened there. Even if they found that the baby really had died, there was no question in Julia's mind by now that Milo and Joyce Shelburn had been up to no good.

She had already compiled a list of adjectives for them: *hypocritical, greedy, oppressive, authoritarian,* and of course *pious* and *virtuous* in their most negative sense. And *villainous*. Julia's words, all of them. None came from Carmen. Her word was a mild one: *strict*.

Though Carmen had believed them in the end, the things she told were more than enough to let Julia know what they were really like. More than anything, it was the pressure they had brought to bear on the girl, when she wouldn't commit to adoption, that convinced Julia they were not to be trusted.

The Shelburns had a speech they gave over and over. It would be unfair to the baby to have a single girl like Carmen for a parent, someone without a home or a job or a car. How was she going to take care of it, feed it, clothe it, get it to the doctor when it was sick? What kind of life could she give a child? And so forth. And think of all the good Christian couples who wanted a baby but couldn't have one—how unfair to deprive them.

Unfair to the baby, unfair to the childless couples, but never a word about the unfairness of taking a baby away from her mother. They weren't used to "balky girls." That was what Milo had told Carmen.

They had narrowed the choice of adoptive couples to four, whom they claimed to be "good matches," which Carmen thought was odd since she had told them so little about herself and nothing at all about the father. They magnanimously told her she could have the final word about which couple got the baby, but she kept saying no, she couldn't meet with any of them yet, she needed more time.

But the strongest evidence in Julia's opinion had to do with the papers Carmen wouldn't sign. "You know, the ones agreeing to an adoption," she had said when Julia questioned her. "They kept trying, and I kept saying the same thing—I had to pray about it some more. And Milo kept saying I didn't need to pray about a *promise*, which I didn't remember ever making in the first place."

Julia didn't know much about adoption, but one thing she did know was that papers like that were signed by a birth mother only after a child was born, never before. And she was pretty sure the mother usually had a certain amount of time even after signing to change her mind. Poor, young, ignorant pregnant girls wouldn't necessarily know this, however.

If she didn't agree to place the baby, they told Carmen, she would have to pay them back for room and board and medical care. Another way to pressure a girl who didn't know better. They kept reminding her, too, of the money they would give her when she left—without the baby—to help her start a new life.

All of this, and yet Carmen had taken their lie to be true. All because they had acted sympathetic when they told her the baby had died. Incredible.

It was almost beyond belief that things like this could happen today, especially in a liberal, progressive state like Massachusetts, which surely must have watchdogs to keep adoption agencies honest. But perhaps it was also true that those who knew the adoption laws best were also best equipped to circumvent them, to resort to duping if a girl refused to cooperate.

O N the radio, a tenor was singing an aria now. Julia turned it down. She was curious about something. "Why didn't you just leave the Shelburns' house and ask someone else for help?" she asked the girl.

Carmen looked puzzled. "Well . . . it never crossed my mind to leave," she said.

"Why? You weren't happy there," Julia said.

Carmen shrugged. "But I didn't blame that on them. I got used to living there. They weren't . . . malicious. They didn't beat me or anything. They let me take walks into town, and I went to church with them—a little church just down the road from their house. They were members there." She paused. "And they were letting me live there free—that's a big thing when you're homeless and pregnant."

Well, yes, of course. That was the only part that made at least a little sense.

· *chapter 20* ·

Lost Children

They drove on in silence and passed through the village of Woronoco, Massachusetts, on the Westfield River—the entrance to Jacob's Ladder, a scenic byway along a thirty-five-mile stretch of Highway 20. Julia looked at the trees along the road, at the height of their autumn pageantry—originally one of the big reasons for this whole trip—yet the view somehow looked more like a flat photograph than a real scene.

Carmen broke the silence. "They have a lot of goat farms up here."

So the girl wanted to talk now. Julia didn't reply.

Another mile or two went by, and then Carmen said, "They make cashmere out of goat hair. But not these kinds of goats."

The briefest pause, then, "Did you know Gil saw his grandmother shot in the back in Poland when he was only six?"

The only Gil Julia knew was her yard man, but she certainly didn't know anything about his grandmother being shot. Sometime in the summer Carmen had taken to working outdoors with

Gil on Tuesdays, and from time to time Julia had seen them standing in the driveway by his truck, talking. She had wondered what kinds of things a peculiar little man like Gil would say to a girl like Carmen. She guessed she knew now.

They drove through Russell and then Crescent, quintessential New England at its picturesque best, yet Julia couldn't even say she felt appreciative, much less awed. Traffic was heavier now, and slower. Clearly they weren't the only tourists driving Jacob's Ladder today.

They entered the town of Huntington, and Carmen slowed to a crawl as they approached the town square. Julia looked at her watch. "Let's stop," she said. "I need to sit awhile."

Carmen laughed. "Uh . . . aren't you already sitting?"

Julia pointed to a gazebo next to a white church. "There. Let's just sit and look around awhile." *And put off getting to Danforth a little longer*—she could have said that, too. But no need for Carmen to know how nervous she was getting.

Carmen pulled into a parking place in front of the white church. Two children were chasing each other around the gazebo while their mother waited for them on the sidewalk.

After a few moments Carmen said, "Did I tell you I peeked ahead in that book—*Ethan Frome*? I should've expected that sled accident, but I didn't." A pause. "Poor old Zeena—I felt sorry for her. She was so . . . hypochondriacal. Is that a word?" She tried a couple of different pronunciations, then laughed. "I went sledding once in Maine. I was holding this dog in my lap, but he flipped out. Both ways."

If the girl had to talk, which apparently she did, at least Julia was glad she was content to carry the whole conversation by herself.

"Hoosier had a hot dog stand in downtown Chicago," she continued. "Well, *supposedly*. I never found him."

Hoosier? All Julia could think of was the state of Indiana.

As if she read her mind, Carmen said, "Lulu's real father. That was his name—Hoosier. I looked for him when I was passing through, but I finally gave up and left." She made a whistling sound. "They don't call that the Windy City for nothing, I'll tell you." A pause and a sigh. "Hoosier Leland LaPierre—that was his name." She said it again, slowly. "*Hoo-sier Le-land La-Pi-erre.* Kind of . . . classy, isn't it?"

Oh, yes, a classy hot dog merchant. Julia glanced at the radio, wondering if it would seem rude to turn it on. There was always an interesting follow-up program after the opera on NPR. Maybe that would quiet the girl, ground her flights of thought.

"I wonder how Josette is," Carmen said.

At least Julia knew who this was. Since the day at the zoo, Carmen had mentioned the little French girl several times.

"Every kid needs a father," Carmen said.

A *good* father, Julia wanted to say. She wondered what Carmen would say if she told her she used to climb under the covers as a child, after angry words and tears, and wish her father would die.

"I heard my daddy sing a song once called 'The Ballad of the Lost Child,'" Carmen said. "Only once. He was playing his guitar. He and Lulu were in their bedroom. They didn't know I was listening, but I heard every word. Did you know that song? I remember Lulu crying, telling him never to sing it again, it was too awful."

Julia leaned her head back and closed her eyes. Maybe Carmen would think she needed to rest and quit talking. She did know the song, and Lulu was right, it was awful—the story of a little boy whose family died off one at a time. And finally, as could be expected in a ballad, the boy, dressed only in rags, also died in the coldest part of winter. Broke through the ice on a frozen lake and drowned. Tragic tripe. Julia still remembered the tune, in a minor key naturally, and all the words. They came back to her now, all of them, down to the last sorry lines: *No one to hear his fearful cry, No one to take his hand.*

It was the song Julia hadn't been able to get out of her head after Jeremiah left home. She would close her eyes and imagine him facing all the worst disasters, alone. Even many years later when they knew he was alive and well, living with a woman and child in Wyoming, she would still sometimes hear the melody when she was lying awake in the middle of the night. Lost children—the saddest thought in the world. And children could be lost in so many ways.

Carmen stopped talking, and they sat quietly for several minutes. Julia opened her eyes again. The mother and the two children had left by now. A matronly-looking woman in a long ashy-gray coat and black lace-up shoes walked by in front of the car, looking down at the sidewalk as she stepped carefully, a large black purse swaying from the crook of her arm.

"That woman looks a little like Stephen's mother," Carmen said. Julia wondered if she meant to say *grandmother*, but she didn't ask. They watched the woman proceed down the street, and then Carmen resumed. "Here's something I didn't tell you. One day when the Shelburns weren't home, I called Stephen. I remembered his phone number. His mother answered. He wasn't home, but I talked to her a little while. She remembered me, said they all missed me at church. She asked if I was okay."

She was running a finger around and around the steering wheel. "It was only a week or two before the baby came," she said. "I suddenly had this wild hope that maybe he and the other girl had . . . *un*pledged, or whatever. I imagined us moving to the West somewhere and living together in our own little house. Painted white. And being a real family." A long pause, and then, "I didn't tell his mother why I was calling. Especially not after she told me she would give everybody at church my greetings, and Stephen, too, the next time they talked—and, oh, by the way, he'd moved to Boston after his wedding a month ago. He had a new job."

No hint of self-pity. The girl lifted her head and looked toward the gazebo. "I don't even remember if I said good-bye to her before I hung up," she added.

Julia could feel the cold seeping into the car. She looked at her watch and saw that only seven minutes had passed. And to think—before Stephen and the little white house out West, the girl had been talking about goats and a man who ran a hot dog stand. Well, she had also talked about lost children.

Within a few minutes they had left Huntington and were making their way slowly toward Chester, then Lee, and from there due north toward Danforth.

D ANFORTH, Massachusetts, was a small town on the Housatonic River in the Berkshire Hills. As they neared it, Carmen began talking again. She knew the town well, had explored it from one end to the other during her stay with the Shelburns. As winter melted into spring and all throughout the summer, she had seen it all—snow, then buds and flowers, even the earliest tinges of autumn color by the time she finally left.

The Shelburns called it wanderlust—Carmen's compulsion to walk about town and countryside every day—but the girl herself called it survival. They agreed to her walking but sternly instructed her not to talk to people. Everyone around here was nosy, they said, and in radical left-wing states like Massachusetts, people disliked anyone with unshakable morals. And adoptions were very private matters, they said, so if anyone asked questions about Babies First Mission or her situation personally, she was not allowed to answer. As it was a small exchange for freedom, Carmen agreed. And they evidently trusted her, for they let her come and go as she pleased.

Every day she rose early and did her assigned duties. As thorough as she was, and as quick to spot other tasks to do without being told, there was little for Milo and Joyce to complain about. The Shelburns' house was on the northern end of town, set back off the road leading to an abandoned paper mill. Milo had purchased the cottage from the former mill owner years earlier and had renovated it room by room. It was sturdy and trim, impeccably maintained, for Milo was very particular.

The nearest neighbors lived a mile away in a yellow house next to the church the Shelburns attended. Carmen liked the pastor, obviously more than the Shelburns did, for Milo always spent a good part of Sunday dinner pointing out the flaws in that morning's sermon.

The yellow house, once the parsonage, was now occupied by two single women in their early sixties about whom the Shelburns had strong suspicions, which they frequently voiced. They might be their nearest neighbors, but they weren't about to make any friendly overtures toward the likes of them.

To Julia, New England seemed like an improbable place for people like the Shelburns, with their Bible Belt mentality, except for the fact that it must have given them ample opportunity to feel superior to everyone else. They would surely have put an end to Carmen's walks had they known that she often stopped at the yellow house on her way into town. Sheila and Hope were the two women who lived there, and the girl sat in their kitchen sometimes for as long as an hour eating their bran and raisin muffins and drinking an herbal tea they grew, one they claimed especially effective for developing a baby's immune system. And talking, of course.

Through their kitchen window over the years, the two women had observed other girls come and go in the company of the Shelburns on Sundays, but none of those other girls had ever walked past their house. For certain none of them had ever opened their gate, entered their yard, pointed to the herb garden Hope was tending, and said, "What are their names?" the way Carmen had. Without looking up, Hope had touched each plant and spoken its name softly, except for the last four, which she sang in a hauntingly beautiful voice: "Parsley, sage, rosemary, and thyme." Carmen recognized the song, of course, for it was one Jeremiah used to sing.

Sheila said they had learned over the years to mind their own business; thus it was no struggle for Carmen to keep her promise about answering questions, for they never asked any.

Carmen sometimes sang with them in the kitchen or on the back porch. Sheila and Hope both played guitar and had given concerts during their hippie days. They taught Carmen some of their songs, and she taught them some of Jeremiah's.

The Shelburns wouldn't have liked the singing either, for in their opinion, any music other than religious and classical was what the Devil played as he led men to hell. And he didn't play a pipe like the Pied Piper; he played a guitar. Carmen had once heard Milo say the only thing guitars were good for was kindling.

All of these facts Carmen imparted as they drove to Danforth. When at last they came to the southern edge of town, she took a deep breath and said, "Well, here we are. It feels . . . surreal." A sign read, *Welcome to Danforth—Home of David Wentworth Haggerty, Beloved Poet of the Berkshires.* As they made their way slowly through the main street, Carmen pointed out places of interest and remarked on a few changes that had taken place since she left.

From the looks of things, Julia concluded that the locals could meet their basic needs here but just barely. A general store, a small diner, a post office. A large boulder beside a flagpole bore a prominent inscription: *Hereupon stood Richard Clay Danforth to deliver his famous Call to Courageous and Humane Action—November 6, 1861.*

"And there's the library," Carmen said, stopping the car in front of what looked like a rust-red clapboard saltbox cottage at the end of a slate walkway. A large sign near the curb identified the building as *The Lottie Cowell Sinclair Memorial Library*, along with a brief biography of the woman, founder of the first one-room school in the region. Clearly, one thing could be said for Danforth: It was proud of the achievements of its citizenry.

"I slept and ate at the Shelburns' house," Carmen said, "but this is where I *lived*." She pointed. "That was my window up there—second floor, far right."

She couldn't begin to guess how many hours she had spent here, but whenever she wasn't at the Shelburns' house or visiting Sheila and Hope or roaming about the fields and hills, this was where she came. She sat in the same old leather armchair every day, beside the same window looking out toward the Housatonic and the hills beyond, and read straight through book after book.

"I wonder if Mrs. Orliss still works there," she said, still gazing at the library. "She was like a hundred years old, but you'd never guess it. I think she knew the call number of every book in the whole library. She had this long gray braid of hair and wore a little blue felt hat every day. She could quote whole sections of *Beowulf* from memory."

Julia said, "Well, before you tell me about her pet bird and her rock collection, let's review the plan again."

There wasn't much to review, but saying it aloud calmed her. To start with, they would stay on the two-lane highway, which Carmen said would take them right past the church. Carmen would get out at Sheila and Hope's house and stay there while Julia drove by herself a mile down the road to pay a visit to the Shelburns.

The plan from there would necessitate some misrepresentation, of course. Julia was still trying to decide what she would actually say when the door opened and she was face-to-face with Joyce or

Milo. She had considered several ways to start the conversation—
which lie to lead with.

It suddenly occurred to her that whereas she had rarely wished
ill of anyone in her life, except her father, there were now numbers
of people upon whom she could inflict suffering without compunc-
tion. She could picture it—every person who had failed or misused
Carmen in any way since Jeremiah's death, standing in a row like
targets, and herself with dead-eye aim, armed with a dart gun.
There was no question that she would have made a horrible parent.
For every offense her child suffered, she would have wanted to
avenge it tenfold.

Carmen drove past the scattered houses on the north end of
Danforth. No more talking now. From the look on her face, only
deep thinking, or more likely deep praying, with some fear mixed
in. They passed stands of trees ablaze with fall color, fields with a
few cows, a shabby barn. Carmen slowed as they approached the
church. The parking lot was empty. Next to it, the front door of the
yellow house stood partly open, and a mud-splattered white Subaru
sat in the driveway.

"They're home," Carmen said. She pulled onto the shoulder of
the road and looked at Julia. "Remember, second road on the right
about a mile down. There used to be a sign, but it was hard to see.
Old Mill Road. Watch the odometer. If you go much over a mile,
you missed it. I'll be waiting for you back here."

"Do you want to make sure they're here first?" Julia said, glancing at the yellow house.

"They are," Carmen said. She gave Julia's hand a quick squeeze
before getting out of the car. "You're not afraid to go by yourself,
are you? I could ask Sheila to go with you."

But Julia said no, she was fine. The Shelburns might disgust her,
but they didn't scare her. Before pulling away, she looked back at

the house. A tall, stout woman was standing on the front stoop now, head to one side, hands on her hips.

J ULIA found the turnoff easily and followed a narrow, winding road until she came to the house. If Carmen hadn't told her it was the only house on Old Mill Road, she would have thought it was the wrong one. The road was a dead end, Carmen had said, two poles and a chain blocking the way to the mill, which had long ago fallen to ruin.

Julia saw the poles and chain, but the house was nothing like she was expecting. From Carmen's description, she had imagined something tidier. This house had a tired, sprawling look, as if some force of nature had picked it up and slung it back down. A pickup truck with a smashed tailgate was parked next to the side door, and bedsheets and pillowcases were flapping on the clothesline.

She pulled up behind the truck and got out of the car. It felt colder and darker amid all the trees. The solemn faces of two children stared at her through a front window. A man pushed open the side door and stood at the top of the steps. He appeared to be in his thirties but was wearing the clothes of an old man—a baggy pair of faded overalls and what looked like the top to a pair of dirty long johns. In one hand he held a kitchen knife covered with something. A large black dog materialized from somewhere and approached Julia with a throaty growl. Through the screen door a thin, witchy voice spoke. "Bobo, you behave!"

The man gave a single sharp whistle and said something. The dog slunk under the truck and lay down.

The whole thing could have been a scene from the backwoods of South Carolina or Georgia. Julia didn't know who these people were, but she felt quite sure they weren't the Shelburns. Still standing by the car, she called over the wind. "I'm looking for Joyce and Milo Shelburn. I thought they lived here. This was the address I was given. Do you know where I can find them?"

The man shook his head and jerked a thumb toward the side door. "We're the Crockers. We live here now. But you can't come in, the wife's sick in the bed."

"Did the Shelburns move?" Julia asked.

The man laughed and spit something over the railing. "I guess you might could say that."

An older woman came out the side door, wiping her hands on her apron. "What does she want? She's not selling something, is she?" It was the same reedy voice that had scolded the dog.

The man scowled at her. "Get on back inside. She's just looking for the folks that used to live here."

The old woman squinted at Julia. "You can't collect from us," she said. "We didn't even know them."

One of the children was outside now, leaning against the man. He looked down and snapped a finger. "Go see what your mama wants. I hear her. All this racket has woke her up." The old woman and child disappeared inside.

Julia's mind was spinning. This certainly wasn't in the plan. They hadn't thought of the possibility that the Shelburns might have moved away.

But there was still hope. "Do you know where the Shelburns are living now?" Julia asked. "Or do you know anybody who might know?" It dawned on her that the post office in town would probably have a forwarding address.

The man licked one side of the knife he was holding, then laughed again. "They're not *living* anywhere. They're six feet under." He bobbed his head toward the highway. "Little piece down the road in a graveyard."

Julia was speechless. She watched the man lick the other side of the knife, then finally said the only words she could think of. "What . . . happened?"

"They got shot dead. In a grocery store over in Pittsfield. Some crazy pulled a gun and started shooting. The mister, he throwed his wife down and laid on top of her, they said, but they both got shot anyhow. Right in the middle of the produce aisle."

Julia was filled with sudden shame at the flippant scenario she had imagined only minutes ago—using the Shelburns and others for target practice. Now she had a sick feeling. "Did they . . . catch him?" she asked. "The one who did it?"

The man shrugged. "He killed hisself at the end. That store was full of dead bodies just strowed everywhere. Didn't you hear about it? It was all over the TV. They called it the Price Chopper Massacre."

Julia's face must have registered horror because the man softened. He laid the knife down on top of the wooden railing, then came down the steps and stood by the pickup truck. "Was they friends of yours?" From inside the house Julia heard a shrill cry. The man turned his head briefly. "She's in a bad fix."

Trouble all around, Julia thought. People sick and suffering. Other people going on killing sprees. Others dying in the middle of a grocery store aisle. And Carmen—left without a clue about her baby.

"No, they weren't friends of mine," Julia said. "I didn't know them, but my niece did. I had some questions to ask them."

"They auctioned off the house, and we got it," the man offered. He looked up at the trees. "Away back here all by itself, but we don't mind. Not much. Gets bad in the winter, though. The wife, she grew up around here. Snow don't bother her. Me, I'm from Kentucky."

"When did all this happen?" Julia said. "To the Shelburns, I mean?"

The man thought a moment. "Just right about two year, same time as now. Maybe a little later." He looked up into the trees. "We been living here going on a year."

Julia considered the timing—so it had been shortly after Carmen left. She couldn't help thinking if it had happened earlier, Carmen might have a little girl today. But it hadn't and she didn't.

"The wife took sick in the spring, been going downhill since," the man said. He put a hand to his ear and listened again to another long anguished cry from indoors. "Her mama's been here a spell helping us out." He looked back at Julia. "Lost my job going on six month now."

"I'm sorry," Julia said. "I'm really sorry." What else was there to say? This man had his own problems, plenty of them. She looked at the house again. One child was still at the front window. She looked down the road past the house and saw the chain stretched between the two metal posts, with a sign that read *No Trespassing*. A dead end all the way around.

She tried again. "Do you know who cleared out the house before you bought it?"

The man shook his head. "It was empty when it come up for auction."

She knew what the answer would be, but she had to ask. "No papers or file cabinets left behind by any chance?"

He shook his head again.

Julia opened the door of her car and got in. The man started back to the steps. Julia pulled a twenty-dollar bill out of her purse and got out again. "Wait," she said. She put the money in the man's hand. "This won't buy much, but maybe it will help."

He stared at it, nodding. "It'll help. It sure will. I'm obliged."

Julia turned the car around and headed back toward the highway. In the rearview mirror she saw the man walking back toward the house, his head bent. Above her, the roof of trees hid the sky, their branches thrashing in the wind.

· *chapter 21* ·

LONG, PURPOSEFUL JOURNEYS

Carmen was waiting at the front door of the yellow house when Julia returned. She waved her inside. She had already told Sheila and Hope why she was here in Danforth—about her dream, her suspicions. And Sheila had told her about the Shelburns. The girl looked dazed. "So much has happened since I left," she said. "Come on in. They're in the kitchen."

Julia had never been in a house with so little space for moving around. The living room looked like a used furniture store. Two couches sat back to back in the center of the room, and lined up against one wall were assorted chairs, stools, tables. Dozens of cardboard boxes and a massive mahogany china cabinet took up most of another wall. A rocking chair was pulled up to face the bay window, in which a veritable jungle of houseplants thrived, long snaky vines spilling down to the floor.

Across the dining room table was spread a mishmash of pottery, linens, record albums, carpentry tools. An old phonograph cabinet, its lid propped open, stood near the doorway into the kitchen, and an LP was playing—a woman's voice, soulful and slow, with a saxophone accompaniment, something about a starry night and a broken heart.

In the kitchen, a plate of pumpkin muffins and mugs of hot cider sat on the table, and Sheila was clearing off one end to make more room. She was a big-boned woman, with a broad, serene face and a thick hank of washed-out auburn hair. After introductions were made, they all sat down and Julia told about her visit to the house on Old Mill Road. When she stopped, no one spoke for a moment. The song finished on the phonograph and a new one came on, something livelier with maracas and bongo drums.

"We didn't know he'd lost his job," Sheila said. "We took a meal down there after we heard she was sick. Then they had a kitchen fire on top of that." She glanced at Hope. "We need to take something else to them. Maybe some of your beef stew."

"His mother is there helping out," Julia said.

Sheila blew lightly into her mug of cider. "She's got her hands full."

Hope got up and brought a blue teapot and a jar of honey back to the table. In spite of her brusque actions, she was a small, delicate woman, no doubt pretty in her youth. Her hair, streaked with gray, was pulled back loosely from her face. She was wearing jeans, an oversized tweed sweater, and suede boots. She set the jar of honey down hard and slid the teapot over to Carmen and Julia. "Echinacea mint," she announced darkly. These were the first words Julia had heard her speak.

Carmen drained the last of her cider and refilled her mug with tea, then drizzled some honey into it. "I can't believe they're really dead," she said, stirring her tea slowly. "What a horrible way to die. That's the last thing you expect to happen when you go to the grocery store." She sipped a spoonful of tea, then added a little more honey and stirred again. "That was a nice thing Milo did— trying to protect her like that. I guess he really did love her."

Hope stood up again suddenly and went to the stove, where she yanked open the bottom drawer and made a racket pulling out a large pot.

Carmen looked at Julia. "Guess what they told me while you were gone? Babies First Mission closed down. Not long after I left. The Thorntons moved away. Mr. Thornton was the director."

"They retired," Sheila said. "Somewhere in Europe, we heard."

"So I guess we won't be talking to them either," Carmen said. She took another sip of her tea. "But the adoption records have to be somewhere. How does that work?"

"If it was legal, the state would have records somewhere," Sheila said. "But if it wasn't . . ." She shook her head, then told about a book she had read that told the true story of a black-market baby who tried to find his biological parents, with nothing to go on but a fake birth certificate. "There was no proof, except his living self," she said, "that he'd ever been born."

"Did he ever find his parents?" Carmen said.

Sheila shook her head. "People who traffic in human life don't usually leave records lying around."

So why write a book like that? Julia thought. Nobody wants to read about a failed effort. Or hear about it either. Why had Sheila brought it up?

Hope stalked to the refrigerator and got a lump of something, which she unwrapped and threw into the pot.

Sheila said, "But you hear stories all the time about people find- ing their real parents." She put her mug down. "We can find out how to look up birth records and sure give it a try." She propped her elbow on the table and rested her chin on her hand. "But if they told you she died, they wouldn't have put your name on a birth certificate as the mother. Not even a fake birth certificate." She frowned. "And death records—we could check for infant deaths on the day she was born, but I'm guessing we won't find anything there either."

No one spoke for a while. There was a clatter at the counter as Hope looked through a drawer of cooking utensils.

Sheila said to Carmen, "For days we didn't know you were gone. You never even told us good-bye."

Carmen set her spoon down slowly. "I know. I wanted to. And I should have, but . . . it happened fast. I'd lost track of time. I didn't even know how many days had passed, but all of a sudden I just knew I had to leave. Right then. I couldn't stay another minute. I overheard Milo tell Joyce they had to drive to Briggsville, for her to go get her purse, so as soon as they left, I called a taxi and went to Pittsfield. I had a little money of my own. I took the first bus out; I didn't even care where it was headed. And then I took another one, and I finally ended up in Bangor, Maine, and . . . but none of that matters now." She reached across the table and touched Sheila's arm. "I'm sorry. I should've told you."

Sheila looked like she was about to cry. "We could have helped you. We *should* have." She took Carmen's hand in hers. "There's such a thing as minding your business too much. We should have gotten involved."

Carmen shook her head. "Oh, Sheila, it's not your fault. None of it. I don't understand it, but none of it was an accident. I ended up here in Danforth at the Shelburns' house—I don't know why, but I did. My steps were ordered by the Lord."

They all stared at her. Even Hope turned around to glower. Julia couldn't put a name to what she was feeling. *Defeated* was too weak a word. Such a pernicious kind of faith and no way to uproot it. The girl could end up in a slave camp in Outer Mongolia and still think it was somehow God's will.

"We were having all that rain then," Sheila said. "So when we didn't see you for a few days, we didn't think much of it. And then when it stopped and we still didn't see you, we wondered if the baby had come. So we waited a little more—but we waited too long." She let go of Carmen's hand and put her napkin to her eyes. "I watched the church on Sunday, but I never saw the Shelburns' car. I waited another day, then drove down to their house. Milo came to the door, and I asked him if you were okay. He didn't like it. Asked me who wanted to know. I told him *I* did. He said you were gone and hadn't left an address." She shook her head. "They were so strange, both of them."

Carmen said, "But deep down Joyce had a soft heart. Lots softer than Milo's, for sure." She took another drink of tea. "But I don't think either one of them meant me any harm personally. They just thought every baby needed a mother and a father."

Of course. Julia might have expected this, the assigning of a justifiable reason for the Shelburns' evil. Fair-mindedness carried to extremes was the same as wrongheadedness. She sighed and looked toward the window over the sink, which faced the church parking lot and an open field beyond. A cover of mottled gray clouds had moved in, leaving only a pale blue fringe of sky near the horizon.

There was a sizzling sound from the stove as Hope jabbed a spatula at whatever was frying in the pot.

Sheila held up a hand. "Listen to me, honey. People who play God are *bad*. If someone steals a baby—if that's really what happened here—they're thinking of just one thing, and it's *not* what's best for the baby. It's what's best for their pocketbook. Forget that nonprofit thing. Believe me, there was profit involved."

"Well . . . we don't know that for sure," Carmen said.

Julia said, "But two things you do know for sure. First, they said your baby died. You heard them say that, right? Second, you said God told you otherwise." She paused. "So now you don't trust *him*?" She could hardly believe she had said such a thing.

Carmen stared into her tea, but it was clear that the words had sunk in.

THE record on the phonograph ended, and there was a crackly pop as the turntable kept revolving. Hope set the pot on another burner and went out of the room. Soon there were sounds from the living room of cupboard doors being opened and closed, of something heavy being dragged across the floor.

All at once Carmen said, "Luna—she might know something." She looked at Sheila. "Do you have a Pittsfield phone book?"

"Who's Luna?" Sheila said.

"The midwife."

Sheila asked, "You know her last name?"

"I do in fact," Carmen said. "I asked her one day, and she told me. Fiorelli. Isn't that pretty? It means little flowers. Her father was Italian. Luna Fiorelli—I loved it. I told her it was *mellifluous*. We laughed about it. It was the only time I remember seeing her laugh."

Sheila unearthed the phone book from a stack of old magazines and newspapers, but there was no listing for anybody named Fiorelli. Carmen tried different spellings, but still nothing. Sheila called information, but they had no listing either.

Another record was playing now—a bluesy rendition of "Paper Moon." Hope returned to the kitchen with a folded newspaper, which she handed to Sheila.

Sheila looked at it. "I didn't know we still had this." She pointed to a small article at the bottom of the page and passed it across the table to Julia and Carmen.

The newspaper was dated two years earlier. The picture was small, but Carmen recognized the man at once. Together, she and Julia read the brief article, which stated simply that Ernest Thornton, director of Babies First Mission, had made a donation to a Pittsfield charity for low-income housing before closing the adoption agency and retiring with his wife overseas.

Carmen said, "That was nice of him to do that."

"People give money to charities for tax deductions," Julia said. "And sometimes to salve a guilty conscience."

All was quiet except for the sounds of something being chopped on a cutting board.

Suddenly Carmen looked at Julia. "Remember when Uncle Butch told us nobody's personal information is secret anymore? He said if you know how to do it, you can find out almost anything about anybody on the computer."

Julia nodded. It was true, Butch had said that.

"We don't have a computer," Sheila said.

Carmen said, "I know, but Uncle Butch does. He knows computers inside out. He's pretty much a genius." She looked back at Julia. "You have your cell phone handy?"

"He'll want to know why you're looking for her," Julia said.

"I'll tell him," Carmen said.

Julia dug her phone out of her purse and handed it over.

The girl turned it on. "Hey, good deal, it's even charged." She stood up. "I'll be back."

CARMEN walked up and down the length of Sheila and Hope's driveway as she talked on the phone, one hand inside her jacket pocket, her hair whipping around her head. Julia watched from the bay window in the living room, struck by the fact that all it took was a windy day and a little distance to notice how long the girl's hair had grown. And to notice how much more mature she looked now than when she had first shown up at the stone house, though part of that was likely due to things Julia knew about the girl now that she hadn't known then. She stopped to count—not even four months ago. In many ways it seemed more like four years. She looked at her watch again. Time was skewed here, too. It seemed like Carmen had been outside much longer than ten minutes.

It was chilly in the living room. Julia could feel the cold emanating off the bay window. She pulled her cardigan up around her neck and buttoned it. She turned and studied the room—the Old Curiosity Shop, New England style. Everywhere she looked she saw something she hadn't noticed earlier. Late sunlight fell across the floor onto an ornate mirror propped between two recliners. Someone had swiped a hand across its surface, which was thick with dust. A birdcage sat crookedly on a pile of blankets in a corner next to a spinning wheel, and on the mantel sat several large conch shells and a collection of clocks, all of them showing different times.

An enormous calico cat emerged from the narrow, dark hallway that tunneled to the back rooms and padded across the living room and through the doorway leading into the dining room. Seconds later from the kitchen Julia heard Sheila's voice: "There's my Lolly baby! Come here to Mommy, you fat cat."

The phonograph was still going, but someone had turned the volume down. A jazzy trumpet was playing faintly. Julia turned back to the window to watch Carmen. She was still walking, bent against the keening wind with the phone to her ear. The sun had dropped to just above the treetops, and beneath the bank of clouds the sky was going red around the edges.

Carmen reached the far end of the driveway, made a quick turn, and started back, the wind behind her now. Julia wished she hadn't gone outside. She wanted to hear her side of the conversation. No doubt Pamela was standing right next to Butch, listening in. No, she had probably switched it to speakerphone so she wouldn't miss a word. She was probably bombarding Carmen with questions.

Here was another way Julia wouldn't have made a good parent. She would have driven a child to desperation, hovering, advising, watching like a hawk for any sign of trouble, leaping to wild, panicky conclusions. Though she wouldn't have been openly nosy the way Pamela was, she would have been very capable of reading diaries and listening in on phone conversations. She would have worried endlessly.

As she watched, she saw the girl lift her head and laugh. Maybe it was the funnel of autumn leaves suddenly spawned by the wind and sent whirling across the front yard, or maybe it was something Butch or Pam had said. But then Julia saw what it was—a V of dark geese flying low against the gray clouds, their great wings laboring, their honks a muffled chorus. Carmen stopped walking and with her index finger traced their flight across the sky.

Migrating birds fascinated her. She could talk about them for hours, as well as all kinds of other creatures that made long, purposeful journeys. Butterflies, salmon, whales. Only weeks ago they had watched a program on the History Channel about the dog team that ran six hundred miles to carry a supply of diphtheria serum to sick children in Nome, Alaska, many years ago. Though that had been a trip supervised by men, it still won her admiration. At the end Carmen had looked at Julia, her eyes glowing. "I wish I could have been one of the mushers on that trip, don't you? Watching those dogs just keep on and on and on for such a good cause—how inspiring!" Julia assured her that she wished nothing of the kind.

Carmen finally headed inside, and Julia moved from the window to the dining room table, where she pretended to be looking through the stacks of old LPs. The jazz album was still playing, now a souped-up clarinet rendition of the Beatles' "Yesterday." Such a gorgeous, yearning tune. Such simple words. *Why she had to go, I don't know, she wouldn't say. I said something wrong, now I long for yesterday.* Like most songs written by young people, it spoke of such small sorrows, nothing close to the kind they would face later, after weathering their first heartbreaks.

She didn't look up when Carmen came in. She tried to sound casual. "So I guess you told them."

Carmen sat down on the dining room floor and leaned her head back against the wall. "I told them everything," she said. "They were . . . incredulous." She laughed. "But not speechless. Definitely not speechless. Especially Aunt Pam. Uncle Butch doesn't think Luna will be hard to track down. He's getting right on it. He knows about search engines most people have never heard of. He'll call back as soon as he finds out something." With both hands she gathered up her hair and scrunched it into a bushy ponytail. "It's a good thing I called when I did. They were just getting ready to go bowling."

Julia tried to form a picture of her sister and brother-in-law bowling. It wasn't anything she would want to watch from behind.

"I'm so nervous I can hardly stand it," Carmen said. She let go of her hair and shook it out. "He's going to check birth records, too, but he doesn't think we'll get anywhere with that. Even if it wasn't done under the table, birth certificates for adoptions are usually amended, he said. That means the new parents' names are on the final record, not the birth parents'."

Sheila came to the doorway between the kitchen and dining room. "We have supper almost ready. You're staying to eat. I'll call you when it's time. Hope's starting a fire in the woodstove." She left, and they heard sounds from the kitchen—thunks and scrapes, the rattle of dishes, the whistle of a teakettle.

· · ·

A SHORT while later they gathered in the kitchen again. Julia wasn't hungry—the muffins and cider had taken care of that—but whatever was cooking smelled good, and somebody had put together a nice salad of greens, dried fruit, and walnuts. Sheila was slicing a loaf of bread at the counter, and Hope stood with her back to them, stirring whatever was in the pot. The cat was curled on a braided rug at her feet.

The woodstove, an insert in a small brick fireplace by the back door, stood somewhat lopsided on little splayed feet of tarnished brass. A rectangle of tempered glass in the door furnished a cloudy view into its interior, and a tin washtub of roughhewn logs sat beside it. Already Julia could feel the kitchen warming up.

"Grab a bowl and serve yourselves," Sheila said.

It was chili, Hope's special recipe that called for venison instead of beef. As they ate, Carmen summarized her phone call. Julia's cell phone was on the table, the ringer volume turned to high.

Presently Sheila began a long, convoluted tale about a folk-singer friend of theirs named Lolly, after whom their cat was named. Lolly, the friend, had a colorful history. Her great-grandmother had been a survivor on the *Titanic* and had read in her horoscope the night before she set sail from England that *The floods of life will not overtake you*. On her deathbed the great-grandmother had given Lolly a silver teaspoon she had snitched from the ship, and Lolly had it made into a bracelet, which she wore every day.

The jumble of details about Lolly was hard to keep up with. Julia wondered if she had missed something—such as why they had named their *cat* after this woman. Sheila went from one story to the next in rapid succession, stopping only occasionally for small, quick bites of food. Even though Julia's attention came and went, she did appreciate what Sheila was doing—filling up time as they waited for Butch's phone call. No need for anyone else to say anything, but no empty awkward silences either.

At some point Hope rose from the table and returned with a fresh pot of tea. "Jasmine," she said as she plunked it down on the table.

". . . and she sells them at different craft fairs all over," Sheila was saying now. Evidently she was still talking about Lolly. "Here's one she made for me last summer." She reached inside the neck of her sweater and hauled out a long chain with ivory Scrabble tiles dangling from it. Some of the tiles were turned the wrong way, so it was hard to tell if the letters spelled anything. She lifted the necklace over her head and laid it on the table. "She buys up all kinds of old board games. Hope has one made out of Monopoly pieces," she said. "Don't you, Hope?" Hope made no reply, didn't even look up from the slice of bread she was sopping in a saucer of olive oil.

On Sheila went. "And she makes these Clue necklaces, with all the colored tokens and the little weapons. The candlestick and the revolver and the knife and the lead pipe and the, let's see, the . . ."

"I didn't tell you exactly what *kind* of dream I had about my baby." Carmen spoke clearly, loudly. "It was more like a vision. I already told Aunt Julia about it."

". . . and there was a wrench and a . . ." Sheila trailed off. She and Hope were staring at Carmen.

Carmen said, "It happened in the hotel in Boston, not at home. I saw a little girl running through tall grass, and then I heard a voice, and then I felt a hand on my face." She gave a short laugh. "Okay, that's not just a *vision*. It was like a whole . . . sensory experience."

No one said anything. Julia was thinking about the girl's use of the word *home*. She had never heard her speak of the stone house that way.

"At first I thought I was just dreaming," Carmen continued, "but then I realized I was wide awake. I didn't open my eyes, though. I just kept still."

"You felt somebody touch your face," Sheila said, "and you didn't scream and jump out of your skin?"

"It was a *little* hand. Right here"—Carmen laid her own hand against her left cheek—"and then it patted my cheek like this, very gently. But first I heard the voice."

The only sounds were the popping and crackling of wood in the woodstove and the dull, hollow susurrus of the wind outdoors.

"What did it say?" It was Hope.

"It was a child's voice, and she whispered, '*I walk the earth.*' But it was a loud whisper, with a little echo to it. Then it faded away, and then the hand wasn't there anymore either."

She looked straight at Hope, then Sheila. Not at all imploringly, but as if she fully expected them to believe her, as if she had just stated a simple fact, something incontrovertible like *Here we are, the four of us, sitting at this table.* "I told Aunt Julia it was a message from God," she said. "And I still think so."

Hope made a sound as if something were stuck in her throat, but no one spoke. There was a soft thump as a piece of wood shifted in the woodstove.

"*For the revelation awaits an appointed time,*" Carmen said. "That's in the book of Habakkuk."

Hope picked up her fork and stabbed vigorously into her salad bowl.

Carmen took a deep breath. "I just want to say this to all of you right now—*He knows our downsitting and our uprising.* That's in the book of Psalms. And he also knows where *she* is right this minute. And I'm going to go out on a limb here and say I believe he's going to let me see her in my lifetime." She threw her head back and looked at the ceiling. "Because he loves me. Even when I make a mess of things, he picks me up and sets me back on my feet. It's something called . . . grace." She looked at Julia. "Like when he led me to you." She looked at Sheila, then Hope. "And you, too."

Before anyone could think of a reply to such a speech, the cat delivered them all by suddenly leaping up onto the empty chair right beside Julia. She let out a startled cry, and Sheila burst out laughing as she reached over to scoop Lolly into her lap. "Bad, bad baby," she crooned, stroking the cat. "Bad Lolly to scare our company like that. One of these days you're going to get too fat to jump." She picked up the Scrabble necklace and jiggled it in front of the cat, who lifted a paw and lazily swatted at it.

And just at that moment, while Julia's heart was still pounding, the cell phone emitted a series of loud tweets. This time the cry came from Carmen, a squeaky "Oh!" She grabbed the phone and flipped it open, then pressed the speaker icon. Julia could have hugged her.

"Hi, Uncle Butch. I'm here. Did you find out anything?"

And then Butch's voice: "I found her. I've got her address. A phone number, too. You have a pencil?"

·chapter 22·

SKEPTICISM OF MARVELS

Carmen wasted no time dialing the number. She kept the speaker on. It would have made a curious picture—the four of them sitting at the table, leaning forward, all eyes focused on a cell phone.

It rang once, twice, three times. Then a woman's voice. "Hello?"

"Luna?" Carmen said.

A moment of silence and then, "Who is this?" *This* was *thee-is*. A decidedly Southern voice.

But Carmen seemed to know it was the right voice. She spoke clearly, eagerly. "Luna, this is Carmen Frederickson. Do you remember me? Two years ago?"

There was such a long pause they thought she might have hung up. But then she spoke. "Yes, I remember you."

"Luna, I need to talk to you," Carmen said. "I have some questions."

Another lengthy pause. "Not over the phone." She spoke so softly it was hard to hear her.

Carmen read off the address Butch had given her. "Is that where you live?"

"Yes."

"May I come to your house?"

A sigh. "Yes."

Carmen told her she was in Massachusetts right now but would get there as soon as she could. Her aunt was with her. They would call tomorrow and give her a time.

After the phone call, it was only a question of how soon to leave. The address was in Roskam, North Carolina, twenty miles west of Charlotte. They must have come within minutes of it on their way to Virginia.

Julia took the phone from Carmen and was soon connected to an airline agent. As the situation called for assertiveness, she told the agent that a family emergency had arisen, of utmost urgency, and it was imperative that they cancel their original flight and instead fly to Charlotte, North Carolina, tomorrow. "On the earliest, fastest possible flight," she stated, then added, "It's a matter of life or death." She wasn't going to feel guilty for that, not when Luna was their only hope of finding out what had happened to Carmen's baby.

The fact that her voice was not quite steady must have motivated the agent, for he flew into action. The earliest he could get them to Charlotte was 10:40 the next morning on a nonstop flight departing at 8:33 A.M. from Hartford, Connecticut, which was only an hour's drive from where they were in Danforth.

Hartford. Julia hesitated. Well, at least they would be there only long enough to catch a plane. The agent must have sensed her reluctance, for he apologized that this was the best he could do, added that the usual fees for changing a flight would be waived. It didn't take long for him to make the changes. At the end he said he hoped they got there "before it's too late."

They were persuaded to spend the night at the yellow house, in
a back bedroom Sheila called "the studio." She led them through the
hall to the room, then set about moving a few things to clear a path
to the bed. Another cramped room, with an easel, guitar cases, and
an old upright piano stacked high with music. A double bed was
shoved into the corner. Evidently the easel was put to frequent use,
for dozens of unframed watercolors and oils stood propped against
the walls, most of them featuring animals: two preening parrots, a
turtle in a brook, a buffalo herd silhouetted against a sunset sky.

After Sheila left, Julia pulled back the bedspread and saw sheets
that looked clean enough. Several quilts were laid across the foot of
the bed. Carmen pressed a fist to her forehead. "I feel like somebody hit me with a sledgehammer." She laughed. "I sure hope we
can sleep with all these animals in the room."

Later, when they were both in bed, Carmen spoke into the dark.
"I canceled all our motel reservations while you were in the bathroom." Such a thing had never occurred to Julia. The idea of the
authors' tour suddenly seemed like something from another lifetime, someone else's lifetime in fact.

Sometime later Julia fell into a restless sleep, then woke to the
sound of howling wind. She wished they were on the plane right
now. She had a horrible thought of pulling up to Luna's house to
find it recently deserted, dust still rising from a gravel driveway
where a car had peeled out for parts unknown. She lay for a long
time with her eyes open, studying the contours of the dark room.
Finally she fell asleep again, but off and on she awoke and looked
at the window for signs of daylight.

I T was close to noon the next day when Julia pulled up at the
address in Roskam, North Carolina. It was a tall narrow town
house, overlooking a park and a tennis court, where a boy was hit-

ting balls against a backboard. There were six town houses in a row, identical except for the colors—a palette of desert hues. Taupe, red clay, sage, mauve, sand, sky blue, all of them with high-pitched gables, balconies, tin chimneys, and small yards. Luna's house, the fifth one, was the color of sand. A pot of yellow chrysanthemums sat on the front stoop. The driveway, Julia noticed, was concrete, not gravel, and she was relieved to see that there was a car sitting in it.

She turned the ignition off, but neither of them made a move to get out. "That's not the car she used to drive," Carmen said, her hands clenched. "I'm so scared. What if she's gone? Or won't talk? Or doesn't know anything?"

"Then we'll figure out something else," Julia said. She laid hold of the door handle. "Let's go." As she stepped out of the car, she heard the sounds of children playing in the park.

Carmen followed her to the front door. Julia pressed the doorbell, and from inside came the barking of a dog, growing louder as it neared the door, then the clicking of claws against hardwood.

"She had a dog," Carmen said. "Sometimes he rode in the car with her."

They heard a voice from inside and footsteps approaching the door. Then the snap of a deadbolt, a twist of the knob, and the door opened a crack, as far as the security chain would allow. Julia, standing in front, saw an eye and part of a woman's face. Not the friendliest of expressions from what she could tell. Meanwhile, the dog scrabbled at the door and continued to bark, its snout jammed into the crack.

"Hi, Luna," Carmen said. She gave a wave through the crack.

"Just a minute." The tone was neutral, cautious, though the words were barely audible over the barking of the dog.

The dog's snout disappeared suddenly, and the door closed firmly. Then the sound of retreating footsteps and the barking grew fainter. Then silence. Carmen shot a worried look at Julia. From farther inside the house, the dog's barking resumed, but less frantic now, a treat-begging bark or a let's-go-outside bark. Then it stopped.

Again, approaching footsteps. Then a soft metallic chatter as the chain was disengaged, and the door opened slowly. And there she stood. Not a tall woman, but striking. She had an olive complexion and a mane of long dark hair, with several slender braids around her face.

Julia found it hard not to stare. She looked like she belonged to another time and place—a prophetess or priestess, and not a very happy one. But maybe it was only the intensity of her deep-set eyes, her absolute stillness, the firm set of her mouth. Maybe it was the long purple robe she wore, an elaborate garment with a plush nap and voluminous sleeves spangled with gold sequins. It had to be a bathrobe—there was a tassel at the top of the long front zipper—but Julia had never seen one quite like it. Not exactly the kind of thing you would throw into the washing machine. The expression on her face said that company was the last thing she wanted right now. Or—it came to Julia as a revelation—maybe it was a mask to cover up something else, like fear.

Luna stepped aside and motioned them in. She closed the door behind them and led them through a hallway into an open, airy living area with a vaulted ceiling. She walked smoothly, fluidly. It could have been a graceful walk but for the fact that under her robe she was wearing clogs, which resounded like hooves against the hardwood floor.

They passed a doorway to a bedroom and proceeded through the kitchen to a sunroom facing the backyard, where the dog was investigating something under a tree. Beyond the yard was a steep embankment, at the top of which Julia could see pedestrians and cars passing. Luna gestured toward a love seat. All of this without saying a word. Julia and Carmen sat down side by side.

Luna moved to a chair across from them, her features still set in stone, her lips slightly pursed now. The brightness of the sunroom revealed her to be older than Julia had first thought. She wore no makeup, and her hair was threaded with gray. Something in Julia had to admire a woman who would do that—seat herself at close range in unflattering light. She wondered if Luna had a husband, if he lived here, too. She had seen none of the telltale signs of a man's presence—little piles of clutter, men's shoes in places they shouldn't be, dishes in the sink.

The sunroom seemed to be tightly sealed against outside noise. A large old-fashioned alarm clock sat on a low white table beside Luna's chair, its vigorous tick-tocks reverberating in the small room.

A few magazines were fanned across the top of a square wooden chest that sat between the love seat and Luna's chair. Luna studied the magazines first, then stared at Carmen's knees for a few moments before slowly lifting her eyes to the girl's face.

S HE didn't die, did she, Luna?" Carmen's voice was soft and pleading. "Do you have any idea where she is?"

The slightest intake of breath, the faintest flicker of an eyelid, but Luna remained perfectly composed, sitting erect. Slowly her gaze traveled upward to a point just above Carmen's head. Her eyes swept back and forth, as if watching the cars. Perhaps she was wishing she were inside one of them.

She looked back at Carmen. "How did you find me?" Again Julia heard the Southernness—the long deep scoop of *how*, the flatness of *find*.

Carmen answered calmly, evenly. "That doesn't matter right now. Please, Luna. You've got to help me—where is she?"

Julia caught the change in the question. The first two had been so neatly sidestepped—*She didn't die, did she? Do you know where she is?*—that they had answered themselves.

Luna's eyes suddenly filled. "I always knew this day would come. I didn't know how we would meet up"—there was that loose, gaping *how* again—"but I knew we would, sometime, some place." With one hand she fidgeted with the tassel of her robe. "I had nightmares about it—looking up and seeing you in a restaurant or on the sidewalk or in a store. I don't know why I never once thought about you calling me on the phone and coming to my house." She looked up at the ceiling, blinking away tears. "I want you to know I've been haunted day and night about what happened. You have to believe that."

To Julia the words were too easy, had probably been practiced many times in the event of a face-off like this. "Carmen has had plenty of bad days and nights, too," she said.

Up to this point Luna had barely acknowledged Julia. She flashed her a hard look now, then addressed Carmen once again. "I knew God would judge us all someday. I told the Shelburns so. They said all they wanted was to give the babies good homes and the girls a chance to start their lives again. But that's not all they wanted." She bowed her head. "I guess you know what happened to them." She looked up again. "But I knew my day of accountability would come, too."

Carmen stood up. She walked around the wooden chest and dropped to her knees in front of Luna. "I know the agency closed down and the Shelburns are both dead. But we didn't come here to talk about all that. All I want to know right now is *where she is*. You know, don't you? You've got to tell me."

Luna stared down at her hands, which were tightly clasped in her lap. Big, capable-looking hands with an enormous topaz ring on one index finger. Lips clamped together, she started nodding, barely perceptibly but keeping perfect time with the loud tocks of the clock. At length she sighed deeply and said, "Yes, I do know."

Carmen touched her hand. "Where?"

Luna looked at the clock. "They should be finishing their lunch about now, and then she'll be going down for a nap."

"How . . . do you know that?" Carmen said.

"She lives two doors down. In the green house."

I N keeping with her skepticism of marvels in general, Julia was slow to take this one in. She heard Luna's words, replayed them, doubted them, replayed them again. *Two doors down. In the green house.* In her mind she saw the six town houses all in a row on the same side of the street, across from the park. She ran through the colors in order. Taupe, red clay, sage, mauve, sand, blue. Then backward. Blue was the last one, then Luna's before that, the color of sand. And they were sitting inside that one right now, their rental car parked at the curb in front. The house on the other side was mauve.

And then one the color of sage. Or cactus. Not a grassy green, or the color of lime sherbet, not even as green as avocados or moss or olives, but more muted, a grayish sort of green. But compared to the other five houses, definitely green. *Two doors down. In the green house.* What else could it possibly mean?

That this qualified as a marvel—their search for Luna so mercifully brief, so rich in dividends—was undeniable. If what Luna said was true, that is. Julia was stalled in disbelief.

Carmen, on the other hand, had evidently processed the miracle with astounding speed. Only a moment of stunned joy, then, "Can I see her?" followed by an immediate revision: "When can I see her?" A slight tremble in her voice was the only evidence that such swift success was the last thing she had expected.

Indeed, on the flight down she and Julia had talked about the possibility of having to travel many miles at great inconvenience, perhaps to another country, to see the child—"if by some chance her whereabouts can even be traced," Julia had said. As soon as the words were out of her mouth, she knew what was coming.

And it did. Another speech on the subject of chance, luck, accidents, and so forth, a speech delivered, as always, with the conviction of an Old Testament prophet, though a shorter version today than usual. Obadiah this time rather than Isaiah. "When we find her," Carmen had said, "it will be by design, not by chance. We're not rolling dice or flipping coins or playing the lottery here."

When we find her, she had said. Oh, the certainty of youth. And as the flight attendant rolled the drink cart down the aisle toward them, Carmen had wrapped up her speech: *"A man devises his way, but the Lord determines his steps."*

Julia had looked out the window at the billowy expanse of white clouds below them and tried to imagine the miles and hours that might be required to track the child down. Or to *try*—she didn't possess the certainty of youth, only the mistrust of middle age. Money wasn't worth a thought. She knew she would sell all she had if necessary. It came to her that whereas she had once worried about how she would fill up a whole year of sabbatical, she now wondered if it would be long enough.

LUNA cleared her throat and looked at the clock again. "After her nap, she usually . . . goes to the park," she said hesitantly, "unless it's bad weather." She lifted her eyes to scan the sky, as if hoping to see a storm moving in. "She's normally awake by three. Her mother will be taking her to the park today. Her father is returning this evening from a business trip. You can see the park from the front window. Upstairs has the best view."

Still on her knees in front of Luna, Carmen shook her head. "No, I want to see her up close." Though courteous, it was a statement of intent, not a request.

Luna placed her fingertips together and studied them a moment. "Of course you do." She paused again, nodding. Her topaz ring glittered in the sunlight. "I like to go to the park when they're there. Sometimes they let me take her by myself, but not often. I need to tell you something else." She looked away and spoke to the corner of the room. "They're not just my neighbors. Her father is my son."

So, another piece of the puzzle.

She looked back at Carmen. "We have to be so careful. They're very protective of her. They went through so much. Four miscarriages and a stillbirth. So many lost babies before they got her, and they know they'll never have another one, so if they thought someone was here who wanted to . . ." She put a hand to her mouth. "I'm so sorry. I know—you lost a baby, too. In the worst way possible." She shook her head slowly. "How can I sit here and say these things to you? You've waited so long and been through so much yourself." She looked toward the door into the kitchen. "I could go to jail for what I did. There's a telephone in there. You could call the police right now and tell them."

Carmen said, "I wouldn't know what to tell them, Luna. Joyce and Milo told me my baby died. That's all I know. You weren't the one who lied to me."

"No, I just . . . took your baby. In a sense." She closed her eyes.

Somewhere in the distance a siren wailed. The dog set up a ruckus in the backyard and another dog from nearby joined in. Julia glanced up at the overhead fan and wished it were on. It was getting warm in the sunroom.

Carmen dropped from her knees and sat on the floor at Luna's feet, as if it were story time. "Will you tell me what happened?" she said. "I need to know. I don't remember much about that night, but you were there, and you were . . . kind."

"Kind!" Luna turned away and took a moment to collect herself. At length she looked back at Carmen and began. Though her style of speech was slow and languorous, and the story full of turns, she kept it moving.

She had gotten the call from Joyce that Carmen's time had come. "Milo wasn't happy you were early. He liked things to run on schedule—his schedule. You were in labor a long time, but you already know that. But you were brave. Teenage mothers aren't always. You did very well." *Very way-ell.*

She swayed from side to side as she talked.

She had delivered numbers of babies at the Shelburns' house, so she knew the routine. The girls were always young, often younger than Carmen, and the babies were always being adopted through the Babies First Mission. Sometimes the girl's parents were there, sometimes the adoptive parents. Occasionally Thornton or his wife dropped by, too. But that night it was only Carmen, the Shelburns, and Luna.

Luna stayed by Carmen's side, coached and comforted her for hours on end. For days it had been raining off and on, and that night it was coming down in sheets, with gusty winds and lightning. There was no window in the birthing room, but she could hear the storm as a distant roar. Sometime during the night a tree went down, somewhere close to the old paper mill, and the fall had shaken the house. The lights flickered but didn't go off.

Joyce was in and out, Milo too, both of them more visibly fretful than usual. When the baby finally came, Luna checked her, then handed her to Joyce to clean up. "She was perfect," she told Carmen. "A beautiful, beautiful baby."

After Joyce left the room, Luna turned her attention back to Carmen. She would have called a doctor right away had there been complications, but her vital signs quickly strengthened, stabilized, and all was normal.

"You kept calling out, saying you wanted to see your baby," she said. "It surprised me. I assumed the girls were instructed not to ask." *Not to eye-esk.*

There were things she didn't like about these births at the Shelburns' house, but Babies First paid her a set fee that included prenatal visits, delivery, and postpartum. She usually took care of filing the paperwork for the birth certificate. Her duties didn't include giving her opinion about the way things were handled. She kept quiet and did her job. Milo liked the appointments to be as short as possible, didn't want a lot of interaction with the girls.

"But my heart went out to them," she said. "So young and so frightened, most of them. And not built for childbirth. Little girls having babies—it was hard on them in every way. Sometimes the girls' mothers were there. Sometimes it was harder on them than the girls. Not a happy time at all. The babies whisked out one door and the girls out another, more or less."

In many ways, however, these births were easier for Luna than regular home births, with family members present in the room, sometimes even little brothers and sisters, and the sounds of everyday living just outside the door. So much activity, so much joy. They had become harder for her over the past few years, to the point that she had been accepting fewer and fewer private patients.

Whenever she handed a mother her newborn and witnessed that first bonding, saw the happy faces of the father and siblings, it made her ache a little more than the last time. To be reminded that her only child, a son, and his wife so deeply and desperately wanted this but would probably never experience it—well, it was getting harder. She often thought of other kinds of work she could do. Or retirement. She had some money put back, and she could start drawing social security soon.

"You had every right to see your baby," she told Carmen. "You were her mother. So I went to the door and called Milo. Then I tried to keep you calm. I told you the baby was fine but you needed to stay in bed. I sat by you and held your hand. I should have done more, but I didn't." Her voice broke. "I should have asked you some questions."

Another adult, Julia thought, who could have intervened but didn't. She wanted to be angry about it but couldn't. She knew firsthand that getting involved was a hard thing to do.

Milo had come in then and told Luna to go. She hesitated because she didn't like to leave a new mother so soon, but he said it was late and she had been here a long time. He told her again to go. Not just go out, but *go*. She checked Carmen once more and left the room. As she closed the door, she heard Milo tell Carmen to lie still and be quiet. It wasn't just a suggestion, but a command.

Joyce had the baby in her arms in the kitchen, wrapped in a blanket. She was sitting at the table trying to feed her from a bottle, and the baby was making little rooting noises. Luna told her she wanted to stay a little longer to make sure everything was okay, but Joyce told her no, if Milo said go, she needed to.

Luna said she would be available by phone, as always, and would come back in two days to check Carmen and the baby, too, if they were still here. Sometimes these babies didn't stay here two days.

But Joyce told her not to come back unless they called. Luna asked about the birth certificate, whether she should fill out the paperwork right now before she left, but just then Milo came out to the kitchen and repeated what Joyce had said, a little more forcefully: Don't call or come back unless she heard from them. They would take care of the birth certificate later. This was a departure from the standard procedure, but she had learned by now not to question Milo. He didn't like anybody trying to tell him what to do, especially women.

So ... I left," Luna said.

When she stepped out and saw it was still raining, she remembered her umbrella, which was propped against the washing machine inside, just off the kitchen. So she slipped back to get it. She tried to be very quiet. She didn't want a scolding from Milo about taking too long to leave.

She paused now and frowned, as if trying to put the details in order. "Just as I picked up my umbrella," she said, "I heard Milo tell Joyce he had given you something to help you sleep. Then he said they had to get the baby out of the house to make sure you wouldn't hear it. At first it sounded like a thoughtful thing to do—so you wouldn't be so upset about not keeping her. I could have left then since I had my umbrella in my hand. I can't really explain why I didn't."

She looked back at Carmen. "Joyce asked him if he had gotten you to sign the papers, and he said no, he hadn't even tried and wasn't going to, it was clear you weren't going to cooperate, so he had gone ahead with plan B. That's what he called it. Plan B. Joyce said, 'So you told her?' She sounded scared. And he said yes. And the only sound for a while was the rain coming down."

Luna stopped talking and took several deep breaths, expelling them slowly each time. Then she continued. "Of course I was wondering *what* he had told you. Joyce suggested taking the baby to the Thorntons' house, but Milo said no, they were out of town until the weekend. And Phyllis couldn't help either. She was the office girl at Babies First. Milo wasn't happy. You'd really messed him up having the baby early. Then Joyce said she was worried, she didn't think they ought to do this, she had a bad feeling about it, and Milo said it was too late, he'd already called the couple in Michigan and told them they had a new baby and they were already making plans to leave. And Joyce must have started crying because Milo said, 'Stop that, you know this is what we have to do. Babies need stable families.' And Joyce said the money wasn't worth it, this just wasn't right, and he said maybe she would change her mind when she heard how much it was this time. He said he only wished the people weren't from Michigan because their laws were harder to work around."

Carmen was taking in every word. She sat motionless, hardly breathing as she looked up at Luna. Though her mind must have been full of questions, she never interrupted. Occasionally she turned her head for a quick look at the clock, as if not knowing which she wanted more—to hear her own story or to see her child.

By now Luna had heard enough of the Shelburns' conversation to know something very wrong was going on. But she couldn't think of what to do and she certainly didn't want to be caught still hanging around, so she left very quietly. She got in her car and wound her way to the end of their long drive, then sat there a good while instead of pulling out onto the road. It was still raining hard.

"I should have called the Pittsfield police right then," she said. *Rat thee-in.* "That's what I should have done. I should have told them what I had just heard and what I suspected—and then let them take it from there. If I had, you would have left the Shelburns' house with your baby."

She was looking down at her ring now, running a thumb over the stone as she talked.

But there was something holding her back, she said—maybe fear of Milo, maybe the slightest doubt about what she heard, maybe just her habitual timidity and indecisiveness. She hated confrontation. What if she was wrong?

So she was sitting at the end of the drive in a dilemma, but afraid to do anything about it, when her cell phone rang. It was Milo. In his usual domineering way, he told her they needed her help. No apology for the fact that he had just pointed her to the door. He went on to say they had a "timing issue" with the adoption and needed someone discreet and trustworthy to keep the baby for a couple of days, and would she mind? There would be compensation, of course.

She agreed. This would give her time to weigh the matter, maybe get up her nerve to do what she knew she ought to do. She agreed to help, so she waited for what seemed the right amount of time, then returned to the house.

As she drove home later, the baby slept in the backseat. She thought of Carmen soundly sleeping in the Shelburns' house, totally unaware of what they were plotting—if her suspicions were right. She thought of what it was Milo might have told her before he put her to sleep—what he *must* have told her. It was too horrible to put into words. She argued with herself. Surely he wouldn't tell her a lie like that. But surely he must have.

She thought also of the couple in Michigan who had received a phone call they had been longing for, who were already making plans to drive to Massachusetts to see their baby, then carry her home after the interstate approval was processed, who probably had a fully equipped nursery waiting with every luxury money could buy.

And then, of course, she thought of her son and daughter-in-law, who also had a nursery waiting, who had come home from the hospital in Framingham only a few months ago without a baby, who were still grieving so much they could barely function.

· chapter 23 ·

ALL THE PARTICULARS

Just then Luna's dog appeared at the back door, jumping up with short peremptory barks, his claws scratching against the screen door of the sunroom, as if used to running the show around here. Luna rose and let him in, at which time he immediately erupted into a frenzy over the discovery of strangers inside his house. Two snaps of her fingers and a stern "Go," however, sent him into the kitchen, where he lay down under the table, with a few resentful woofs to let them know he was still on guard.

Thankfully, Luna left the back door open so that cooler air wafted in through the screen, along with sounds of traffic from the road above the embankment. It was an ideal October day, with some early autumn reds and golds. Somewhere nearby a bird was chirping aggressively. It was hard for Julia to believe she had shivered under blankets through the previous night in Massachusetts.

Luna excused herself and went to the kitchen. She returned with three glasses of ice water on a tray, which she set on the wooden chest. Carmen moved back to sit on the love seat, and Luna pulled her chair a little closer, then took a long drink of water and settled herself again, arranging the folds of her purple robe. Another deep breath, and she resumed.

Milo called the next day to check in and to tell her they still needed her help. He reminded her that it was best not to be taking the baby out of the house, that if she needed anything, to let them know and they would bring it over. The adoptive parents were on the road now. They would arrive the next day sometime. It was a long way from Michigan.

Meanwhile, though Luna was still in a quandary, she was clear on this point: She knew she had to talk to Carmen. She had to find out if Milo had told her the lie she suspected, and, if he hadn't, whether she had willingly agreed to place the baby for adoption. She also knew that in Massachusetts a birth mother couldn't sign relinquishment papers until four days after the birth, so if they had gotten her to sign anything yet, that was a major red flag. Depending on what she found out from Carmen, Luna would know whether to notify the authorities. But if she couldn't talk to Carmen, she would have no choice but to call for help. She couldn't take a chance since time was running out.

So she told Milo she needed to talk to Carmen briefly and remind her of some instructions they had gone over. He said she was sleeping and he didn't want to wake her up. Joyce was checking on her regularly and she had eaten a good breakfast, so things were fine. Another "don't call us, we'll call you," and he hung up.

Besides being tied in knots with worry, something else was going on with Luna. "She was the sweetest baby," she said. "I was falling in love with her." Her voice quavered a little, and she smiled, the first smile she had offered. "Milo hadn't counted on that, and I hadn't either. Of course, I liked babies—they were my life's work. But I was always happy to hand them over and go back to my quiet house. This one, though—she was different." She paused. "I called her Little Princess."

M ILO phoned late the next morning, greatly agitated, and reported that the adoptive parents had been involved in a freeway accident, nothing serious but they had to switch out cars and it was holding them up. He talked as if they had done it on purpose. It was clear that his only concern was for the inconvenience this was causing him. He sighed and said they probably wouldn't be here until early the next morning now, so he would be back in touch. Did she need anything? Could she keep the baby a little longer? It was the first time he had asked instead of telling.

She told him she could, and then said if they didn't want her to come over, then at least she needed to talk with Carmen by phone. Not now, he said, she was taking a little walk in the driveway and needed her exercise, but maybe Carmen could call her back later. Another brush-off.

"So then I asked to speak with Joyce just a minute. I told him I wanted to review with her the special problem these young girls had with breast milk—unless he wanted me to explain it to him and he could relay the message. I hoped that might embarrass him enough to let me talk to her, and it worked."

He handed the phone to Joyce, but it was clear that he was standing there monitoring things. Luna asked several questions about Carmen's progress, and after one of them Joyce hesitated and said she didn't know. Well, could she go out to the driveway and ask her? Luna said, hoping Milo wouldn't follow and she could get Joyce to hand the phone to Carmen. She wasn't in the driveway, Joyce said. Then she immediately changed her story and said, oh, well, maybe she was, or maybe she had walked a little farther.

So they weren't going to let her speak directly to Carmen. No use driving out there. Milo would simply meet her at the door and tell her to leave. She still had a little time, but not much. She had already looked up the phone number for the Pittsfield police and had it written down. And she still had the baby—another reassuring thought. She could use the baby for bargaining if she had to: *I keep the baby until I talk to Carmen.*

Milo took the phone back and told Luna they had to hang up. They would be away from home for a few hours that afternoon but would be back by early evening, and Carmen was going with them.

Carmen interrupted. "That's not true. They drove to Briggsville, but I didn't go. That was the day I left."

"He was cagey," Luna said. "He just wanted to make sure I didn't call back or come over while they were away."

That same night she got another call a little after eight o'clock. Her heart started racing when she saw it was from Milo. She assumed he had been in contact with the couple from Michigan and now he was going to give her a time to meet them tomorrow. She knew this was it. Time for a showdown. She was taken aback, therefore, when he told her they were heading over to get the baby in a few minutes and would keep her at their house from now on.

"Then it hit me," Luna said to Carmen. "I knew you must not be there anymore, or else they wouldn't want the baby there. I felt so stupid. I had never thought of this happening. Sometimes the girls did leave after a day or two, but those were always the ones whose parents came to get them. I knew you didn't have any family, so I guess I was just thinking . . . well, I obviously wasn't thinking."

Meanwhile, Milo was on the phone waiting for a reply and wondering why he wasn't getting one. He raised his voice and told her again they were getting ready to leave, so have the baby ready in about fifteen minutes.

"So I made up something on the spot," Luna said. "I told him I had to go pick up a prescription at the drive-through pharmacy, so

I would just bring her over to save them a trip. He said well, okay, but not to forget to bring all the things they had sent along—the blankets, the diapers, formula, and so forth. Knowing Milo, he was probably going to take inventory to see how many diapers I'd used."

But she had to know if her hunch was right, that Carmen had left, so before they hung up she asked him. Not "Did Carmen leave?" but "When did Carmen leave?" Two questions in one. He paused just a second, then told Luna what she knew must be another lie, that Carmen had caught a bus in Briggsville and headed off to New York City to start a new life.

Carmen nodded. "Yep, another lie. I did catch a bus, but in Pittsfield, not Briggsville, and not to New York."

"If only I had driven out to the house that day," Luna said. "I might have seen you before you left." She heaved a sigh and picked up with the story. Milo told her to hurry up and bring the baby, they would be waiting. They were both tired and wanted to go to bed early and get a good night's sleep.

She laughed dryly. "Milo always expected everybody to follow his timetable. Even a little baby."

SHE was kneading her hands as she talked. "So, there I was. You had disappeared, and I was convinced Milo was about to have a big payday off your baby. I had failed to save her for you." Remorse was written all over her face. "I should have gotten help right away. That was my mistake. Hindsight . . ." Her hands went still. "I was beside myself when I hung up. But . . . then I saw something."

She paused. "This is the part that's hard to tell." *Hard to tay-ell.* "I saw a picture on the table beside my sofa. Of my son and his wife. They were living in Massachusetts at the time, close to Boston, in Framingham. Later his job transferred him down here to Roskam."

She swallowed hard. "I don't know how to say this except to just say it. I was scared to death of what I was thinking, but once I started justifying it, I couldn't stop. You were gone, and nobody knew where. Maybe you could be tracked down, but maybe not. Probably not, I told myself. And even if you could, maybe you would tell them yes, you had thought it over and agreed to give the baby up and had signed the papers early so you could leave."

She stopped again and hung her head. Her hair fell around her face. After a few moments, she looked up. "I've never been a very daring person, and I've always moved slow. But that night I hatched a plan faster than you would believe."

Sitting on the sofa staring at the picture of her son and daughter-in-law, she seized the idea, thought about it for a few frantic moments, and then stood up and proceeded to carry it out. She jotted a few notes to herself, then got a drink of water to calm herself, checked on the baby—she was sleeping—and picked up her telephone.

"I don't know where I got the courage," she said. "I've never been a risk-taker. Well, I take that back—I do know where I got the courage. I was looking into the room where Princess was sleeping. There were two things on—a night light and a CD of Mozart. And as I dialed the Shelburns' number, I kept my eyes on her, and I never took them off the whole time I talked."

It wasn't a long phone call in that there wasn't much two-way talking. Joyce answered, and Luna was glad for that, though her script would have remained the same either way. She asked her to put the phone on speaker and call Milo since this was for both of them. Joyce said he was sitting right there.

"I knew this would be the speech of a lifetime," Luna said. "I had to be strong, I couldn't grope around for words, I couldn't act unsure for even a second. So I kept my eyes on the baby and started talking. I know it helped that it was over the phone, not face-to-face.

I might've lost my nerve if I'd had to look at him. First, I said I knew everything. I repeated it: *Everything.* I said, 'You told Carmen the baby died, but I'm looking at her right now and she's very much alive.' I told them I knew they were planning to forge and notarize your signature on the surrender papers and secure a false birth certificate. I said I knew all about the exorbitant amount the couple from Michigan was paying for the baby. And even though I hadn't planned to say this part, I took another gamble and told them I knew this wasn't the only time Babies First had been involved in something like this."

She paused, shaking her head. "I'll tell you the truth, I could hardly believe I was saying those things since I didn't know any of it for sure. I still can't explain it. I really can't." *I rilly cain't.* "Milo must have wondered what in the world had happened to me in the space of a few minutes since we'd last talked. I still can't believe I did it." She picked up the glass of water and took another drink.

Julia didn't know what to think. She thought of Luna's earlier words: *No, I just took your baby* and *Her father is my son.* She wanted to despise this woman. She didn't want to be drawn into her story. And what a story anyway. Far stranger and less plausible than many she had doubted in the past. She looked at Carmen. No time now for even a quick consultation with her: *Do you believe her? Do you think she's making all this up?*

She turned to Luna again. There she sat in her purple robe, her shoulders back, her dark eyes steady, looking for all the world as if she were telling the truth. Julia didn't want to believe her, but for some reason she did. She certainly didn't want to like her, but she couldn't hate her either.

Luna continued. "Milo denied it all, of course. He told me I was delusional and he had no idea what I was talking about. But I interrupted him. Told him to stop and take a good look at Joyce's face right then and ask himself how well he thought she would hold up under interrogation when I called law enforcement and they started investigating." Luna shrugged and laughed. "Don't ask me where *that* came from. I was not . . . myself that night."

Milo had nothing to say to this. Luna could hear Joyce crying, but she let them squirm a little longer by reminding them that a conviction of baby selling would mean large fines, jail sentences, who knew what else. Public humiliation, of course. Their lives would be in shambles.

"Now it was time for my proposal," she said. "I knew if they didn't accept it, I was digging a pit for myself, too. They could bring me down with them. We could be in jail together. I wish I didn't have to tell you this part."

There was one way out, she told them. She could tell she had their attention, so she let the pause extend a little longer than necessary. The first step was to call the couple from Michigan and tell them the adoption had fallen through. The birth mother had refused to sign the papers.

The second part was to facilitate a different adoption with another couple whose names she would supply. They were good people, but they weren't wealthy, so there would be no big payoff. She would personally guarantee payment of modest legal fees, but that was all. She didn't know all the required procedural steps to make it happen, and she didn't want to. But the Shelburns did, and the Thorntons, too, and they could expedite things—the home study, any necessary paperwork. This other couple lived in Massachusetts, so she assumed it would be simpler in some ways. She knew it couldn't happen tomorrow, but they could get it started tomorrow. It had to be finalized legally, every jot and tittle. There couldn't be one single snag. The couple was never to have the slightest inkling that anything was out of order.

And the Shelburns' reward for doing this? Well, they would be spared having their good name dragged through the mud. She would tell no one what she knew about them or Babies First. Provided, of course, that Babies First quietly closed its doors.

"I know—it was blackmail," she said. "I looked that up in the dictionary to make sure. *The extortion of money or something of value by threatening to expose something dishonorable.* I told myself it wasn't as bad as what they had done, but I know it was still wrong. It was full of lies and deceit, and I knew the adoption would involve forgeries and false documents. And I knew you had been deprived of your baby." She studied her hands a moment. "They were doing what they did for money. I was doing it for love. But it was a crime either way."

S HE looked up at Carmen. "So that's it." She lifted her hands as if to say, *Here I am, judge me as you see fit, I deserve it.* "I could have done so much in the beginning to help you," she said, "but I held back. And then I ended up taking the very thing I had wanted to save for you. I cut off any possibility of trying to find you, to give you back what was yours. At times I've almost been able to forget what I did, but then I would always remember again—we had your baby, and you didn't. And I would know this day was coming sooner or later."

She had been so remarkably composed for so long that it came as a surprise when she suddenly covered her face with both hands and bent forward, her head on her knees.

Carmen said nothing at first, but after an interval of silence she spoke. "So that couple from Michigan—all their hopes and dreams came crashing down that night."

Luna raised her head and nodded. "I don't know how Milo handled that, I really don't. I tried to tell myself they were rich, everything would work out for them, they would get another baby, but I didn't even know for sure that they *were* rich. I was only guessing.

If they were so rich, why weren't they flying instead of driving? Anyway, the truth is that rich people hurt, too."

Carmen said, "And your son and daughter-in-law. They . . . were happy?"

Luna looked at her for a long moment. "I'll never forget the looks on their faces when they held her for the first time." Her voice dropped to a whisper. "They don't know a thing about any of this. All they know is that I found out about a baby that was available for adoption and they were blessed to get her. They call her . . . their miracle."

"You didn't have to tell me all that, you know," Carmen said at length.

At first Julia thought she was referring to all the particulars. It was true, it could have been a much shorter story. But Carmen wasn't talking about the length of the story. "You could have told me the other adoption went through," she said to Luna, "and you didn't have any idea who the people were or where they were from. You could've said you never talked to the Shelburns again after that night, so you didn't know what happened. You could've said the baby really did die. I never would've known the difference."

Luna shook her head. "I'd already lied enough." She looked away. "I've never told any of this to a living soul. It feels like I've laid a burden down."

A brief silence, and then Carmen said, "Just think. If it hadn't been raining."

Luna looked quizzical.

"I mean, if you hadn't needed your umbrella that night," Carmen said, "you wouldn't have gone back in the house and heard them talking. I might not have ever found out what happened. And Babies First might still be in business." She nodded. "'He laid the foundation of the earth. He sends the wind and the rain. His ways are unsearchable.'"

All was quiet except for the ticking of the clock.

"What's . . . her name?" Carmen said.

Luna looked at her and said, "Elizabeth. We call her Lizzy."

Julia knew that in the days to come she would often wish for a transcript of every word spoken in the sunroom that day, first to keep all the details straight, but in the end to remind herself that even in the darkest human trials there could be brief gleams of triumph.

· chapter 24 ·

A Faster Way to Kill

"There they are," Luna said. "Finally." It was a little past three thirty. Luna and Julia stood at the upstairs window and watched as a fair-haired woman walked hand in hand with a pink-capped toddler down the front sidewalk of the green house to the street. In addition to the pink cap, the child was wearing brown overalls and a yellow shirt. At the street the woman picked the child up and carried her across, then set her down on the other side and took her hand again.

Carmen was already in the park, sitting in one of the larger swings situated perpendicular to the smaller bucket swings and facing the row of town houses. She had been there for close to an hour now, swinging gently from side to side, bumping into the empty swings on either side as she watched the green house.

Though Julia longed to see the child up close, she knew the girl wanted, and deserved, this time to herself. At least the lookout from the upstairs window was excellent, and with the binoculars Luna had provided, the view was even better. Luna was clutching the edge of the curtain, clearly nervous, no doubt fearful that Carmen would forget what they had discussed and approach the child directly.

"It's going to be okay," Julia said to her. "You can trust her."

"But look what I've done to her," Luna cried. "Just *look*! She has to sit there and pretend she doesn't know her own daughter. Everything about that is wrong!"

There was nothing to say to that. It was true.

Julia looked back at the woman below. She refused to think of her as Lizzy's mother, not with Carmen sitting in the swing, forced to feign disinterest. The woman was stooping in front of the child now to pull the pink cap down over her ears, a precaution that seemed unnecessary on such a mild day.

Vanessa Fiorelli—it could have been the name of a cocktail waitress, a dance instructor, a B-movie actress. But Julia scolded herself. Here she was again, making appraisals based on something a person had no control over. Regardless of her flamboyant name, Vanessa Fiorelli looked sensible, conscientious, responsible. The kind of woman who took care of business. Somewhere in her thirties, attractive enough, but pale, her light hair pinned back on the sides. The type who didn't try very hard to make the best of her assets.

"The pink cap will come off," Luna said. "It won't last five minutes."

Vanessa took the child by the hand again and held her in check as they walked toward the tunnel slide. Lizzy strained forward, reaching out with one hand. Finally Vanessa let her go, and away she went in a toddling gait. She mounted the steps, then plopped down, pushed herself off, and spilled out the other end of the tunnel before Vanessa could get there.

"She's absolutely fearless," Luna said. "Wants to do everything by herself. And she's not a whiner. If she falls, she gets right back up and tries again."

Lizzy stood up, brushed her overalls off, knees and bottom both, and then scrambled back to the ladder for another turn. Julia smiled—how would a two-year-old know to brush off her clothes like that?

"She's quite the little imitator," Luna said. "You should hear her talk. One day last week she said the word *inappropriate*, or her version of it. Left out only one syllable. She saw a boy hit his little sister over the head, and she turned to her mother and said, 'That's in-propriate.'" Luna laughed. "It's something she hears her parents say."

Another trip down the tunnel slide, and then she was off toward the sandbox, where a boy was busy scooping shovelfuls of sand on top of a toy truck while another was twirling around in a circle kicking sand everywhere.

"She's full of energy," Luna said. "She wants to do everything at once. And very observant. Doesn't miss much. And curious about everything—her mental gears are constantly turning." Lizzy picked up a toy shovel and struck it against a large plastic pail several times. She put the shovel inside the pail, then added a funnel, then a scoop, then a sifter, then dumped them all out and put them back in again one at a time. She shook the pail up and down, then tossed it aside and squatted down to dig out a ball half-buried in the sand, which she threw toward the swings. Julia didn't know a two-year-old could throw a ball that far. A wail rose from the boy playing with the truck, and he pointed to the ball.

Vanessa, who had followed her to the sandbox, said something to her, and Lizzy took off at once in the direction of the ball. Vanessa trailed behind. The ball rolled to a stop a few feet from the swing where Carmen sat. It must have taken every ounce of willpower she had not to get it and hand it to the child. But she stayed put.

Lizzy picked the ball up and held it out to Vanessa, who said something and pointed back to the boy in the sandbox. Lizzy set off with it and returned it to the boy, who snatched it from her so hard she almost lost her balance.

"As cheerful as the day is long," Luna said. "And very obedient. I keep watching for signs of the terrible twos, but I haven't seen them. Yet."

F ROM there Lizzy headed to a miniature house of bright molded plastic. She stuck her head out the window and waved to Vanessa, then closed the shutters, then opened them again and waved. Next it was on to a row of large tractor tires, which she proceeded to climb over, and then to a gray plastic whale mounted on a big coiled spring. As soon as Vanessa lifted her onto it, she grabbed the handles and began rocking with all her might. After that she toddled off toward the bucket swings.

As they came closer, Carmen stretched herself out full-length in her swing and leaned back to look up at the sky. Though Lizzy and Vanessa were now near enough that she could have talked to them, she gave no sign that she even noticed them. After Lizzy was installed in her swing, Carmen gave herself a push in her own swing and began pumping to gain height.

Vanessa stood behind Lizzy in the bucket swing and pushed, gently at first and gradually higher. And then Lizzy must have noticed Carmen, for her head began to move back and forth in time with the long arc of Carmen's swing. She held out a hand longingly as if to say she knew a superior swing when she saw it. She must have said something, for Vanessa laughed and pushed her a little higher.

Suddenly Lizzy put a hand to her head, and the pink cap went flying, revealing a fine, staticky cloud of blond hair.

"That was closer to ten minutes," Luna said. "A record."

The cap landed well in front of the bucket swings and off to the side, close to the bigger swings. Though Vanessa couldn't have missed the flinging of the cap, she kept pushing Lizzy—a fact that impressed Julia. So Vanessa Fiorelli could take things in stride. Carmen was still swinging high, and Lizzy was still watching her, still leaning forward. An airplane passed overhead, diverting her attention momentarily. She pointed to the sky and said something.

"She's smart," Luna said. "Has an amazing vocabulary."

Julia laughed. "She's probably saying, 'Look at the contrail, Mommy.'"

Luna said, "Or maybe, 'What exceptional aerodynamic lift.'"

For the first time in her life, Julia had a glimmer of understanding about the unqualified admiration of grandparents for their grandchildren. Though she had avoided children for most of her life, she was already favorably disposed toward this child— charmed by her would be closer to the truth.

It made no sense. She couldn't even see the child's face clearly, for heaven's sake. Luna's glowing commentary must have accounted for part of her fascination, though she had heard other grandmothers' glowing commentaries, plenty of them, without being smitten by their grandchildren, all of whom had seemed quite ordinary in her estimation. Luna's praise was understandable, for she had a history with Lizzy. She had been the first person to hold her, had seen her almost daily for over two years now, loved her as a grandmother. Julia had seen her for what—maybe ten minutes? She lowered the binoculars and scanned the park from one end to the other. More than a dozen children playing on this crisp October afternoon, but not one to equal Lizzy.

The thought came to her that if she had known a child like Lizzy all those years ago when Matthew brought up the subject of having a baby, might she have answered him differently? Might she have been willing to take a chance on the redemptive power of a child, and might she be a different person today? She lifted the binoculars again and looked back at Lizzy in her bucket swing, her face upturned, her head still moving back and forth as she watched Carmen sail through the air.

It was a mystery why the simplest truths often came so slowly. Julia should have realized this one immediately—that her feelings for Lizzy had their origin in her feelings for Carmen. So that was the way it worked with grandparents. They didn't have to wait to get to know a grandchild before loving it; they loved it instantly because it was the child of their child. If she had harbored any doubts about her feelings toward Carmen, this would have dispelled them, that from a distance, within mere seconds, she had taken Carmen's child into her heart. From now on she would have to omit something she had always told her Creative Writing students before they wrote their first stories: *There is no such thing as love at first sight*.

Carmen stopped pumping and gradually began to slow. She was still quite high, however, when she launched herself out of the swing and landed in a gymnast's crouch within feet of the pink cap. She retrieved it, then stood and twirled it around on her index finger.

Luna breathed in sharply. "Oh, no. She wouldn't . . ."

But evidently she would, for she started walking toward the bucket swing, still twirling the cap. She appeared to be saying something to Vanessa or Lizzy, or both. She couldn't have forgotten the guidelines they had talked about, so obviously she was choosing to ignore them.

Luna braced her hands on the windowsill.

Vanessa stopped pushing the swing and came forward, her hand extended. She looked pleasant enough. She took the cap and said something to Carmen, who said something back. Vanessa looked back at Lizzy, and Carmen laughed and said something else. Lizzy held out both hands and wiggled her fingers. Vanessa handed her the cap, which she laid against her cheek and petted like a kitten. Vanessa said something to Carmen, gesturing and smiling as she spoke, not in the manner of an anxious, overprotective mother but like someone completely at ease.

Carmen said a few words in response, then waved to Lizzy, turned around, and walked away. Luna relaxed at once and stepped back to sit on the edge of the bed. Carmen stopped at the water fountain by the seesaw and took a long drink, after which she lifted her head, looked directly at the upstairs window across the street, and nodded slowly. Then she walked to the picnic shelter near the tennis court. Though farther away from Vanessa and Lizzy now, she could still see them, and she sat there until they left the park.

JULIA and Luna were in the kitchen putting together a quick meal of tomato soup and grilled cheese sandwiches when Carmen came back. She walked to the window and looked out into the backyard. "Sorry for what I did over there," she said at last, "but I had to. I had to hear their voices."

She sat down at the table. "I don't know if you could tell, but the cap had little ears and eyes. And a little snout-looking thing. It's supposed to be a pig. When her mother handed it to her, you know what she said? She said, 'Thank you. My Piggy Wig is soft. I like it. Nice Piggy Wig.' She *cuddled* it. Did you see her?" She laughed. "Her mother said she has a love-hate relationship with it. When it's on her head, it's pretty much hate. When it's not, she treats it like her favorite teddy bear. She even sleeps with it sometimes." She put her head down on the table, buried it in the crook of one arm. "Did you *see* her? Isn't she incredible?" It wasn't clear whether she was laughing or crying.

Luna walked to the table and put a hand on Carmen's head. "I don't know what I was thinking to ask you not to talk to them. Now that you've seen her, you must hate me more than ever. And you have every right to. I don't blame you one bit." *One bee-yit.*

Carmen looked up at her. "Hate you? No, I don't hate you. I know there's a deep mercy at work here, and I don't want to miss it."

Luna sat down beside her. "Please, it would be easier if you hated me. You could . . . get her back, you know." She spoke with conviction, a tremor in her voice. "The courts would be on your side. Any judge in the country. And I'll take whatever punishment I have to. She's your child. You could take her away and have a life with her."

They looked at each other a long time, and then Carmen said, "You're right, I could." She paused. "I could take her away and rip out her parents' hearts." She looked toward the window. "Or I could just get a gun and shoot them both. That would be a faster way to kill them."

In the silence that followed, Julia stood at the stove and stirred the soup. The sandwiches were ready to grill, and the griddle was hot, but now wasn't the time for the sound of food being prepared. No sizzling or scraping.

At length Carmen said, "I . . . like her. A lot."

Luna must have been as confused as Julia, for she said, "You *like* her?"

"Vanessa," Carmen said. "I like her. She's nice."

Nice. It was the same thing she said about so many people. Maybe it was true about Vanessa, but Julia also knew that a big part of other people's niceness was Carmen herself. Always friendly and generous, always ready to give anyone the benefit of the doubt.

"Something inside me didn't want to like her," Carmen continued, "but another part wanted to, desperately. That's why I had to talk to her. If I could like her, it would be such a help." She laughed suddenly, a bright and brittle laugh. "And then I got a bonus. I got to hear Lizzy say, '*Thank you. My Piggy Wig is soft. I like it. Nice Piggy Wig.*' Of all the things she could have said, she said *that*." She was still laughing as she spoke, but there were tears in her eyes. She stopped all at once, swiped at her cheeks with both hands, then said, "When did you say your son was getting home? I've got to talk to him, too. I can't leave until I do."

Luna nodded. No argument, no warning. "He should be home by six. I usually take my newspaper down there in the evening. Vanessa likes to do the crossword puzzle. She doesn't care if they're old. It's not the news she wants, just the puzzle."

Carmen said, "She likes crossword puzzles? See, didn't I say she was nice?"

"We can watch for his car, and you can take it to him when he pulls into the driveway," Luna said. "Tell him you're visiting me."

They ate their soup and sandwiches and later sat in the living room with the drapes open, watching for his car.

CARMEN wasn't gone long, and her report was brief. "He was very polite. Said to thank you for the paper. We talked a little, but I could tell he wanted to get inside, and I was glad to see that. I told him I saw his wife and little girl at the park, and his whole face lit up. He has a good face and big, manly hands. I like his eyes." She looked at Luna. "They look like yours. They scrunch up at the corners when he smiles. I like his smile, too. And his voice. Does he sing?"

She looked straight at Luna, waiting. Unlike some of her questions, this was evidently one she wanted an answer for.

"Yes," Luna said. "He sings in their church choir. He also took piano lessons in school, then cello. He plays in a community orchestra over in Charlotte."

Carmen nodded. "That'll do." She squeezed her eyes shut. "Okay, I have a picture in my head now. Robert. Vanessa. And Lizzy. The Fiorellis. A very, very nice family."

· *chapter 25* ·

GREAT LENGTHS

The week before Christmas, on a late Saturday afternoon, Julia was in the kitchen of the stone house making a fruit salad called Olympian Nectar. She was working her way through the recipe, slicing, dicing, chopping. Strawberries and blueberries weren't as good this time of year, but they looked pretty and would taste fine in a recipe that called for so many other things. The bowl already held the berries, pineapple, bananas, and golden raisins. Next came the cup of grape juice, the applesauce, shredded coconut, maraschino cherries, and pecans.

The salad was the last thing to put together. All the casseroles were ready to go into the oven in shifts, and Carmen had made two loaves of bread that morning. Julia couldn't remember the last time she had given a dinner party, and she wouldn't be giving one now if Carmen hadn't begged.

The whole idea had been set in motion when Luna had invited Julia and Carmen to come to her house in Roskam the Saturday after Thanksgiving. Dinner had been a quietly happy and elegant affair that day, made happier by the fact that it was mild enough afterward to go over to the park, and more joyful yet, though not at all quiet, because Robert, Vanessa, and Lizzy, along with their houseful of company, had all trooped over to the park also. Vanessa's family had driven to Roskam for Thanksgiving Day, and several had stayed over the weekend.

Somehow Carmen had ended up playing tag and Red Rover with the children, pushing them on swings, going down the slides, organizing races. She had taken a picture on Julia's cell phone of all the cousins climbing over the tires, with Lizzy right in the middle, wearing her pink cap, her little tongue stuck out the side of her mouth with the effort of keeping up with the big kids.

From time to time even now, Carmen stopped midsentence and said things like, "She sure doesn't hold back, does she?" or "Remember when she was chasing her cousin and she *caught him*?" She seemed particularly pleased that the cousin was a boy, and a whole year older than Lizzy.

That Carmen would ask for a dinner party, given her general indifference toward food, had surprised Julia, but she had readily agreed, hoping it was a sign of things to come. Who knew what other changes might follow? Maybe she could convince the girl to buy some new clothes one of these days. Or take a bath in a full tub of water instead of only a few inches.

But most likely the motivation behind the dinner party had more to do with Carmen's firm belief in reciprocation. Luna had spread a feast for them in November, so nothing would do but to return the favor and invite her to Beckett. And many weeks before that, Pamela had fed them well at her house in Virginia, so this was to be a double reciprocation, for Pam and Butch were driving down and were due to arrive within the hour.

It couldn't be just a regular meal at the kitchen table. No, Carmen had to make it into a Grand Occasion. In between studying for her GED test, which was scheduled for March, she had thrown herself into the dinner plans, had been at it off and on for weeks. She went through cookbooks and recipe files, took stock of Julia's china, and drew up a guest list, which Julia had at first mistakenly assumed would include only five of them.

When Carmen asked if the dining room table had an extra leaf, Julia said uneasily, "How many people are you thinking of inviting?" and the girl responded with "How many *can* I invite?" Evidently she wasn't to be deterred by a minor detail such as the fact that nobody else in Beckett, South Carolina, knew Luna, Pamela, and Butch. Gradually she narrowed the total to thirteen and drew up a seating arrangement, which she revised numbers of times.

In Julia's opinion, it was going to be the least homogeneous assortment of thirteen people ever convened, but Carmen was proud of the diversity, especially age-wise, the youngest guest being five and the oldest sixty-three. Julia had questioned her about the number thirteen, not because it was considered unlucky— Carmen would laugh at that—but because only twelve chairs would fit around her dining room table. Not a problem, Carmen had said. They could squeeze in another chair at one end.

The table was ready now except for the centerpiece, which Carmen was in the process of assembling in between checking on the ham, which was cooking slowly on the grill outside.

Julia mixed the maraschino cherries into the salad, then went to the refrigerator to get the bag of pecans. On her way back she paused at the door of the dining room for another look. She was still trying to see the table objectively. Did she like it because it really looked good, or simply because it was the product of Carmen's quirky imagination?

The girl must have been afraid she would never have another opportunity to sit in Julia's dining room and eat off her good dishes, for she had decided to use place settings from three different patterns of china, alternating them around the table. Nothing Julia would have ever thought of doing, though she had to admit the result wasn't bad. Thankfully, the three patterns coordinated nicely—a white set, a blue Spode, and red cut glass. Hardly a Christmas look, however, especially with the navy blue tablecloth and the white napkins, folded like sailboats, with a place card sticking out of each one. It looked more like a Fourth of July dinner, but Carmen said the centerpiece would set things straight concerning the season. And the sailboat napkins, she explained, were a reference to a Christmas song. Hadn't she ever heard of "I Saw Three Ships Come Sailing In, Plus Ten More"?

All of this from someone who had never shown the slightest interest in anything remotely fancy. It had taken an amazing amount of labor, most of which Carmen had done herself. Julia wasn't worried about the meal—it was a good menu, better than anything she had put together for a long time—but she feared that Carmen might have set her hopes too high.

Though she had forgotten much of what she once knew about the art of giving dinner parties, one sure principle Julia remembered was that even if every dish turned out perfect, there were always things you couldn't plan for—awkward silences around the table, guests with strange food allergies, spills and breakage, verbal gaffes, late arrivals or no-shows.

Well, if the whole thing was a flop, it would still be something to remember, maybe to laugh over someday. Regardless of how it turned out, it would be another manifestation of Carmen's tendency to take anything she did to great lengths.

J ULIA looked out the kitchen window. A fleet of white clouds floated through the pale blue ocean of sky above the treetops, which, except for the evergreens, were mostly bare now. The two little girls across the street were out in their yard again, jumping in piles of leaves.

Julia glanced at the thermometer mounted outside the kitchen window. Fifty-two degrees. A perfectly poised temperature for a December day. Twenty degrees colder and it would be freezing; twenty higher and it would be balmy. At dessert time maybe they could move to the living room and turn the gas logs on. Or maybe not. Maybe with all those people in the house, they would need to open the windows instead.

The Olympian Nectar was finished now, a pretty salad with all the fruits purpled by the grape juice. Julia covered it and put it in the refrigerator. She took the casseroles out and placed them on the stove, then turned the oven on to preheat. She went to the back porch to check on Carmen's progress with the centerpiece.

On the wicker table sat a toy sleigh made of red tin, filled with cascades of ivy. Carmen was adding pinecones, holly berries, and miniature blue Christmas balls, moving around the table to study the effect from every angle. She had dug the sleigh out of a box of old Christmas decorations in the attic, had asked Julia if it was okay to ditch the Santa Claus and reindeer, several of which were missing their antlers.

Carmen saw her and looked up. "Does it look okay?"

Julia laughed. "Fetching." She was no longer surprised at anything Carmen did. She could take an old sock and somehow turn it into a work of art, which was exactly what she had done for their Christmas stockings now hanging from the mantel in the living room.

"What did you do with poor old Santa?" Julia said.

"Left him in the attic with the reindeer," Carmen said. "They're up there conspiring. I heard Prancer tell Blitzen they're going to crash the party." She laughed and stuck a sprig of holly in her hair. Even that looked good.

• • •

IT was funny how everyone seemed to arrive at the same time, as if they had traveled in a caravan. Pam and Butch pulled into the driveway first, followed by all the others in close succession, with Luna being the last by only a few minutes. By six thirty they were all seated in the dining room, except for Carmen, who was standing to deliver a few opening remarks. She started by introducing each guest, though they had already met informally in the living room. She circled the table as she spoke, touching the chair of each person in turn.

She started with Julia, then Luna. Then Colleen, their neighbor across the street. Then Colleen's two little girls, Jackie and Nicole. "They sometimes let me play with them if I beg hard enough," she said. The little girls, usually full of chatter, smiled shyly as if this Carmen couldn't possibly be the same one who played hopscotch with them and talked in funny voices.

She proceeded to Dr. Boyer, who bobbed his head primly and offered the same smile that had always struck Julia as self-satisfied. He was wearing a limp houndstooth sport coat and black vest, with a pocket watch on a fob, which he had already pulled out once to consult.

Carmen moved on. "And my pastor and his wife, Chris and Christy—I promise I'm not making that up—and their two sons, Jared and Jay, who look like twins, but fortunately their parents had a year after Jared to catch their breath and try to regain their sanity."

Jay spoke up. "Yeah, and then they said, 'Okay, let's try again, I know we can do better than that.'"

Everyone laughed.

"And when *that* didn't work out," Jared said, "oh, well, oops, they were stuck with both of us."

More laughter.

"And my highly esteemed Aunt Pamela," Carmen was saying now. Pamela flapped her napkin and said, "Woo-hoo!"

"And her husband, Uncle Butch," Carmen added. "They gave up a bluegrass Christmas shindig to drive all the way down from Virginia."

Carmen smiled and looked around the table. "Okay, so now that everybody knows everybody else, you can all share your deepest, darkest secrets while you eat."

Dr. Boyer looked worried. He pulled out his pocket watch again and looked at it.

Pamela exclaimed, "I've got a secret! Butch and I have lost fifty-three pounds between us! In just *nine* weeks!"

She stood up and took a little bow amid a flurry of congratulatory remarks and applause.

Julia joined in, even though she felt like pointing out to Pamela that something one bragged about constantly hardly qualified as a secret. But she was glad for her sister, she truly was. If she weren't looking at the proof with her own eyes, she wouldn't have believed that a water exercise class could really help people lose weight. Pamela had told her on the phone recently that she and Butch were having a contest now, carefully checking each other's weigh-ins to make sure there was no cheating. The loser had to take the other one on a cruise. Pamela thought this was hilarious. "See, we're guaranteed a cruise either way!" she had crowed.

After Pamela finally sat down, Carmen asked Pastor Chris to say grace, and then she started bringing the food in from the kitchen. She was dressed in all red tonight—a pullover sweater of Julia's and a pair of red pants, not exactly the same shade of red, though she declared them "close enough." Her face was bright, her mass of curls still sporting the sprig of holly. She showed no signs of being as high-strung as Julia had always been when she used to host dinner parties.

Julia wanted to pull her aside and warn her not to presume on the fact that everything had gone smoothly so far, to remind her that the evening was far from over and anything could happen. She could tell her about the time many years ago when she had knocked herself out putting on a dinner for the English department faculty, only to have the dean's wife get suddenly, violently ill right as the beef Wellington was being passed around the table.

But no, she couldn't do that. Let the girl have her pleasure while it lasted. Let her find out for herself how quickly a dinner party could take a turn for the worse. For now, Julia meant to relax and enjoy it. Not being in charge was a good way to start.

T HE food was good—the fatted pig, as Carmen called the ham, the Olympian Nectar salad, the homemade bread, the mint tea, the potatoes au gratin, the green bean–carrot–corn medley, and the squash casserole. There were no lulls in the conversation, no embarrassing slips of tongue, no glasses tipped over, no unwelcome surprises of any kind. No one seemed to be in a hurry. Even Dr. Boyer seemed to forget about his pocket watch.

Afterward, Carmen asked Jackie and Nicole to help her clear the table. The conversation, which had earlier revolved around a single topic at a time, had now fractured into several different ones. When Pamela started telling Colleen about an article she had read concerning chicken pox vaccinations, Julia got up and went into the kitchen to help with the coffee and dessert. The countertops were covered with dirty dishes—always the discouraging part of a big dinner. Carmen was at the kitchen table, slicing the cake they had put the finishing touches on late last night. Carrot pumpkin cake with cream cheese frosting. Julia began pouring the coffee while Jackie and Nicole helped Carmen carry plates of dessert into the dining room.

The cake, like the rest of the meal, was a hit. Christy and Luna both wanted the recipe, but Pamela said, "Not me. I would be too tempted to make it!" Both she and Butch nevertheless ate a whole piece each. "You can't stick to a diet when you're at somebody's house," Pamela said. "That would be downright *rude*."

Pastor Chris was the first to start breaking up the party. "Some of us have to work on Sunday," he said, smiling affably. "I need to go over my sermon some more. Might have to add another couple of illustrations you good folks provided tonight."

A few at a time they got up from the table and wandered into the living room, still talking. Julia went back to the bedroom to get coats and jackets, and within a few minutes everyone had left except Luna, Pamela, and Butch. Pam and Butch were staying overnight, but Luna was driving home tonight, and she appeared ready to get on her way.

"Can't you stay just a minute?" Carmen said to her at the door. "We haven't had a chance to talk. Did you have a good time tonight?"

Luna took Carmen's hands in hers. "It was wonderful," she said. "Thank you."

"How is she?" Carmen asked.

"She's fine," Luna said. "Just as beautiful as ever. She *counted* for me the other day. Very precisely—*one, two, free*. All the way to twelve. She's getting a tricycle for Christmas, and she's singing in a program at church. The two- and three-year-olds are going to be . . . a choir of little angels."

Carmen hugged her again. "Oh, Luna, that's a *good* thing. It's nothing to cry about." She helped her with her coat, then walked her out to her car. The last thing Julia heard her say was "I'm so glad you came. You need to get out more, you know." From the kitchen window Julia saw her standing at the end of the driveway in the faint glow of the streetlight, watching Luna's car all the way down Ivy Dale.

· *chapter 26* ·

SOMETHING WORTHWHILE

It seemed in many ways like just any other day, this cold drizzly Wednesday in late March, but it wasn't. Though it was early, Carmen had been up for well over an hour already, and now she was eating her breakfast, chewing slowly after every bite. Julia was sitting at the kitchen table with her, ready to talk if she wanted to but looking at the newspaper to show she didn't have to.

She had fixed the girl a hearty breakfast of scrambled eggs, toast, ham, and grits. She thought it was funny how Carmen had grown to like grits. A little butter, salt, and pepper, and she could eat a plateful. Today she didn't seem to be aware of what she was eating, however, only that on such a big day as this, she needed to eat. As for Julia, she couldn't imagine eating anything right now with her stomach in knots.

The day of reckoning—that was how Carmen had referred to it for the past several months. She was taking the GED test today, all five parts, almost eight hours' worth. She was wearing a pair of jeans and an old sweatshirt of Julia's with the Phoenix Suns logo on it, along with the words *Phoenix—A Capital City for Basketball.* Her hair was pulled back and secured with a rubber band at the nape of her neck, though a multitude of curly wisps had escaped. She looked at Julia. "Well, it's here. I feel ready. I think."

"You're ready," Julia said. She heard herself say the words, quietly, confidently, saw her steady hand lift her cup of coffee, was aware of her reassuring nod and smile, all the while wondering how she could fake such calm. She knew parents must wage a lifelong battle against nerves, for how was it possible *not* to feel your children's dreams and desires as intensely as your own, not to feel your heart pounding when they put themselves on the line in some important endeavor?

They had already looked into the GED before their trip last fall, but when they located Lizzy, Carmen's interest in taking the test suddenly turned into something close to obsession. And not just to pass it, but to pass with flying colors. "It's time to get serious," she had said. "I should have done this a long time ago." She allowed herself no excuses. Never mind that she had been trying to keep body and soul together for over four years, an explanation she brushed aside as nonsense when Julia mentioned it. "I could've done it if I'd wanted to bad enough," she had said, then corrected herself. "Badly enough. Where there's a will, there's a way, and all that. Bottom line, I wasted a lot of time."

Now, after months of preparation—poring over books, studying late into the night, taking practice tests—the day had arrived. She had been told she could spread the test out over two or three days, but she had wanted to take it all on the same day. You don't slay a dragon, she said, by chopping off a foot one day, then a leg, then eventually getting around to the head. You sharpen your sword and go in for the kill.

She took a long drink from her glass of milk. "I probably shouldn't have taken those two weeks in December off."

"You needed them," Julia said. "Besides, it took time to plan the party, remember? And the party was nice, wasn't it?"

"I could've gone through that history book at least another couple of times," Carmen said. She was referring to a study manual she had ordered, titled *Around the World in Eighty Pages: A Condensed History of Civilizations Past and Present*. Condensed indeed, but it had helped her get the big picture, to see what was going on in China, for instance, during the French Revolution.

"You already know it like the back of your hand," Julia said.

It was the history section of the test the girl seemed most concerned about, more than the science or math or language arts. Certainly more than the essay. She was actually looking forward to the essay, couldn't wait to see what the topic would be. Over the past months she had written dozens of practice essays for Julia to read and comment on. It had become like a game for her, a way of rewarding herself at the end of each night's study session.

She knew the real topic wouldn't be any of the ones she had found online, but she had practiced all of them. For Carmen, the challenge wasn't trying to come up with something to say; it was streamlining all the ideas that flooded her mind, keeping her answers within the time and word limits. She sprinkled her essays with vivid words—*bellicose, arcane, fulminate, poppycock, salutary*. It was amazing how she could slip them in with such precision, never giving the impression that the word was more important than the idea it was developing.

She had even started making up questions of her own to write about, and more recently had asked Julia to give her some. Though Julia had resorted to a few frivolous questions, some of them had yielded useful information—for example, *If you had a thousand dollars, what special thing would you buy for yourself and why?* That one had resulted in Julia's purchase of a guitar for Carmen's birthday in

February, something she never would have known the girl wanted if she hadn't assigned the question for an essay.

Y OU'RE sure you know how to get to the right place?" Julia asked now.

"Is that another essay question, or do you really want to know?" Carmen asked. But she must have guessed it was a hint to watch the time, for she glanced at the clock, then finished up and carried her dishes to the sink.

"Leave them," Julia said. "I have all day. You don't."

Carmen went to get her things. Julia forced herself to remain at the table. Carmen was twenty-one now. She didn't need her aunt fussing around as she left, checking to make sure she didn't forget anything. Julia had fixed her a good lunch, had put it in a tote, along with three bottles of water. It was sitting on the kitchen counter. Carmen would pass right by it when she came back through the kitchen on her way to the garage. Julia would stay put until she left, would keep her voice low and even as she said good-bye, would refrain from test-taking reminders—and, of course, would watch to make sure she didn't forget her lunch.

Carmen was putting on her jacket as she came back into the kitchen. "I hope they don't think I'm cheating," she said, pointing to her sweatshirt. "I mean, what if one of the questions is 'What's the capital city of Arizona?'" She had a small canvas purse, which she unzipped now. "Okay, pencils, two forms of ID, gum, large sums of cash to buy them off if I flunk." She shot a grin at Julia, then took the car keys off the hook by the back door. "Oh, and this." She walked back to the counter and picked up the tote. "Thanks, Aunt Julia, I'll see you when I see you." She blew a kiss and was gone.

Julia took her coffee to the window. As the car pulled away, she waved and was answered with a light beep of the horn. She stood there a long time, watching the rain come down. *What are the advantages of a rainy day over a sunny one?* That had been another question she had given Carmen to write about. She remembered the first main point of her essay: "A rainy day is more conducive to contemplation than a sunny day." *So here it is,* Julia thought, *a whole day for contemplation laid out before you.* As if she could contemplate anything, knowing Carmen was sitting in a room taking a test that meant so much. Julia hadn't felt this jittery at her own dissertation defense almost thirty years ago.

She needed a new project to occupy her mind, or at least her hands. Or maybe an old project not yet completed. She would clean up the dishes, then get dressed and see what she could find to do.

Sometime later, after finishing some ironing, cleaning out the refrigerator, and talking with Pamela on the phone, she passed by Carmen's bedroom and noticed that the guitar case was open. So maybe the girl had at least taken time to hold the instrument. She had been overwhelmed by the gift a month earlier, had immediately thought of her essay and apologized profusely. "I never meant to be hinting, I promise!" she said over and over. "Oh, this is too much, way too much!"

Julia had told her not to worry, she hadn't paid a thousand dollars for it. And it was true, though not by much.

She stepped into Carmen's bedroom. She never came in here since there was never a reason to. Carmen kept it clean, folded her own laundry and brought it to her room to put away. Julia picked the guitar up and strummed it. She had been totally ignorant of what to buy, had no idea there were so many factors to consider— types of wood, strings, body styles. The sales clerk at the music store had walked her through the basics, then asked her how much money she wanted to spend, after which he had gone to a back room and returned with this instrument, just acquired on a trade-in, he said, the same way it worked with cars.

"This is going to be *so* frustrating." That was another thing Carmen had said when she first held the guitar.

"Wait, didn't you say you already knew how to play some?" Julia said.

Carmen explained. The frustration was going to come from having to wait until after the GED test to really enjoy it. If she started playing it now, it would take up time she needed to use for studying. But it would be an incentive, she said. A prize for finishing the test. Every time she looked at it, she would study harder.

Julia ran her hand over the wood now, plucked a few strings, then set it gently back in the case. Maybe tonight Carmen would get it out and play something. She had a book of folk songs somewhere, something that had come with the instrument. And then she saw it. It was on the table next to the bed, on top of other books. She walked over and picked it up.

Folk Tunes Everyone Should Know. Julia detested titles like that, as if anybody could make a list of things *everyone* should know. But evidently Carmen had found it interesting enough to browse through while sitting in bed.

J ULIA looked at the other books on the table. Most of them were study aids for the GED test. And a novel titled *Home*, which Luna had given her for Christmas. And Carmen's Bible, of course. And her journal, which Julia hadn't seen since their trip to New England. She wondered if Carmen still wrote in it.

Before she stopped to think, she pulled it out of the stack and opened it to a page near the back. *She's not mine, but I love her so. I pray that she'll grow to be as beautiful inside as she is outside. I never knew how hard it was to find a treasure you couldn't keep, but I'm so thankful we—* Julia closed it quickly. What did she think she was doing?

After a moment she opened it again to another page. *I dreamed last night that I was married. We lived in a house just like Aunt Julia's. I was in the kitchen working, and I could hear the birds singing in the backyard, and then I realized it wasn't birds at all. It was my children playing and laughing.* Julia closed it again. How low could she sink to pry into Carmen's private thoughts this way? Sneaking into her room while the girl was away doing something worthwhile and honorable.

She started to put the journal down, but opened it once more. *God's Mercies* was written at the top of the page, and under it a numbered list all the way to the bottom. Julia scanned the list. *Forgiveness, Justification, Sanctification.* Those were all on one line. *Finding Aunt Julia.* That was farther down on a line by itself. And a few lines later, *Finding Elizabeth Sarah Fiorelli—my daughter Lizzy, age 2 yrs. 1 mo. 8 days when I found her.* And on the very next line, *Robert and Vanessa Fiorelli—Lizzy's parents.*

Overcome with shame, Julia closed the journal and put it back on the table. She couldn't remember where it had been in the stack of books, but she knew it wasn't on top. Compounding her guilt was worry. What if Carmen noticed things had been tampered with? She would know Julia had been snooping.

Julia didn't know why she was crying all of a sudden, whether from the disgrace of what she had just done or from the heartache of the words she had read or from her sudden, deep longing for a soul as clear and free and honest as Carmen's. She rearranged the books, hoping it was close enough. It comforted her somewhat to realize that although she knew exactly which four books were currently stacked on her own nightstand, she didn't have any idea what order they were in. So maybe Carmen wouldn't notice anything amiss.

At least Julia remembered that the book of folk songs had been on top. She adjusted the stack so that it didn't look so neat, then opened the folk song book and leafed through it. All the standard songs, with chords written above the staves. "Greensleeves," "Shenandoah," "On Top of Old Smoky." She turned a page. "The Girl I Left Behind," "Hush Little Baby." She slapped it shut and walked to the door. She knew for sure the door had been open all the way, so at least she didn't have to worry about that.

She checked the clock. Carmen wasn't even close to half done with the test by now. Julia suddenly realized she ought to eat something since she'd had nothing but two cups of coffee early that morning. She found a small container of leftover chicken salad in the refrigerator and ate it on a few crackers, then washed it down with a glass of ginger ale. She tried to do the crossword puzzle in the newspaper but couldn't concentrate. Besides, Carmen liked to do the puzzle. She would save it for her.

S HE walked from the kitchen back through the hallway again. All the closets and cupboards and drawers were sorted and straightened. All the laundry was done, all the housework caught up. She couldn't work outside in the rain. Carmen had the car, so she couldn't go to the grocery store even if she needed to, which she didn't. She returned to the kitchen.

She thought of calling Marcy Kingsley. They had talked several times since Christmas, mostly about things going on at Millard-Temple. Old Dr. Kohler had died in her sleep over Christmas break, so Marcy had been asked to teach her two Shakespeare classes this semester, on top of her regular British Literature classes. Dean Moorehead's wife had fallen coming down their back steps and broken both wrists. That Vera person, the adjunct professor filling in for Harry Tobias, had been asked to stay on next year and develop some new graduate courses in psychology. And Julia's classes were smaller this year, which Marcy interpreted as "everybody's waiting till you come back in the fall." Marcy was always upbeat, and, unlike Pamela, didn't get testy if Julia suddenly wanted to end the conversation. She picked up the phone to dial her number, but then remembered what day it was. Marcy taught all day on Wednesdays.

She put down the phone and looked around. There was another idea, of course. A quiet, rainy day would be perfect for writing. Over the past month or so, she had cautiously, secretly begun writing a story about a husband and wife drifting apart, adding only a few sentences at a time so as not to let it get ahead of what she felt rising slowly within her—hope maybe, and the beginnings of confidence. She liked it so far. She didn't know where it would lead, but she was determined to follow. Perhaps her strongest motivation was a recent thought: that fiction writers could, in a sense, revise the mistakes of their past through their stories.

But she knew writing was out of the question today. Her mind was too scattered. She might get stuck, and then discouragement would undo her.

It suddenly hit her that part of the problem right now was that it was too quiet in the house. That she hadn't thought to put on any music or turn on the radio was proof that she had not been thinking straight today. She went back to the living room and looked through the CDs. Rachmaninoff, Shostakovich, Beethoven, Handel, Mussorgsky, Prokofiev—none of them seemed right for a rainy day when she couldn't sit still. She needed something to take her far away from the stone house, the musical equivalent of a cyclone to blow her from Kansas to Oz. And then she saw it. The CD titled *Space for All*, which included everything from Holst's *The Planets* to John Williams's *Star Wars* to Rimsky-Korsakov's *Dance of the Comets*. That should do it.

And almost simultaneously, she had another thought. Her eyes swept across the wall of bookshelves. She had cleaned and reorganized every inch of the house except, for some strange reason, these bookshelves. It was enough to make her laugh. It was almost enough to give rise to a Carmen-like thought: *This was a task especially reserved for today, forgotten until you needed it most.* Well, if that was so, why hadn't it come to her earlier, before she started prowling around in the girl's bedroom?

She put the *Space* CD on, then stood back and studied the bookshelves again. This would be a good time to weed out some of these things. She would work from left to right, top to bottom. Just like reading a book.

T HREE weeks later, a few days before Easter, Julia was looking through the freezer for a package of lunch meat when Carmen came in from the backyard. "*Look* what I found," she said. "Did you know these were back there? Do you know what they're called?"

Julia stopped rummaging and turned to look. It took a moment to call up the name. "Lily of the valley," she said. "I had forgotten all about them." It came back to her now, one of those scenes still lodged in the recesses of her mind, still capable of rising from the dead, so to speak, making it hard to keep breathing normally, also making her wish once again that she had a different kind of memory than the one she had. People with bad memories were spared so much. She turned back to the freezer and aimlessly moved a few things around.

Matthew had shown her the picture in a plant catalog—a whole bed of lily of the valley nestled beside a walkway—then had gone on at some length about how his grandmother used to grow them in her little patch of a flower garden in Tennessee, about how pretty they would be in early spring if he planted some in their own backyard.

Like so many other times, Julia had listened without responding. One thing she had learned long ago was that Matthew could talk on and on, especially if someone acted too interested in what he was saying. He could be almost as excitable as a woman, remarking on common things you saw every day. "Whoa, look at that cardinal on the fence—such a big guy!" he might say. Later in the day she might see him sitting on the back step putting a new switch on her bedside lamp, and she would feel a brief stirring of pity and gratitude for all the small kindnesses he did, for which he must know by now he would receive no thanks.

He had ordered the lily of the valley from the catalog—pips, he had called them, not bulbs—and when they arrived, he went on at length about the chance he was taking, since South Carolina wasn't the ideal growing zone, though they should do all right along the creek bank in the partial shade and good rich soil, moist enough but not too moist, and so forth and so on. She was glad when he had finally stopped talking and gone outside to plant them.

But Julia had never seen them in bloom, hadn't given them a thought since the day he planted them, whenever that was.

She heard the clink of glass and looked back to see Carmen stooped in front of the cupboard under the sink, where all the vases were kept. "I don't see how anybody could forget about these," the girl said, laughing. "Have you ever *smelled* them?" She took out a small blue cream pitcher, filled it with water, and brought the flowers over to Julia.

Julia leaned close and breathed in, then shook her head in wonder. "No, I would remember that." She stared at the tiny bell-like blooms. It seemed impossible that so much fragrance could come from flowers no bigger than pearls. And equally impossible that she wouldn't know that something so exquisite was growing in her backyard. It must have been one of the last things Matthew had planted, now that she thought about it, maybe even on the same day he collapsed in the flower bed. If that was so, they would have bloomed last spring. But, of course, she hadn't been in her right mind last spring, going through the motions of teaching, trying to imagine how she would survive a sabbatical. No doubt she had been unaware of a lot more than the lily of the valley quietly opening along the bank of the creek.

Carmen set the flowers in the kitchen window. "I do believe these are the last ones, though," she said. "A lot of them are already dried up. I can't believe I missed them. They must not bloom very long."

Ah, yes, Julia thought, another metaphor for the way life works. You wake up too late to find you missed something good, or almost missed it. She closed the freezer door hard. "I know I bought some sliced turkey and ham, but I can't find it," she said. "Want to walk over to Del's with me and get a sandwich?" It was well past one o'clock, late for lunch. Maybe that was why she felt so cranky all of a sudden. Driving would be faster, but the walk would do her good and it would allow a little more time for Del's to clear out from the lunch crowd, if there was one today. With spring break starting tomorrow, maybe the students were already on their way to the beach or wherever it was they were going to waste their time and money.

Carmen glanced at the clock. "You mean right now?"

"Right now," Julia said. "I'm hungry. Are you?"

Carmen shrugged. "Well, okay, I guess I could eat a sandwich."

"We can decide what to do about supper later," Julia said.

As if meal schedules were of any importance to Carmen. Julia didn't know what or when the girl had eaten today, only that she had been down on her knees with a bucket of sudsy water scrubbing the floor when Julia had come into the kitchen that morning for her first cup of coffee. The whole house smelled like Pine-Sol. A little later she had seen her in the driveway examining an old bicycle—a rusted relic she had pulled out of the loft in the garage.

"CAN we go this way?" Carmen said when they got to the end of the driveway. She pointed left. That would mean taking the long way to Del's, but it was okay. Walks with Carmen didn't happen that often. Besides, there was no pressing business to get back to.

They headed west on Ivy Dale, soon passing the house with the wide porch and all the wind chimes. There wasn't much breeze today, however. A man was sitting on the porch, tipped back on the rear legs of a ladder-back chair. He had on an old hat, pulled down low. He looked like he was asleep, but then he dipped his head and touched the brim of his hat.

"Has she made you another one of those pies yet?" Carmen called. "Naw," came the answer. His wife made good sweet potato pies, she explained to Julia. Then, from the man, "You heard back yet from that test you took?" Carmen told him the scores still weren't posted. "Shouldn't be long now," she said.

A little later she said to a woman watering a plant, "Is it hot enough for you?" The woman called Carmen "darling," told her they were predicting upper eighties on Easter Sunday, said it was way too early for that.

Approaching the Presbyterian church, they heard the children before they saw them. "Those are the K–4 kids," Carmen said. "They play outdoors after rest time."

Julia laughed. "Do you know the whole day's schedule?"

"Pretty much," Carmen said. "Sometimes they mess me up, though, and switch things around, like on the days they have group chapel."

Julia couldn't help wondering what the Presbyterians did for "group chapel" with children so young, what with all the whining and wiggling around and such. Would there be a sermonette? A catechism drill?

Carmen was still talking. ". . . and some of them get picked up at twelve thirty. But a lot of them stay all day. A different group of fours come after lunch for an afternoon session. And it's not just babysitting either—they teach them all kinds of things. It's like real school." She had obviously hung around here a good bit. More evidence that she had another life besides the one she lived with Julia in the stone house. "They're smart kids, too," she said. "One of the teachers told me she was showing the threes and fours a video not long ago and needed to pause it. She was fumbling around with the remote when the little boy sitting next to her leaned over and said, 'Just push the button with the parallel lines on it.'"

They turned by the church to cut back through the neighborhood and head in the direction of Millard-Temple. They could see the playground now, and they slowed as they passed it. A little boy close to the fence waved at Carmen, then pointed to Julia and asked, "Who's she?"

"My aunt," Carmen said. "Do you have an aunt?"

"Aunt Penny," he said. "She's fat."

"I'll bet she has a nice, soft lap, doesn't she?" Carmen said.

"She doesn't have a lap," he said gravely. He waved again and took off for the swings.

They continued on their way. "How many two-year-olds are there?" Julia asked at length.

"Seventeen," said Carmen. "Cute kids." Then, half a block later, "No, not a single one can hold a candle to her."

chapter 27

FULL IN A DIFFERENT WAY

As Julia had hoped, Del's Deli was almost empty. At a table by the door, a boy sat by himself, his eyes glued to the screen of his laptop. At another table, two girls were laughing as they gathered up their trash to leave. Julia recognized one of them as the student who had made an F in Creative Writing a couple of years earlier, something that rarely happened, even to those with the imagination of a boulder. The girl glanced at Julia, then stopped laughing and ducked her head quickly.

Julia suggested ordering a whole sub and splitting it, to which Carmen replied, "Hey, yeah, cool, no problem, like, let's split, L-O-L, you know, dude?" an obvious reference to a recent comment of Julia's about the sloppy vocabulary of so many young people today.

They ordered, got their drinks, and found a table.

"New paintings," Julia said, looking around. "I think I'll digest my food better today."

Carmen nodded. "These were left over from the midyear art

show." She pointed to a picture near their table. "This is my favorite. This guy is really good. He won some kind of big prize at a juried show in Charleston."

It was quite a large piece, a backyard scene—toys scattered across the grass, a hound sleeping under a tree, a rusting swing set, clothes hanging on a sagging clothesline, an overgrown vegetable garden beyond, with a few pie tins strung around it.

"Imagine that," Julia said. "Something you can actually recognize. Obviously the product of a dull, limited mind."

Carmen caught the irony. "For real. He must be such an embarrassment to the art department."

As they ate, Julia looked around at the other paintings. More representational pieces than usual. She wondered what it meant. Was there a new wind blowing through the art world? If so, she might start going to student art shows again. Not that she thought realism was always best, not at all. Many of her favorite pieces were abstracts, but not the bleak, random, angst-ridden things she saw so often these days—ugly stuff she didn't want to look at, much less buy and hang on her wall. Not an opinion she would ever voice on campus, though, for no professor wanted to be stuck with the leprous label of "traditionalist," especially in the arts. Heaven forbid that you should prefer performances where you saw or heard something hopeful, something you understood.

She looked again at the painting of the backyard. It was obvious that the artist had a fine eye for proportion, perspective, line, color. Not anything she would want to take home, though. All those signs of a tired, broken-down life—why would she want to look at that every day?

"I wish I could live there," Carmen said. She was still studying the painting. She took a small bite of her sandwich and chewed awhile. "I don't know why I like old things so much. But that right there is the kind of life I've always dreamed about."

The girl didn't sound like she was teasing, but with her you never knew. "What kinds of dreams?" Julia said. "Good ones? Or bad?"

Carmen didn't laugh. "You know for sure that the woman who looks out her kitchen window and sees a yard like that has a very full life."

"Then I guess my life is very empty," Julia said.

Carmen looked at her. "No, I didn't mean that. Not everybody wants a life like that. Your life is full in a different way. And I like your house anyway. I have dreams about it, too, sometimes. Good ones."

"It's fine," Julia said. The kind of vague comment that could mean almost anything. What she meant, she supposed, was that her own life was fine, Carmen's dream was fine, and everything in between the two was fine.

LOOKING away, Carmen spoke to the opposite wall. "Yesterday morning at the grocery store," she said, "I was in line behind this woman. There was a baby in the buggy gnawing on a box of animal crackers and two other little kids standing behind her fiddling with all the candy bars and gum in the rack. Her buggy was jammed full—cereal and diapers and milk and apple juice and all the rest of it. I started thinking about her older kids coming home from school in the afternoon and her husband coming home from work, and she'd be getting supper ready—maybe hot dogs and baked beans or chicken legs and mashed potatoes—and then they'd all sit down and eat together and everybody would be talking at the same time and one of the kids would spill something and the baby would make them all laugh, and then they'd all pitch in and clear the table, and . . ." She stopped and looked back at Julia. "Well, I guess it must sound like a pretty silly dream to you."

Julia shook her head. "I wouldn't call it silly." How could she say this next part tactfully? It was something that needed to be said. Carmen was twenty-one, not twelve. It was surprising, distressing really, that someone with her background could still be so emotionally young. It struck her as a sad, willful kind of blindness. All these months they had spent together, and Julia still hadn't taught her much that really mattered.

She proceeded carefully. "Any dream has a way of . . . growing old when it becomes reality. The romance fades. That woman you saw in the grocery store is probably dreaming of a different kind of life than the one she has." She gestured toward the painting. "And the one looking out that window probably wishes some magician would show up and get the laundry off the line and cook supper and give her money to buy a decent swing set." She went on for a little while longer until she realized she was repeating herself.

Carmen was listening politely. How could it be, Julia wondered, that the words she was saying—words she knew in her heart to be true—sounded so empty and unconvincing, even to herself? And what a conversation to be having in Del's Deli anyway. She came to the end of a sentence and stopped. No one else was in the shop now. The boy behind the counter had disappeared into the back.

Carmen ate a few chips. "Did I tell you there was a job opening on the yard crew on campus? I talked to the man in charge the other day. I might apply for it when I get my test scores back."

Yard crew? Julia thought. Why did the girl keep talking about applying for jobs instead of for college? Here was something else that needed to be said—again. Somebody with Carmen's mind needed at least a master's degree. She could major in anything she wanted to, ace any course, from math to music.

But just as Julia opened her mouth to speak, two boys entered the deli. One of them, a dark handsome kid in a pair of plaid pants, was talking quite loudly: "And so he tells me to mind my own . . ."

He stopped long enough to yank the cord of the cowbell just inside the door and say, "Hey, hey, here we are, everybody, now the fun can start," before picking back up with ". . . mind my own business, and I tell him it sort of *is* my business, see, since that's my dad's car he just rear-ended, and he says . . ."

He broke off suddenly and struck a pose like a lookout sentry. "Hark, is that really Charmin' Carmen sitting over there?" The other boy, tall and thin, looked over at Carmen and waved.

They walked over to say hello, the dark-haired boy talking the whole time, pausing only long enough for Carmen's introduction. The boys' names were Hardy and Joe Leonard, she told Julia, and their gospel quartet sang at her church sometimes. When she introduced Julia as "my aunt, Dr. Julia Rich," Hardy, the dark-haired kid, said he was glad to meet her because he'd been wanting to ask a doctor about a pain in his gall bladder.

Hardy was like a very immature, very smart, very hyperactive child. Besides his plaid pants, he was wearing a T-shirt with a faded picture of Beaver Cleaver on the front. Around his neck was a long chain with a collection of dog tags on it. Literal dog tags. One of them read, *My name is Sydney. Please return me.* There was a phone number, too.

Julia had fallen into the habit of sizing up every boy she saw these days as a potential match for Carmen. She sincerely hoped the girl wasn't interested in this one, though. The other one was better, though it was odd to see a college boy who still blushed as he did when he cleared his throat and said to her, "Dr. Rich? Are you the one who teaches Creative Writing at Millard-Temple? I think my girlfriend was in your class last year. She really liked it." His ears were bright pink by the time he finished. Julia asked what his girlfriend's name was, and he proudly said, "Kelly Kovatch."

"Yes, I know her," Julia said. "A nice girl and a very good writer."

His whole face turned pink.

"Hey, now, you've gone and embarrassed my bud here," Hardy said, laughing as he clapped Joe Leonard on the back. "Joe Leo's trying to convince me to transfer to Mill-Temp next year, so he's been showing me around campus today. And, say, I like to write! Who knows, I might be in one of your classes next fall."

Julia could only hope that wouldn't happen. She couldn't imagine being able to concentrate with a boy like him in class.

"How's your grandmother?" Carmen asked Joe Leonard. To Julia she said, "Joe Leonard's grandmother is one in a million. She came to our church to hear them sing one time."

"She's doing fine," Joe Leonard said. "My parents are going to take her to Atlanta to a Braves game for her birthday. She's hoping to catch a foul ball."

Hardy started telling a story about Joe Leonard's grandmother, something that involved a bag of popcorn on an escalator at the mall, but he was laughing so hard Julia didn't catch half of what he was saying. After that he said he knew a joke that would "curl your hair," but then he looked at Carmen and said, "Oh, wait, you must've already heard it, like, a thousand times." By the time the boys went to order their food, Julia felt like she had been in a crowded room pulsing with strobe lights and loud rock music.

"Hardy is a great guy but totally out of his mind," Carmen said, in a tone that bordered on fond.

"Does he have a girlfriend?" Julia asked.

To her relief, Carmen nodded. "He's engaged to a girl in Mississippi."

Julia gave Hardy another long look from across the room. On second thought, he might actually be fun to have in class. After all, she knew by now that a student's appearance wasn't a reliable indicator of how well he wrote. Hardy might just write the kind of wacky but insightful stories that could take your breath away.

And he sang in a gospel quartet—that was what Carmen had said. Julia was almost curious enough to want to hear it.

O NE Saturday in early May, Julia hurried in through the front door with two bags of groceries and took them to the kitchen. She left the car running in the circular drive since she was headed back out to buy a wedding gift for Marcy Kingsley's son. As she set the groceries on the kitchen counter, she heard Carmen playing her guitar and singing out on the back porch.

So this must be the song she had finally decided to sing in church tomorrow. She had been practicing several all week, but she kept coming back to this one—"What Wondrous Love Is This."

Sweet was the only word to describe Carmen's singing voice. The high notes floated light and easy and landed right on pitch, and the low notes were smooth and sure. A very natural voice, never breathy, never showy. Very little vibrato. Like clean, pure water. It was a voice Julia could listen to all day.

She stood very still so she could hear the words. The song was slow and measured, the chords changing frequently. Carmen was near the end now. *"And when from death I'm free, I'll sing and joyful be, And through eternity I'll sing on, I'll sing on, And through eternity I'll sing on."* The last note died away and all was quiet. Such a strange combination—happy words sung in a minor key, slowly.

With the car still running, Julia had meant to take time only to put the milk away, but she found herself reaching into one of the bags and pulling out the first thing her hand touched. A box of grits. She set it on the counter. Maybe if she waited just a moment or two, Carmen would sing again. But she didn't. The back door opened and the girl entered the kitchen, whistling. "Oh, hi, Aunt Julia, I didn't know you were back already." She ambled over to the sink.

Julia looked down at the box of grits. "I'm not staying. I'm just dropping some things off. But look what I did—I just noticed. I bought instant instead of regular."

Carmen shrugged. "That's okay, they'll just cook faster." She got a juice glass out of the cupboard. "Did you hear the joke about the undertaker? He took all the ashes from the cremations and sent them to the cannibals so they could have Instant People for breakfast."

"That's an old one," Julia said. She took the milk to the refrigerator.

Carmen filled the glass with water, then drank half of it and stopped. "Guess what?" She started drinking again.

Though it was one of the girl's favorite questions, Julia felt a sudden surge of hope. Maybe this was the day they had been waiting for. For weeks now Carmen had been checking online several times a day to see if her GED scores were posted yet. She had even found a phone number and called to ask about them. Evidently she wasn't the only one who had called, for there was a recorded message: They were "experiencing a delay" in reporting all test results, due to the high volume of spring test-takers and a programming error in the electronic grading equipment, which necessitated rechecking. The voice apologized for the "inconvenience" and said tests were being regraded in the order taken.

So maybe today was the day. Maybe while Julia had been out buying groceries, Carmen had found her scores online, and now she was about to break the news that she had passed, maybe even with honors.

JULIA took some cans of soup out of a bag and tried to act calm as she said, "What?"

"There's a new color of iris that just opened up," Carmen said.

"It's the color of cherry cola, and it's all frilly. It's right under your bedroom window. Did you see it?"

As a matter of fact, Julia had seen it. She hadn't put a name to the color, but cherry cola was as close as anything she could think of. She nodded. "Gil said he's going to pull up all the irises and separate them after they've finished blooming. He says they're too crowded." She took several more items out of the bags.

Carmen ran a little more water into the glass and drank it down. "Yep, I'm going to help him. We're tagging the stems so we'll know what color the bulbs are. Guess what else?"

"What?"

She pointed to the colored tiles of the backsplash above the sink. "I finally figured out the pattern. I don't know why it took me so long. See, if there was another row going down over here on this side, it would start with white, then gray, then blue, then white, then red. See? And on the other side, it would be blue, gray, yellow, white, red. That's because every fifth tile going across is gray and every third is white and in between . . ."

"Okay, I'll take your word for it," Julia said.

"Oh, and you know the thousand longest rivers in the world?" Carmen said.

Julia looked at her, puzzled.

"Remember—that big tapestry thing we saw in the art museum in New York?" Carmen said. "By Somebody Boetti."

Oh, that. *The Thousand Longest Rivers in the World.* Julia tried not to sound disappointed. "What about it?"

"Well, guess what I found out?" Carmen said. "Turns out Mr. Boetti hired *women* in Afghanistan to embroider the names. Just as we suspected."

"Imagine that," Julia said.

"And guess what else?" Carmen said.

"What?" Julia knew this could go on indefinitely if Carmen had been on the computer this morning. Now that she had finished retyping all of Julia's class notes, she was exploring the web just for fun. She loved the way she could find answers for the most trivial questions.

"I also Googled lily of the valley," Carmen said, "and you know what? It said it's poisonous if ingested but it's also used as a folk remedy in small amounts. For things like ulcers and earache and fevers. Isn't that weird? And it's a symbol of humility. Oh, and guess what else? I Googled that woman's name—the one who gives the news on NPR at noon. You know we were talking about how to spell it the other day? Well, it's L-a-k-s-h-m-i S-i-n-g-h. So we both missed it, but you were closer. It showed a picture of her, too. She's pretty. Oh, and she's not Indian or Pakistani. Her parents were from Puerto Rico and Trinidad. *Lak-shmi Singh*." Carmen said the name clearly, slowly, savoring each syllable. "I wonder if Lakshmi is a common name where she grew up. Maybe it's like Mary in the U.S."

"Why don't you Google 'common girls' names in Puerto Rico and Trinidad' and find out?" Julia said. She stuffed the empty plastic bags into the pantry with the others.

Carmen laughed. "Maybe I will. Oh, and that house next to Dr. Boyer's is listed for a hundred fifty-nine thousand, and . . ."

Julia laughed and held up a hand. "Save the rest for when I get back, okay? The car's still running out front. I shouldn't be gone long." She headed out of the kitchen.

"Okay," Carmen called after her, "I'll wait till you get home to tell you about my GED scores."

Julia came back to the doorway. "You'd better not be teasing."

Carmen held the glass up to the light and studied it. "No, I'm serious. I'll tell you when you get home. You know, I thought there was a crack in this glass, but I believe it's just part of the swirly pattern. Cool."

Julia pointed in the direction of the front door. "Go. Now. Turn the car off. I'll wait right here." She sat down at the kitchen table.

"Are you feeling *sick*?" Carmen said. "Why don't you lie down and let me run your errand for you?" She laughed. "Stay right here. I'll be back in two seconds."

A perfect score on the GED was 4000 points. To pass with honors, you had to score 3200 points or higher. Carmen's score was 3940. Science was the only part of the test she hadn't aced. She thought she might have missed a question about the effect of temperature on solubility and maybe one about carbon dating, but that one wasn't really fair, she said, because its premise was that evolution was true. "You can retake any section to try to do better," she said, "but I guess I won't."

So this, thought Julia, is how parents feel when their children excel—the initial "I must be dreaming," quickly countered by "No, it's true, she really did it," back and forth many times, until in the end it wasn't blood pumping through your veins, but pure euphoria. It was a joy that couldn't be contained. If you didn't talk about it, you would explode. Already Julia was making her list: Pamela and Butch, Luna, Marcy, Sheila and Hope, Colleen, Dr. Boyer. She would tell them first.

And children, no dummies when it came to handling grownups, could get a lot of mileage out of a single achievement. They could ask for anything in the following days and get it. Which could have been why Carmen asked Julia to go to church with her the next day. For sure it was why she got a different answer than the one Julia had given all the other times.

・*chapter 28*・

Sinking Down

Pulling into the church parking lot the next morning, Julia wondered again whether Carmen realized today was Mother's Day. They hadn't talked about it, but it was the kind of event that would be hard to miss with all the commercial hoopla surrounding it. She wondered if it would be a hard day for the girl, another reminder that she was a mother but had no child to show for it.

It wasn't a day Julia had ever celebrated, certainly not on the receiving end and only rarely on the giving end in the form of a few cards sent to her mother. Never the sentimental kind of card, though, and never any personal note beyond a generic "Happy Mother's Day" and her name. Pamela had always done much better. Flowers and gifts, always planned so as to arrive in plenty of time, followed up by a phone call on the actual day, all of which she talked about at length in the weeks and days before, with the obvious intention of spurring Julia to similar outpourings of gratitude.

If she had given more thought to it, Julia might have made an excuse for today and promised instead to go with Carmen the following week. But it was too late for *ifs* since they were now walking to the front door of the church. She could only hope that Pastor Chris wasn't the type to make a big deal out of Mother's Day, a hope that was dashed as soon as they stepped inside, where two ushers were presenting a long-stemmed rose to each woman with a smile and a greeting: "Happy Mother's Day! We're giving these to all the ladies today."

Julia took hers mutely—a salmon pink, tinged with yellow—and followed Carmen to a seat near the front. She was already wishing the morning away. The only thing she wanted to hear was Carmen's solo.

But there was much to be endured both before and after that. Songs and announcements, a choir number and responsive scripture, in which one of the lines read by the congregation was *that our daughters may be like cornerstones adorning a palace.*

Then a prayer, and offering plates were passed as the organist grappled with a piece that was beyond her ability. Another prayer, this one longer, and, finally, Carmen's solo. No theatrics, no microphone, just Carmen's voice and the guitar. She sat on a stool on the platform. The sanctuary was small, and her voice filled it. She was wearing a skirt as she did some Sundays—not her necktie skirt this time, but a green print, gypsy-style, long and flowing—and a white peasant blouse with a braided belt, all from Julia's closet of castoffs.

Julia wondered if everyone else was as disappointed as she was when the three stanzas were over. She wished she could leave now, but Carmen returned to sit by her and Pastor Chris stood up for his part.

Julia had never wondered how students could sit in her classes and hear so little of what she said, judging from their performance on papers and tests, for she knew from experience what flights her own mind was capable of taking. And so it was today. Instead of listening to the preacher, she kept replaying Carmen's solo. *What wondrous love is this, O my soul . . . When I was sinking down, sinking down . . . And when from death I'm free, I'll sing on . . .* She kept seeing the girl on the platform, sometimes bending her head to her guitar, sometimes lifting it to look out at the people.

And the happy news of the previous day—Julia relived that, too. A score of 3940 out of 4000—intelligence as well as beauty and musicality! And inevitably she found her mind wandering to the future. Carmen could enroll as a student at Millard-Temple for the fall, perhaps take one of Julia's writing classes at some point. There might be a scholarship of some kind for her high GED score. And perhaps Julia could put together a case to present to the financial committee so that Carmen might be considered a "faculty child" and therefore qualify for a tuition discount. She would write out a proposal first, then ask her dean to set up a meeting with the committee to discuss the matter. She even composed the opening few sentences. *For twenty-seven years I have taught full time at Millard-Temple . . .*

And then she was suddenly aware that the pastor must be concluding his sermon. Class was almost over, the bell was about to ring, and if she were to be given a quiz on today's lecture, she knew she would surely fail, for she had heard only isolated snatches, along with some communal laughter. Now he was wrapping things up with a prayer that God would raise up from among their midst "women of honor." He repeated the phrase several times, enough so that she knew his sermon must have been at least loosely related to the occasion of Mother's Day.

The prayer was still going when Julia felt a slight rustling beside her. She looked over to see Carmen wiping her eyes. Clearly, she had been listening. Julia was suddenly and deeply ashamed for her self-focus. What a host of sad thoughts must have been aroused in the girl by a sermon about mothers. What a sinking-down feeling.

I F Julia had thought that Carmen's quiet, brooding spells were a thing of the past, she was wrong. But what a time for melancholy—right on the heels of an academic triumph, just when they needed to be making plans for the months to come. Evidently word of her GED score had already been issued from some official source, for a reporter from the newspaper called the next day to talk to her about doing an article and coming by to take her picture. She told him to call back in a week or so.

Two days passed as the girl came and went, aloof and morose. She went for long walks, disappeared to her room early in the evening, played and sang only a few songs over and over, an odd rotation. "Rock of Ages," "Michael, Row the Boat Ashore," "He's Got the Whole World in His Hands." At supper she tried to put on a smile when she joined Julia at the kitchen table. They talked—about the gardenias budding, a neighbor's new fence, an accident on I-85, the price of gasoline. A few times they resorted to talking about the weather.

There was nothing to be done except wait it out. Whatever the cause, it had to be linked to the sermon on Sunday, the sermon Julia hadn't heard. She wouldn't think of asking the girl outright: *What's wrong? What's on your mind?* She knew, of course, that it ultimately related to Lizzy. And what was there to say about that?

On the morning of the third day it occurred to Julia that she could attack one last pocket of disorder at the stone house—the attic. She lowered the folding steps in the hallway and climbed up. There was a light with a pull chain, so she turned it on and looked around. Standing on the top step, she felt something almost like disappointment. As attics went, hers was probably less disorderly than most, certainly less so than she remembered.

Only seven boxes were stacked along one side. On the other side were several old suitcases, coated with dust, a large ice chest, and a lumpy stack of door wreaths wrapped in plastic garbage bags. Ah, yes, Julia remembered a time in her life when she used to change the wreath on the front door with every season. And next to the wreaths were the bins of Christmas decorations. Lying beside them was the artificial tree, each section neatly wrapped inside a plastic dry cleaning bag.

It suddenly struck her why things looked tidier than she had expected. Carmen had been up here before and after Christmas. She had gone through the boxes of decorations, had brought the tree down, taken it back up, and obviously done some reorganizing while she was at it. Julia looked back at the stack of boxes. The word *BOOKS* was scrawled on the side of one, but she knew such labels were never to be trusted when it came to attics. She made her way over to investigate. She could sort through whatever was inside them, probably discard most of it.

As she knelt to open the first one, she couldn't help thinking of all the "attic epiphanies" her students had written in their stories over the years. The main character goes to the attic to get something, only to stumble across something else that conveniently solves a mystery or helps him put his shattered life back together. *You're forcing a resolution.* Julia had written it on so many stories that she had considered having a rubber stamp made to save herself time and effort.

BEFORE long she was sitting down, surrounded by scores of useless things. There was something dispiriting about handling them all. What had ever possessed her to keep an old rolling pin?

A shoeshine kit with ancient tins of hardened wax and smudged rags stuffed inside? Matthew's old fondue pot from his bachelor days? A framed needlepoint of a kitten?

She went through five of the boxes, consolidating into a single box the few things she wanted to keep and shoving the others over toward the steps. She opened the sixth box, the one labeled *BOOKS*, and saw that it did indeed contain some books and quite a few magazines. Whose idea had it been, she wondered, to store *books* in the attic? She pulled one out and saw that the years had done to it exactly what would be expected in such a humid climate. Several she recognized as Matthew's, some as hers, but none were of any value or interest. The same with the magazines, no doubt. She picked up a few and looked through them.

If someone had asked her before today where the magazines containing her two published stories were, she would have thought about it briefly before admitting, "I don't know." Never would she have guessed they were in a box labeled *BOOKS* in the attic, but here they were. Two different issues, a year apart, of a magazine titled *Green River*. She opened one of them and found the story by "J. Frederickson Rich." Jeremiah's story. She stared at the picture some artist had deemed an appropriate illustration—the top of a tall rundown apartment building with articles of clothing hanging on balcony rails and heavy rain falling at a slant.

Well, so much for epiphanies. None here. No mysteries unraveled, no broken pieces of life put back together, no resolution of anything. Only a reminder that no amount of time or remorse could wipe away sullied honor.

"Aunt Julia?"

The sound made her jump. She looked up to see Carmen standing at the top of the ladder.

"Sorry, I didn't mean to scare you," the girl said. She climbed up into the attic and sat down facing Julia. "Can we talk?"

Julia's eyes fluttered down to the magazines in her lap, then back to Carmen's face. "Sure," she said. "This can wait. I was just going through these boxes." She tried to be nonchalant as she laid her hands over the magazines.

"I need to go to Wyoming," Carmen said.

It took Julia a moment to find her voice. "Wyoming?" she said. "When? Why?"

Carmen took the questions in order. "Yes, Wyoming. Right away. Among other things, to honor my mother." She must have read confusion in Julia's eyes. "You know, Pastor Chris's sermon on Sunday—he was preaching directly to me." She paused, then tried again. "What he said about how a woman who wants to honor God always honors the woman who gave her life—you know?"

"Oh, right," Julia said.

"But when he said it's never too late to make things right," Carmen continued, "I felt like standing up and saying, 'Uh, excuse me, what if your mother is *dead*? Isn't it a little too late then?'" She stopped again as if hoping for a reaction, at least a flicker of agreement, perhaps wondering if the same kinds of thoughts had crossed Julia's mind. She went on. "But then it was like I had asked my question out loud because remember the next thing he said?"

No, Julia didn't remember the next thing he said, and she didn't want to be told, but she knew she was about to be anyway. She felt a wave of dread, for she knew now where this was heading, especially since the thesis had already been stated: *I need to go to Wyoming.*

Carmen was evidently picking up on the fact that Julia hadn't heard much of the pastor's sermon, for she started summarizing. "He said if your mother's dead, maybe there's someone else back home you need to make things right with, which might mean making a trip. A *literal* trip. Life is too short, he said, to carry grudges around in your heart. Spiritual freedom always requires forgiveness.

He also said you might need to write out a confession or apology and read it out loud at her grave."

Julia raised her eyebrows but said nothing. Maybe Carmen was testing her, throwing in something preposterous to see if she would take issue. Surely the preacher hadn't really suggested a graveside speech, but if he had, maybe that was good. Surely Carmen could see the absurdity of that. Surely that part would make the whole idea of a trip sound a little silly. Especially such a long trip.

The girl continued. "But he said you should start by asking God to forgive you for not showing her the respect she deserves. And by remembering the good things about her and being thankful for those." Carmen looked down at her hands, closed into fists. "So I've been doing a lot of remembering. I tried for a long time to forget all the good things about Lulu because deep down I was still so angry at her." She looked back up at Julia. "But now I feel like I owe it to . . . Lizzy to do this." She paused and swallowed. "It didn't make sense at first—I mean, Lizzy won't ever even know me, and for sure won't ever know if I honored my mother, but I can't get away from it. I owe it to Lizzy to honor her grandmother. And to do that, I need to go to Wyoming."

If only Julia had been attentive enough on Sunday to hear even the gist of the preacher's sermon, she might have been able to forestall all of this drama and soul-searching. She could have initiated a conversation that very day, could have gotten it all out in the open, could have asked Carmen about some favorite memories of Lulu, and—though this part would have been especially hard—could have also dredged up some good memories to share about her own mother. By focusing on the positive, she might have distracted the girl enough to keep her from falling into such gloom and making such a drastic decision.

But she hadn't. Instead of support, she had given Carmen space—that is, solitude—and in so doing had left her defenseless against the kind of grief and misguided resolve brought on by regret. So now, this: *I need to go to Wyoming.*

JULIA quickly began constructing an argument. She had to be careful, of course—controlled and organized. Tone was as important as substance. The most logical starting point was easy: *How can a child be at fault for not honoring a mother who rendered herself ineligible for honor?* She hesitated, though. She knew Carmen well enough to anticipate her answer to that. She could mimic not only the girl's exact words but also her delivery, prompt and confident—the slight elevation of pitch, the lift of chin, the unflinching gaze, all of it so typical of the kind of mind that allowed no shades of gray. She could hear her now: *You do right because it's right, not because it's what somebody deserves or doesn't deserve. Wrong is always wrong. The fifth commandment says to honor your father and your mother. Period.* So skip that point; it was a lost argument. Besides, hadn't Carmen just said Lulu had some redeeming qualities?

A more promising idea came to her, though she realized even as she said it that it was a minor point. "Lulu may not even have a grave. She had your father cremated, remember. If they did the same for her, what would be the point of going back?"

Carmen's look said, *Weren't you listening to what I just said?* But she answered patiently, politely. "I can talk to Ida, maybe Effie, too. I was the one who started all the trouble by leaving home all those years ago. Left Lulu high and dry. Ida, too. They depended on me. I didn't even leave them a note. Just took their car and their money and Daddy's guitar and disappeared, then . . ."

"You were sixteen," Julia interrupted. "Sixteen-year-olds do foolish things."

Carmen held up a hand, shook her head. ". . . and then I show back up and say, 'Oops, my bad, things didn't work out, can I live here again?' Think about it—why *wouldn't* they say, 'Get lost, kid, it's not that easy'? I mean, I *stole* from them. And they didn't have that much."

Julia thought of something else that might work. She made herself talk slowly, calmly. "You said one time that Ida and Effie hated you because they hated Jeremiah. You said they turned Lulu against you. Well, let's imagine that a year or two later Lulu started wishing she could see you again. That would be the most natural thing in the world—to want to see your child again. She probably thought about you day and night."

Carmen was listening, her eyes fixed on Julia's face. She looked to be on the verge of tears.

Julia continued, cautiously. She didn't want this to become too emotional, but it had to have more than a purely rational appeal. "Did Lulu . . . ever pray?" she asked.

Carmen nodded. "All the time before Daddy died, a lot of times out loud. Afterward, mainly to herself. She cried a lot."

Tears and prayers—that evoked a tender scene. A little pathos was good. "So after you went back and they turned you away," Julia said, "Lulu probably spent hours praying for you and wishing she knew where you were so she could ask you to come back."

Carmen looked down. "Well, maybe but . . . Ida was still calling all the shots."

Julia suddenly lost sight of wherever she had been heading with this line of thought. She paused, then quickly improvised. "Well, my point is that if Lulu were still living, a trip home would make perfect sense. There would be a strong bond there already, and you could build on that. Both of you would be older and wiser now. Ready for a reconciliation. An answer to her prayers, forgiveness all around."

A squirrel skittered across the roof above their heads. Julia glanced up at the cobwebby attic beams, then at the drifts of insulation between the joists. It was surprising how clearly she could hear the chirping of birds through the roof. She looked back at the small floored area where they sat, surrounded by boxes, bins, dusty miscellany. Another odd setting for a conversation with Carmen.

"But she died," Carmen said. "No use thinking about if she hadn't."

"My point exactly," Julia said. "Lulu's not there, so there can be no appeal to her motherly instincts. So let's say you go all the way back to Wyoming and they slam the door in your face—again—or don't even open it in the first place. What good has that accomplished? It will be a lot of money and time for nothing."

"I'm paying for it," Carmen said. "I have enough saved up to buy a plane ticket. Or I might start out by bus. I haven't decided yet."

Julia didn't like the wording: *I'm paying for it*. It sounded like a decision already made. Furthermore, how could that be? Though Carmen was thrifty, how could she have saved that kind of money from her neighborhood jobs? But Julia rebuked herself for mentioning money. That wasn't the issue here. She needed to steer the conversation back to her main point—the futility of the trip. Yet still very carefully, gently.

"It might be wiser to start with a phone call," she said. "I have the number somewhere around here. Butch found it for me last year. You can tell a lot about Ida over the phone, and she can tell a lot about you. She can see how much you've changed and grown up, and . . ."

"I don't want to call," Carmen said. "I want to go. I want to see her face-to-face."

"She might not even still live there, you know," Julia said. "Effie was at death's door when I talked to Ida—didn't I tell you that? And hadn't Ida come out there originally just to help Lulu after your father died? Wasn't she from the South somewhere? So why would she want to stay in Wyoming after Lulu died?" Julia could hear the strain in her voice, the faster pace. How quickly a simple goal like staying calm could be abandoned.

CARMEN leaned back against one of the boxes, shifted a little so she could rest an elbow on it. She gazed up at the rafters. "This is kind of a peaceful place up here, isn't it? You could make yourself a nice little studio loft." She pointed. "That's called a ridgepole. I learned that when I worked on a roofing crew one day in New Hampshire." She laughed. "*One day.* They were hard up for help. They paid me in cash at the end of the day. Good money, too. They told me I was coming along pretty well for a newbie and things would start up again at seven the next morning if I could come back. But I said I was heading on down the road the next day, which was a decision I made right there on the spot. I was so sore I couldn't lift my arms." She looked at Julia. "You've always lived in the South, haven't you?"

Julia sighed and nodded. It was vintage Carmen to veer off the subject, sometimes when she sensed tension and sometimes for no apparent reason at all.

The girl closed her eyes. "I guess there's really no way anybody who hasn't been to Wyoming could understand why people like it there." She paused, then, "I miss it so much. Especially Sweetwater County. That's where Painted Horse is."

Julia was taken aback. Never once had she imagined such a thing. To her, Wyoming sounded like a place you would want to get away from, not return to. She used to have an old map game as a child, with removable pieces for all the U.S. states. Wyoming was a brown rectangle, she remembered that. Maybe that was the source of her impression that it was a dull, nondescript state.

"I miss every part of it," Carmen said. "The cottonwoods and the wind and meadowlarks and all the wide open country." She was gesturing a little, her eyes still closed, as if seeing it all in her mind. "The sky is so big and so blue, and the mountains and the sunsets—you've never ever seen a sky like that." She opened her eyes. "And all that clear, clean air, and the wild horses and bison and antelope and sheep and cattle and all the ranches." She had dropped the dreamy tone now. "And the *fishing*—Daddy took me all over the state. Lakes and dams and beaver ponds everywhere. Trout and splake and sunfish and catfish, even some crawdads at Moon Lake. Once Daddy caught a landlocked salmon—that far from the ocean! And he would make a little fire and we'd eat whatever we caught right there straight out of the water."

She sat up straighter. "And rivers and waterfalls and trails—I mean, *real* historical pioneer trails, where *real* pioneers carved their names on rocks. And in late spring we get a little rain and all these pretty flowers spring up, like they're growing straight out of the granite. And all the mountains and hills and buttes—I can't begin to name them all. The Rockies and the Tetons and Flaming Gorge and Honeycomb and Flattop and . . . the tumbleweed and the elk and the rodeos and . . ."

She stopped abruptly and laughed. "Okay, I know—my organization stinks." She made a gushing sound and with her arms pantomimed an eruption. "Sorry for the geyser. I got carried away big time. I guess it's just been building up inside me. I know it doesn't sound like anything special to you, but for me it's just . . . home. Not a single day goes by that I don't think of it." She took another deep breath and let it out.

Julia said nothing. What could be said after a speech like that? Maybe she should start humming "Home on the Range."

chapter 29

ANY OTHER SPRING DAY

But Carmen wasn't done talking. "I guess when I left the second time, it was a little like getting kicked out of paradise. Not that home was this . . . utopia or anything, but I knew I'd been bad and didn't deserve to be there. I guess I thought there were angels with flaming swords posted all around the border or something." She paused. "*Paradise Lost*. But it hit me the other day—*I can go back*, I really can. And I want to. I want to see it all again. Especially the sky. Whenever I think of heaven, I imagine this huge domed ceiling, with all the colors of a Wyoming sunset." Her voice faltered, but she gathered herself quickly and covered it with a laugh. "Okay, now, that's humiliating—getting all choked up over the *sky*. Sorry."

Julia couldn't say at what point during the girl's monologue she had begun to catch on, but by the time it was over, she knew she could talk herself blue in the face and never convince Carmen not to make the trip. *I need to go to Wyoming*, she had said, and that was exactly what it was. A need, like the kind that involves physical suffering. As in *I need surgery*. As if she would die without it.

"I had no idea," Julia said. But it came to her all at once that she should have. She thought of the days in New England last fall, when her eyes were beholding such beauty all around her, while her heart was already longing to get back to South Carolina. She hadn't realized she loved it so much until she got so far away from it. So why did it never occur to her that Carmen might feel the same about the place she knew best?

Now that Julia knew what she was up against, her worry was full-blown. A visit to Wyoming could be dangerous—the same way it was for an alcoholic to walk past a bar. She gave a rueful laugh to gain time. "I guess I could have found all this out if I had asked you the right question for a practice essay: *If you could choose another state to live in, which would it be, and why?* I guess I just assumed everyone knew South Carolina was the perfect place to live."

Carmen smiled. "It does have some pretty spots. The whole East Coast does, but, well, I hope you won't take this wrong . . . but you do understand that the Appalachians and the Smokies and all the rest aren't *real* mountains, don't you? And I don't have anything against trees, but isn't there any such thing as moderation? I mean, you have to wait till winter around here to see the sky. And speaking of moderation, when *summer* gets cranked up, it's like . . . an inferno. And the singing of the cicadas—well, it's sort of cute, but I like the sound of coyotes a lot better."

The telephone rang downstairs. Both of them looked toward the attic stairs, but neither of them moved. The answering machine came on, then a voice. The words were indistinguishable, but Julia could tell it was Pamela.

"And all this time, I thought you liked it here," Julia said.

Carmen laughed. "Well, it's not a *horrible* state. I'm sure there are worse."

"So all this isn't only about honoring your mother, is it?" Julia said. She didn't mean to imply the girl hadn't been truthful. She

knew how desire for one thing could lead to desire for another
without canceling out the first.

"Well, no, not completely," Carmen said. "But that's how it all
got started. Pastor Chris got me thinking, and then it was like
everything came together."

"So even if you found out Ida wasn't still there and Lulu wasn't
buried in a grave," Julia said, "you would still want to go, just to see
it all again. Right?" She already knew the answer.

Carmen nodded. "I'll tell you what I want to see more than anything. I want to see home. I mean, specifically. Did I ever tell you
it was a trailer? Daddy had it anchored and insulated tight, and he
had these big semi tires bolted to the roof, but sometimes you could
still feel the wind shaking it. I guess that should've been a little
scary, but it never was. I loved feeling the power of the wind but
knowing we were all safe inside. I want to walk through it again and
sit outside on the step at night, where Daddy and Lulu read me
stories and sang songs and told me the names of the stars. And the
moon—you've never seen anything like it. All that sky to show it
off." She sighed. "I want to see the moon again."

"I'm pretty sure it's the same one we have here," Julia said.

Carmen laughed. "Daddy's favorite folk song was 'Michael,
Row the Boat Ashore'—did I ever tell you that? In the summertime
he would play his guitar and sing it under the moon."

"What if home isn't still there?" Julia said. "They call them mo-
bile homes for a reason, you know. Maybe somebody hooked it up
and moved it somewhere else. Or if Ida still lives there, she may
not . . ."

"Yeah, I know. She may not let me in the front door, but I've got
to try. And even if there's just a bare spot where it used to be, I can
still stand there and look out in every direction as far as I can see
and talk to Lulu and . . ." Carmen broke off and looked at Julia. "I

told you she grew up in Arkansas, didn't I? And when she ended up in Wyoming, she said she knew that was exactly where she was meant to live for the rest of her life. She loved it. But I don't guess Ida ever forgave her for leaving Arkansas. Or refusing to leave Wyoming after Daddy died."

Julia spoke before she could stop herself. "I could go with you." She knew it was her heart talking, not her head. She also knew Carmen would be kind as she said no.

"This is something I need to do by myself, Aunt Julia," she said. "But thank you." She laid a hand on top of Julia's.

Julia nodded. Another irony of life. A year ago, she had tried her best to talk the girl into going back to Wyoming, and now she would give anything to keep her here. But maybe this was the best time for a visit after all. She could get it out of her system and be back in plenty of time to get enrolled at Millard-Temple for the fall. This time next year she could have a year of college under her belt.

C ARMEN said, "I prayed so hard a year ago that God would help me find you. And he did. And you let me stay. I'm thankful for that. I was so tired of being a . . . peripatetic. Is that the right word? You've taught me so much, Aunt Julia. You've helped me face some hard things, even when I didn't have the courage." She laughed and put a hand on her jaw. "The latest one being that dentist appointment. Ouch."

Julia knew Carmen was only trying to soften the blow of rejecting her offer to go along. She also knew the girl had ten times the courage she had.

Carmen was looking at the magazine in Julia's lap. "Cool," she said, pointing to the title. "There's a Green River in Wyoming. It's not far from Painted Horse. Is that a magazine about Wyoming?"

Julia shook her head. She would show Carmen the stories in the magazine sometime. She owed it to the girl to honor her father by admitting what she had done. "No," she said. "There must be a lot of Green Rivers. This one happens to be in Kentucky."

There was a question she had to ask, of course. "When are you going?"

"Soon," Carmen said. "I have to help out with something at church on Sunday, but as soon after that as I can. I need to check flight schedules and all that."

"I'll buy your plane ticket," Julia said. "You need to save your money." Carmen started to protest, but Julia waved her off and kept talking. "Pamela says Butch is a whiz at hunting down good airline tickets, so I'll call him right away and . . . wait a minute—there *are* airports in Wyoming, aren't there?"

"Ho ho, very funny," Carmen said. "Aunt Julia tells a joke." She got up from the floor and half crawled to the attic ladder. "Tell him the nearest one to where I live is in Rock Springs." She let herself down two or three steps and stopped to look back. "But I'm going to pay for my ticket. You need to save your money for your own. You can come visit me in July, and I'll take you to Frontier Days in Cheyenne. We can go every year. It can be like our . . . family tradition."

Julia stared at her. Come visit her? What was she talking about?

"Oh, and Aunt Julia, the South isn't *all* bad," Carmen said. "I mean, I did find out how much I like sweet tea and grits." She laughed and disappeared. Julia heard her whistle her way down the hall and through the kitchen. She heard the back door open and close.

For a long time she sat there without moving. All this time she had been assuming it was only a short-term visit Carmen was talking about. But it was a one-way trip, and one she meant to take soon. Julia couldn't think of anything as sad as that.

• • •

I T was late the next morning when Julia finally came to the kitchen to get her coffee. The washing machine was going, and the
ironing board was set up by the kitchen table. Several shirts and
pairs of pants were hanging on the door of the laundry closet. Carmen was on the back porch, sitting cross-legged on the glider,
talking on the cell phone. Or holding it to her ear. She didn't see
Julia. There was an occasional "uh-huh" or "right," then a long
period of nothing, then another "uh-huh" and "well, yes, maybe
so." With her free hand, she was plucking at her hair, stretching out
curls to their full length, then releasing them to spring back into
place.

"I don't know, probably not," she said now. She looked up and
saw Julia in the doorway. She pointed to the cell phone and
mouthed *Aunt Pamela*, then made a face that said, *Wow, she's on a
roll.* "Oh, sure, except for . . ." she said, but was evidently cut off.
Another long wait, then, "Hey, but think of this—bluegrass music
doesn't stop at the Mississippi, you know, so you and Uncle Butch
can just . . ." Another apparent interruption.

So Pamela knew she was leaving. Julia wished she didn't—she
wouldn't have told her until after the fact. For one thing, she
couldn't have spoken the words without breaking down, which
would have brought Pamela flying to her side—a prospect she
couldn't face right now. For another, she knew Pamela, true to her
way of handling any setback, would want to talk the subject to
death, as she was obviously doing now.

"Yes, I've thought about that," Carmen said. Then another
lengthy pause. "No, that's not going to happen."

It struck Julia that she had been in such a trance after coming
down from the attic yesterday that she had forgotten about calling
Butch about a plane ticket. Even if she had remembered, she knew

she couldn't have gotten the words *one-way ticket* out of her mouth. Nor had she ever returned Pamela's call, which was probably why Carmen was on the phone right now. Pamela's motto concerning phone calls was always "If at first you don't succeed, leave a long, long message and then try, try again."

Julia took her cup of coffee and left the kitchen. Looking into Carmen's room, she saw a few items laid out on the bed, neatly folded. One of the suitcases from the attic was sitting on the floor, unopened. There were only four books on the bedside table now, the journal on top. Besides the shame of it, Julia wouldn't have thought of opening it now, for she knew it would hurt too much to see what the girl had written over the last few days: *Finally, I'm leaving the South! Wyoming is where my heart is!*

She took her time getting dressed, stopping often for non-essentials: straightening a lampshade, removing empty hangers from her closet, picking something up and setting it down again. She pulled a navy sweater over her head and then realized she was wearing black pants, so she changed pants. She dabbed a little makeup on, tried to fluff her hair with a brush. No examining of the brush this time—she couldn't do anything about hair loss anyway. She noticed in the mirror how pale and tired she looked. She needed to decide sometime soon whether to keep coloring her hair herself or give it over to a hairdresser. Or just forget it and let it go gray.

She opened the draperies and immediately felt resentful that everything outside looked like any other spring day. The sun was shining, the leaves on the trees were green, the clouds white in the blue sky. She saw the bits of yarn tied around the iris stalks under the window and couldn't imagine ever caring again what color her flowers were.

She finished the last of her coffee, which had already cooled off. Before leaving her bedroom, she looked in the mirror again for a long time. "You are an adult," she said aloud. "You will be mature about this. You will not play the victim and try to make her feel guilty." On the chair beside the dresser, she saw the two *Green River* magazines she had brought down from the attic yesterday.

The door between the kitchen and back porch was still open, and Carmen was still on the phone. "No, money's more important than time," she said. "I've waited this long, I definitely don't need a direct flight." She paused, then, "Well, thanks. Aunt Julia said you were the best." So she must be talking with Butch now. "I'll give you the money when you come."

Julia's heart sank. *When you come?* There was only one thing that could mean.

Carmen came into the kitchen when she got off the phone. "Guess what? Uncle Butch says he has some connections with a couple of airlines. He thinks he can get a discount price on a plane ticket."

A clever way to put it, Julia thought. It probably just meant he was using credit card points or frequent flier miles. "Well, that's good," she said. Natural and sincere—that was how she hoped she sounded. Neither miserable nor falsely cheerful. "They're not planning to come down, are they?" It was an old habit of hers—posing a negative to verify the affirmative.

"Oh, yeah, Aunt Pam wanted to talk to you, but I told her you weren't handy, so she's going to call back later. They're leaving on Saturday to visit Butch's sister in Memphis—I think it's for a nephew's graduation—so they might swing by here first to say bye."

Swinging by South Carolina on the way from Virginia to Memphis—that was a joke. But Julia knew there was no use fighting it. If Pamela had it in her mind to come, nothing would keep her from it. She poured another cup of coffee, then busied herself with cream and sugar, and much stirring, so that she didn't have to turn around. "What day are you thinking of leaving?" she asked.

Carmen was pulling clothes out of the washing machine and putting them into the dryer. "Next Thursday or Friday," she said. "That'll give me a whole week."

Another demonstration of a youthful perspective. *A whole week.* Spoken as if it were an eternity.

PAMELA and Butch pulled up in front of the stone house two days later around eleven in the morning. Thankfully, they truly were just stopping by since they needed to make it all the way to Memphis that evening. It was clear from the moment Pamela stepped into the house that she was still full of alarm and disapproval that Carmen was going "back there to *that place*," which turned out to be the only way she would allow herself to refer to Wyoming.

Carmen had prepared an early lunch, which they ate together in the kitchen. Sandwiches, chips, drinks, grapes. Butch had found a plane ticket for her, of course. He gave her the boarding pass and itinerary he had printed out but wouldn't take the money she tried to give him. "No lie," he said, holding up both hands, "it was free. I got a deal. I know people in high places." And though Pamela was still mad, she mustered enough momentary good cheer to say, "That's the honest truth. Butch can pull more strings than . . . a puppeteer." She even managed to chuckle over her little witticism.

Smart girl that she was, Carmen had Googled all the upcoming bluegrass festivals in Wyoming. Armed with this information, she permitted no opportunity during lunch for dead time, which she must have known would be seized upon by Pamela for argumentative purposes. The girl rattled off the names of bluegrass groups—Stringdusters, Long Way Home, Big Hollow Band, Haunted Winds, Bearfoot Boys—and told exactly when and where in Wyoming they were scheduled to sing during the summer.

And it worked. Both Butch and Pamela were drawn in. "*Rosebud and the June Bugs* are going to be there?" Pamela exclaimed at one point. "I love them!"

After lunch Carmen walked them out to their car. When she came back to the kitchen, she emitted a long whistle. "You would've thought I was about to *die* instead of just move to Wyoming. Wow, I'm sure glad you're not falling to pieces over this like Aunt Pam is."

Julia was shaking out the place mats over the sink. "She does know how to carry on, doesn't she?" she said, adding a little laugh for a breezy effect.

S UNDAY came and went, and then they were down to four days. On Monday Julia went back up to the attic and brought down the boxes full of useless things she had weeded out. She set them by the back door. One of her errands today was to drop them off at the Goodwill donation center.

"Hey, what's this for?" Carmen said, pulling out the fondue pot. It was avocado green with a wooden handle and Teflon interior.

Julia explained the concept of fondue, showed her the long-handled forks of different colors, told her about the fondue parties Matthew loved when they first got married, well past the fondue craze of the seventies.

Carmen laughed. "Cool. Can we try it out one night before I go?"

So Julia set it aside. That would be their last supper together. A trip back in time for herself, a novelty for Carmen. Maybe it would brighten up what could be a difficult meal.

The last few days were filled with odd sensations. It was curious how a bland, tuneless word like *departure* could suddenly turn onomatopoetic; say it aloud and it sounded like something ripped in half. And there was no explaining how she could feel both heavy and empty. Warring wishes were another mystery: one minute, wishing she could have more time to prepare herself for Carmen to leave and, the next, wishing it were already a thing of the past. The waiting was terrible, yet she clung to each day. She felt a dread that was nearly tangible, as was her relief upon waking each morning and thinking, *Not today, not yet.*

And hopes collided with hard truths. Her dreams for Carmen to stay with her, go to college, distinguish herself as a star student, be like a daughter to her—all of that set against the realization that a twenty-one-year-old didn't need a supervisor like the one she would be, caring too much about every aspect of the girl's life.

There were other contradictions: one day, watching Carmen intently across the table or room or yard, trying to memorize every gesture, every vocal nuance, every comical thing she said and did, and, the next day, turning her head, refusing to even look at her. Or one day, drawing near to listen to her play and sing through all the verses of a song and, the next, leaving the house as soon as she heard the first few notes.

One of the songs Julia never walked away from was "Michael, Row the Boat Ashore." That one made her go still every time, for she somehow felt closer to Jeremiah every time she heard his daughter sing one of his favorite songs.

Julia had never before realized it was a song about going to heaven. Or so Carmen told her. Nor did she know that Michael was one of the archangels and he was rowing the boat across the Jordan River. Or that the song was actually an African American spiritual. For some reason Julia had always associated it with hippies and communes and Joan Baez.

The way Carmen sang it reminded Julia of a gathering storm. She started it slow and soft, like a friendly rainfall, increasing the tempo and volume ever so slightly with each verse, from the brother lending a helping hand and the sister helping to trim the sail, right on through the mother and father waiting on the other side. By the time she got to the verse about the Jordan River, it was considerably livelier, especially the line "Kills the body but not the soul!" And at the end, when the trumpet was sounding the jubilee, it was like a tempest, though more spectacular than terrifying. She even did some hand thumps on her guitar for a little rhythmic flair.

And then there was the French folk song Carmen had learned from Dr. Boyer a few weeks earlier. Julia always listened to that one, too, though she didn't know at first that it was actually a carol about a shepherdess who had been to the manger in Bethlehem, had seen the baby, Mary and Joseph, the animals, the angelic hosts. Julia was no judge of the girl's French pronunciation, but it sounded convincing enough.

And then only three days remained. On Tuesday night Carmen sang the French song again on the screened porch. Julia was watching the news in the living room but crept into the kitchen to listen. It was just after ten o'clock, and through the back door she could see the twinkle of fireflies in the cool dark of the yard.

The girl started the second stanza, more slowly than usual: "*Est-il beau, bergère? Est-il beau? Plus beau que la lune, Aussi le soleil. Jamais dans le monde on vit son pareil.*" All at once she stopped singing. Julia waited for more, but all remained quiet. She returned to the television and soon heard Carmen in the kitchen, then footsteps in the hallway, then a door closing.

Sometime the next day Julia found a sheet of paper on the floor in front of the glider. She turned it over and saw it was the French song written out by hand, with the English translations under each line. She looked at the second stanza: *Is he fair, shepherdess? Is he fair?* And then the answer: *Fairer than the moon, fairer than the sun. Never in the world has such a one been seen.*

So that was why Carmen had stopped singing. It was easy to see how one uniquely beautiful child could remind her of another.

And in Julia's mind, this was the most perplexing part of the girl's decision to leave, yet one she couldn't bring herself to mention. Wyoming had to be more than fifteen hundred miles from Roskam, North Carolina. How could she bear to put so much distance between herself and Lizzy? Perhaps the same question was troubling Carmen, for she grew pensive the next day, disappeared for an extended walk after lunch, and went to her bedroom early that evening. Her guitar case stayed closed up tight.

A ND then they were down to the last day. Julia rose early, full of purpose. She had made her plans during the night. She wouldn't mope. She wanted Carmen's last memory of her to be something positive and admirable, not pathetic. She got dressed, went to the grocery store and bank, and was home shortly after ten. She set about making a Coca-Cola cake, something she hadn't done in many years, an idea perhaps triggered by the thought of the fondue supper. While fondue had been Matthew's favorite supper, Coca-Cola cake had been his favorite dessert.

The time for interrogating the girl was over. Julia had asked all her questions during the past week, trying to slip them in offhandedly but utterly failing, sounding instead like the middle-aged worry-wart she was. *Where will you live? What will you do for money? Do you still have friends in Wyoming? Will you call if you need help? Will you let me buy you some new clothes and shoes? A cell phone? A laptop?* The last three were answered with a firm but gentle "Oh, no, thank you, I want to travel light."

They both knew that all the questions came down to one: *How will you ever make your way in the world?* And though the girl offered no specific answers, she gave confident, optimistic ones, always in Old Testament terms: *I will follow the fiery pillar, the Red Sea will part, manna will fall, I will mount up with eagle's wings, angels will attend me.*

Clearly, Carmen had plans for this last day also. Having rallied from the previous day, she showed no signs of sadness, nor anticipation, only good-natured determination to put these final hours to practical use. After lunch she spent a good while outside, cleaning the rest of the windows, climbing onto the roof to check the gutters, tagging the last of the irises, sweeping the front walk.

She was washing the Buick in the driveway when Gil pulled up in his pickup, on the pretext of leaving some bags of fertilizer, which he could just as easily have brought on his regular yard day next week. He and Carmen talked for several minutes, Gil holding his battered hat against his heart like a gentlemanly old suitor. Before he got into his truck to leave, he took a step back and gave a courteous little bow. Carmen, her hands clasped under her chin, bowed several times in return.

Julia, watching from the kitchen window, was tempted to laugh, though it occurred to her at the same moment that it was only further evidence of Carmen's unerring instincts about people. That Gil adored her was obvious. And just as obvious was the fact that any kind of physical contact would have overstepped a boundary and discomfited him. So there they were, a Polish yard man and a girl from Wyoming, saying their farewells like two Buddhist monks.

In the middle of the afternoon, Carmen took the Buick for an oil change. She wasn't gone long. "Once again Jiffy Lube lives up to its name," she said when she walked onto the back porch, where Julia was sitting with a book in her lap, though not reading. "I would've been back even sooner, but Ricky was telling me all about his wife's trip to China."

Julia motioned to the wicker table, where she had laid the two *Green River* magazines. "There are a couple of things in there I want you to read—if you don't mind. I marked the pages. It won't take you long. They're stories."

"Oh, bummer," Carmen said, laughing. "You know how much I hate stories." She walked to the table. "I'll do it right now." She picked the magazines up. "You know what Ricky told me? His wife went to this open-air market in China, where they had all these live *scorpions* impaled on the end of sticks, and you could pick which one you wanted *to eat* and the vendor would fry it for you right there in this big pot of oil."

Julia gave her a look. "If that's a hint, it's too late. We're just having steak and chicken for our fondue tonight."

Carmen said, "I'm going to miss your sense of humor, Aunt Julia." She sat down on the glider and opened one of the magazines. "Hey, you wrote this?" She looked up at Julia. "I thought you said you didn't write."

"Just read them, and then we'll talk," Julia said.

W HEN Carmen finished reading, Julia told her. It seemed that it should have taken much longer to confess a shame carried around for so many years, but it was over quickly.

Carmen was nodding before she was done talking. "I remembered the one about the boy at the rodeo. Daddy read parts of it to me while he was writing it. I didn't remember how it ended, though. And I didn't remember much of the other one at all, except for that girl that killed all the chickens."

Such a logical thing, of course—that Carmen would have heard or read the stories and, with a mind like hers, would have remembered them—yet a possibility Julia hadn't considered.

Carmen gave herself a little push in the glider and looked up at the fan. "So that's why you don't write," she said matter-of-factly. "Guilt. Punishment. Maybe some fear mixed in."

"So *anyway*," Julia said, "I put an envelope on top of your suitcase while you were gone. It has money in it—what I got paid for your father's stories, plus some extra for interest. You have to take it. It's yours, and it's one small way you can help me."

Carmen looked at Julia. "Daddy wanted you to have them. They were yours. They would never have gotten published if . . ."

"Don't," Julia said. "Please don't."

"But, think of it, they would've just sat somewhere in a box. Or been thrown away. That's what Ida wanted to do with them, but Lulu said . . ."

"What I did was dishonorable. I need to hear you say you forgive me," Julia said. "For your father's sake. I could have published them under his name, but I took credit for something he did." Saying it aloud made it sound worse. In her years of teaching, she had given more than one student a failing grade for turning in a paper written by someone else.

Carmen spread her arms wide. "Oh, Aunt Julia, *of course* I forgive you. Now you need to forgive yourself. Didn't you give me a little talk about that one time? You need to just put it behind you and move on. Enough wandering in the wilderness. It's time to lay down your fear and guilt and cross over into the good land of Canaan."

Sometimes Julia had to smile at the girl's simple way of thinking, as she did now. Not that it was funny, but what else was there to do?

· chapter 30 ·

ATTENDING ANGELS

This was Julia's meal to prepare. She banished the girl from the kitchen, told her to take a hike but be back by six. After she heard the screen door slam, Julia closed her eyes tight for a moment. She couldn't let herself think about how quiet the house was going to be after tomorrow. No one to talk to, or to talk to her. No bantering, no singing, no sharing of Google tidbits, no discussing books or listening to music together, no sounds of the girl's coming and going. She moved to the kitchen window.

At the end of the driveway, Carmen stopped and looked up into the trees, then turned right and started walking. Probably off to say good-bye to neighbors up and down Ivy Dale.

Well, time to get to work. She opened her cookbook to the page she had marked. She would make the sauces first: parsley butter sauce, blue cheese, bearnaise, and one called spicy hot. The sounds of *The 1812 Overture* wafted into the kitchen from the CD player. That was good. Tchaikovsky would keep her moving.

By the time Carmen returned, things were almost ready. The

rice casserole and bread were in the oven, the broccoli and cauliflower were in the steamer, and the Caesar salad was in the refrigerator. The table was set, the fondue pot in the middle, filled with oil and ready to heat. She turned it on now.

"Look what Dr. Boyer gave me," Carmen said from the kitchen doorway. "It's a little French dictionary." She held it up. "And Jackie and Nicole made me this." She lifted a beaded string around her neck. "Hey, am I too early? I can hit the road again if you're not ready for me."

"Five minutes," Julia said. "Just enough time for you to put on some new music and then see if you can squeeze your gifts into your suitcase." It was a joke, of course. Carmen was taking so little with her that she had switched to a smaller suitcase. Even then, Julia kept telling her she needed packing peanuts to fill up all the extra space.

There was nothing quick about a fondue meal, which suited the purposes for a last supper. As did the candles and the brightly colored Fiesta ware. Julia had also set out yellow napkins and two ceramic salt and pepper shakers that looked like little bluebirds. The tablecloth was white with polka dots of every color.

Maybe for Julia's benefit Carmen was only pretending, or maybe she had somehow developed an interest in the taste of food over the past couple of months, or maybe the retro look was the key, but whatever the cause, the whole meal seemed to delight her, especially the fondue. She loved the idea of cooking her meat in bites, tried all the sauces, declared the spicy hot her favorite.

And as they ate, they talked. First, small talk, then gradually bigger. Or, as Julia thought of it later, first wading in shallow water, and then barely able to touch bottom. And who was to say revelations were too late? They came when they came. She couldn't say how it happened, for neither of them said at any point, "Okay, let's dispense with the chitchat, this is our last time to really *talk*." The leisurely nature of the meal must have contributed. Or perhaps it was simply the proving of a paradox Julia had once read: *Living together erects barriers; separation tears them down.* Maybe Carmen's imminent departure had started a demolition.

All she knew was that in one breath Carmen was talking blithely about a cucumber-eating contest she had read about and in the next she was asking Julia if she knew what "sweetbread" was made out of and didn't that sound revolting? And did she know that there could be as many as *fourteen hundred* strains of bacteria in a person's belly button? And had she seen the peonies in Dr. Boyer's yard with fat round buds the size of baseballs?

And then somehow, suddenly, the girl's face clouded and she was talking to a slice of bread, turning it around and around in her hands, tearing off little bits of the crust and putting them in her mouth. "I never told you that the last time I called home was a year ago," she said. She paused to chew, then, "Ida answered, but I couldn't get any words out. She kept saying hello, hello, louder every time, and somebody in the background was saying, who is it, who is it? And then I heard Lulu just as plain as day, like she was all of a sudden standing right next to the phone. She said, 'If it's Carmen, let me talk to her. I want her to come home.'"

She stopped to chew again, then continued. "And then I felt all that old anger again, and I wanted to scream, 'You wouldn't even *talk* to me when I really needed you! You wouldn't even let me in the door!' And I hung up without ever saying a single word. And I never called back. Then when I got here, you told me . . . she was dead."

There was a long silence. The girl looked at Julia sadly and said, "You were right—she did want me to come home. I knew I ought to, and the funny thing was I wanted to see her, too, I *needed* to. I was sick and tired of roaming around all over the place. But I was stubborn. I wanted to make her wait. So I thought I'd come down here and look you up first, and then . . . well, you know the rest from there."

She sighed, took another bite of bread. "So my little speech yesterday about wandering in the wilderness? Well, that's a place I know pretty well, believe me. I go back there for regular visits. I find where I hid my bundle of guilt and pick it back up and carry it around in circles for a while. And then it hits me again: *Wait, I'm a child of grace, I don't have to do this anymore!* So I put it down again and head back to the good land. And then the cycle starts all over."

She looked at Julia. "You probably wanted to clobber me for sounding so teachy-preachy. So wise and . . . *instructive*, like I have it all figured out. But I don't. I sure don't. I still have so many things to . . ." She trailed off.

"So do I," Julia said. "Everyone does, I guess."

There was silence again, except for the background music. The girl had chosen all her favorite CDs for dinner music. Incongruous to say the least—a talk about regret and guilt accompanied by Copland's *Billy the Kid*. Most likely Bizet's *Carmen* was in the mix somewhere, too.

CARMEN stood up. "I want to show you something." She left the kitchen and returned a minute later with a book. From between the pages she took out what Julia thought at first was a bookmark and held it against her heart. "I never showed you this," she said. "I don't know why, really. I didn't mean to be hoarding it, but I guess that's what it amounted to. I guess I just wanted to look at it, not talk about it. Luna sent it to me in with my birthday card, so I've had it for a while. She sent me some money, too. I guess I never told you that either. She wrote a nice note saying it was just to help out whenever I needed it."

She handed Julia what she was holding and said, "It was taken at the Christmas program." It was a snapshot of Lizzy in a white angel costume, complete with iridescent gauzy-looking wings and a tiny gold halo. Her fine blond hair, charmingly messy, framed her sweet face and curled around her ears. She was looking up at something, her lips parted, her eyes alight with wonder, as if the heavens above her had split open to reveal real angels descending. She was in the very center of the photo, obviously the main reason for it, though parts of other children could be seen around her. The boy next to her had his whole hand in his mouth, and a girl behind her was crying, her halo lopsided. If it were Julia's photo, she would get a pair of scissors and carefully cut around Lizzy and throw the rest away.

"Did you know Luna could sew?" Carmen said. "She made the costume."

Julia couldn't speak. She could only stare at the photo.

Carmen opened the book she was holding. "I've been reading this. I found it on the bookshelf in the living room."

Julia glanced up. She recognized it—a slim volume with a blue cloth cover, titled *Essays on Living Well*. It had been among the few books Matthew owned when they were first married, one of those books you kept more for looks than contents, though she shouldn't judge the contents of this one since she had never read the first word. She only knew she wasn't interested in reading essays by a man with the unremarkable name of Bill Smith, especially with a *Rev.* in front of it. At least he could have dignified it a little by using William instead of Bill.

"Here's the part I keep reading over and over," Carmen said. "Listen to this. It's from a chapter called 'Honor Thy Children.'" She began reading. "*Letting your child go is the ultimate act of love, demanding of parents the kind of seasoned courage that acknowledges the presence of evil yet believes in the greater power of good. A parent who releases his child must first release himself from fretting over past failures, present fears, and future dangers. A parent who views his child as an extension of himself becomes greedy for perfect performances, seeing the child's success as his own. Letting go, then, starts with a giving up of one's pride. As at the end of a weary day, the parent must lay aside his busy efforts and schemes, rest his head on the pillow of faith in a wise and good God, and trust attending angels to guard his precious one through the uncertain night ahead in a place beyond his reach."*

She stopped reading but didn't lift her eyes. "There's more, but that's the part I keep coming back to." She looked at Julia. "I know he's talking about older children here, but he's talking to me, too. I have to give her up."

Julia didn't mean to sound so full of wrath and panic. "She was *taken* from you!" she said. She was surprised to hear her voice shaking. "Why should you have to give her up again?"

Carmen didn't answer right away. She looked back down at the book, studied the page. Finally she said, "She's another reason I have to leave. The main reason, really. I didn't tell you that part. I can't keep reliving the past and wishing things were different. I can't live my life through her and make her responsible for my happiness, which is what I would do if I stayed here." She looked at Julia again. "I would live from visit to visit, hoping to see her in the park, or hoping maybe she would be at Luna's one day when I was there, and maybe even some wonderful, glorious day would come along when I could actually pick her up and hold her. But if I went to Luna's and didn't get to see her, I would cry, and if I did, I would still cry, maybe harder. And then her parents might start . . ."

"You have every right to see her!" Julia said. "They need to know who you are. They need to know what *you've* been through."

Carmen looked horrified. She was the first to break the silence that followed. "They *can't* know, ever. That's the whole point. Don't you see? How could I do that to them? I've made Luna promise not to tell them, and you can't either. You've got to promise me that, Aunt Julia." Her eyes brimmed with tears.

Julia turned away and said nothing. She felt an astonished kind of fury, that the girl could be so willing to turn her back on something so dear, so undeniably hers.

"I've thought this through, and I know I'm right," Carmen continued. "I've tried to imagine how Vanessa would feel. She would look at Lizzy every day and know she was . . . taken away from someone who loved and wanted her. How would it feel to know every minute of every day that your joy wasn't really *yours*, it was stolen from somebody else? Why should I want to make them live with that?"

Answers sprang to Julia's mind at once—because it was the truth, because what had happened was so painfully wrong, because Carmen shouldn't have to suffer alone. But they weren't really answers. The girl's line of thought didn't take into account her rights, but it was right, of course. It was driven by love, and there was no arguing against love and mercy and sacrifice. They were their own justification.

One final thought, though. "Lizzy will need to know who you are sometime in her life," Julia said. "What if she wants to find you someday?"

"Someday isn't today," Carmen said. "Right now she needs to be happy. And that means her parents need to be happy, too." More childish, simplistic reasoning, yet true. "*For our affliction will bring about an eternal glory*," she added. "*We walk by faith, not by sight. We fix our eyes on things that are not seen.*" More of her Bible verses, no doubt. Nothing to be gained by arguing with those either.

CARMEN closed the book and set it on the table. "Leaving her behind is going to take every ounce of faith I have. But I've seen her, and she's happy and loved. And I've seen her attending angels. I've talked to them both. Their names are Vanessa and

Robert. God is good." She laid a hand on the book. "I just wanted you to know all this. I couldn't talk about it before. It's taken a long time to sort it all out. But you deserve to know."

Julia handed Carmen the photo. Her thoughts were still whirling. She said the only thing she could think of to say. "Well, thank you."

Carmen blotted the corner of each eye with the sleeve of her T-shirt. "No problem," she said, with the smallest of smiles. "And Luna's going to write me. And send me pictures."

Julia stood up and started clearing the table, and Carmen rose to help. Phrases from the book kept playing through Julia's mind: *the ultimate act of love, seasoned courage, the uncertain night ahead.* She could have picked the essay apart for its reliance on generalizations, its scattered organization, its affectations, the obvious effort of the Reverend Smith to sound earnest, literary, deeply moving, and whatever else he was trying to be. And the crowning touch, the laughable metaphor at the end about the pillow.

Nevertheless, behind the self-conscious rhetoric, there was something there. In the girl's own interpretation, she was the parent, but in Julia's she was the child. Reverend Bill Smith had a point. Letting Carmen go wouldn't be easy, but it was the good and right thing to do.

THEY sat on the back porch later with their coffee and Coca-Cola cake, Carmen on the glider, Julia in the wicker rocker. They ate and drank quietly, as if at the close of a ceremony. They certainly weren't eating because they were still hungry. It tasted good, though, and they took their time. Daylight was fading, and all was quiet except for the occasional swat of an insect against the screen and a faint shushing sound, a mingling of breeze and brook. The music had stopped inside.

"This was Matthew's favorite dessert," Julia said. Maybe Carmen's earlier openness was responsible for the remark, or maybe Julia would have said it anyway, at the end of their last supper together. Maybe it was the twilight setting that encouraged it—the trees stirring, the water lapping high on the creek banks from late spring rains, memories of the past year like warm, sweet air all around them, and the coming years spread out like the sky behind the trees, streaked with coral, a reminder that sunrise always follows sunset.

Whatever the case, Carmen was instantly interested. "Yeah? What else did he like to eat?" and "Did he ever do any cooking himself?" and "Did you sit together out here on the porch in the evenings?" Other questions followed, along with answers. And then a long pause, before Julia said, "I used to think I never should have married him, but now I only wish I had been a good wife to him. He was a good man, worthy of a woman's love and respect."

"He never knew about the . . . little boy who died," Carmen said. Not a question but a fact, offered reluctantly yet sympathetically, as if to remind Julia that her regrets as a wife had their source in an accident, not in a cold heart or whatever she was implying.

"No, but still." What was the point of saying more? The fact stood that Matthew had deserved better, and—the hardest part—that there was no way to make it up to him. More silence, and then, "I asked him for the circular driveway, but never told him why. I hated . . . backing out of driveways." She paused. "It was expensive, but he did it. Never asked why, just did it."

"Life goes on," Carmen said. It could have sounded flippant if spoken a different way, but it was meant as comfort. A simple, reliable truth, a mercy really, in the complicated matrix of an unpredictable universe.

"Yes," Julia said. "Yes, it does." Curiously, she had a sudden recollection of a videotape Matthew had watched over and over—a basketball game his favorite team had lost by a single point. One day after critiquing it again, he sighed and said, "Oh, well, I guess the score's not going to change, is it?" A funny thing to remember right now, yet relevant. You could replay and analyze the past endlessly, but you could never change it. The only hope was for tomorrow. A cliché, of course, but clichés were always grounded in truth.

Julia finished her coffee, set the cup down beside the dessert plate. Hers was bright yellow, Carmen's orange. "These dishes belonged to my mother. They're called Fiesta ware—not exactly a word that would describe our home growing up. No fiestas there. They were her everyday set. I haven't used them for years."

She knew she was opening the way for more questions, and Carmen delivered. "What was your mother like?" and "Did she like music?" And "What did she look like?" And "Did she tell you stories?" Answers for each, and then this question: "Do you have a special memory of her?"

Yes, she did. As a child, Julia was easily frightened, prone to terror, especially during nighttime storms. She would lie in bed trembling, with visions of being swept away by floodwaters, struck by lightning, sucked up into the sky. Sometimes it wasn't a real storm but only a dream of one that woke her, made her cry out. And she remembered how her mother would always come to her room and slip into bed with her. They wouldn't talk, but her mother would take her hand and lie with her until she fell asleep again.

Julia shared the memory, and others, and at last found herself saying, "I didn't honor my mother as I should have. I blamed her for everything. I thought she should leave my father and take us with her, at least stand up to him and do a little yelling and screaming herself. But that wasn't her way. The last time I saw her alive, we had a terrible argument. She looked so old and beaten down. At the end she said something I'd never heard her say before. She told me she wished she had done better by us. *Done better by us*—it was an apology, I suppose, but it made me mad that she wouldn't come out and say she had been *wrong*, which was what I wanted to hear." She shook her head, then added, "Growing up, I was always thinking of myself, never what it must have been like for her."

"You were just a kid," Carmen said.

"A selfish kid," Julia said. "And afraid of my own shadow."

"Kids are born selfish. And when they're afraid, there's usually a reason."

"It's strange, though," Julia said. "Pamela was younger, yet she weathered it all fine. She never was scared like me. Never cried when our father scolded her, just let it roll off. She called him Daddy. Even sat in his lap sometimes."

"People handle things different ways."

"My mother paid my tuition all the way through college," Julia said, "even though I never went home. She had some money of her own, from her parents. She always sent me little notes with the tuition checks. I never wrote or called, but then finally the grudge visit, to make a point: *See, I made something of myself in spite of the wretched years I spent here in this house.*" She paused. "If only I hadn't . . ."

"It was an accident," Carmen said.

"Accident or not, he still died."

"You don't know what his life would've been like if he'd lived," Carmen said. "It might have been a sad life."

"Or it might have been happy," Julia said.

"All our transgressions are carried away," Carmen said. "He stretches out his hand to the needy. He rides the storm and divides the waters. We are troubled on every side but not in despair, cast down but not forsaken. He commands light to shine out of darkness."

Julia had a feeling she was cobbling bits of verses together,

maybe even making up some of her own for want of anything better to say. But somehow it was uplifting. And it reminded Julia of
something in her possession, the small ray of light in her darkness.

"Wait here. I have something to show you, too."

S HE went to her bedroom and came back with a sheet of paper.
She handed it to Carmen and turned on the fan light. "After
Butch tracked down Luna for you, I had an idea one day. I called
him and asked if he could find out something about the Hammon-
trees. They were the family that lived next door to us in Nadine,
Alabama. The ones with the little boy."

Carmen studied the paper. "And he found them."

Julia had remembered their first names, which had helped, not
to mention the fact that Hammontree wasn't a common last name.
She also knew Anthony Hammontree had been a firefighter,
remembered that Marta's birthday was the same day as the
accident—the newspaper had made a point of that—and of course
knew their old address.

Butch had located them and compiled a brief report, which he
e-mailed to her. Julia had printed it out and kept the paper folded
inside a book on her nightstand.

Not many words, but enough. *Anthony David Hammontree,
Marta Ellen Fisher Hammontree. Currently reside in Patchett, Ohio.
Four children, ages 26, 21, 18, 13. Occupations: Anthony—fire chief of
Patchett Fire Department, Marta—licensed practical nurse at Patchett
Regional Family Clinic.*

Julia had read it over numbers of times. She was most interested
in the children, of course. Not that any number of other children
could erase the grief of the one they lost, their first, but it helped
her to know there were more. Though past sorrows could never be

canceled out, the nature of time was such that it could at least furnish subsequent joys. She knew this to be true.

Carmen looked up and nodded. "Life goes on," she said again.

JULIA turned the light off. They had finished their cake by now but remained on the porch, watching as night crept in. The first stars glimmered as the moon rose—flashbulbs around a luminous celebrity. An owl in a nearby tree called and was answered by another farther away.

"What are you going to do this summer, Aunt Julia? Will you be okay?"

"Oh, I have some things in mind," Julia said. "I'll be fine." She had in fact given the matter a good deal of thought over the past week.

"The invitation to come to Wyoming for Frontier Days is still open," Carmen said. "That's in July. I'll be settled somewhere by then."

Such a rosy outlook. All week Julia had tried to block out the image of Carmen wandering around Wyoming with a hobo stick over her shoulder. "Maybe I'll wait till next summer for Wyoming," she said. "I have to start teaching again in three months, you know. The dust is probably an inch thick in my office."

She would review all her class notes, then ask Marcy Kingsley to show her how to do PowerPoint slides. And just that morning she had seen an advertisement in the newspaper for a summer fitness and recreation program at the YMCA, with a special price for "seniors," a term defined as fifty-five and older. Well, that was all right. She might not appreciate the label, but she didn't mind the discounts.

She also had a story to finish writing. She hadn't told Carmen about it yet, but it was coming along and might turn into something more than just a story. And there were always books to read, besides a little traveling to do. Not a second try at New England—that would be for another summer, too—but a few short drives: a day trip to Thomas Wolfe's home in Asheville, a play or two in Abbeville or Flat Rock, maybe another trip to Andalusia, a couple of visits to Roskam. Thankfully, Carmen had asked only for a promise about what she couldn't tell Robert and Vanessa. No mention of staying away from their neighborhood. After all, Luna was her friend now. They had discovered they had much in common. A love of classical music, for one. Both of them had lost their husbands, for another. They both liked to read and had grown up in the South. And, of course, they both loved Carmen and Lizzy.

Carmen had asked her for another promise—to visit her church at least once a month and let her know how things were going. Julia knew the girl was hoping for more, of course, and praying, too. But she could promise her this small thing, and she did.

"I'm praying about college," Carmen said now. She laughed. "Yes, Aunt Julia, we do have colleges in Wyoming." Another laugh. She had narrowed her choice of majors to five, she said. She would keep Julia posted. "Say, did I ever tell you there are more men than women in Wyoming?" she added. "Who knows, maybe someday I'll find a man as good as Daddy." She paused. "Well, I would probably have to train him a little bit first."

T HERE was one more trip Julia would take before school started. One to Nadine, Alabama. She would drive down the street where she grew up. She might park the car and look at the house, and the one next door. She would go to the cemetery and pay her respects to her mother. Carmen's grandmother and Lizzy's great-grandmother. She would find her father's grave, too. No speeches, though. Just a brief, silent vigil to honor the ones who had brought her into this world, imperfect though it was, imperfect though they were.

And from time to time she would stand outside and turn her eyes to the night sky, so faithful and accommodating, always ready to close off an old day and give way to a new one, and she would remind herself that it was the same sky that sheltered everyone, the same moon that shone down on the whole world.

READERS GUIDE FOR

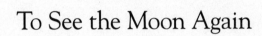

To See the Moon Again

BY

JAMIE LANGSTON TURNER

DISCUSSION QUESTIONS

1. Describe Julia Rich at the beginning of the novel. Is she a likable woman? Would you like to have her as a teacher, a wife, a friend, or a sister? Why or why not?

2. Julia dreads her sabbatical time. If you had a year off, what would you do? How would you fill your days? Discuss the things you would want to accomplish and the people you'd want to see.

3. Why is Julia so fearful about Carmen's arrival? What do you think makes her change her mind and let the girl stay with her?

4. In what ways are Carmen and Julia alike? In what ways are they different? Do you think they are more similar than not? Discuss their thoughts on children; their attitude toward religion; their hobbies, habits, and childhoods.

5. Carmen frequently quotes Bible verses while talking to Julia, often to reinforce her point, and it is clear she has a strong faith in God. What is the role of religion in the story, and in the relationship between Carmen and her aunt?

6. Julia says, "Many years ago, she had read a description of guilt that had stuck with her, the gist of it being that guilt is an irresistible thing humans latch on to and carry around like precious cargo." How do the characters in this book carry around their guilt? What moral compasses do Julia, Carmen, and Luna use to determine what makes a mistake a crime, or an act of love a sin? How do they justify or reconcile their guilt in their daily lives? Do you believe one of them deserves to suffer more than the others for her actions?

7. Discuss the importance of the many catastrophic events of Julia's life: her traumatic relationship with her father, Jeremiah's disappearance, the fight with her mother, the accident, the plagiarism of Jeremiah's story, and Matthew's death. Which one of those things do you think had the biggest effect on her, and why?

8. How do you think Julia's life would have been different if she hadn't had the accident in her parents' driveway that killed a little boy? Would she have let herself have kids? Would she have married Matthew? Would she have reconciled with her family?

9. When trying to convince Carmen that she needs to find out if her baby lived, Julia says, "Sometimes the same thing can bring good and evil." How is this statement relevant not only to Carmen's situation, but also to other situations the characters have encountered? Consider Julia's accident, Jeremiah's death, and any other events that had both a good and bad effect on the characters' lives.

10. Carmen always manages to see the positive in a situation, and is confident in God's plan for her life. After Luna confesses to

taking Lizzy as her own grandchild, Carmen reacts by marveling at how God orchestrated that plan so she could find out the truth about her child. Were you surprised at Carmen's reaction? What would you have done in her situation? Does Carmen's interpretation of Luna's actions as "a deep mercy" seem frustratingly naïve to you, or is it something to be admired?

11. As an English professor, Julia frequently analyzes situations or conversations as they relate to creative writing, or the stories and essays her students might write. Why do you think the author refers so often to literature and writing technique? Do her references affect the way you read certain passages in the book?

12. Forgiveness—particularly the ability to forgive oneself—is a big theme in this novel. Why is it often easier to forgive others before forgiving yourself? Do you think Carmen and Julia were finally able to forgive themselves? How did Julia's views on forgiveness change throughout the book, if at all?

13. Julia believes she "forfeited her right to have children" when she had the accident, and doesn't believe she would have been a good mother. After seeing her develop a relationship with Carmen, do you agree or disagree with her assessment? Why?

14. How has Julia changed by the end of the book? How are her attitudes, relationships, and feelings different than they were before she met Carmen? In what ways do you think she will be a different kind of teacher when she returns to the classroom in the fall?

15. Julia's relationship with her husband was not warm and open. Whose fault was that? What were their reasons for marrying

each other? Have you ever known anyone in real life who learned to appreciate someone only after that person died?

16. Another theme in the book deals with "letting go." Do you think it's fair to say that women tend to hang on to their children more than men? Why or why not? How can parental possessiveness damage both the child and the parent? Besides Carmen, what else does Julia let go of?

Notes

Notes